THE GOLDEN YEARS

TILL now, bringing to life the fabulous women of history – Mary, Queen of Scots, Queen Elizabeth I, the Empress Josephine, Lady Hamilton, Marie Antoinette – has been F. W. Kenyon's *métier*; to each of their stories he has given dramatic immediacy. Now in *The Golden Years*, he turns to one of the most exciting poets of history, Percy Bysshe Shelley, whose life would have been called unbelievable had a novelist dared to suggest it.

Born to wealth and the promise of a minor title, Shelley was always a rebel and an iconoclast. Expelled from Oxford for publicly proclaiming his atheism (in which he only half believed himself), he soon rushed into marriage with pretty, vapid Harriet Westbrook. Together they wandered on impulse from place to place until Harriet, unable to bear Shelley's headstrong irresponsibility any longer, was persuaded by her malicious elder sister to come home to London.

Shelley, with his unbounded readiness to act upon what he considered right principles, fell in love with the brilliant Mary Godwin and eloped with her. From these well-known facts, F. W. Kenyon has now re-created the romantic adventures of this fascinating circle which also included Leigh Hunt, Lord Byron, and Mary's beautiful, strong-willed stepsister, Jane Clairmont, who became famous as Byron's mistress and mother of his ill-fated daughter, Allegra.

Shelley, the poet, has often been analysed and interpreted. But here is Shelley the man, handsome and impetuous, and made vividly human.

F. W. KENYON

The Golden Years

A novel
based on the life and loves of
Percy Bysshe Shelley

HUTCHINSON OF LONDON

HUTCHINSON & CO. (*Publishers*) LTD
178–202 Great Portland Street, London, W.1

London Melbourne Sydney
Auckland Bombay Toronto
Johannesburg New York

★

First published 1960

*This book has been set in Baskerville type
face. It has been printed in Great Britain on
Antique Wove paper by Taylor Garnett
Evans & Co. Ltd., Watford, Herts, and
bound by them*

PART ONE

Harriet

One

I

'HERE comes that young fire-brand Shelley! I wonder what mischief he's up to now?'

'Something crazy, we can count on that, my dear chap.'

The Reverend John Walker, a Fellow of New College, Oxford, was strolling in the High with a colleague, enjoying, as were many others, the crisp clear air of a March afternoon in the year of grace, 1811. They paused for a moment as the long-legged young man, hair in wild disarray, swept past them. Turning, they watched him as he came to an abrupt halt at the premises of the Oxford booksellers, Munday and Slatter. He stared indignantly at the display of books in the window, took a firmer grip on the parcel beneath his arm, shrugged contemptuously and flinging open the door disappeared within the shop.

'As you say,' the Reverend Walker remarked, 'something crazy, we may count on that.'

With the doorbell still jangling in his ears, Percy Bysshe Shelley, a youth who would be nineteen next August, demanded an immediate interview with the senior partner, Mr. Munday, and presently that gentleman, smiling benignly, made his appearance from the back of the premises.

'You've been eating biscuits,' Shelley declared.

'Indeed I have.'

'And sipping tea!'

'I admit it, I admit it.'

'I can see evidence of both on your whiskers.'

'Dear me, you *can*?' Mr. Munday hastily brushed his whiskers. 'And now, my dear Mr. Shelley, what may I have the pleasure of doing for you this afternoon?'

'A favour, Mr. Munday, a very great favour. I have here a number of newly published pamphlets. I want you to display them in your window.'

Mr. Munday glanced uneasily at Shelley's parcel. 'With what subject do they deal, sir?'

'Atheism,' Shelley said sternly.

'Atheism?' Mr. Munday looked aghast. 'You say *atheism*, sir?'

'*Atheism*, Mr. Munday!'

'Dear me, dear me, a somewhat daring subject,' Mr. Munday wailed.

'Anything unorthodox, anything controversial, is always daring. That, if nothing else, will make my pamphlets sell.'

'You, then, are the author.'

'A certain Jeremiah Stukeley is the author.'

'An unpleasant sounding name, sir.'

'One, you must admit, that goes well with godlessness. But come, I shall help you at once to make a fitting display. The centre of the window will do admirably.'

Mr. Munday gazed into the young man's excited eyes and was all but lost. They were large, luminous and as blue as the Mediterranean sky in summer. Fearing that if he gazed into them a moment longer he would cast all caution aside, he gave careful attention to Shelley's clothing. It was fashionable and expensive, but so crumpled and stained that it might well have been salvaged from some rag heap.

'Mr. Munday!'

'Very well, let me see the pamphlets,' the bookseller said miserably.

Shelley tore open his parcel and presented Mr. Munday with the topmost copy, the title of which, that gentleman saw in mounting horror, was *The Necessity of Atheism*.

'You quake with fear, I see that clearly,' Shelley chuckled.

'You ask too much of me, 'pon my soul you do!'

'Then you are not a man of your word,' Shelley accused warmly. 'When my father brought me to Oxford and introduced me to you he beseeched you to encourage my literary leanings in every possible way. *And* you promised! By heaven you did!'

Mr. Munday laughed shakily. 'Your esteemed father's exact

words were these: "My son has something of a literary turn; I pray you to indulge him in his freaks of writing."'

'Freaks of writing! *Freaks!*' Shelley tore at his long hair, making it more dishevelled than ever. 'My father is a purblind orthodox blockhead!'

'Dear me, what a way to speak of Mr. Timothy Shelley, and he so distinguished a Member of Parliament.'

'There are no *distinguished* Members of Parliament, not unless one regards stupidity as a prime distinction. But come, Mr. Munday, are you or are you not prepared to display these pamphlets?'

'The subject is scarcely to my liking,' Mr. Munday stammered.

'What of it? A bookseller is in business to sell books.'

Mr. Munday began to back away. 'Answer me one question – are you really an atheist?'

Shelley laughed airily. 'I am everything and nothing. My mind, which is in a state of flux, is seeking one thing only. My mind, Mr. Munday, is seeking Truth.'

'A very noble aspiration, sir.'

Mr. Munday backed still farther away. The young man's eyes were boring into him now, fascinating him, imposing upon him the violent will of this incredibly violent undergraduate. Moreover, a raging storm had turned the Mediterranean blue to an ominous grey. Mr. Munday was ready to swear that he could hear the thunder and see the lightning. The gods of a certainty were shaking with anger. Never before had he seen young Shelley like this, for normally, even though prone to little fits of excitement, he was gentle, courteous and kindly. *Atheism*, Mr. Munday thought, and gathering a faltering strength from the black horror of it all was thankful that he was a hardened man of business, not a susceptible young girl.

'I must consult my partner first,' he gasped, and fled.

Shelley laughed contemptuously. He knew quite well what the result would be. Mr. Slatter was a much harder-headed man than Mr. Munday. 'Fools!' he raged, but soon he was laughing in delight and looking cunningly about the shop, for a most entrancing idea had occurred to him. Slipping behind the counter he flung open the door of the window, reached forward and seized a pile of books from the centre display. It was a simple matter then to fill the empty space with the pamphlets, the title in broad and sinister evidence. This done to his satisfaction he made a parcel of some of the displaced books and tucking it under his arm returned to his former position in the centre of the shop.

'I very much fear—' Mr. Munday began, reappearing unhappily.

'As do I, as do I,' Shelley murmured sadly.

'Mr. Slatter feels—'

'Say no more, my dear Mr. Munday. I recognize defeat when I see it. Jeremiah Stukeley is at least a hundred years ahead of his time. England is not yet prepared to accept him.'

Mopping his brow in considerable relief, Mr Munday escorted Shelley to the door, shook him by the hand and watched him as, half-running, he disappeared from sight along the High.

' 'Pon my soul, the narrowest escape of my life,' he whispered fervently.

2

'Shelley, I say, Shelley!'

'Oh, it's you, Hogg.'

Shelley got up from his chair by the fire and smiled blandly at his friend, Thomas Jefferson Hogg, who, an awed expression on his face, hovered uncertainly at the door.

'Do you mind if I come in, Shelley?'

'My dear fellow, have I ever minded?'

'It's not that, Shelley, it's—'

'In a word, the Dean.'

'What a disgusting faculty you have for stealing a chap's thunder,' Hogg complained.

'The Dean wants to see me.'

'He does, Shelley, and let me warn you, he's in one of his towering rages.'

'Dripping righteous anger from every pore, no doubt.'

Hogg giggled suddenly. 'From every pore, and from both nostrils. He has a heavy cold.'

Shelley glanced at his friend with casual affection. They had met six months ago when Shelley, a freshman, had sat next to Hogg at dinner, Hogg himself having been at Oxford only a month or two longer than Shelley. Lingering in the hall they had argued, Shelley hotly, Hogg calmly, over the merits or otherwise of German literature. The argument had been carried forward in Hogg's own rooms, interrupted while Shelley went hastily to a forgotten lecture, resumed an hour later and concluded only after the clock had struck the hour of midnight. German literature had given place to the mysteries of chemistry, which Shelley swore would in the course of time produce enough artificial food to keep the human race alive for centuries, chemistry to the galvanic battery, which would cure all ills, and the galvanic battery to aerial balloons which, he was absolutely certain, would one day carry men to the moon and beyond. Friendship, punctuated by many other such arguments, had developed rapidly, the more so since Hogg had evinced, almost from the outset, a growing admiration for what he secretly termed the 'uncontrolled genius' of the impetuous Shelley.

'I suppose it's about those pamphlets,' Hogg ventured.

'Of course, what else?' Shelley said with relish.

'Aren't you just a little afraid, old man?'

'Afraid?' Shelley echoed reproachfully. 'You ought to know me better than that, Hogg.'

'The Dean can be very scathing.'

'Pooh! So can I!'

'What if he asks you outright if you're an atheist?'

'I sincerely hope he does!'

'You're awfully fearless, Shelley. I think that's one reason why I admire you so much.'

'When a man starts out in search of Truth,' Shelley declaimed, 'he *has* to be fearless.'

Hogg took Shelley's hand in a warm grasp. 'We're in this together, remember that, Shelley!'

'Whatever the outcome?'

Hogg laughed jauntily. 'Whatever the outcome!'

3

'I can only conclude—'

But before he could say more the Dean was overcome by a shattering fit of sneezing. Papers fluttered on the desk before him; some, which Shelley graciously retrieved, drifted to the floor.

'Thank you,' the Dean gasped, and began, with terrific trumpet-like noises, to blow his nose.

Watching with interest, Shelley fell to wondering if the Almighty, whom the Dean on occasion affected to represent on earth, ever caught a cold. It would be hard, he decided, for a mere mortal to accept the authority of a sneezing, nose-blowing Almighty.

'I can only conclude,' the Dean went on at length, 'that you are fully aware of my reason for summoning you.'

Shelley shrugged easily. 'I have been reprimanded several times already, sir, for the untidiness of my rooms.'

'Arrogance will gain you nothing, young man!' the Dean thundered.

'My lack of punctuality has also been called into question,' Shelley added smoothly. 'As my esteemed father often remarks, sir, my sense of time is lamentably poor.'

'Bah!'

'I beg your pardon, sir?'

'Yesterday, Shelley, an obnoxious pamphlet entitled *The Necessity of Atheism* was advertised in the *Oxford Herald*. At the same time copies were received by the Vice-Chancellor, the bishops of the bench and the head of each house. With each copy was a letter extending the compliments of the author, Jeremiah Stukeley.'

'*Most* interesting, sir!'

'Hold your tongue! Later yesterday, in the afternoon, copies appeared on display in the window of Munday and Slatter. Fortunately the Reverend John Walker, ever a vigilant gentleman, observed them, compelled Mr. Munday to remove them and stood over him while he burnt them. Do you deny that those copies were placed in the window by you yourself?'

'By no means, sir.'

'Is it correct that you claim friendship with this Jeremiah Stukeley?'

'Quite correct, sir.'

'Have the kindness to give me the man's address.'

'I have no knowledge of it, sir.'

'I expected you to say that. However—' the Dean, threatened

by another sneezing fit, drew in his breath sharply. 'However—'

'Sir—'

'Silence!'

'I was only about to suggest, sir, that the pressing of one's forefinger beneath one's nose is often a timely way of averting a sneeze.'

As if compelled beyond his will, the Dean did this at once, gulped, shuddered and recovered himself.

'To continue,' he said, giving Shelley a baleful look, 'I have here a sheet of paper and a pen. Take up the pen and write according to my dictation.'

'Very well, sir.' Shelley took up the pen.

'Write, "With the compliments of. . . ." '

' "With the compliments of . . ." ' Shelley repeated, as he wrote. 'Anything further, sir?'

'Add the name "Jeremiah Stukeley".'

' "Jeremiah Stuke—" ' Shelley looked up inquiringly. 'L-Y or L-E-Y, sir?'

'L-E-Y.'

'Thank you, sir.'

The Dean, leaning forward eagerly, laughed in ungodly delight. 'Exactly as I thought! I have here a specimen of the supposed Jeremiah Stukeley's handwriting. His and yours are identical.'

'Imagine that, sir.'

'Do you wish to deny it?'

'Hardly, sir, since you have gone to such pains to make denial ridiculous.'

The Dean rose majestically. 'Little more need be said. You stand exposed as the author of *The Necessity of Atheism*. It would seem to me that you *sought* exposure, sought it knowing full well what the result would be. In short, Shelley, you courted disaster—'

'As one would court a fascinating woman, sir – yes!'

'Courted it de—' The Dean once more pressed his forefinger beneath his nose – '*de*liberately.'

'*De*liberately, sir.'

'Your arrogance and insolence quite apart, Shelley, I have no recourse but to—'

'One moment, sir, one moment!'

It was Thomas Jefferson Hogg bursting headlong into the room.

'And what, pray, is the meaning of this unwarranted intrusion?' the Dean demanded indignantly.

'Sir,' Hogg gasped, 'I want you to know that I am implicated equally with Shelley, that I desire to share whatever penalty you see fit to impose upon him.'

'The pamphlet was a joint effort?'

'A joint effort, sir!'

'Then I have no recourse but to pronounce a joint penalty.'

'Expulsion, sir?' Shelley asked airily.

Too late, the Dean brought his finger up to his nose. Papers were scattered in all directions. With the utmost fastidiousness, Shelley wiped his cheeks with the back of his hand, and Hogg, quite unnecessarily doing likewise, laughed shrilly.

'Expulsion!' the Dean gasped, and fell back helpless in his chair.

Saying 'Thank you, sir,' Shelley took Hogg by the arm and led him from the room, noticing as he did so that his friend had grown quite pale and was even trembling.

'Expelled,' Hogg whispered, 'expelled. . . .'

'I never felt more exhilarated in my life!' Shelley chortled.

'What do we do now?' Hogg asked faintly.

'We go forth,' my dear fellow, to face our respective and no doubt highly wrathful fathers.'

'Highly wrathful!' Hogg exclaimed. 'Mine will be that, certainly.'

Shelley glanced at him in faint amusement. 'If you wish I'll go back and tell the Dean the truth. I'm sure he'll believe me if I assure him that *I* am the sole author of *The Necessity of Atheism*.'

Hogg rallied quickly. 'No, no, I won't allow that, Shelley, but do please tell me one thing, you aren't really an atheist, are you?'

Shelley frowned. 'Confound the Dean, he lacked the grace to ask me!'

'You do believe in God, don't you?'

A slow, sweet smile crossed Shelley's face. 'If God is Beauty, I believe in God. If God is Truth, I believe in God.'

'If, Shelley, *if*—?'

'God *is* Beauty, God *is* Truth. Of course I believe in Him.'

'Then, Shelley, why—?'

'Why did I write and publish *The Necessity of Atheism*? I had several reasons. Oxford today is not a seat of learning so much as a mausoleum of the past, and all the past's mistakes – mistakes, mark you well, before which one is expected to genuflect. At Oxford, providing one conforms, there is far too much smug safety for *my* liking.'

'Oh, and mine too, mine too!'

'Here the dons are dead and need the lighting of a mild explosion beneath them. Oh, I could go on and on for hours! Sufficient to say that I wanted to be expelled. *Wanted*, my dear Hogg.'

'As I did,' Hogg avowed staunchly.

'Then the sooner we start packing the better; the sooner we leave this mausoleum the happier we'll be.'

Hogg looked at his friend uncertainly. 'Do you intend to go home and face your father at Field Place immediately?'

'No, not immediately. I had London in mind, London, my friend, and – freedom!'

Two

I

'You are Percy, of course.'

Shelley looked at the girl in surprise.

'Percy the atheist,' she added, pointing a slender finger at him.

'Whoever *you* might be,' he said haughtily, 'one thing is all too clear.'

'And that?' she asked pertly.

'You're a member of the enemy camp.'

'Nonsense!' cried Hogg, who had followed Shelley into the hall. 'She's far too pretty to be anybody's enemy.'

With this Shelley began to study her carefully as she stood before him, her back to the long, gilt-framed mirror. Pretty, he thought, was an altogether inept description. She was short and slim, and though she was obviously no more than sixteen there was a womanly maturity about her rounded limbs and small full breasts which the simplicity of her pale yellow gown emphasized rather than hid. Her back, the reflection of which he caught in the mirror, was straight and slender; it gave him the impression of strength, yet at the same time vulnerability. He looked at her light brown hair and was entranced by the sheen of it in the mellow candlelight.

'Ask her what her name is and what she's doing at Field Place,' he commanded Hogg brusquely.

The girl stamped her foot indignantly. 'What insufferable rudeness! First you stare at me as if I were some strange sort of insect, then you refuse to address me directly.' She turned with flashing eyes to Hogg. 'Pray tell Mr. Percy Shelley that I am his sister Mary's school-friend, Harriet Westbrook.'

'And tell *her*,' Shelley retorted icily, 'that I dislike the name Harriet even more than the name Percy.'

'There was a time, and not so long ago,' Hogg whispered, 'when he absolutely adored the name Harriet. My own name, by the way, is Hogg, Thomas Jefferson Hogg.'

'So I assumed, Mr. Hogg, and let me warn you at once that Mr. Shelley senior will be very angry indeed to find you here at Field Place. He is quite convinced, you see, that you and you alone were responsible for Percy's scandalous behaviour at Oxford.'

'If Miss Westbrook must call me anything,' Shelley snapped, 'let her call me Bysshe.'

The girl inclined her head. 'But tell me, Mr. Hogg, why did Bysshe once adore the name he now dislikes so intensely?'

Hogg hesitated, mindful now of his loyalty to his friend.

'Tell her if you must,' Shelley said loftily.

'He had hoped at one time to become engaged to his cousin, Harriet Groves,' Hogg whispered, 'but the wretched girl chose in the end to spurn him.'

'Nonsense!' Shelley cried indignantly. 'It was *I* who spurned *her*. She behaved outrageously. She and I published jointly a book of poems, upon which I discovered to my horror that her own poor efforts were not entirely original. At least one ballad had been taken from the work of Matthew Gregory Lewis. Infamous, you must agree. Naturally, I spurned her after that.'

Harriet Westbrook sighed elaborately. 'There must be thousands of girls called Harriet. Must all suffer because of the iniquity of a single one of them?'

Shelley turned and faced her fully. 'A reasonable enough piece of rhetoric, Miss Westbrook. Please forgive my churlishness.' He peered at her closely. 'I realize, naturally, that only one Harriet could have hair like yours.'

Harriet nodded her agreement. 'Pretty hair, that I've often been told.'

'*Pretty!*' Shelley expostulated, and taking her by the shoulders shook her violently.

'My dear fellow—!' Hogg protested.

Ignoring him Shelley continued to shake the girl, while she for her part began to scream. He was still shaking her and she was still screaming when his mother and Elizabeth, the eldest of his three young sisters, came hurrying into the hall.

'Why, Bysshe—' Mrs. Shelley faltered.

Shelley gave Harriet a final shake.

'She infuriated me,' he said blandly.

'I hate him, hate him!' Harriet sobbed.

'Little goose,' he said softly, 'I was only trying to convince you that your hair, far from being merely pretty, is hair such as only poets could dream of, and dreaming become inspired.'

Harriet looked up at him in tremulous amazement. His smile was the most charming and guileless she had ever seen. A final sob died in her throat. It seemed to her that this strange young man, now of a sudden so gentle, was smiling at her in a way he had never before smiled at anyone else. Lost entirely in the compelling gaze of those large blue eyes, she knew that whatever he might ask of her she would do at once, and gladly.

'Poor little Harriet, I didn't mean to hurt you.'

'But obviously you did,' his mother said dryly.

He turned abruptly. 'Has Father gone to bed?'

'No, Bysshe, he's waiting for you in the study.'

'Drinking port?'

Elizabeth Shelley smiled broadly. 'The second bottle.'

'Oh, splendid! I knew if I came late enough he'd be easier to deal with.' He beamed upon Hogg. 'Come, my dear chap, now's the time to beard the lion in his den.'

2

'Help yourselves to the port,' Mr. Shelley senior invited.

Smiling confidently, his son filled a glass for Hogg, another for himself.

'Your very good health, Father.'

Timothy Shelley cleared his throat. 'Make no mistake, Bysshe, my anger is in no way mitigated.'

Wondering hastily if his speech was in any way slurred, he took another sip of wine. He would have been both indignant and amused had he known that these two young scoundrels had presented themselves with the intention of bearding the lion in his den, for at sixty there was nothing in the least lion-like about Timothy Shelley. Taller than his son, he was of slight build – he flattered himself that his fondness for port would neither fatten him nor give him gout – with greying wispy hair that had once been fair and the characteristic blue Shelley eyes. At forty he had married the beautiful Elizabeth Pilfold, who had borne him seven children, six of whom were still living: Percy Bysshe, the first-born, four girls and five-year-old John, the last-born. A satis-factory enough family, he reflected, with the sole exception of Percy Bysshe. A God-fearing man himself, it grieved Timothy that he had failed lamentably to instil in his eldest child the respect which a Shelley should feel for orthodox Christianity.

'As I said in my letter,' he declared heavily, 'atheism is blasphemy.'

'And what of bigotry and intolerance?' Shelley asked warmly.

Timothy, having long ago learnt that he was no match for his son when it came to an argument, found himself fumbling for words.

'You *did* receive my letter?' he blustered.

'Yes, Father. Otherwise we would not be here now.'

On reaching London from Oxford, Shelley and Hogg had taken lodgings at a Piccadilly coffee-house from which, because of the expense, they had moved to modest rooms in Poland Street. Here, breaking the news of their joint expulsion, they had written to their respective fathers. Hogg senior, who lived in Yorkshire, had commanded his son to return home at once, but Shelley had persuaded his friend to come first on a visit to the Shelley country house, Field Place, which lay near Warnham in Sussex.

'You received my letter,' Timothy rasped, endeavouring to work himself into a temper, 'yet you saw fit, being as ever a law unto yourself, to ignore the most important of my instructions.'

'There were so many instructions, Father,' Shelley sighed. 'To which one in particular do you refer?'

Timothy glanced as balefully as he could at Hogg. 'I informed you in plain enough language, Bysshe, that your friend would not be a welcome visitor at Field Place.'

'Oh, *that!* I intend him to marry young Elizabeth, so, naturally, welcome or unwelcome, he simply had to come.'

Mr. Shelley half-rose in his chair. His hand shook so violently that wine was spilt on his breeches. Sinking back, he looked down balefully at the spreading stain.

'It would seem,' he stuttered sarcastically, 'that I am no longer the head of my own family.'

'I do assure you, sir,' Hogg said in embarrassment, 'that I knew nothing of the prohibition you had placed upon me, otherwise I should not have come to Field Place. Nor,' he added lamely, 'did I know anything of Bysshe's desire that I should marry Elizabeth.'

'Oh, it was just a passing fancy,' Shelley said airily, 'my best friend, my favourite sister.' With a sweet smile he refilled his father's glass. 'I suggest, sir, that we leave this interesting discussion until tomorrow and permit you to enjoy your port in peace.'

'Peace will never be mine again with this dreadful scandal hanging over me,' Mr. Shelley said sadly. 'I have tried, not once but many times, to regard it as a horrible nightmare from which I shall presently and gratefully awake.'

Shelley shrugged elaborately. 'Every man is entitled to his own point of view. My new theology, for instance—'

'Your—*what*, sir?'

'My new theology, Father. It—'

'New theology fiddlesticks! Be good enough, please, to confine your experiments and flights of fancy to poetry and story-writing. I see my mistake, of course. I have been, I fear, a far too indulgent father. However, all that is at an end. I shall assert my authority from now on, belatedly, yes, but sternly.'

'Very well, Father, if you must.'

Mr. Shelley sipped again at his port. Sternly, he thought, *sternly*. He ran his tongue round his mouth, savouring the wine. But how could he practise real sternness when his son, lounging at ease before him, reminded him so strongly of his wife Elizabeth, not as she was today, though she was still a beautiful woman, but as she'd been twenty years ago? He looked at the second bottle, now almost empty, and wondered how many more of this most excellent vintage still lay in the cellar. Not enough, he was sure of that.

'Father—'

'Silence!' Mr. Shelley tried to thunder.

Yes, he thought, Elizabeth as she was twenty years ago. The same small, fine hands, the same slender neck, the same chin, still boyishly chubby. He steadied himself; there was no room now for sentiment. Atheism, he thought, *atheism!*

'Father, you demanded a full explanation—'

'Hold your tongue, Bysshe! Whether or not I shall inflict upon you some form of punishment – and punishment you richly deserve – will depend entirely on your future conduct. For the moment I have two commands, both of which you will instantly obey. Young Hogg here is a bad influence. The friendship will therefore be discontinued.'

'Oh come, Father, you should know me better than that.'

'Better than *what?*'

'It was I who was what you call a bad influence. *I* am never led astray by others. I, in fact, lead others astray: that is to say, I do my best to make others worship at the shrine of Truth.'

'The only truth at the moment, Bysshe, is that I am angrier with you than ever before.'

'Be that as it may,' Shelley said grandly, 'Hogg lied like the loyal friend he is. I, Father, am the sole author of *The Necessity of Atheism.*'

Timothy looked uncertainly at Hogg. 'Is this the truth?'

'It is, sir,' Hogg admitted.

'Dear me, then I owe you an apology.'

Shelley stifled a yawn. 'Do please tell me your second command, Father.'

'A public apology, Bysshe. By heaven, yes! A public apology to be made in the *Oxford Herald*. Otherwise—'

'Otherwise?' Shelley echoed softly.

'Are you or are you not prepared to obey?' Mr. Shelley fenced.

'A public apology, *any* sort of apology, is out of the question.'

'Very well, then. Your allowance shall be discontinued at once—'

'*Discontinued?*'

'You shall be confined to Field Place—'

'Outrageous!'

'A suitable tutor shall be appointed—'

'Dear heaven!' Shelley cried melodramatically. 'Field Place a prison, the tutor a warder!'

Mr. Shelley smiled grimly. He had gained the upper hand at last.

'You have the alternative of starving in London,' he added rashly, 'or existing, if you can, on your literary activities.'

'Splendid!' Shelley laughed. 'I shall, I expect, do a little of each. Starvation will be good, not only for my literary activities, but for my soul. Starvation will turn me into a real poet. Thank you very much, Father, for showing me so clearly what I must do.'

Mr. Shelley rose hurriedly. 'Wait, Bysshe! I—'

'Good night, Father,' Shelley said softly. 'I'll tell them to bring you another bottle.'

3

'You really do intend to defy your father?' Harriet said admiringly.

'Naturally!'

Harriet, catching sight of Shelley from her window, had dressed hurriedly and come out to join him in the garden. His refusal at first to notice her had left her quite disconsolate, but doggedly she had walked at his side, turning when he had turned, stopping when he had stopped, and presently, when at last he had deigned to smile upon her, she had found herself trembling with joy.

'Your mother thinks you ought to make that public apology,' she ventured.

'And *you*?'

Harriet shook her head. 'The humiliation would be insufferable.'

'Insufferable,' Shelley agreed.

'Of course, I know you aren't *really* an atheist,' Harriet added.

'Do you indeed!'

'It's something I feel, deep down in my heart.'

'Ah! Feminine intuition!'

'Perhaps.'

Shelley looked earnestly at Harriet. 'Believe me, if all the theological questions of the world could be solved by the feminine

intuition of a girl so absolutely feminine as you, there would be
no such beings as atheists.'

'I – I don't quite know what you mean by that, Bysshe.'

'I mean that your sweetness and beauty would make anybody
believe in God.'

Tears sprang to Harriet's eyes. 'You – you aren't joking?'

'You are the sweetest, the most beautiful person I have ever
seen.'

'If you aren't joking,' she faltered, 'you must be trying to
flatter me.'

'Flattery is evil. I hate it.'

'What a strange young man you are!'

Shelley laughed in delight. 'All poets are strange. Strange
and a little mad. Even at Eton I had the reputation of madness
and people were afraid of me. You see, I refused to fag and led
a rebellion against that iniquitous system. Eton was shaken to
its ancient foundations and for a time I was in danger of being
expelled. Are *you* afraid of me, Harriet Westbrook?'

'I was last night when you attacked me.'

'And you still are?' he asked hopefully.

'No, I don't think so.'

Shelley lowered his voice to a whisper. 'If you met me in a
dark lane on a moonless night and I screamed like a banshee,
surely then you would be afraid.'

'I've never heard a banshee scream.'

'Something like this—'

And Shelley screamed with all the force of his lungs.

'Please don't,' Harriet begged.

'You have not yet answered my question!'

'I should quake with fear,' she said, and forced herself to
shudder.

'Splendid!'

They continued to walk up and down the spacious garden together. It was a bright and cloudless morning with the sun
sparkling blindingly on the dew-laden grass. Behind them loomed
the eighteenth-century country house with its row of tall windows
sentry-like above the open portico. Standing at one of them,
unnoticed either by Shelley or Harriet, was the master of Field
Place. There, in nightshirt and nightcap, he shook with anger,
for he had been rudely torn from sleep by his son's screaming.

'Isn't a banshee a sort of fairy?' Harriet asked.

'A very special sort. Irish, and female to boot. Every family has a banshee attached to it. Her task is to shriek and wail just before somebody dies.'

Harriet drew closer to him. 'How horrible!'

'Nonsense! Banshees aren't the cause of death, they merely warn one about its approach. For instance, when my baby sister lay desperately ill, I heard our own particular banshee wailing here in the garden. She died the next day.'

'Nothing so horrible as a banshee should be called a fairy,' Harriet asserted.

'But surely you believe in fairies?'

'I've always believed in fairies,' she whispered.

'On the moon, *fairies on the moon*?'

'Oh, not on the moon, surely!'

Shelley stopped and, turning, glared at her. 'And I don't suppose you believe that some day you and I and everybody else will be able to fly?'

Harriet shrank back nervously. 'What a s – silly idea.'

'There's nothing in the least silly about it!'

Nervous still, Harriet began to laugh, upon which Shelley seized her by the shoulders.

'Stop laughing, or I'll shake you till your pretty teeth fall out.'

'They very nearly did fall out last night. If it pleases you I'll willingly believe that you and I and everybody else will be able to fly some day. I – I'll even believe in fairies on the moon, t – too.'

Shelley stopped shaking her but still held her firmly by the shoulders.

'Just believing it to please me wouldn't be believing it at all,' he said sternly. 'You must believe it with all your heart and soul, the way you believe in God. You *do* believe in God, of course?'

'Of course!' she cried, writhing under his grip.

'Ah, but why? *Why* do you believe in God, Harriet Westbrook?'

'Because – Oh, what a silly question to ask!'

'That's what everybody says, and that's why everybody calls me an atheist because I ask it. *You* believe in God because your father and mother do, because your family has believed in God for countless generations. But I' – a dreamy look came to his eyes and all anger fell from his voice – 'I believe in Truth and Beauty, and you, being Beauty, are half of my belief.'

Tears sprang to Harriet's eyes again; no one else in the world, she felt sure, had this power to frighten her one moment yet melt her heart with love the next.

'I've never met anybody like you, Bysshe,' she sobbed.

'Nor will you, if you live to be a withered, shrunken old crone of ninety.' He was looking at her now in a strangely brooding manner. 'Unbutton the front of your dress and slip it off your shoulders,' he commanded. 'I want to see for myself.'

'What do you want to see for yourself?' she stammered.

'How delightfully you blush!' he laughed. 'Come, do as I say!'

'Oh, Bysshe, what a thing to ask of me!'

'Idiot!' And reaching out as she stood hesitantly before him he unbuttoned her dress and dragged at it until her white and rounded shoulders gleamed in the morning sun. 'So I did hurt you last night.'

'Dreadfully,' she exaggerated.

He stroked the bare shoulders gently. 'I can see several bruises. What a brute I was.' He took her contritely in his arms. 'Forgive me, Harriet, please.'

'Oh, gladly, gladly!'

Shelley kissed her shoulders and l er neck, and holding her away from him he looked at her pleadingly.

'Are we friends now, Harriet?'

'Friends, yes,' she said shakily.

'You look so child-like. How old are you?'

'I'll be sixteen on the first of August.'

'A sensible month to be born. I'll be nineteen on the fourth. We're friends? You do promise me that?'

'With all my heart, Bysshe.'

A doubtful look crossed his face. 'Are you saying it just to please me?'

'I'm saying it to please myself. I—' Harriet broke off. 'Bysshe, I can hear somebody coming.' She began hastily to button her dress. 'Oh, I do hope nobody saw us!'

A discreet cough made Shelley turn quickly. Standing hesitantly a few paces away was his father's valet.

'Well, what is it, Davis?'

'Your father, Master Bysshe. He wants to see you immediately.'

'In the study?'

'No, Master Bysshe, the bedroom. Breakfast in bed, that's the order. Not feeling too well this morning. Proper poorly, I'd say, and temper ticklish.'

When the valet had departed, a broad grin on his face, Shelley offered Harriet his arm.

'I think you're still a little frightened of me,' he said, looking at her quizzically.

'Why should I be frightened of a young man who thinks my hair is like a poet's dream?' she countered. 'Unless, of course, you didn't mean it.'

'I meant it, I meant it! One of these days I'll write a verse or two about your hair.'

'Will you really?'

'I could almost do it now.'

'Elizabeth showed me some of your poems yesterday.'

'Did you like them?'

'We-ll—'

'Come! Tell the truth!'

'*Must* I?' Harriet asked, unhappily.

'You may please yours;lf, but if you lie I'll know it instantly.'

'Oh, Bysshe, you'll probably think me stupid, but I – I didn't understand them.'

'Splendid!' he laughed, surprising her beyond measure. 'I don't understand them myself, now.'

'Your father will be growing impatient,' she told him.

'So he will!'

Shelley kissed her on the brow and, turning from her, broke into a run. Entering the house as if competing in a race, he took the stairs two steps at a time, reached his father's door breathlessly and flung it open.

'Congratulations, Father!' he gasped.

Timothy Shelley was sitting up in bed, a scowl on his face. He looked much older, Shelley thought, in the nightcap. His eyes were bloodshot, his lined cheeks twin patchworks of red and white.

'What the devil do you mean – congratulations?' he glowered.

'It's a splendid thing to know that one's father is a three-bottle man. I'm proud of you, sir.'

'I tackled a fourth,' Mr. Shelley said miserably.

'Better and better!'

Suffering horribly, his mouth dry as dust, his tongue feeling twice its normal size, Mr. Shelley began to give his son a sharp little lecture on the virtue of moderation. He was, he knew, expostulating with himself, and grew more querulous as he continued.

'Oh come, Father,' Shelley said propitiatingly, 'what is excess in one man is certainly moderation in another. It's simply a matter of a man's capacity. You, sir, are surely more than moderate if you confine yourself to three bottles, less than excessive if you embark upon a fourth.'

'Enough!' Mr. Shelley snapped. 'I sent for you to discuss a very different subject.'

'So I imagined, Father,' Shelley sighed.

'Answer me at once, Bysshe: were my eyes deceiving me, or were you actually on the point of stripping that chit of a girl when I sent Davis out to intervene?'

'By that chit of a girl you mean Harriet Westbrook?'

'Of course I do! By heaven, Bysshe, if you *must* indulge in a bit of fiddlefaddle with a wench, have the grace to do it privately, not in full public view.'

Shelley was instantly appalled. Harriet, he realized suddenly, even in acute surprise, was desirable in the way his father was suggesting, but in searching for the bruises he had intended nothing like that.

'A complete stripping,' he said airily, 'especially in the early morning, with dew on the ground, would be dangerous. One might well catch cold.'

'Your poor grandfather,' Mr. Shelley moaned.

'I beg your pardon, sir?'

'Atheism, and now *this*. I can't imagine what your grandfather will have to say about it all, 'pon my soul I can't.'

Shelley smiled broadly. Whenever a crisis arose in the Shelley household that was the invariable cry: I can't imagine what your grandfather will have to say about it all!

'One of the oldest families in Sussex,' Mr. Shelley added, snatching off his nightcap, 'and our honour never more at stake.'

Shelley laughed derisively. 'You seem to be forgetting the wickedness of a certain Sir Thomas Shelley, who died on the scaffold.'

'A political crime, merely,' Mr. Shelley said indignantly.

'And another was surely committed when grandfather bought a baronetcy.'

Timothy sat forward in horror. 'Bought, you say *bought*?'

'From the Whigs, and that, in the eyes of the Tories, was sheer perfidy.'

Sir Bysshe Shelley, after whom his grandson was named, had married twice, the lady in each case being an heiress. He lived in retirement now and was growing more and more eccentric, for though he had spent the best part of a hundred thousand pounds on building a grand mansion for himself he passed all his time in a cottage at Horsham with only one servant to look after him.

'You seem to forget,' Timothy complained, 'that the title, which your dear grandfather earned rather than bought, will be yours some day.'

'A sobering thought,' Shelley admitted solemnly.

Deceived by this, his father looked at him hopefully. 'Turn over a new leaf, Bysshe, and I'll promise to do all I can to keep the news of your scandalous conduct from reaching your grandfather's ears.'

'If the devil had been offering titles at the time,' Shelley chuckled, 'grandfather would gladly have become an atheist to gain one.'

Timothy looked as stern as he knew how. 'I am referring in this instance, Bysshe, to Harriet Westbrook.'

'Pooh! Grandfather is a man of the world. He must have had many bits of fiddlefaddle with many pretty little wenches.'

Timothy cocked his head on one side. 'Is that your sole intention as far as the Westbrook girl is concerned?'

'I don't quite know what you mean, Father.'

Mr. Shelley stirred himself to anger again. 'The girl shall be sent packing, whatever your intentions are.'

Shelley began to suspect his father's drift.

'My intentions are entirely honourable, sir,' he said primly.

'That makes it even worse. Her father, old Westbrook, is a retired publican.'

'Comfortably retired, Father?'

'Apparently. He—Bysshe, I refuse to be sidetracked like this!
'Pon my soul, you'd twist me round your little finger if I didn't
watch you carefully! By honourable' – his voice rose in horror –
'you mean . . . *marriage*?'

Shelley chuckled softly. Not a lion to be bearded, but a bear
to be baited!

'You think her beneath me, Father?'

'I most certainly do.'

'What nonsense!'

'When you marry, your wife must be worthy of your position.'

'If I were heir to a dukedom instead of a mere Whig baronetcy,
Harriet would still be worthy of my position.'

Mr. Shelley sprang out of bed, staggered and clung to the
nearest bedpost.

'Fortunately you are under age,' he said, controlling himself.
'I can do nothing, I admit, to turn you from atheism but I *can*
forbid you to marry without my consent.'

Shelley smiled sweetly. 'Harriet is a charming and beautiful
girl. Publicans' daughters often are. But as for wanting to marry
her, I hadn't given the matter a moment's thought – until now.'

'What the devil do you mean?'

'You put the idea into my head yourself, Father.'

Mr. Shelley clutched his brow with one hand, his stomach
with the other.

'I feel ill,' he said.

'Let me help you back into bed, sir.'

Unresisting, Mr. Shelley allowed himself to be placed on the
edge of the bed, then rolled unceremoniously into it. Presently,
with the bedclothes tucked beneath his chin, he looked pleadingly
at his son.

'Ill as I feel,' he said faintly, 'my resolution has in no way
deserted me. Your allowance, as I threatened, shall be discontinued. That, for sure, will clip your wings. Your unorthodox
ideas and your shocking contempt for your social position have
been allowed to grow uncurbed, but from this moment on things
will be very different. Your re-education shall begin at once.
You shall be taught, before your wilfulness carries you too far,
to place a true value on the importance of your position. You
shall be made to understand, whether you like it or not, that you
are the son of a gentleman.'

'Three hearty cheers for the gentlemen of England!'

'Your sense of humour is both perverted and misplaced.'

'A gentleman, a *gentleman*!' Shelley raged suddenly.

'Which I am, and which indeed you are yourself, by right of birth.'

'Right of birth indeed!'

'Only by birth does a man become a gentleman.'

'Ah, you would say then that God made me a gentleman!'

'Undoubtedly.'

'God Himself being a gentleman?'

'Bysshe, I am far too ill for this sort of thing.'

'More than just that, but an *English* gentleman?'

'Bysshe—'

'But better still, whether or not there are politics in heaven, a *Whig* gentleman?'

Mr. Shelley covered his face with the sheet. 'Go away,' he begged.

Shelley thought of something else. 'Grandfather was born in America. Grandfather, in effect, is an American. Would you say that he can, at the same time, be a gentleman?'

There was silence for a moment, then plaintively, his voice muffled by the sheet, Mr. Shelley spoke up, as valiantly as he could.

'All things considered, your grandfather and all of us being of English stock, there *must* be gentlemen in America.'

Shelley remembered the Declaration of Independence. 'But an *independent* gentleman?'

'Your grandfather was always independent.'

'And so was his grandson,' Shelley laughed, and still laughing ran from the room, collided with Davis, who bore a breakfast tray, slid wildly down the banister and leaping from it at the bottom of the stairs came abruptly face to face with Harriet. 'A gentleman, would you say I was a gentleman?' he demanded.

'You were born one,' Harriet said, uncertain as ever of his mood.

'And so, by the grace of God, I must remain one,' he said sadly.

'Poor Bysshe, was it a very trying interview?' she ventured.

'Not trying, darling, exhilarating! But imagine it, I'm to be turned into a gentleman, even though I'm one already by right of birth. A gentleman of gentlemen, in short!'

'How indignant you sound, Bysshe.'

'Think of it, a poet to be turned into a gentleman!'

'But can't a man be both?' she asked reasonably.

Shelley flung his arms round her. 'What a blessing you are! Of course he can, providing he remains independent.'

'You'll always remain that, Bysshe.'

'Always! Now tell me, when are you going home?'

'Well, I came here for a week—'

'Where do you live in London?'

'Chapel Street, Grosvenor Square.'

'A fine address for a retired publican.'

'You're making fun of me, Bysshe.'

'Is your father, while not being a gentleman, *independent*?'

'Goodness, yes. Quite frightenly so, at times.'

'Then I'm not making fun of you, darling.'

Harriet shook her head in despair. 'I'll never know what to make of you.'

'Pooh! I never know what to make of myself. But you and I together, in this instance, can make at least *this* much: I'm going back to London today, to starve, and starving write pages and pages of exquisite poetry.'

'Are you, Bysshe?'

'Most certainly I am. And do you know why?'

'No, Bysshe.'

'Because the daughter of a retired publican has inspired me as never I was inspired before. I—' He broke off. 'What number in Chapel Street?'

'Twenty-three.'

He released her and bowed sweepingly. 'The number is inscribed upon my heart. I love you, Harriet Westbrook, I love you!'

Three

I

Gᴏᴛ a kiss for your old father?' Mr. Westbrook chuckled.

Harriet, home at last from Field Place, ran eagerly to her father and flung herself into his arms.

'Here, now, not so rough!' he admonished.

Eliza Westbrook, Harriet's elder sister, watched fondly from the door. She had met Harriet at the coach and during the short journey to Chapel Street had listened tolerantly to her breathless chatter. The holiday at Field Place had clearly been an exciting experience. Eliza was thirty and had come during the last ten years to take her mother's place in the Westbrook household, Mrs. Westbrook being a colourless, ineffectual woman whose presence, if actually noticed, was rarely taken seriously.

'You'll strangle poor Papa,' Eliza laughed.

She adored her young sister with an intensity which at times she found frightening. Having mothered Harriet from the first, she was often moved strangely to feel that the child was not so much a sister as a daughter, and this feeling had been deepened by the conviction that she, known at times as the haughty Eliza Westbrook, would never like a man sufficiently to want to marry him.

'Plain as the nose on my face you had a good time with the Shelleys,' Mr. Westbrook laughed.

'Oh yes, Papa!'

'Naturally she did,' Eliza said. 'You see, Bysshe was there.'

'Bysshe?'

'Percy Bysshe Shelley, poet and gentleman, but a most reluctant gentleman, by all accounts.'

'Him that's an atheist, you mean?'

'Oh, but he isn't, Papa!' Harriet broke in.

'He'd better not be,' said Mr. Westbrook, who was a staunch Methodist. 'Not if this family is going to have any truck with him.'

'I think we can take it that he isn't, Papa,' Eliza smiled. 'He believes in Truth and Beauty—a poetic way of saying that he believes in God. Harriet, it seems, is half of his belief, Harriet being Beauty in *his* eyes.'

'What an odd young feller.'

'I've never met anyone like him before, never!' Harriet cried.

'Clear as day why you enjoyed yourself so much. Did the young jackanapes steal a kiss or two when nobody was looking?'

Harriet blushed richly. 'Oh, Papa!'

'Well, well, that's enough of that. It's back to school at the end of the week. More lessons to be learnt – deportment an' whatnot. Miss Fenning hasn't finished the job yet.'

'Papa,' Harriet pouted, 'I don't want to go back to school.'

'You don't, my pretty?'

'I'm too grown up for school.'

'Well, fancy that. A week with the gentry an' you're grown up of a sudden.'

Harriet smiled secretly. A day with Bysshe had been sufficient for that! Nay, just a few moments when he'd kissed her shoulders and neck. And even before that when, making her hate him, he had shaken her so violently. *Bysshe loves me, he said he did*, an insistent little voice sang in her ears. Yet another voice which she tried to ignore warned her just as insistently that he had probably forgotten all about it by now.

'Off you go an' see your mother,' Mr. Westbrook instructed. 'She's busy upstairs at her needlework. Maybe she won't take much heed of you, but kiss her dutifully all the same.'

Eliza was looking steadily at her father, thinking that he was growing stout in his old age but was still an attractive man. It was from him that she had inherited her own black hair, brilliant dark eyes and olive skin, whereas Harriet's fairness came from their mother's side of the family. His eyes had narrowed, she noticed, and now as she studied him a smile touched his lips. Only too well from past experience did Eliza know that narrowing of the eyes, that contemplative smile.

'Papa,' she said, when Harriet had gone in search of her mother, 'what mischief are you planning now?'

John Westbrook shrugged with the eloquence which, combined with his swarthy appearance, caused old friends to call him 'Jew' Westbrook.

'Not half so keen on redcoats any more, our Harriet, I'll be bound.'

London, in these days of the Napoleonic wars, was crammed with soldiers, and Harriet, like most of her romantic young friends, found the sight of a redcoat utterly entrancing.

Mr. Westbrook rubbed his hands together as if drying them on a towel.

'Real nice to have a title in the family, eh, me girl?'

'How vulgar you make it sound, Papa,' Eliza protested.

'He's the eldest son, isn't he?'

'Percy Bysshe Shelley? Yes, Papa.'

'Then he'll get his grandfather's title, one of these days. Lady Shelley! Can't you just see the little Harriet carrying it off a fair treat?'

'I can't see the Shelley family permitting it, or finding it a "fair treat",' Eliza said dryly.

'There's always ways and means, me girl.'

'For you there is, Papa.'

'I usually get what I want.'

'It's what Harriet wants in this case, Papa,' Eliza warned.

'Meaning it's what you want for her,' Mr. Westbrook chuckled.

'Perhaps, and I'm not even sure that I want young Shelley for Harriet. How can I be when I haven't seen him yet?'

'You'd like to see Harriet well set up, wouldn't you? You an' me's got to put our heads together in this, see eye to eye.'

Eliza fell silent for a moment, thinking of all Harriet had told her about Percy Bysshe Shelley. So vivid had been her description that she could almost see those luminous, compelling eyes, dreamy one moment, flashing angrily the next. It was plain enough that Harriet was in love with Bysshe Shelley, an emotion she was feeling with all the intensity of her susceptible, romantic nature.

'How to bring them together again, that's the question,' Mr. Westbrook said thoughtfully.

'That won't be difficult,' Eliza decided. 'Young Shelley is in

London, living alone in lodgings in Poland Street. He quarrelled with his father. I expect he's very much at a loose end, and rather lonely. It wouldn't do any harm to call on him.'

'Taking Harriet with you?'

'Yes, Papa.'

'Let's hope you like the look of him,' Mr. Westbrook chuckled.

Eliza gave her father a tight little smile. 'If I don't, Papa, there's no chance at all of our putting our heads together, title or no title.'

Mr. Westbrook looked at her without rancour. 'I've got most of the things I want in this life without help from nobody. You remember that, me girl.'

2

'Harriet, how splendid!' Shelley cried.

Harriet, hesitating on the threshold, stood aside for Eliza to enter.

'I've brought my sister with me,' she explained.

Shelley stared unseeingly at Eliza. 'Ah, a chaperon.'

'One must observe the proprieties,' Eliza said dryly.

'Did you come in a carriage?' Shelley demanded.

'We did.'

'Your own, or hired?'

'Our own.'

'Then the carriage is waiting below.'

'Of course.'

'Excellent! The proprieties notwithstanding, the only place for a chaperon is in the carriage below.'

Ordinarily the harshness of his tone would have angered Eliza, but the smile which accompanied it, a smile she found irresistible, completely disarmed her. Studying him as carefully as she could, she saw that he was dressed informally, his shirt open at the neck, his hair in child-like disarray. The smoothness of his brow and the fineness of his slender neck affected her strangely. Biting her lip, she realized that she was on the point of feeling tenderly protective towards him. He was such a boy, irresponsible without a doubt, younger in appearance, even, than the now prettily blushing Harriet.

'I doubt if you have the strength, Mr. Shelley, to carry me down to the carriage.'

'Ah, a veritable termagant!' he laughed.

He invited the sisters into the cramped little room, a room made even smaller in appearance by the large writing-table, the two large leather-covered chairs and the stacks of books which stood irregularly against the walls. Ushering each into a chair, he placed himself with his back to the small fireplace where a fire spluttered fitfully.

'I fear we must have interrupted the flow of your thoughts,' Eliza remarked, her eyes on the writing-table.

'It scarcely matters,' Shelley said, with a loftiness that again reminded her of his boyishness.

'Work such as yours,' she said gravely, hoping that her eyes revealed none of the gentle amusement she felt, 'must suffer badly when broken into so rudely.'

'Thank you for calling it work,' he said earnestly.

He was looking at Eliza now with real interest. His first impression was that she was exceedingly prim, his second that she was only prim because at times she liked to affect that attitude, his third, as his eyes lingered on her face, catching for a moment the hint of a twinkle in her dark eyes, that there was nothing whatever prim about her. A certain sternness, yes, but that, he was sure, arose out of nothing more serious than a sense of responsibility.

'To call it work,' he went on eagerly, 'poses an interesting question. If one enjoys one's work, is it really work? Work is drudgery, and I, thank heaven, have never been guilty of that particular form of self-righteousness.'

'Let us say, then,' Eliza decided, 'that the only work worth while is the work that one enjoys.'

'Are you engaged upon a new poem?' Harriet ventured, her eyes devouring him.

He shook his head. 'A letter to Hogg. I write to him almost daily, telling him all my thoughts, my hopes, my ambitions. He went off to Yorkshire, as you know, and has been flung by his wretched father into a solicitor's establishment.'

'Poor Hogg,' Harriet murmured.

'Oh, he has a bent for law. I expect he'll do quite well for himself, end up fat, florid and pompous. What news do you bring from Field Place?'

'Your mother and sisters were in excellent health when I left but very anxious on your behalf.'

'And my venerable father?'

'Somewhat queasy,' Harriet giggled.

'And angry still?'

'Dreadfully.'

'To be queasily angry, or angrily queasy, is surely most uncomfortable.'

Harriet giggled again. 'Elizabeth sent you a message. She wants you to know that she and the other girls will stand by you whatever happens.'

Shelley smiled tenderly. Elizabeth, the spokeswoman, had presented him with some money before he left Field Place, enough for his immediate needs, and later, all of them having jealously hoarded their pocket-money, more would be forthcoming. Life on the whole was exceedingly pleasant in London. There were poems to be written, a union of intellectual liberals to be formed and speeches to be made at the British forum. His mind was seething with a multitude of ideas, and to so great an extent that he found it impossible to sleep for more than a few hours each night. And now, he thought, glancing enthusiastically from Harriet to Eliza, there was the additional prospect of a delightful social intercourse with the Westbrook sisters.

'I think it a pity,' said Eliza, 'that because of the quarrel with your father, you should find yourself confined to such dingy lodgings.'

'Even if I hated it, which I don't,' Shelley cried gallantly, 'it would be well worth while, wringing pity as it does from a heart as kind and compassionate as yours.'

Eliza felt the colour rising in her cheeks. It was easy to understand why Harriet had become so quickly besotted. If she were Harriet's age she would, she knew, become a willing victim herself. But *victim*, she thought, that was hardly the right word to use. Nevertheless, she was ready to believe, even on so short an acquaintance, that she would like young Shelley for Harriet.

'Papa wants you to call at Chapel Street,' Harriet said softly.

'And so I shall, and so I shall!'

'Harriet goes back to school tomorrow,' Eliza pointed out, and added with an archness that made her feel vaguely uncomfortable, 'I doubt if you would care much for the company of an old man, one, moreover, with whom you can have very little in common, and that of his spinster daughter.'

'I have everything in common with your father and yourself,' Shelley asserted dramatically.

'Everything, Mr. Shelley?'

'Harriet, no less! And in addition, Miss Westbrook, I think we shall discover, on further acquaintance, that you and I have many intellectual interests in common also.'

Harriet, at first displeased that Shelley should be giving so much attention to Eliza, decided that he was surely making fun of her sister.

'My thinking is often confused,' Eliza said dryly. 'You will, I hope, find me an apt and eager pupil.'

'I ask nothing more, except, of course, enthusiasm.'

'My search for Truth,' Eliza added, 'shall be nothing if not enthusiastic. But I warn you, if we become close friends I shall insist on taking you to church.'

'Shall you indeed!' Shelley laughed.

It was Eliza now, Harriet thought, who was surely making fun of Shelley.

She said quickly, 'Eliza visits me at school every Sunday afternoon. You, of course, will want to visit your sisters.'

'More than ever, now, my sweet Harriet.'

This was better, much better. The gallantry now was being turned in her direction, and with an underlying suggestion of real intimacy.

'I can't imagine why, sir,' Harriet said coquettishly.

For a moment Shelley looked as if he were about to thrust out his tongue at her.

'I shall visit the school,' Shelley laughed, 'whether or not to see my sisters, whether or not to see you, in the company of a most adequate chaperon.'

Eliza rose and offered him her hand.

'My services are entirely at your disposal, Mr. Shelley,' she said.

Four

I

'Love,' Eliza Westbrook pronounced, 'was ever a most absorbing topic of conversation.'

The three of them – Eliza, Harriet and Shelley – were strolling leisurely on Clapham Common, a Sunday afternoon occupation which Shelley during the last few weeks had grown to enjoy enormously. Eliza, it was true, was inclined at times to argue a little, but amiably, whereas Harriet, whether or not she grasped the significance of his words, looked at him always with devotion in her eyes, agreed with his words of wisdom and laughed delightedly at his jokes.

'*L'amour, l'amour!*' Eliza exclaimed, her accent execrable.

In faint irritation Shelley wondered why of a sudden she should introduce this subject yet again. They had discussed it so often before, and from so many angles. One whole afternoon had been taken up with the argument that love in its purest form was that of a mother for her child, love in that respect being the noblest form of self-sacrifice. At other times they had touched on brotherly love, self-love, platonic love, the romantic, deceiving love of sweethearts and the more sober, everyday, matter-of-fact love of those long married. They had even, though in Harriet's absence, dwelt at length on immoral love, analysing, as far as they were able, the pain the Prince Regent must have caused the poor creatures who had partnered him in his many notorious *affaires*.

'I thought we had worn the subject threadbare,' Shelley said sharply.

'To a woman that could never happen,' Eliza assured him. She wondered, nevertheless, if she were persisting too obviously and thus preventing what she was striving to bring about, a passionate declaration from Shelley of his love for Harriet. It seemed to her that he had forgotten – as indeed he had – that he had once told Harriet that he loved her; worse, it seemed that friendship merely was to be the outcome of his interest in her sister. 'Give him time, don't frighten him away,' her father had cautioned, but it had occurred to her long ago that young Shelley, so sudden in his enthusiasms, was not the sort of person to whom, if one wanted anything from him, one should give any time at all. With Percy Bysshe Shelley one struck, however great the risk might be of frightening him away, while the iron was hot.

'Love,' Shelley pronounced, his manner suggesting that he was disposing of the subject once and for all, 'must be free, entirely unrestrained. Otherwise, my dear Eliza, it ceases to be what it undoubtedly should be, an idyllic and heavenly emotion.'

'It has been said,' she ventured coyly, 'that true marriages are made in heaven.'

'As are all good and worthy things,' Shelley agreed. 'But tell me, pray, what is, and, for that matter, *where* is the heaven you speak of?'

Eliza smiled wryly. He was off now with a vengeance, and the fault was entirely hers. He would spend the rest of the afternoon talking about heaven which, as he'd said often enough before, had nothing whatever to do with orthodox theology.

'Heaven,' Harriet tried hopefully, 'is where one's heart is.'

'That is one kind of heaven,' Shelley admitted loftily.

'And when two hearts are in the same place it must be very heaven indeed,' Eliza exclaimed.

Shelley turned and began to retrace his steps; Eliza and Harriet turned with him.

'Love, like thinking, should be as free as the air we breathe,' he declaimed.

Eliza sighed gratefully; he had forgotten all about heaven.

'To say that one is a free-thinker, as I do, is excellent,' he said broodingly, 'but to be one, in the *full* sense of the word, is another matter.'

'Yes indeed, my dear Bysshe,' Eliza agreed.

'How can a man think, really *think*,' he asked warmly, 'unless he is free to do so?'

'How indeed!' Eliza agreed.

'I am, myself, of course,' he said with relish. 'That's just another of the many reasons why people call me crazy.'

'Gracious heaven, here comes Papa!' Harriet exclaimed.

'And with him, unless I am very much mistaken, my own venerable father.'

'Both of them with faces as black as a thunder cloud,' Eliza pointed out.

The two gentlemen approaching were indeed Mr. John Westbrook and Mr. Timothy Shelley, a most ill-assorted looking couple – a rhinoceros and a giraffe, Shelley thought, taking an uncomfortable and silent, yet grimly purposeful walk together.

'This means trouble for somebody,' he predicted.

When at last the two parties came face to face – the attackers and the attacked, it almost seemed – Shelley greeted both his father and Harriet's with well simulated deference. Neither was in the least impressed; Timothy Shelley scowled, John Westbrook looked as if he badly wanted to spit.

'I was unaware,' said Shelley, addressing himself cheerfully to Eliza, 'that our respective and – ah – respected fathers knew each other.'

'Miss Hawkes, that Fenning woman's underling, introduced us,' Timothy growled.

Miss Fenning was the proprietress of Church House, the select Clapham academy at which Harriet and the younger Shelley girls were being educated – or 'diseducated', as Shelley called it.

'A stringy, dried-up creature, Miss Hawkes,' he suggested brightly. 'Neither man, woman nor beast, and suffering, I'll be bound, from some obscure but everlasting liver complaint.'

Harriet giggled instantly.

'Hold your tongue,' Mr. Shelley told his son.

'Stop that silly snickering,' Mr. Westbrook reproved his daughter.

'I knew you were in London,' Shelley said imperturbably, 'but I didn't expect you to come out to Clapham.'

'Miss Hawkes requested the pleasure of my company,' Mr. Shelley said, in part explanation.

'Mine, too,' Mr. Westbrook added.

'How delightful for you both!'

Mr. Shelley was fumbling in his pocket and presently

brought out a well-worn sheet of writing paper. Spreading it out he flourished it at his son.

'Did you write this?' he demanded.

Shelley glanced at it. 'Indeed I did. A letter to Harriet, and as such her own private property. May I ask how it came into your possession?'

Mr. Shelley waved it in Harriet's direction. 'Miss Hawkes found it among the girl's things.'

'By "the girl",' Shelley said politely, 'you mean Harriet?'

'By "the girl" I mean Harriet.'

Eliza glanced hastily at her father. Mr. Shelley's rudeness was more than enough to bring an angry flush to his cheeks, but to her amazement he showed no sign of anger. Indeed, as she held his eyes for a moment, he winked expressively. It was the sort of wink which, as she knew of old, said plainly: Keep out of this me girl, leave everything to me.

'It will be more than sufficient for me to read only a few words,' Mr. Shelley snapped, and scowling anew he read: '*Rest assured, my dear Harriet, that the mass of mankind are Christians in name only; their religion, a mockery in the eyes of the Almighty, has no reality.*'

'Insolent young puppy,' Mr. Westbrook exploded.

Mr. Shelley looked at him with distaste. 'I am bound in this instance to agree with you, Westbrook.'

'And having agreed,' Shelley asked warmly, 'may I ask, Father, what all this pother is about?'

'To come to the point,' Mr. Shelley said impatiently, 'Mr. Westbrook's daughter, as well as your sisters, are in grave danger of being expelled.'

'Because of my letter to Harriet?'

'The views expressed in it being nothing short of blasphemous, yes.'

'Seems Harriet's been letting the whole school read it,' Mr. Westbrook put in. 'First thing Miss Hawkes heard of it was a complaint from one of the parents. Church of England clergyman, no less. Talking of taking it up with the Archbishop of Canterbury, he is.'

'And as a result,' Timothy Shelley broke in, 'Miss Fenning or Miss Hawkes, it matters not which, has issued an ultimatum. Westbrook's daughter will be expelled and I shall be asked to withdraw your sisters unless you promise not to visit the school again and refrain from writing to any of the girls.'

'Infamous!'

'There's more to it than that, far as I'm concerned,' Mr. Westbrook said heatedly. 'You're never to see Harriet again – here, Chapel Street or anywhere else.'

'Oh – *Papa*!' Harriet wailed.

'I am, of course, in complete agreement,' Timothy asserted. 'A most unsuitable association.'

'For Harriet, you mean?' Mr. Westbrook challenged.

'No, my dear sir, for my son.'

'That's rich, him being an atheist!'

Leaving the two fathers to glare at each other, Shelley turned to Harriet and gave her his most charming smile.

'Do *you* regard me as an evil influence, my dear?'

'You know I don't, Bysshe! I – I'd rather be expelled than never see you again.'

'You won't see him again whatever happens,' Mr. Westbrook growled.

'Oh, Bysshe!' Harriet moaned, and flung herself into Shelley's arms.

He held her gently, but before he could murmur any words of comfort, the two irate fathers descended upon them. Mr. Shelley seized Harriet by the shoulders and Mr. Westbrook tugged ineffectively at Shelley's coat tails.

'You keep your hands off my girl!' Mr. Westbrook roared at Mr. Shelley.

'Unhand my son!' Mr. Shelley roared back.

The fathers changed positions and thus, after much heavy breathing, Shelley and Harriet were separated.

'Bysshe . . .' Eliza whispered, and taking him by the arm led him a few paces away. Knowing much of the devious workings of her father's mind, she still wondered why he should have changed his attitude so suddenly as far as Bysshe was concerned.

'If you love Harriet, even only as a friend,' she said, 'do the one thing that will make this distressing situation easier for her.'

'And that, Eliza?'

'Go to our ridiculous fathers and promise to do exactly what they ask.'

'Capitulation!'

'With anything but capitulation in mind. The next school holidays are not too far distant. Meanwhile, I shall see to it that she comes home for an occasional weekend.'

'You'll bring her to Poland Street?'

'Of course.'

'Very well, I'll do what you want.'

Like an actor throwing himself wholeheartedly into a new and interesting role, Shelley walked in seeming humility to his father, hung his head for a moment before speaking, then murmured brokenly that he was ready, even though it would break his heart, to do what was demanded of him.

'Amazing!' Mr. Shelley ejaculated.

Shelley turned sadly to Harriet.

'Farewell, little friend,' he cried, flinging out his arms extravagantly. 'I shall never see you again, but I shall never forget you.'

Eliza thought he was rather overdoing it, the more so since it reduced Harriet to a fit of weeping, but she found herself deeply moved by the beautiful sadness of his voice.

'Come, Eliza, you too, Harriet,' Mr. Westbrook said briskly.

For several moments Shelley and his father stood together in silence watching Eliza and Mr. Westbrook lead the still-weeping Harriet away. Timothy cleared his throat self-consciously; there was a suspicion of tears in his eyes, for he too was deeply moved.

'I must thank you, Bysshe, for meeting my wishes in this unfortunate matter,' he said at length.

Shelley bowed graciously. 'Most handsome of you, Father.'

'I can – hum – make no promises at this stage,' Timothy went on, 'but possibly we shall now reach a more amicable understanding.'

Shelley repressed a chuckle. The atheism of which he was still suspected was clearly more acceptable to his father than the interest he had shown in Harriet, a retired publican's daughter.

'Why not return with me to Field Place?' Timothy suggested.

'A command, Father?'

'Does it sound like one? I take no pleasure in our being at loggerheads. As the Duke pointed out, you are in many ways a young man of exceptional ability. In point of fact, he—'

'You discussed our quarrel with the Duke of Norfolk?'

'His Grace asked after you. I could do no less.'

Shelley made no attempt this time to repress a chuckle. His father, like his grandfather, was one of Norfolk's ardent supporters and deferred to him on every possible occasion.

'If the Duke asked you to stand on your head naked in Piccadilly,' Shelley declared, 'I'm sure you'd do it.'

'His Grace would never dream of making so unreasonable a request,' Mr. Shelley said, in shocked tones. 'You show the utmost disrespect in suggesting such a thing.'

'Disrespect for the Duke, or for you, Father?'

'For the Duke, naturally.'

'You must remind me to genuflect the next time I meet him.'

Mr. Shelley laughed unexpectedly. 'You are determined to bait me, Bysshe.'

Shelley laughed too. This meeting on the Common had made him realize how much he had missed the stimulation he always felt when baiting his father. On the whole, a few days at Field Place would be quite enjoyable, and apart from that his landlord at Poland Street, complaining daily of the rent owing to him, was growing more than truculent.

'I'll come home with you, Father,' he said, with alacrity.

2

'I can't imagine why you treated Bysshe so harshly, Papa,' Eliza remarked.

'Can't you, my dear?' her father chuckled.

Having left the tearful Harriet at Miss Fenning's, Eliza and her father were now travelling back to Chapel Street in the Westbrook carriage.

'You treated poor Harriet harshly, too,' Eliza added.

'I had to, me girl. Not that I liked it, but if she knew I was only pretending she wouldn't be clever enough to go on looking miserable. It's like this, Eliza. When I found out what the trouble was at Miss Fenning's I put on me thinking cap. She's staying on at school, is Harriet, but she's under a cloud. Miss Hawkes said she was. When things get real bad for her, you'll tell young Shelley how unhappy she is. That's stage one. She'll come home in tears, but I'll send her back, and you'll tell the boy how heartless I am. That's stage two.'

'And then, Papa?'

'Elopement.'

'Elopement?' Eliza echoed.

'We'll never get 'em married any other way.'

'Mr. Shelley would never give his consent, I know that, but Bysshe will come of age in a little over two years and will be able to please himself then.'

'What if he changed his mind?'

'There's that, certainly.'

'Seems to me he hasn't made it up in any case. Needs prodding, he does.'

'In other words, Papa, you want to arouse his sympathy.'

'That's right.'

'He's romantic and impulsive,' Eliza said, pondering on this. 'Highly dramatic, too. Life isn't life to him without a touch of drama. Or perhaps I mean melodrama. You might be right, Papa.'

'Course I'm right. Opposition from his father, *and* from me, an' there you are! Harriet persecuted, as it were. I can just see his eyes flashing with black anger. He'll feel like a knight of old, real keen to rescue the maiden in distress.'

Eliza was silent for a moment.

'Well, I hope we're doing the right thing, Papa,' she said soberly.

3

'This is a damn' fine port, Timothy,' Captain Pilford declared heartily.

'I never tasted a finer,' Mr. Shelley agreed. 'The pity of it is, there's but a few bottles left.'

'I laid in a stock at the same time,' the Captain reminded him. 'I've still got twenty dozen in the cellar.'

'Twenty dozen!' Mr. Shelley exclaimed enviously.

Captain Pilford, Shelley's maternal uncle, had ridden over from Cuckfield that afternoon, and now, having declared his intention of spending the night at Field Place, was sitting up late with Shelley and his father. Taking Shelley aside earlier he had told him, in his usual bluff, good-natured manner, that he was determined, one way or another, to set things to rights before he went back to Cuckfield. Shelley had always liked and admired his uncle who, retired now from the Navy, had fought under Lord Nelson, having been in command of the *Ajax* at the Battle of Trafalgar.

'There's no better way of settling an argument than over a bottle or two of port,' the Captain remarked warmly.

Mr. Shelley, who had promised himself that he would go no further than one bottle, but was now well advanced with his second, agreed just as warmly.

'Nevertheless,' he said, his mind somewhat hazy, 'I can't recollect that we were arguing about anything whatever.'

'The necessity or otherwise of atheism, that was one argument,' Captain Pilford chuckled. 'Politics, that was another. Let's have one last look at Bysshe's provocative ideas and have done with them once and for all.'

Mr. Shelley gave his brother-in-law a pained look. 'If we must, confound you.'

'Start me off,' Shelley warned, 'and I'll keep you up till daybreak. Either that or till both of you are snoring under the table.'

'Then keep your mouth closed and let others have their say,' the Captain growled.

But since he accompanied the growl with an owlish wink unseen by Mr. Shelley, his nephew thought it might be amusing to remain silent for once and see if the tactics which had won the Battle of Trafalgar could be applied to good purpose here.

The Captain placed his elbows solidly on the table. 'It's a funny thing, this appreciation you have for a good port, Timothy.'

'I see nothing funny about it. Bless my soul, I've been drinking port for more years than I can remember.'

'What I mean is this,' the Captain went on thoughtfully: 'you like it, but *how* do you like it?'

'To ask me *why* I like it would be more to the point.'

The Captain chuckled deeply. 'Good lord, man, I know *why* you like it. What I want to know is how. *How*, you understand, not *why*.'

Mr. Shelley was quite at a loss. Indeed, he was beginning

to think that his brother-in-law, though he'd never shown any sign of it before, had a poor head for wine.

'I'll tell you, Timothy,' the Captain went on, 'you like it through your sense of taste.'

'That's simple enough, of course I do,' Mr. Shelley agreed.

Shelley looked at his uncle with increasing admiration. Captain Pilford had read *The Necessity of Atheism* and in a letter had admitted himself shaken by its basic argument. It seemed obvious now that he was twisting that same basic argument a little in an attempt to get the better of his brother-in-law.

'Sight comes into it as well as taste,' he went on. 'Sense of smell too. It has a lovely colour and a lovely smell. Did you ever smell anything better?'

Timothy held up his glass and admired the colour of the port; he placed it beneath his nose and with a sigh of pleasure inhaled the rich bouquet.

'What I'm getting at is this,' the Captain added softly: 'You know all about wine because of your senses. They carry the knowledge to your mind. In other words, the senses are the source of knowledge, whether it's wine you're concerned with or anything else.'

'That's true enough— But wait a moment.' Timothy was frowning now. 'I seem to have heard *that* argument before.'

'Of course you have. It's your son's, my dear Timothy.'

'You're a cunning devil,' Mr. Shelley complained.

'Rubbish. I'm only trying to be fair.'

Timothy looked unhappy, for he was beginning to feel most confused. He could see no connexion between a belief in good wine and a belief in God, though wine as excellent as this was surely nectar of the gods. Looking sombrely at his glass he all but wept at the thought that only a few bottles were left. Wine on the one hand, he grumbled to himself, atheism on the other. Belief in wine, but *dis*belief in God; that seemed to be the argument. He struggled to clear his mind of the muddled thinking. If your knowledge of everything came to you through your senses, how then could you believe implicitly in God? The thought shocked him; he rose shakily to his feet.

'You're trying to turn me into a sceptic,' he groaned.

'Nothing of the sort, Timothy. What I'm getting at it is: Bysshe, thinking freely for himself, has a right to his ideas.'

'I'm shaken, badly shaken.'

'Glad to know I've made some headway,' Captain Pilfold chuckled.

'Looking at it from your own point of view, Father,' Shelley chirped up brightly, 'if God created us he created our senses too.'

'Thank you for that, Bysshe,' Timothy said, and began to feel happier.

Captain Pilfold gave his nephew an approving glance. 'Open another bottle for your father, Bysshe.'

Timothy sank back into his chair and looked hazily at his son. It was true enough what the Duke had said, Bysshe *was* a young fellow of exceptional ability. A bit hair-brained, yes, but the clever ones usually were, till they settled down. Maudlin tears filled his eyes: a son to be proud of. He took up his glass, replenished now by the Captain. The Duke had said something else too, made a useful, attractive suggestion.

'Bysshe,' he said, leaning forward eagerly, 'the Duke, God bless him, has a warm spot in his heart for you. He wants you to stand for Parliament. There's more than room for another Shelley in the House of Commons.'

Shelley sprang to his feet instantly. 'So you want to bind me hand and foot, shackle my mind until I haven't a mind of my own left to think with. Never, Father, never!'

Without wasting another moment Captain Pilfold slipped quickly round the table, seized his nephew from behind and trundled him to the door.

'Young hothead!' he growled. 'Out you get and out you stay.'

But before the door closed on him Shelley turned and saw the twinkle in his uncle's eyes, and lingering heard his father being assured that more headway would be made with Bysshe out of the way. 'It's like this, Timothy, Bysshe will argue against anything, given the chance, but left alone he'll argue *for* it.'

Smiling, Shelley began to pace up and down, pausing from time to time to listen to the indistinct rumble of voices within the room. Presently, in obedience to the urgent ringing of the bell, a footman panted up the stairs and entered the study. Whatever the man had done, Timothy Shelley, by the sound of his voice, was in a furious temper.

'What's troubling the old gentleman?' Shelley asked, when the footman reappeared.

'I had the unenviable task, Master Bysshe, of informing your
father that he had made a mistake.'

'Mistake, Thomas?'

'That there wine,' Thomas wailed, forgetting his carefully
cultivated accent, 'ain't no more of it left.'

'Then heaven help us all!' Shelley laughed.

But help, as it turned out, came from Captain Pilfold, not
from heaven. He emerged from the study five minutes later, took
his nephew by the arm and led him to his room. He was stagger-
ing a little, was the Captain, but his speech was still unslurred.

'How does it feel to have two hundred pounds a year?' he
asked.

'What on earth do you mean, Uncle?'

'That's your new allowance.'

'You're joking!'

'Word of honour, I'm not.'

'I'm not going into Parliament, not even for two hundred a
year.'

'You don't have to. The money's yours unconditionally.
Fifty pounds paid into your bank every quarterday. You may live
where you please, do what you like. You're a free agent, my boy.'

'You're a worker of miracles, Uncle,' Shelley gasped. 'Tell
me how you did it.'

Rocking on his feet the Captain smiled reflectively. 'Things
are always a bit difficult with the second bottle. It's what I've
been saying for years. One's enough, two's too many, three's not
enough. That's why I held back my broadside till the third was
empty.'

'But there isn't a single bottle of that best port left,' Shelley
pointed out. 'Your broadside, whatever it was, must have been
powerful enough to blast the entire French fleet out of existence.'

'Remember my own supply. Twenty dozen bottles.'

'You actually offered them to Father?'

'*And* he accepted.'

'But, Uncle, what a sacrifice!'

Captain Pilfold placed his hands on his nephew's shoulders.

'I couldn't love you more, Bysshe, if you were my own son,'
he said emotionally. 'And apart from that, there's nothing to
stop me from coming regularly to Field Place while the supply
lasts, now is there?'

Five

I

THE Westbrook carriage was turning from Oxford Road[1] into Poland Street when Eliza caught sight of Shelley. Seeing instantly that the young man was behaving in a most peculiar manner, she bade the coachman stop on the corner. Oxford Road was at its busiest, with coaches and carriages of all descriptions forced by the congestion to move at a snail's pace. This, apparently, suited Shelley's purpose admirably, though as she watched him Eliza found it impossible to decide just what that purpose was. She peered more closely. There he stood in the midst of the traffic, waving his arms wildly and – goodness gracious yes! he was flinging sheets of paper into the carriages as they rumbled slowly past him.

'Go back into Oxford Road,' she instructed the coachman. 'Drive on in the direction of Charing Cross, then turn and come back to Poland Street.'

And so presently, when the flow of traffic permitted it, the Westbrook carriage came level with the excited, gesticulating Shelley, and a sheet of paper – some verses were printed on it, she noticed – was thrust into Eliza's hand.

'Bysshe!' she said sharply.

'Ah, Eliza Westbrook!' he cried, recognizing her but faintly.

'Get in, Bysshe,' she said, still sharply. 'You're making a disgusting spectacle of yourself.'

Laughing, Shelley leapt into the carriage and flung himself down at her side.

'I enjoy making a disgusting spectacle of myself, Eliza!'

[1] Now Oxford Street.

She shrugged helplessly; his laughter, as usual, was irresistible.

'I do hope it isn't another pamphlet about atheism,' she said.

Shelley fell serious for a moment, considering this. 'No, not about atheism, but an attack on an *atheist*.'

'Well, that's a change!'

'Oh, he doesn't call himself one. *He* thinks he's the greatest Christian in the land.'

'Who on earth are you talking about, Bysshe?'

'His Royal Highness, the Prince Regent, no less.'

'Bysshe, you're incorrigible!'

'It's a satire. I wrote it and had it printed at my own expense. Read it and have the grace to compliment me.'

Eliza's eyes fell on one verse only.

> For he is fat – his waistcoat gay
>   When strained upon a levee day
>   Scarce meets across his princely paunch
> And pantaloons are like half-moons
>   Upon each brawny haunch.

'I like "princely paunch", don't you, Eliza?' Shelley asked eagerly.

'You'll get yourself into serious trouble,' she said.

'Pooh! Too many other attacks, really deadly ones, are being made for the law to take any notice of *my* efforts.'

This was true enough. The Prince Regent, who had been raised to that exalted position because of the King's insanity, had never been as unpopular as he was today, his vast debts being no less a scandal than his licentiousness. He was still called the First Gentleman in Europe, but that description now had as distinct a ring of satire in it as anything Shelley might write.

'Why are you taking all this trouble?' Eliza asked.

'It makes me angry that such a hypocrite, a mock-Christian, no less, should be set up to rule over us.'

'You look amused, not angry.'

'It's possible to be both! Sometimes the most effective sort of anger is the laughing sort.'

The carriage had now stopped at Number 15 Poland Street. Shelley leapt out and handed Eliza down.

'You were coming to see me, of course?'

'Of course, and I have a letter for you from Harriet.'

'Poor little Harriet, still cooped up in her prison,' he said casually.

His manner both annoyed and pleased Eliza. She had grown accustomed, during the last few months, to having Shelley entirely to herself. Her father, when told of the proposed secret meetings, had forbidden them, quite wrongly, she thought, for Shelley, caught up in so many other interests, seemed now to have relegated Harriet to the back of his mind. He was sorry that she was unhappy at school – he said that often enough – but not sorry enough, obviously, to be really deeply moved. Nevertheless, Eliza always felt a strange stirring of delight, a quickening of the pulses, when alone, as now, with Shelley.

'Here it is,' she said, giving him Harriet's letter when they were seated in Shelley's untidy, cluttered-up lodgings.

Opening it, he began to skim through it, casually at first. Harriet was more miserable than she had ever been before. Miss Hawkes never lost an opportunity of lecturing her on the error of her ways, that error being her persistence in declaring that he, Bysshe Shelley, was and always would be her Dearest Friend.

Shelley began to feel uneasy, and read on hurriedly. The girls at school, spurred on by the example set by Miss Hawkes, continually taunted her, calling her the Atheist's Friend, an Abandoned Wretch, and even accused her of being an Unrepentant Atheist herself. This treatment, she said, was enough to make her one, but she was determined, come what may, never to renounce him.

'Read it!' Shelley cried, thrusting the letter at Eliza.

Eliza took it and read it.

'It's covered with tear stains,' he shouted.

'I can't see any, Bysshe.'

'It is, I insist it is! The poor child will fall into a decline.'

'That does seem possible,' Harriet agreed. 'There's a PS.; did you read it?'

Shelley snatched back the letter. The PS. read: *I fear you have quite forgotten me; you failed even to remember my birthday.*

'How could I remember it when it was never known to me?' he demanded indignantly.

'I thought it was, Bysshe. Harriet attached so much importance to the fact that you were born on the fourth of August and she on the first.'

'Ah, yes! I do remember now! What a thoughtless brute I am!'

It was now the middle of August, Eliza reflected. Bysshe was nineteen, Harriet sixteen. Their joint ages – and this thought made her frown – amounted to only a few years more than her own.

'I remember something else, too, Eliza! You were going to bring Harriet to see me, arrange secret meetings. Or did I dream it?'

'Papa forbade me.'

'If the meetings were to be secret, how could he do that?'

Eliza bit her lip. 'Papa suspected my intention. He is a very shrewd man. He accused me of planning secret meetings and kept a strict watch on me.'

'How is it then that you yourself are able to come so freely to Poland Street?'

'He only watches me when Harriet is at home.'

Shelley gave her a savage look. 'I begin to suspect that she is persecuted as much at home as at school.'

Eliza endeavoured to bring a sob to her voice. 'She is, poor child, she is.'

'Methodists!' Shelley stormed. 'Ranting, hidebound Methodists!'

Eliza hid a smile. Her father was certainly a Methodist in one respect, and that entirely irreligious. And his method was at last beginning to show results. The thing to do was to keep Bysshe at this white-hot pitch of indignation.

'Harriet is coming home this weekend,' she said. 'I'll defy Papa as never before and bring her to see you.'

'You promise, Eliza?'

'I promise.'

Shelley tore at his already disordered hair. 'This devilish persecution! The fault is mine, all mine!'

'Tell her that, Bysshe, and give her at least a little comfort.'

2

'Eliza!' Harriet cried. 'It's Bysshe! And he's running down the street, actually *running*!'

Eliza joined her sister at the window. There was no doubt about it, the youthful figure, hair flying in the breeze, coat-tails streaming out behind him, was unmistakable.

'By the look of it he must have run all the way from Poland Street,' she said.

It was Sunday afternoon. Less than an hour ago, on her father's instructions, Eliza had sent the Westbrook coachman with a brief note to Shelley. In it she had said that a secret meeting was impossible. She and Harriet had been caught attempting to leave Chapel Street last night, and today servants had been set to prevent them from making another move. This would be enough, both she and her father had hoped, to bring Shelley flying in anger to Chapel Street, but for good measure she had added, without exaggeration, that Harriet was ill and looked but a piti-ful shadow of her former gay and cheerful self.

'He's at the door now,' Harriet whispered, a deep flush staining her pale cheeks. 'If Papa hears him he won't let him in. I know he won't!'

'I'll go down and see what can be done about it,' Eliza said confidently.

Her father joined her in the hall below; thunderous knocking was already shaking the front door.

'Young Shelley?' Mr. Westbrook asked, with a grin.

'Yes, Papa.'

'I'll let him in. You know what to do, Eliza?'

Eliza nodded – she was well rehearsed in the small part her father had set her to play – and slipped to the back of the hall while her father went to the door and flung it open.

'Monster!' Shelley shouted, all but falling into the hall.

'Hold hard, young feller!' Mr. Westbrook roared, and seizing the lapels of Shelley's coat held him at arm's length. 'Either you go quietly, or I call the watch, that's what!'

Shelley tore himself free, tugged a pistol from his pocket and waved it in Mr. Westbrook's face.

'Either you let me see Harriet,' he shrieked, 'or I'll shoot you like the villain you are, *that's* what!'

Eliza ran forward, alarmed by this quite unexpected development, and placed herself between Shelley and her father.

'Dear Papa,' she said urgently, 'do please try to understand poor Bysshe's agitation. You were hot-headed enough yourself in your youth, remember that. And Harriet is ill, remember that, too, Papa.'

Mr. Westbrook controlled himself. 'I like a young feller to have a bit of spirit,' he admitted, 'but lord love us all, I can't say I like the look of that pistol.'

Eliza, catching Shelley unawares, snatched the pistol from his hand.

'*Now* do you feel any easier, Papa?'

In his turn, Mr. Westbrook snatched the pistol from his daughter's hands.

'Why, it's unloaded!' he laughed.

'I could have knocked your brains out with it, all the same!' Shelley asserted.

'Papa—' Eliza begged.

'Very well,' Mr. Westbrook conceded, with every show of unwillingness, 'he can have a few minutes with Harriet.' And remembering in time one of the lines he had rehearsed he added scathingly, 'But if he thinks he's a knight in shining armour flying to the rescue of a damsel in distress he's much mistaken. He can see her this once, but never again.'

Eliza beckoned to Shelley and led him quickly upstairs to the richly furnished over crowded withdrawing-room which was reserved for the exclusive use of herself and Harriet.

'Be gentle with her,' she beseeched.

'Would I ever be anything else?' Shelley asked indignantly.

Thrusting Eliza aside he flung himself into the room. Harriet, in what appeared to be a half-fainting condition, was lying languidly on a sofa. She had grown quite thin, he saw that instantly, and her eyes, unnaturally large in a face that had never before been so pale, reflected much of the pain she had suffered and was still suffering. Frantically he remembered Eliza's words: *a pitiful shadow of her former gay and cheerful self.*

'Harriet!' he cried, falling on his knees at the sofa.

'Dearest Bysshe!' Harriet sobbed.

'I suspected nothing of your suffering, nothing!'

'As if that matters now.'

'You scorned the world for my sake.'

'But proudly, Bysshe, proudly.'

It was a beautiful, heart-rending scene, Eliza thought as she watched the two of them breathlessly. Never on any stage, though her theatre-going was sternly disciplined by her father, had she seen anything like it. Harriet, making crooning little noises, began to run her fingers through Shelley's tousled hair; he for his part let his head fall into her lap and embraced her round the waist. So much in sympathy was Eliza with her sister that the silky feel of Shelley's hair clung to her own hands. She reached out impulsively, then checked herself. She was being carried away to a ridiculous extent, wanting now as she did to snatch Shelley from Harriet and embrace him.

'The fault was mine, all mine,' Shelley groaned.

'Dearest Bysshe, does it matter whose fault it was? Has it not brought us together again?'

Eliza compressed her lips; a queer unwelcome sort of anger was gripping her now.

'Let us at least be practical,' she said tartly. 'Papa has no intention whatever of your meeting again.'

Shelley leapt to his feet. In spite of John Westbrook's jeering remark he *was* a knight in shining armour, he *was* flying to the rescue of a damsel in distress. To have lived in the days of the Crusades – how grand that would have been! He looked wildly at Harriet. All his anger against the world, against the mock Christians, the torpid ineffectual politicians, the fat and lecherous Prince Regent, became centred in this new and urgent problem.

'Papa is adamant,' Harriet said woefully. 'I begged him not to send me back to school but he refused to listen.'

'Conditions at school can scarcely be worse than conditions at home,' Eliza put in sadly.

'Very well, then, let us at least be practical!' Shelley cried, and seizing Harriet by the arms dragged her from the sofa. 'Look at me, Harriet!'

Big tears were rolling down Harriet's cheeks. 'Oh, Bysshe. . . .'

'Promise to do anything I ask.'

'I – I promise.'

'Repeat after me, "I have nothing whatever to fear".'

c*

'I have nothing whatever to fear.'

' "Neither at home nor at school." '

'Neither at home nor at school.'

'You actually *want* her to go back to school?' Eliza asked indignantly. 'How heartless of you!'

Shelley ignored her. 'Now repeat, "My fate is entirely in your hands".'

'Oh, it has been, Bysshe, ever since I met you.'

'Repeat it, repeat it!'

'My fate is entirely in your hands.'

'Now hold your head up proudly and say, "I'll go with you wherever you please, whenever you please".'

Harriet flung her arms round his neck. 'Oh gladly, gladly!'

'This is being anything but practical,' Eliza remarked dryly. 'Where, for instance, do you propose to take her?'

'A thousand miles from here. *Ten* thousand if necessary.'

'That you should want to rescue Harriet from all the misery she has suffered is very noble and self-sacrificing,' Eliza said carefully, 'but what of her reputation? Would you not by taking her away expose her to further persecution?'

'My wretched father would never consent to our marrying, you know that.'

Eliza hid a smile. That Shelley himself should be the first to speak of marriage was excellent.

'Nor would *my* father,' Harriet sobbed.

Shelley threw out his arms in a grandiloquent gesture. 'We shall elope, then!'

Eliza nodded her head slowly. That he should be the first also to speak of elopement was excellent too. She almost wished that her father was behind the curtains, listening approvingly to the skilful way she was handling this ticklish situation.

'You can't marry without your father's consent,' she said, 'nor can Eliza marry without her father's.' She sighed gently. 'At least, not in England, but what of Scotland, where the law is different?'

'I had Scotland in mind myself,' said Shelley, not having thought of Scotland until Eliza mentioned it.

'Then once again you force me to say, let us at least be practical.'

'Be as practical as you wish,' Shelley said airily.

Eliza saw – in time, she hoped – that resentment was creeping into his mind. Harriet, his manner suggested, was *his* responsibility; he, not her sister, was the one to make plans, and making them achieve a dramatic rescue.

'Dear Bysshe,' she said softly, 'tell me what I can do to help you.'

Shelley beamed on her instantly. 'I need your help in one thing only.'

'And that?'

He glanced about the room. 'Harriet's escape from this intolerable prison. We must get her away at once, at once!'

'With Papa standing guard in the hall, and servants at the back door? I do admire your forcefulness, Bysshe, but we must use a little guile.

At that moment a knock was heard at the door and with it Mr. Westbrook's disgruntled voice.

'Out you come, young feller. Enough's enough!'

'You see how impossible it is?' Eliza whispered. 'Go back to Poland Street, Bysshe. I'll contrive to call on you tonight. Papa will be out visiting friends—'

'In that case I see nothing to prevent me from rescuing Harriet this very night.'

Mr. Westbrook was hammering on the door now.

'It would be too late then to catch the Edinburgh mail,' Eliza said urgently. 'Where would you take Harriet? Poland Street? Papa would follow her there. Please do as I say. Hurry back to your lodgings, make careful plans and be ready to tell me about them when I call.'

'Eliza!' Mr. Westbrook roared.

'Coming, Papa, coming!' she cried gaily.

3

Shelley, running continually from his writing-table to the window and back again, was penning a hasty letter to his friend and confidant, Thomas Jefferson Hogg. Back at the table once more he began to read the few lines which he had already written.

The decision is taken! My excitement is at fever pitch. The role of knight-errant may seem to you to fit oddly upon my shoulders, yet assume it I must, and joyfully.

'Joyfully?' he asked himself, aloud.

He snatched up the pen and in the margin wrote: *Yes, joyfully!*

The next sentence he had written then captured his attention. *The only thing that makes life worth living is self-sacrifice.* He dwelt on this. It was a noble thought, but what precisely did it mean?

Seizing the pen again he wrote: *Here I must examine myself, look deep into my mind. Now more than ever before I must know myself.*

He remembered having told Eliza once that love must be free, entirely unrestrained. Usually he forgot most of the things he said soon after saying them, but he remembered this because he had enjoyed saying it. Enjoyed it and meant it too? *Know yourself, Shelley, know yourself!* Very well, then, most certainly meant it too.

And now – what? How depressing to contemplate the undoubted fact that marriage – marriage as sanctioned by the customs and laws of society – spelt anything but freedom! At least, as far as the average man was concerned. Might it not be different with a man like himself? His mind was like a see-saw, he thought, thumping down on the ground of unorthodox conduct one moment, orthodox conduct the next.

He sprang up in torment and ran again to the window. A hackney carriage was in the street below and Eliza Westbrook was stepping fastidiously down from it. Time was running out. He must make up his mind without further delay. Harriet, the poor little victim! He saw her in his arms, sobbing as if her heart were broken. To love was one thing, to be in love quite another. He remembered vaguely that once, when shocked that his father should have suggested an impending seduction, he had thought Harriet desirable. An abstract thought, surely! To be 'in love' meant physical craving and he had never even dreamt of possessing her physically. The sober truth was this: he was not in love with Harriet but he did most certainly love her and want to protect her.

There was a knock at the door.

'Come in!' he cried desperately.

Eliza, her skirts swishing ominously, swept briskly into the room. Shelley, darting forward, pointed a quivering finger at her.

'The only thing I have against marrying, Eliza Westbrook, is marriage itself.'

Eliza stared at him in alarm. His mood was such, she decided quickly, that he must be provoked at once to violent contradiction.

'My poor Bysshe,' she said scathingly, 'that is surely what a man says after marrying, not before.'

He took fire instantly. 'By heaven, are you trying to turn me from the firmest resolution I ever made in my life?'

'That depends on the sort of marriage you have in mind. I told you once, remember, that true marriages are made in heaven.'

Shelley's eyes grew dreamy. 'No, it was Harriet who said that.'

Eliza breathed more easily. To argue would be silly. She had achieved her object, or so she hoped.

'The dear child also said,' he added tenderly, 'that heaven is where one's heart is.'

'She said more than that,' sighed Eliza, and glibly repeated her own words: 'she said that when two hearts are in the same place it must be very heaven indeed.'

'And heaven, in this case, is Scotland!' Shelley cried.

'You have made your plans, then?' Eliza asked carefully.

'We leave for Scotland tomorrow, Harriet and I,' he said instantly.

'How fortunate, then, that Harriet is not to be sent back to school tomorrow, after all. I called in a physician and he and I between us persuaded Papa that Harriet was too ill to be moved from Chapel Street.'

But Shelley was scarcely listening. 'The Edinburgh mail leaves at seven in the evening.'

'Do you propose that Harriet should meet you at the mail-coach?'

'No, at the coffee-house in Mount Street where you and I have sometimes taken a meal together.'

'I shall miss those meals together,' Eliza said sadly.

Shelley was staring at her unseeingly. 'Mount Street, convenient enough to Chapel Street.'

'The coffee-house in Mount Street, then.'

'But how to get Harriet out of her prison? *How?*'

There would be no difficulty in that, but Eliza kept up the

pretence. 'Harriet shall declare that she is ready, after all, to return to school. That will put the carriage at our disposal and we shall start off, to all intents and purposes, for Clapham.'

'Splendid!'

'And the time of the rendezvous?'

'Six o'clock. I shall have a hackney carriage waiting to take us to the Edinburgh mail.'

'Then no more need be said. Everything is arranged.'

Shelley flung out his arms dramatically. 'So the knell has struck!' He remembered something from *Macbeth* and shuddered violently. 'You remember the scene,' he said, as if Eliza were fully conversant with his thoughts.

'What scene, Bysshe?'

'The bell rings. Macbeth is all too aware of its meaning. The murder of Duncan lies before him.'

'Really, Bysshe, this talk of murder!'

Inserting his own name in the lines Shelley lowered his voice to a tense whisper.

'Hear it not, Shelley, for it is a knell that summons thee to heaven or to hell!'

'To heaven, surely!'

Shelley embraced her wildly. 'If it be hell, I shall turn it into heaven. That I swear!'

4

'Being sensible at last, my pet,' Mr. Westbrook murmured.

'I do hope so, Papa,' Harriet sighed.

The three of them, Mr. Westbrook and his two daughters, were grouped together in the hall. The coachman had already carried Harriet's small portmanteau out to the carriage.

'Keep a stiff upper lip,' Mr. Westbrook warned.

'I'll try my best, Papa.'

Harriet flung her arms round his neck. It hurt her now to think that she was deceiving him so shockingly. She hoped and prayed that when the truth came out his anger would not last too long and that in the end he would forgive her and make her husband welcome once again at Chapel Street. Husband, she thought wonderingly, Bysshe my husband! It needed no more than that to check the tears which had sprung to her eyes.

'Good-bye, Papa!' she cried.

Mr. Westbrook held her at arm's length and looked at her unsteadily. He regretted as never before the harshness in which he had forced her to believe. Perhaps he would tell her some day that it had all been one big pretence and they would laugh about it together, he repentant at the temporary hurt he had caused her, she grateful that her old father, clever as a cageful of monkeys, had conjured up happiness for her out of much sorrow and many tears.

'Be a good girl,' he said, as unemotionally as he could.

Harriet and Eliza were soon at the Mount Street coffee-house. Eliza, who had been troubled with the fear that Shelley might change his mind, or even merely forget the important rendezvous, saw the hackney carriage waiting in the street, and Harriet herself, with a little cry of joy, caught sight of her husband-to-be.

'There he is, Eliza, there he is!'

Shelley was standing at the coffee-house door. Evidently he had just had a meal, and with a pile of oyster shells clutched to his breast he was tossing them one by one in the direction of the hackney carriage.

'Here, you try!' he cried impishly as the sisters approached him.

'Try *what*, Bysshe?' Harriet stammered.

He thrust four shells into her hand. 'See if your aim is better than mine. I'm trying to land as many as I can in the carriage.'

'Oh, Bysshe, what a scream you are!'

'It's very important,' he said earnestly. 'Out of twenty-four shells, more than half must land in the carriage.'

'But *why*?'

'It's like counting the leaves of a flower. This year, next year, sometime – never! Only simpler. Thirteen shells in the carriage, and we go to Scotland; less than thirteen and we forget all about it.'

'Dearest Bysshe, what a tease you are!'

'I'm deadly serious,' he said huffily.

'How many shells have you landed in the carriage already?' Harriet asked anxiously.

'Ten,' he admitted.

'Then watch me!' she cried.

She took careful aim and tossed the first of her shells. To her immense relief it landed squarely in the carriage. The second missed, and so did the third. Desperate now, she concentrated with all her might. Her last shell wobbled on the door, then fell within the carriage.

'But that's only twelve!' she moaned.

'Wait!' Shelley laughed, and tossed another.

He began to feel desperate himself when it fell short of the carriage. He tried again, and again he failed. He *wanted* to take Harriet to Scotland, he was *determined* so to do, but it looked as if Fate were deciding otherwise. With a shaking hand he tossed another shell.

'Bravo, bravo!' Harriet shouted, jumping up and down in her excitement.

'Thirteen is an unlucky number,' Eliza murmured slyly.

Shelley looked at her in shocked amazement. 'I thought you were far too intelligent to be superstitious.'

'*I*'m not superstitious,' Harriet said stoutly, trying to ignore a twinge of apprehension.

'Of course you are,' Eliza said sharply, appalled none the less at the sudden perversity of her mood. 'You never cut your nails on Friday, you always avoid walking under ladders and on the thirteenth of every month you go about in fear and trembling.'

Frantic with worry, for Shelley was looking at her as if she were some strange and repulsive insect, Harriet wracked her brains for a denial which might please him.

'That was my Methodist upbringing,' she said. 'I'm not a Methodist any more so I'm not superstitious any more.'

Shelley's face cleared; he laughed in delight.

'Come, darling, let's get started.'

Harriet embraced her sister hurriedly; Shelley offered her his hand.

'Thank you for all your help,' he said graciously.

Standing back, Eliza watched them scramble into the hackney carriage. Eager children, both of them, she thought, their laughter carefree and infectious. Tears misted her eyes. Life without them would be dull and monotonous. Their going meant that a vital part of her was being rudely torn away. They looked back and waved to her.

'Good-bye,' she called miserably, 'good-bye.'

Six

I

HARRIET woke suddenly to find that she was being shaken, not by the large dog in the dream which still clung to her, but by Bysshe. Vastly relieved, she yawned and stretched.

'Where are we, Bysshe?' she asked.

'York,' he told her. 'They're changing the horses. We'll be on the road again in a few minutes.'

'It's awfully dark. What time is it?'

'Midnight.'

She remembered then that they had been in the mail-coach since seven o'clock on Monday night, that this was Tuesday night. She wondered inconsequently if her father had discovered that she had not returned to school. London seemed part of a life that had never been hers.

'Have you any money?' Shelley asked.

'I don't think so, Bysshe. A few shillings, perhaps.'

'Then I'd better write a brief note to Hogg. He's working in York, as you know, slaving at some ridiculous occupation called conveyancing. I'll ask him to send ten pounds to me at Edinburgh.'

Harriet yawned again. 'Haven't you any money either, Bysshe?'

'A pound or two, no more.'

'But what are we going to do when we reach Edinburgh?'

'Find a charitable landlord and throw ourselves upon his mercy.'

'Oh dear, that might be very awkward.'

'Ah, the thought of our straitened circumstances alarms you!'

'No, Bysshe,' Harriet said stoutly. 'I have the greatest faith in your resourcefulness. All the same, even a charitable landlord will have to be paid some time.'

'Fifty pounds will be deposited at my London bank within a matter of days. I left instructions for it to be sent on to Edinburgh.'

'Are you *sure* you did?'

Shelley gave this a moment's hurried thought. 'No, I didn't *leave* instructions. I sent them back from one of the posting stations.'

'In that case we have nothing whatever to worry about,' Harriet said confidently, and promptly fell asleep again.

2

'My dear sir,' Shelley asked warmly, 'what is the whole of life but mutability?'

His voice reached Harriet but hazily, and wriggling in her corner seat she tried once again to find a more comfortable position. Shelley himself, she noticed through half-closed eyes, seemed in no way disturbed by the rigours of the journey. He was sitting forward at her side, wagging a finger at the gentleman opposite, a Scotsman who had joined the coach at York. She had been roused several times by their voices, so evidently they had been arguing on and off all night.

Shelley turned to her suddenly. 'You agree, Harriet?'

'Indeed I do,' she hastened to reply.

Relieved that he pressed her no further she closed her eyes and tried desperately to remember what the word 'mutability' really meant. If by some mischance she were forced to admit her ignorance, dear Bysshe would be absolutely appalled.

'Nothing endures but mutability,' she heard him assert.

The wretched word again! It was quite unfuriating. Nevertheless she smiled happily to herself. Whatever it might mean she was sure of one thing enduring, her love for Bysshe.

'That sounds like a contradiction to me,' the Scotsman murmured placidly.

'You miss the fineness of my point,' Shelley said impatiently.

'Look, for example, at this child here. She appears to be sleeping peacefully.'

Harriet kept her eyes tightly closed. How ridiculous that he should call her 'child' when she was only three years younger than he was, and almost a married woman, too.

'I concede that she appears to be sleeping peacefully,' the Scotsman said in a puzzled voice, 'but what—'

'She may well be dreaming too, and a dream can poison sleep. That in itself would cause a change, however small, in her brain cells. And tomorrow when she wakes, what of yesterday? Our yesterdays are never the same as our tomorrows. Change again, you see!'

'My dear young man—'

'Wait! Yesterday you might have picked a flower and loved its beauty, but tomorrow it will be dead, dead! Nothing endures but change, nothing! Constancy is a sort of lightning – lightning that mocks the night.'

'Lightning that mocks the night . . .' the Scotsman pondered. 'My dear young man, you have a most poetic turn of speech.'

'Why, thank you, thank you!' Shelley said gratefully.

Harriet relaxed in her seat. Dear Bysshe, how wrong he was. Many things might change, but not love, not *her* love. Unchanging, it would endure for ever.

'My dear sir,' Shelley cried excitedly, 'I'm sure you said earlier that you were an advocate.'

'A prosaic enough occupation, to be sure,' the Scotsman laughed.

'Prosaic or otherwise, you're the very man I must talk to. I have a personal problem of great importance. It concerns the Scottish marriage laws. You shall tell me everything and put my mind at ease, then I shall know exactly what to do.'

Sleep was claiming Harriet again and, drifting into it, floating on gently lapping waves, a new dream took control of her mind. They were at the next posting station. Bysshe was standing at her side, holding her hand in his. The sun was shining with a brilliance such as never before had been seen, and the Scottish advocate, his face creased in a beatific smile, was pronouncing them man and wife.

3

Harriet woke with a start. For a moment she thought she was still in the mail-coach, then she saw the man who was pacing up and down the room. He was brandishing a pistol in each hand. Worse, for she had never seen such a sight before, he was completely naked. Too frightened even to scream she slipped deep into the bed and dragged the sheet over her face. Slowly, as the sound of drunken singing reached her ears, she began to remember all that had happened since York. Many changes of horses had taken place and after a total of four nights and three days Edinburgh had been reached at breakfast time. She knew now exactly where she was. Bysshe had indeed found a charitable landlord. She was in bed in one of the ground-floor rooms of a house in George Street. And goodness, she thought, Bysshe and I were married this morning! The drunken singing became less frightening. The landlord and his friends were celebrating the ceremony with a lively party. Cautiously she uncovered her head and sat up.

'Bysshe, how you frightened me!'

Still brandishing his pistols he was standing at the door, listening intently. Fascinated now, Harriet stared at him in silence. Unhampered by clothes, his body gleaming in the candle-light, he looked more youthful than ever.

'They were trying to break in,' he muttered. 'The Scots have some barbaric marriage customs. If they do break in I shall warn them once, then shoot.'

'How fearless you sound!'

Shelley turned and pointed a pistol at her accusingly. 'You were asleep, Harriet.'

Harriet sought hurriedly for a reasonable excuse. 'After they carried us in, then carried you out again, and I heard you singing with them, I – well – there was nothing else to do but get into bed. After that I fell asleep.'

Shelley came slowly towards her, kicking aside his clothing which littered the floor.

'Harriet, you're blushing.'

'Am I?' she stammered.

'Your face, your neck. All over, I'd say. You're trembling too. Are you nervous?'

Harriet glanced beyond him at the door. 'A little, Bysshe.'

'I'm not talking about those noisy ruffians out there,' he said sternly.

Harriet turned and buried her face in the pillow.

'Nor am I,' she mumbled.

'I'm sure you don't know a thing about what's going to happen.'

'There was a lot of talk at school, but of course I can't be *sure*.' She half-turned her head. 'Are you nervous too, Bysshe?'

'Certainly not. I slept with at least a dozen girls during the short time I was at Oxford.'

'Oh, *Bysshe*!'

'Fifteen in all,' he boasted, making the lie a bigger one.

'Won't you catch cold like that?' Harriet asked faintly, her face completely buried in the pillow again.

'On a night as warm as this? Nonsense!'

'Besides, it isn't decent.'

'What isn't decent? Being warm or being cold, you mean?'

'Walking about with nothing on.'

'Little goose of a Methodist!' he laughed.

Harriet rolled over on her back and sat up.

'I'm not a Methodist any more, you know I'm not!' she cried indignantly.

'Now you're angry, so you can't be quite so nervous.'

'It's because I'm nervous that I'm angry.'

He bent over her and kissed her brow, then gently bit the tip of her nose.

'There's no real reason for being nervous, darling.'

She flung her arms round his neck. 'Oh, Bysshe, I do so want to be a good wife.'

'And I a good husband.'

She stroked his smooth, firm shoulders. The coolness of his flesh beneath her hot palms filled her with a joy she had never felt before. Conscious of a sudden that he was trembling beneath her touch, she felt a little upsurge of confidence in herself.

'Bysshe, you're just as nervous as I am!'

4

Harriet woke to find the morning sun streaming through the window. Propping herself up on one elbow she looked down in wonder at the still sleeping Shelley. His face in sleep, rosy and untrammelled, filled her with tenderness. Bending over him she kissed his brow and gently stroked his cheek. He opened his eyes after a moment and smiled.

'I'm so happy, darling,' she whispered.

'So am I, Harriet.'

'Just think,' she said dreamily, 'nine months from now I shall have a baby.'

'As soon as that?' he laughed.

'The girls at school said nine months.'

'For all we know it may be never.'

Harriet gazed at him in wide-eyed disbelief. 'But Bysshe, after what happened last night—!'

Shelley pulled her down against him. Her childlike ignorance was endearing her to him all the more. Whispering in her ear he told her precisely how, when the time came, she would know she was going to have a baby.

'One of the older girls said the same thing,' she whispered back, 'but we didn't really believe her.' She took his hand and placed it over her navel. 'She was sure, too, that when you had a baby it came out here.'

'Amazing.'

'It didn't seem quite possible. There was an awful argument. Your sister Helen asked Miss Hawkes.'

'Did *she* know?'

'We never found out. She was absolutely furious and made each of us write a hundred lines, something about promising never again to ask impertinent and indecent questions. It made us all the more curious. We thought it more likely that a baby came out – well – farther down.'

'Less painful than from the navel, certainly.'

'Don't you know for certain either, Bysshe?'

'Of course I do. It comes out through the nose. You catch a

heavy cold when everything is ready. A terrific sneezing fit does the trick.'

'Now you're teasing me,' Harriet giggled.

'You should have asked your mother, not Miss Hawkes.'

'I did, but she looked at me vaguely and said she couldn't remember.'

'Did you think of asking Eliza?'

Harriet nodded her head against his breast. 'Poor Eliza was even more furious than Miss Hawkes.'

'Perhaps your sister doesn't know.'

'I think she does. She blushed horribly.'

'I'll make a point of asking her next time I see her.'

Harriet snuggled closer against him. 'The girls used to argue about something else. Most of them were sure you would only have a baby if you enjoyed it.'

'I don't think women enjoy having babies.'

'Silly! I don't mean *that*. I mean what happened last night.'

'You enjoyed it yourself, my sweet?'

'Not the first time,' Harriet said solemnly. 'Nor the second, quite. But the third time very much indeed.'

She had been too petrified the first time, she thought, so very frightened at the amazing change that had taken place in him as he kissed and fondled her. The girls had giggled about that sort of thing happening to a man but she had considered it impossible, even ludicrous. It was different now, though. There was something magical about it, something that filled her with admiration and awe, as well as the most urgent desire in the world.

'I'm glad you soon found it enjoyable,' Shelley murmured.

'So am I, Bysshe. And thinking what I did you can't blame me for believing I was going to have a baby right away.'

'As far as I'm concerned it ought to be three babies.'

'Three!' Harriet shrieked. 'Oh please, not three all at once! And why *three*, pray?'

'I enjoyed it each time.'

'How very unfair!'

Shelley laughed and took her fully in his arms. 'You'll forget all about the unfairness the fourth time. It's going to be better than ever, for both of us.'

Seven

I

THOMAS JEFFERSON HOGG knocked a second time at the door but again received no call to enter. Smiling, he stood there listening to the familiar, unceasing drone of Shelley's voice within the room. The dear fellow was obviously caught up in some new enthusiasm and his young wife, whose voice had not yet been raised, was just as obviously a silent and admiring listener.

Opening the door softly Hogg stepped into the room. Harriet, a book open before her, was seated at the table, her chin cupped in her hands, her eyes following Shelley as he paced up and down the room. He was talking excitedly, Hogg discovered, about the Godwin theory concerning physical love.

'I agree with him entirely,' Shelley cried. 'There must be no monopoly whatever.'

'But dearest Bysshe,' Harriet murmured, 'do you mean that I must be prepared to share you with any other girl who might take your fancy?'

Shelley threw up his arms. 'Even as I must be prepared to share *you* with any other man who might take *your* fancy.'

Hogg laughed uproariously. 'A strange conversation to be taking place between a husband and wife who have been married only sixteen days.'

Shelley flung himself on his friend and embraced him warmly. 'This is splendid, Hogg, splendid!'

Harriet came forward and shyly offered Hogg her hand.

'Bysshe was talking nonsense, as usual,' she murmured.

'I was completely serious,' Shelley avowed sternly. 'Now tell me what brings you to Edinburgh. Have you turned your back on that wretched conveyancing, like a sensible fellow? Edinburgh is a marvellous city! I find I can write here as never before. Inspiration swamps me, absolutely swamps me! I shall remain in Edinburgh for the rest of my life. What the devil are you smiling at, Hogg?'

'My dear Bysshe, it occurred to me that Edinburgh has had nothing whatever to do with inspiration.'

'If not Edinburgh, then what, pray?'

Hogg gave Harriet a courtly little bow. 'What else – that is to say, who else, but your charming wife?'

'What an extraordinary idea!' Shelley gasped.

'Oh come,' Hogg chided, 'you must surely have written a few verses already in Harriet's honour.'

'Have you, Bysshe, oh, have you?' Harriet asked eagerly.

'Little goose, of course I have.'

'Oh Bysshe, how lovely,' she sighed.

'And now we must have some tea,' Shelley decided. 'We drink tea at all hours of the night and day. Ring the bell, Harriet.'

Tea was brought in by an untidy, snub-nosed little maid whose Scottish accent brought a howl of protest from Shelley. Clapping his hands over his ears he demanded that she should be sent away, and while she lingered, giggling uncontrollably, he flung himself under the table.

'This happens several times a day,' Harriet told Hogg. 'I can never be sure whether the sound of her voice hurts him or he's just teasing her.'

'Has she gone?' Shelley moaned, from under the table.

'Yes, but she'll be back in a moment with the kettle.'

'You mean kittle. She calls it kittle, always *kittle*. I shall remain here until the agony is completely over.'

When at last they were seated at the table, Hogg, who had remembered little of Harriet from the first and only meeting at Field Place, fell to studying her with interest. She looked incredibly young, even virginal still, he thought. Her eyes shone with happiness and her lips, as she poured the tea, were parted in a little secret smile. Catching his eye, she looked down demurely, and a faint blush stained her cheeks. He found himself envying Shelley and was amazed, when he took the cup and saucer from Harriet's hands, the way his own shook so unsteadily.

'You haven't told us yet why you came to Edinburgh,' Shelley remarked.

'My dear Shelley, have you given me a chance?'

'Out with it now, then!'

'Did you receive the money I sent you?'

'I did indeed, and many thanks, Hogg.'

'I hesitate to upset you by mentioning your father,' Hogg went on carefully, 'but have you written to him?'

'My father is more likely to be upset by mention of me than I by mention of him,' Shelley chuckled. 'Yes, I wrote to him.'

'Did he reply?'

Shelley glanced vaguely at Harriet. '*Did* he, my sweet?'

Harriet shook her head. 'Nor has my father yet replied to my own letter to him. Both, of course, will be terribly angry.'

'Shelley's father is, make no mistake about that,' Hogg said grimly. 'He wrote a complaining letter to *my* father, hinting that *I* was responsible for the elopement. He begged my father, Shelley, to do everything possible to keep us apart, and he urged him to make certain that I gave you no assistance whatever.'

'Ah,' Shelley cried in delight, 'so you came to Edinburgh in defiance of parental commands.'

Hogg shook his head. 'No, Shelley. You see, in my father's eyes I am for the moment a model son. In any case he was angry when he read your father's letter.'

'Did he let *you* read it?'

'More than that, he gave it to me. I have it here.'

Hogg took the letter from his pocket and gave it to Shelley who, having skimmed through it, picked out sentences here and there and read them aloud.

'*My son is in Scotland with a young female*. That, Harriet, is you. Not a young lady, mark you, but a young *female*.' Shelley seized upon another sentence. '*By such an arbitrary action he has withdrawn himself from my protection*. Protection! I can imagine the sternness of father's face when penning those ridiculous words!'

'Protection to the extent of two hundred pounds per annum,' Hogg said soberly.

Shelley thumped the table till the teacups rattled. 'My poor Hogg, why per *annum*? Why not per *year*?' He turned dramatically to Harriet. 'That, my dear, is what happens to a man when he starts conveyancing. Per annum indeed!'

'Annum or year, the fact remains that your allowance has been discontinued,' Hogg said warmly.

Shelley shrugged unconcernedly. 'That is obvious on two accounts. My father refers to it in this letter, and the sum of fifty pounds due to me has not yet been paid into my London bank.' He glanced again at the letter. 'I see I am not to communicate with him directly in future, but only through the family solicitor. I shall, of course, do nothing of the kind. Protection, my father talks of protection! And so do you, Hogg! Have the goodness, please, to remember that I am heir to an entailed estate – *entailed*, mark you! – worth six thousand pounds per annum. Yes, per *annum*, since you love the word.'

'Two hundred pounds a year is worth more to you now,' Hogg pointed out, 'than six thousand in years to come.'

'Starvation!' Shelley raged. 'My father proposes to bring me to heel by starvation!'

'Whatever he proposes,' Hogg pointed out, 'the position is a serious one.'

'Pooh! Money, what do I care about money? Think no more of it, my dear fellow. I myself am completely unconcerned.'

Hogg glanced at Harriet. 'You have your wife to think of, Shelley.'

'I am just as unconcerned as Bysshe,' Harriet averred stoutly.

'Ah, then no more need be said,' Shelley remarked with satisfaction. 'Have you seen the comet, Hogg?'

'Several times, but not very clearly.'

'Then you shall go out with us tonight and gaze up at it in rapture. The Edinburgh air is crystal clear. You must settle here, Hogg, I absolutely insist upon it!'

Hogg explained, much to Shelley's indignation, that he had no intention of giving up conveyancing, but the indignation passed when his friend added that this being the long vacation he could spend at least a few weeks in Edinburgh. A vacant room was immediately found for him on the top floor of the house, and the rest of the morning was spent in a visit to Holyrood Palace. The afternoon was given over to reading and more tea drinking; the evening to a stroll in Princes Street and the promised viewing of the comet. Before returning to their lodgings Shelley insisted on a call at the post-office to see if there were any letters. There were two, one for himself, the other for Harriet.

'My sister's handwriting,' Harriet exclaimed. 'Papa himself must have been too furious to write.'

And this was precisely what Eliza said in her letter, though she added encouragingly that their father, if given a little more time, would become accustomed to his younger daughter's new status and cease to grow purple in the face at the mention of her name.

'We appear to be in funds again,' said Shelley, looking up from his own letter.

'Has your father relented? Oh, I can't believe it!'

'Father hasn't relented. This is from my uncle, Captain Pilfold. A most cheerful letter, and look, Harriet, a bank-post bill for fifty pounds!'

'How very generous of the Captain.'

'You understand what it means, of course?'

'Your uncle is willing to stand by you until your father relents.'

'That, yes,' Shelley said impatiently, 'but more important still, we are no longer tied to Edinburgh. We are as free as the comet up there. We have new wings and can use them. Edinburgh, how I loathe the place!'

'But, Bysshe, you said—'

'Whatever I said is of no importance whatever now. We shall go back with Hogg to York. York, I think, is the most beautiful city in England.'

'Dearest Bysshe,' Harriet said patiently, 'we only saw it in the dark.'

'Pooh, does *that* matter? Even in the dark the atmosphere, so gentle and kind, reached out and touched me with the soft and caressing fingers of a passionate lover. Hogg, of course, will find us lodgings there.'

'Gladly,' said Hogg.

'Perhaps in the house where you lodge yourself?'

'Nothing,' murmured Hogg, looking reflectively at Harriet, 'would give me greater pleasure.'

2

'Haven't you found him yet?' Harriet asked, when Hogg came back to the post-chaise for the third time.

'No,' he said, shaking his head crossly. 'He seems to have disappeared completely from the face of the earth.'

Harriet shrugged unconcernedly and taking up the novel which lay open on her lap went on with her reading. They were at the Berwick posting-station, and Shelley, as was his habit while the horses were being changed, had rushed off alone in search of what he called local colour. It had sometimes seemed during the past three weeks that Shelley had forgotten all about his decision to go to York, but the little party was *en route* at last, and taking the journey leisurely would spend one night at Belford and another at Darlington. Hogg had protested that to travel by private post-chaise was an unnecessary extravagance, but Shelley, declaring himself to be the richest man in England, had insisted.

'There are times,' said Hogg, getting into the post-chaise and seating himself at Harriet's side, 'when I find that husband of yours the most exasperating of fellows.'

'Why that, Thomas?' Harriet asked, in surprise.

'He has no conception of the meaning of time.'

'We should both of us be used to that by now.'

'He exasperates me on your account rather than on my own.'

'If I accept it, so should you,' Harriet said, with considerable asperity.

Hogg, a contrite expression on his face, took her hand in his.

'Please don't blame me too much, Harriet, for feeling concern on your behalf.'

'I feel none myself,' she said, and tried unsuccessfully to release her hand.

'Shelley is a dear fellow,' Hogg went on, his voice unsteady, 'but his neglect – and he does neglect you, Harriet – hurts me deeply.' He raised her hand to his lips and kissed it clumsily. 'Please do believe in my sincerity.'

Harriet rose in an attempt to escape from the post-chaise, but Hogg caught her and drew her back into his arms. Sickened by his hot breath on her cheeks as he sought to kiss her, she squirmed and kicked and at last, by feigning a sudden weakness, caught him unawares. Nevertheless, she was a little frightened, for her sudden violent push had sent Hogg backwards from the post-chaise, and there he lay now rolling in the roadside dust.

'Are you hurt?' she gasped.

'I think my back is broken,' Hogg said, scrambling to his feet.

'You seem to have no difficulty in standing,' she said in relief, 'so it can't be, can it?'

Hogg hesitated for a moment, then approached the carriage again.

'Unless you leave me alone I shall scream,' Harriet warned, 'and that will bring people running to my aid.'

Hogg smiled admiringly. 'Little wildcat!'

Tears of vexation sprang to her eyes. 'I shall tell Bysshe and – and that will be the end of you. He'll get out his pistols and shoot you without the slightest hesitation.'

'Perhaps, perhaps not. It would depend on his mood. Remember what he said before we left Edinburgh. The three of us are inseparable and must remain so for the rest of our lives. He and I, he said, are to share our possessions equally.'

Harriet picked up her book, the only weapon within reach, and flung it with all her strength at Hogg. It struck him square in the face, causing him to gasp in pain and surprise.

'Are you hurt?' she asked once more.

Glowering at her, holding his hand tenderly over his left eye, he turned on his heels and hobbled away.

'I'll go and look for Shelley again,' he flung back at her.

'You're limping!' she shouted.

'I told you my back was broken!'

Harriet watched him until he disappeared from sight, then sank weakly into her seat. The tears were rolling down her cheeks and soon she was laughing hysterically. Bysshe and Hogg to share all their possessions, she being one of them! Bysshe hadn't meant it like that, she was sure he hadn't.

'Where's Hogg?' said a voice.

Harriet smothered a scream. 'Bysshe!'

She saw that he had picked up the book which Hogg had left lying on the ground.

'Did you throw this away?' he asked.

'I – yes, I must have.'

'Very sensible of you. Your habit of reading so many trashy novels was beginning to alarm me.' Taking casual aim, Shelley sent the book skimming across the road. 'Well, where *is* that wretched Hogg?'

'He went to look for you, Bysshe.'

'Really, was I lost?'

'Is anything the matter, darling? You sound quite angry.'

'And so I am,' said Shelley, getting into the post-chaise. 'Angry and despondent.'

Harriet's heart missed a beat. Without a doubt he had witnessed her struggle with Hogg, but had seen it not as a struggle on her part but an act of willing submission.

'I went for a walk on the Walls,' Shelley said sadly. 'I felt in need of gaiety, and nothing is gayer than the sea when the sun is shining. Those little white-caps, the carefree curve of the tiny waves – laughter, sheer laughter.'

'I often thought the same myself,' said Harriet, lying hopefully.

'Ah, but a mist has shrouded the sun. The sea is flat and grey. I saw nothing anywhere but sadness and tears. I came close to weeping myself.'

'*I* did weep,' said Harriet, striving to excuse the tears on her cheeks.

Shelley looked at her vaguely. 'How like Hogg to keep us waiting. I've half a mind to start off without him.'

'It would certainly serve him right if we did.'

The despondency fell from Shelley. 'What a delightful joke!'

'A better one if we returned to Edinburgh and left him to search for us in vain at York.'

'That would be carrying things a bit too far,' Shelley frowned.

Harriet set her jaw stubbornly. 'We can manage quite well without Thomas Jefferson Hogg.'

Shelley was silent for a long moment. 'So I was right. You don't like my friend.'

'I wasn't aware of having shown it,' Harriet said nervously.

'But you don't like him?'

'I loathe him.'

'How extraordinary. *He* likes *you*.'

'*I loathe him*,' she repeated.

Shelley looked puzzled. 'Are you pregnant? Women behave queerly when pregnant.'

'I'm not pregnant, you know I'm not,' and she added despairingly, 'I don't think I ever shall be.'

'We have only been married five weeks,' Shelley pointed out reasonably. 'Ah, *I* know what's disturbing you. It's Willie again.'

'How silly you are,' Harriet cried in exasperation. 'Willie came two weeks ago. There are two more weeks to go.'

'An amusing name, isn't it! Did I think of it, or was it you?'

'Please don't change the subject, Bysshe.'

'We seem to be quarrelling,' Shelley said mildly.

'Yes, and all because of Hogg!'

'Give me one reason why anyone should dislike poor Hogg,' Shelley said warmly.

Harriet very nearly told him the truth then, but realized in time, in a groping sort of way, that Shelley would be anything but pleased. Perhaps he *would* get out his pistols and kill the faithless, disloyal Hogg. On the other hand, since he seemed to place more trust in his friend than his wife, he might press the pistols against her chest and pull the triggers unmercifully.

'*Well?*' Shelley demanded.

'He frightens me,' she stammered.

'That's because of his name, poor fellow. I see quite clearly that it clouds your vision. Do you see him as some queer, squat animal, with short thick legs, a hairy body and a grotesque snout?'

Harriet shuddered. 'I didn't, but no doubt I shall, now you have drawn my attention to it.'

'Very well, then, we shall ask him to change his name. I have it! Angelo! Thomas Jefferson Angelo!'

'How ridiculous you are,' Harriet giggled.

'Angelo conjures up quite a different picture. Gone are the thick legs, the hairy body, the grotesque snout. Wings in their place, Harriet, snow white wings. Wings, and a golden harp tucked under one of them. Ah, here he comes! Hurry, Hogg, hurry! I want to ask you an important question.'

Hogg, limping still, approached in considerable nervousness.

'Can you play a harp?' Shelley demanded.

Hogg's face showed immediate relief. 'I can't play any sort of musical instrument.'

'Well, no matter. The point is this: Harriet dislikes your name. In fact, it frightens her, almost gives her the vapours. You must change your name, my dear Hogg. Wait, though! I know what the trouble is. Harriet isn't frightened at all. She's jealous.'

'Jealous?' Harriet asked indignantly.

'Of our friendship, Hogg's and mine.'

'Incredible,' said Hogg.

Shelley stared at him in surprise. 'What on earth have you done to your eye?'

Harriet saw that Hogg's left eye was now inflamed and watering.

'Yes, what *have* you done to it?' she asked, with a boldness that set her heart fluttering wildly.

Hogg gave her a sly look. 'I tripped and struck it on a book.'

Shelley roared with laughter. 'Good lord, you don't mean that stupid novel she threw away?'

'She certainly threw it away,' Hogg murmured.

'Then Harriet herself did the damage. We must procure a raw steak for you immediately and strap it over your eye, otherwise it will grow purple before we reach Belford.'

Shelley rushed into the tavern which adjoined the posting-station, and after only a few moments emerged, much to Hogg's and Harriet's amazement, with a slice of uncooked steak. Whipping out a large handkerchief he placed the blood-dripping meat over Hogg's left eye and bound the handkerchief firmly into place. This done to his satisfaction he assisted his friend into the post-chaise, ordered the postilion to proceed and leapt in himself.

'My dear,' he said, looking earnestly at Harriet, 'I do beg you not to be too jealous of Hogg. Just as virtue is frail, except of course in your own case, so is real friendship rare, one of the rarest things on earth.'

'But I'm not jealous of Thomas,' Harriet insisted.

Shelley looked questioningly at his friend. 'Do you believe her, my dear chap?'

'Harriet is no more jealous of me than I am of her,' Hogg said carefully.

'Then there's only one thing for it. You simply must change your name. Henceforth you shall be known as Angelo.' And raising his voice Shelley chanted unmusically, 'Angelo, An-gel-o, An – gel – oh!'

3

Harriet, stirring sleepily, pushed away the hand that lay lightly across her breast, but it was there again in a moment, the fingers firm and probing. Seizing it once more she discovered a ring on one of the fingers. That was peculiar, she thought, for she had never known Bysshe to wear a ring. She sat up suddenly. Bysshe had left that morning for London.

'Don't be frightened,' a voice whispered.

'Thomas!'

Hogg chuckled softly. 'You were sleeping so soundly you scarcely moved when I got in beside you. And when you pushed my hand away the first time I was sure you thought I was Shelley.'

Indignant rather than alarmed, Harriet peered at him in the darkness. He had moved – she could see only a dim outline of his head and shoulders – and was sitting now on the edge of the bed.

'You can't be sure what actually happened just now while you were asleep,' Hogg suggested.

'Unless you go at once I'll scream,' Harriet warned.

'And rouse the house and cause a terrible scandal?'

Harriet shuddered. To be caught like this with Hogg would indeed cause a terrible scandal. More than likely the three Miss Dancers, in whose house lodgings had been found, would throw them into the black cheerlessness of the night. A vision of the hawk-eyed, tight-mouthed spinsters flashed through her mind. Worse than that, they would surely summon the watch.

'You're being very hateful,' she complained.

'Only because I'm angry with Shelley. Admittedly it pleases me that he should rush off to London, but at the same time his extreme neglect angers me beyond endurance.'

Harriet tried not to listen. Bysshe, she was sure, had meant no neglect. His money had dwindled away during the ten days they had been at York. There had been nothing for it, he'd decided, but to pay his father a visit and try, if only for her sake, to patch things up.

'Please go away,' she begged.

'I love you, Harriet. I absolutely adore you.'

'What a despicable way of showing it!'

'You love me too. That's why you've been avoiding me.'

'Your conceit is quite ridiculous,' Harriet sneered.

'If it be conceit to admire you as no girl has ever been admired before, than I am the most conceited man in the world. Just one little thought of you, and heaven is all about me, yet a frown on your brow, a harsh word on your lips and heaven gives place to the blackness and despair of hell.'

Harriet sneered again, but could but wonder at Hogg's

amazing flight into lyricism. Bysshe, poet that he was, had never uttered such words as those, nor had there at any time been the same tremulous throb in his voice.

'Knowing how I fell,' Hogg said passionately, 'can you blame me for wanting to marry you?'

'How crazy you are. Have I not a husband already?'

'A marriage celebrated in Scotland isn't necessarily legal in England.'

'But lots of people run away and get married in Scotland.'

'I know they do, but the validity of your own particular marriage is in considerable doubt. I made inquiries in Edinburgh about the clergyman who married you. He has an unsavoury reputation. His activities, some people think, might yet bring him before the courts.'

'What a fiend you are, trying to frighten me like this!' Harriet cried.

'I'm not trying to frighten you. All I want to do is convince you that you can accept my protection by marrying me in England.'

'That would be bigamy.'

Hogg leant forward suddenly and seized her hands. 'You love me! You want to accept my protection. Otherwise you would not be searching so desperately for excuses.'

He had his arms round her now and was forcing her down on the bed. Squirming helplessly she felt the pressure of a bare hard leg and discovered that he had apparently stripped to his shirt.

'You want to kill me,' she sobbed. 'What use would I be to you dead?'

Hogg relaxed his grip for a moment, thus enabling her to free her arms. Flinging them round his shoulders she ran her hands down his back, found herself touching bare flesh and arching her fingers dug her nails deeply into it. His muffled cry of pain filled her with exultation, and twisting as the weight of his body was lifted she succeeded in slipping from the bed. He caught her as she reached the door, but not before she had managed to fling it open.

'Why struggle, Harriet, when your heart is set on submission?'

Acting instinctively now, sobbing that there was little resistance left in her, she threw her arms round his neck and drew his face down to hers. Presently, by twisting in his arms as if in an ecstasy of delight, she succeeded in placing him with his back to the open doorway, and murmuring that his kisses were bringing on an attack of vapours slid through his arms to her knees.

'Help me,' she pleaded woefully.

As he bent to do so she sprang forward, butting him so sharply in the stomach that a pain shot through her head and down her spine. The rest was easy. A quick push at his shoulders and he was rolling on his back in the passage. She closed the door and barred it, and in sheer exhaustion this time sank to the floor again.

'Harriet . . .' she heard Hogg whisper.

She made no reply.

'Harriet,' he added, in what sounded like a whimper of defeat, 'I want the rest of my clothes.'

Lying there, listening at length to his receding footsteps, it came upon her that she had never felt so miserable in her whole life, nor so lonely. Bysshe had deserted her, had said not a word about when she could expect him back. Tears of self-pity filled her eyes. If Bysshe had really deserted her she would either die at once of a broken heart or shoot herself.

Later she cried herself to sleep, and waking at dawn, remembering all that had happened, a great longing for the old familiar surroundings of Chapel Street filled her heart. She sprang out of bed, intent on packing and catching the first mail-coach to London. Then she remembered that her father had not yet relented. He would either imprison her at Chapel Street or send her back to school. Except for one person she possessed not a friend in the world. Eliza, she thought, I'll send for Eliza!

4

Shelley paused for breath at the door, then slowly and carefully he began to open it. Newly arrived in York, he had run all the way from the posting-station and rushed headlong into the house, but was determined now to steal softly into the room and give Harriet the surprise of her life. To his intense relief, for he had feared that she might be out walking with Hogg, his eyes fell on the back of a high chair which had been placed at the window, the skirt of a yellow gown just visible on either side of it. Creeping upon it on tiptoe he uttered a piercing scream and flung his hands over the occupant's eyes.

'I give you one guess, just one!'

With a smothered cry Eliza Westbrook jumped to her feet and faced him with heaving breast.

'Good lord,' he laughed comically. 'Surely this is Coney Street, York – or have I strayed by some mischance to Chapel Street, London?'

'This is certainly Coney Street,' Eliza told him severely, 'though I must say it surprises me that you should have found your way here.'

Shelley gave her his most charming smile. 'Dear Eliza, how cross you sound. What can I have possibly done to displease you?'

Eliza found herself weakening at once. How utterly impossible he was to deal with! The irresistible Shelley smile was enough to melt the stoniest of hearts.

'Bysshe,' she faltered, 'this is the middle of the afternoon. The London coach usually arrives at midnight. Where have you been meanwhile?'

Shelley laughed gaily. 'I missed the coach at some posting-station or other. I can't for the life of me remember the name of it. I was engrossed, you see, in a most interesting argument with a clergyman and came close to convincing him that he was a professional hypocrite. He offered me a room for the night and we argued again until the small hours. His claret was excellent.'

'But how did you travel to York?'

'By post-chaise, of course.'

'You had enough money for that?'

'Certainly. I happen to be rich again. My uncle lent me ten pounds.'

'Oh, Bysshe, what an irresponsible boy you are!'

'By the look of your eyes you love me dearly, but your voice sounds cross again.' Shelley embraced her warmly, kissing her on each cheek. 'Tell me what it is I'm supposed to have done and I'll do all I can to make my peace with you.'

Eliza freed herself. 'I have every reason to be cross with you for the way you deserted Harriet.'

Shelley tore at his hair. '*Deserted* her?'

'You were thoughtless rather than cruel. That much I do admit.'

He looked at her in amazement. 'But I simply had to go to London, and I knew Harriet would be safe with Hogg.'

Eliza repressed an indignant rejoinder, remembering in time that she had promised Harriet, who had confided in her fully, to make no reference whatever to Hogg's despicable behaviour.

'Where is Harriet?' Shelley asked. 'Out walking with Hogg?'

'Certainly not.'

'But it's a beautiful afternoon.'

Eliza sighed in exasperation. 'How careless you are of the proprieties. The poor child is in bed.'

'In *bed*? Is she ill?'

'Harriet is in a highly nervous state. I thought it necessary for her to rest as much as possible. Mr. Hogg distressed her by casting doubt on the strict legality of your marriage. That was why Harriet sent for me.'

'What nonsense! Hogg is over-anxious on our behalf. The marriage was recorded at the Register House in Edinburgh. But enough! I must see Harriet at once. The true reason for her nervous condition is all too obvious.'

Laughing merrily at this new thought Shelley hurried to the bedroom, tore open the door, slammed it behind him and shot the bolt into place.

'Bysshe! You're back! I can't believe it, darling!'

Harriet, who had been lying in bed reading a book, sprang up to greet him. They flung themselves into each other's arms, Harriet sobbing in relief and joy, Shelley laughing gaily.

'I flew to you in a golden chariot drawn by six winged horses. They were talking horses, too. Moreover, they had the gift of second-sight. They knew everything about you, Harriet, everything!'

'Did they?' Harriest asked uneasily.

'They knew you were in what Eliza calls a highly nervous state. They knew the reason for it, too.'

'They must have been very wise horses,' she said faintly.

' "We must hurry," they kept saying, "otherwise it might be too late." '

'Too late, Bysshe?'

'Their mission, you see, was a matter of life and death. Harriet Shelley was sinking fast. Only one thing could save her.'

'I can't imagine what that could be.'

'Is Willie with us?'

'Willie? No, of course he isn't.'

'There's your answer then,' said Shelley, and began to throw off his clothes.

Later, deliriously happy, Harriet lay in his arms purring, Shelley declared, like a basketful of well-fed kittens. Placing his ear over her heart he added that he could still hear nothing but the sound of purring. When the time came for her to have a baby, he chuckled, it wouldn't be a human creature at all but a litter of kittens – red kittens, blue kittens, purple kittens, the most beautiful kittens in the world.

'I do so love your craziness,' Harriet sighed.

'Am I forgiven? Eliza insists that I deserted you.'

'What a stupid sister she is.'

'Stupid, yes. She says Hogg upset you by casting doubt on the validity of our marriage. Could anything be more valid than this?'

'Nothing, darling.'

But the mention of Hogg was alarming, the more so because, in a fit of remorse, he had wanted to write to Shelley and confess everything. He had agreed in the end to restrain himself, but since he had appeared to be enjoying a dramatic appreciation of his perfidy Harriet feared that the sight of Shelley would loosen his tongue.

Later, during tea, Eliza asked pointedly if Shelley had made any progress with his father. He shook his head and told her that while staying with his uncle at Cuckfield he had visited Field Place several times but had never been admitted.

'Everyone at Field Place was afraid of me,' he said gleefully. 'Servants were set to guard all entrances and my mother and sisters were sent up to the attics for safety. And when I walked in the village mothers snatched their children from the streets, fathers appeared armed with clubs and old men, too doddery to make their escape, fell on their knees and begged for mercy. I am as notorious in my own way now as the Prince Regent is in his.'

'Oh, Bysshe, how you do exaggerate!' Harriet squealed.

'Exaggeration is the spice of life, and I enjoy it hugely,' Shelley laughed, 'but I give you my word, Father vowed that unless I left the district he would swear in special constables and set them between me and Field Place.'

'If you went about brandishing pistols,' Harriet suggested, 'everyone would naturally be afraid of you.'

'I did something much more terrifying. I deposited a pile of Necessities in Warnham Church.'

'*Necessities?*'

'That pamphlet of mine, *The Necessity of Atheism*. In short, I unfurled the flag of intellectual freedom and that, in England, is a greater sin than the stealing of another man's wife, a wife being property, for property is the golden calf before which all God-fearing Englishmen – the landed gentry especially – bend the knee and bow the head in abject worship.'

'You appear to be in excellent talking form,' Eliza remarked dryly.

'Then why interrupt me? Hogg never does, except to add a few wise words of his own. Hogg, I sometimes think, is my other self. And that reminds me, surely today is Sunday? Where, then, is Hogg? He should be here taking tea with us.'

Harriet tried to keep her voice steady. 'He could scarcely have known that you would return today.'

'Even so, he would surely join you for tea.'

Harriet looked uneasily at her sister.

'Your Mr. Hogg,' Eliza said quickly, 'has found lodgings elsewhere.'

'You speak of him as if you hate him. Did you drive him away?'

Harriet's uneasiness increased. It was necessary to say something and say it quickly before her husband, whose eyes were flashing angrily already, provoked Eliza into telling him the truth.

'We quarrelled with him,' she invented. 'You wanted him to change his name, remember? I begged him to, Eliza did likewise. He refused.'

'Ah yes, Angelo! But darling, a quarrel about *that*? Hogg was never petty. Something much more serious must have happened.'

'Really, Bysshe—'

'Tell me his new address.'

Harriet told him, and when he had rushed off impetuously to see his friend she threw herself into her sister's arms. All was happiness a moment ago, she wailed; now there was nothing but misery.

'If Hogg tells the truth,' Eliza said, 'Bysshe will thrash him soundly.'

'No, he'll forgive him and blame me, I know he will.'

'I very much doubt it, child. It was perfectly clear when you came to tea arm in arm with him that he loves you more than ever.'

'He was very sweet this afternoon,' Harriet sniffed.

'He certainly turned a frightened shrinking girl into a happy and radiant young woman. I never saw such a change in anyone before.'

'That was the lovely remedy he prescribed.'

'May I ask what it was?' Eliza said curiously. 'I suffer at times from nervous prostration myself.'

Harriet, feeling an irresistible urge to shock her sister, laughed as impishly as Shelley in one of his teasing moods.

'We slept together, Eliza. That is to say, we didn't actually *sleep*, but you do understand what I mean.'

'How disgusting!' Eliza gasped, a queer, constricting sensation running through her stomach. 'Not only in broad daylight, but on the Sabbath, too!'

5

'Bysshe, is that you?' Harriet asked breathlessly.

There was no reply, but the fumbling at the door handle still went on. It was long past midnight. Harriet and Eliza had sat up late waiting, hopelessly it seemed, for Shelley to return from his visit to Hogg's new lodgings. Finally Eliza had put Harriet to bed and had gone unwillingly to her own room.

'Bysshe, don't frighten me like this!' Harriet begged.

The door swung slowly open and Shelley stumbled into the room. His face was haggard, his clothing in greater disarray than ever, and there was mud on his boots. Harriet sprang out of bed, snatching up her dressing-gown and wrapped it tightly about her trembling body.

'I have suffered a devastating blow,' Shelley said.

Harriet looked at him with new hope. The tone of his voice suggested that he was enjoying – oh, in a very sombre manner, of course – the drama of what had taken place between him and Thomas Jefferson Hogg.

'Do please sit down,' she said, taking him by the arm and leading him to a chair.

'How kind and gentle you are,' he said, sinking heavily into the chair. 'I am utterly exhausted, both physically and mentally.'

The new hope faded a little. He spoke now in a weary monotone. Had he said 'vile and faithless' it would have told her no more than 'kind and gentle'.

'We must have walked for miles,' he added.

'You and Hogg?' she faltered.

'Yes. In the fields. Up and down, up and down. We rested only once, when we stopped to throw stones in the river. Flat stones, you understand, but such was our mutual agitation we failed to make them skim across the water's surface. They fell heavily, like dead things. Hogg said fancifully that the stones were as dead as our hearts within us. A promising poet is lost in Hogg.'

He still spoke in a monotone. Harriet shuddered; the atmosphere of the room was growing frighteningly eerie.

'I think you should go to bed,' she ventured. 'I'm sure you'll feel better in the morning.'

'*Bed?*' Shelley's voice rose indignantly. 'I have told you nothing yet, nothing! However, if you prefer not to listen. . . .'

'Dearest Bysshe,' Harriet faltered, 'I want to hear all you have to tell me.'

Shelley sighed. His voice became a monotone again.

'Hogg confessed everything, and gained some small relief, poor fellow, from laying bare his soul.'

The 'poor fellow' brought a quick question from Harriet.

'Did you forgive him?'

'I did, Harriet, but not immediately. My fury at first knew no bounds. I flew at him. I shook him violently. I flung him to the ground. He offered no resistance. Indeed, he lay there moaning and begged me to draw my pistol and make an end of him. I raised him up as gently as I could and he wept in my arms. I reproached him sadly, telling him that I had held him in the highest esteem, regarded him always as the most noble of beings. There were tears in my own eyes when I added that he had shattered the most precious ideal of my life.'

Shelley was striding about the room now. His eyes were flashing, his gestures were extravagant. Living the moment over again, his voice rose and fell in one beautiful cadence after another.

'He said that he was the basest of criminals,' he went on. 'I agreed for a moment, and then I saw that only the crime, not the man himself, was base. I assured him that if he was truly repentant there was hope for him still, and for me, too.'

'Why for you, too, Bysshe?' Harriet asked in surprise.

'He being my friend, and I still loving him. I hastened to assure him that I pardoned him fully and freely. His face was lit then, for one tiny, fleeting moment, with a look of wonder. It was a beautiful and inspiring sight. We shook hands, retraced our steps in silence to his lodgings and, if I remember rightly, drank a bottle of wine.'

'Still in silence?' Harriet asked, on the point now of hysteria.

'There was little left to be said. It was in a sense a Last Supper. We agreed, I seem to recall, that the time would come when each of us would forget with joy and gratitude the disgust we felt for the crime he had committed.'

'In a sense a Last Supper?' Harriet asked.

Shelley took her in his arms and gazed fondly on her face. He was seeing her now with new eyes. This, then, was the lovely creature he had loved but with whom up to now he had not been in love. That he could have been so blind was incredible, yet how disappointed he was in himself that he should have been brought to this glorious 'in love' feeling only because another man should have desired her.

'Bysshe . . .' Harriet began uncertainly.

'What is it, darling?' he asked gently.

But afraid now to persist, to ask him if he had decided never to see Hogg again, she pressed her head against his breast and to her intense satisfaction wept quite genuinely.

'Poor little Harriet, how you must have suffered.'

'Hogg hurt me grievously,' she sobbed.

'Darling, he swore he caused you no physical harm.'

'Nor did he, Bysshe.'

'Nevertheless, you must be prepared in future to repulse effectively any other man who might be tempted to attack you.'

'I butted Hogg quite effectively in the stomach.'

'Partly winding him, yes, but had he been a more powerful man your little head would have caused scarcely any damage. On any other occasion use your head if you must, but I think your knee would be better.'

'My knee?'

'No, on second thoughts, not your knee. You're such a little thing you wouldn't be able to bring it up with sufficient force. Use your head but strike lower.' He showed her where to strike. 'This is the most vulnerable part of a man's body, his Achilles Heel, as it were.'

'What a funny place for a man's heel,' Harriet giggled. 'Now tell me please what you meant by "Last Supper".'

Shelley sighed deeply. 'It is all too clear that we can remain no longer at York. The temptation must be removed, for your sake as well as Hogg's. We shall go away at once.'

'To London, Bysshe?'

Shelley looked at her in horror. 'London is a sink of iniquity, a stinking den of vice. And by vice,' he ran on warmly, 'I refer, not to the sexual licence of the Prince Regent and his cronies, but to political chicanery, money grubbing commercialism and'– he sought vainly for an example of even deeper perfidy, failed to find one and added somewhat lamely – 'and the insufferable posturings and prancings of Beau Brummell and his fellow fops.'

'I think we should go to bed now,' Harriet decided. 'You said you were exhausted, both physically and mentally.'

'Mentally I am more alert than ever. My mind is seething with ideas. I could talk and talk all night.'

'Mentally, yes, but . . . physically?' Harriet asked slyly.

Shelley saw the soft look in her eyes, marvelled at the spreading darkness of the pupils in the candlelight and laughed delightedly.

'Physically, darling, I'm anything but exhausted – yet.'

Eight

I

'I LIKE Keswick,' Shelley pronounced. 'I shall stay here for the rest of my life.'

Harriet smiled at him tenderly. 'You said that the first day we arrived.'

'And every day since,' Eliza added.

Shelley was lying on his back in front of the log fire; Eliza, busy with her needlework, was sitting in a rocking chair close by, and Harriet, looking very much the schoolgirl she had scarcely ceased to be, was working valiantly at the French lesson her young husband had set her.

The three of them had come to Keswick because Shelley had suddenly decided that he must breathe the same lakeland air that the poets Wordsworth, Coleridge and Southey breathed, and he was especially excited by the fact that the latter lived near Keswick, for Robert Southey, a man of letters who held decidedly republican beliefs, had long been one of his heroes.

Eliza had accompanied the young couple with the intention of remaining only a short time, but now, nobody quite knowing why, she seemed to be firmly settled in Keswick and was gradually assuming control of Cheshunt Cottage, the little furnished dwelling Shelley had rented on the Penrith road.

'Bysshe,' she said, venturing after many days of hesitation to bring up the subject of Shelley's financial problems, 'do you realize how long we have been here?'

Shelley shook his head. 'I've been too engrossed in my Inquiry to count the days.'

The Inquiry, as all three of them had come to call it, was a lengthy examination of the causes of the failure of the French

Revolution to be of lasting benefit to mankind. Having inadvertently reminded Shelley of it now, Eliza knew that unless she diverted his thoughts at once it would be hours before she could get a word in edgeways.

'We've been here eight weeks,' she said quickly.

'Amazing!'

'And are you aware that when we arrived you were all but penniless?'

'What nonsense! I received ten pounds from my uncle during the first week.'

'It dwindled away very rapidly, Bysshe.'

Shelley sat up and warmed his hands at the fire. 'We appear to be managing quite nicely.'

'I expect we are in debt with the trades-people,' Harriet suggested.

'No,' said Eliza, 'we don't owe anyone a penny.'

'Then a small miracle must have happened,' Shelley chuckled. 'I know! It's that well at the bottom of the garden. I've seen you standing there, Eliza, with a peculiar witch-like expression on your face. You throw in a penny, utter some horrible incantation and fish out a crown.'

'Do be sensible, Bysshe,' Eliza laughed. 'The truth of the matter is that I myself am paying the rent and the housekeeping accounts.'

Shelley moaned in mock despair. 'I knew it, Harriet, we live on charity.' He pointed a finger at Eliza. 'And does that frightening ogre, that retired publican moneybags, your esteemed papa, countenance such rash and daring generosity?'

Eliza tried to look severe. Her father, ordering her to keep the matter secret, was supplying her with an increased personal allowance. He was prepared, when he judged it expedient, to grant Harriet herself the sum of two hundred pounds a year, but Timothy Shelley, he had said in a recent letter, must first grant his son the same amount.

'Papa,' Eliza lied glibly, 'knows nothing of what you call my rash and daring generosity. But I can tell you this much, he misses Harriet very much and will gladly forgive her once he knows that her husband is providing for her fully. More than that, I can promise a supply of pin-money for Harriet.'

Shelley leapt indignantly to his feet. 'Even that would be charity.'

'An allowance from your father would be charity too,' Eliza said, expecting and receiving an immediate denial.

'Indeed it would not? I shall some day inherit my grand-father's money and title. An allowance would be part of my expectations, no more, no less.'

Eliza tried not to smile. Theorists such as Bysshe were any-thing but practical. Liberty, equality, fraternity – that was his constant cry. He raged against property and sneered at the commercialism of men who, like her father, had worked hard to amass a fortune. Yet he laid claim, indignantly and violently, to money which he himself had done nothing to earn. True enough, he declared that he would give all the Shelley money away when it came to him, but the actual possession of a large estate would, she felt sure, make him change his mind.

'Since Harriet will inherit half of Papa's estate,' she murmured, 'anything she might receive before his death would be part of her expectations also.'

'Precisely what I meant,' said Shelley, contradicting himself shamelessly.

'In that case,' Eliza pointed out, 'you should be able with a clear conscience to approach your father once again.'

'That mistaken man, my father, is as implacable as ever. He would refuse, as before, to receive me.'

'And you, in your own way, are as implacable as he is.'

'Nonsense! I am the most gentle of beings.'

Shelley's eyes were flashing now with the characteristic but ever-attractive anger. Staring at his sister-in-law wildly, he thought himself a fool for having permitted her to come to Kes-wick. He glanced in distaste about the room. Everything had changed from those far-off days when he had lived in pleasurable untidiness at Poland Street. And who was responsible? Eliza, of course, Eliza with her passion for orderliness. She had wrought orderliness in his life to such an extent that it was *his* life no longer. She held the ridiculous belief that there was a place for every-thing and everything must be in that place. Rarely these days was he able to find anything he wanted, whether it were a manuscript, a coat, a pen or a shoe.

He leapt to his feet and strode to the window. The view no longer delighted him, for the mountains beyond the lake seemed to be crowding down upon him, crawling forward on invisible legs. Moreover, the sky was leaden and thunder clouds were shrouding the mountains in a black and ominous veil. No wonder Eliza felt at home in such a dismal place; he, for his part, was beginning to detest it.

'Why not write to your father?' Eliza suggested. 'A dutiful and contritely worded letter might work miracles.'

'Never!'

'Perhaps if you went for a walk—' Harriet said hopefully. 'I mean, you generally solve your problems when walking.'

'There'll be a downpour in a matter of minutes,' Shelley complained. 'I know this wretched climate only too well. However, since you seem bent on my going to an early grave, walk in the rain I shall. The result will be high fever and that, to everybody's delight, will be the end of Percy Bysshe Shelley.'

He rushed headlong from the room, leaving Eliza to remark that she feared she had done more harm than good. However, after an absence of two hours, during which the clouds had drifted away and the mountains had become bathed in pale winter sunshine, Shelley returned and bounded into the room crying at the top of his voice for tea. His cheeks were gleaming with health and his eyes shone radiantly.

'Godwin is alive!' he cried. 'Imagine it! William Godwin alive and I thought him long since dead!'

'And who, pray, is William Godwin?' Eliza asked.

Shelley looked at her in astonishment. 'I never heard of such ignorance. William Godwin is a famous philosopher, the author of that tremendous work, *Political Justice*. But for Godwin, my pamphlet, *The Necessity of Atheism*, would never have been written. Godwin alive – I can scarcely believe my good fortune!'

'How could you possibly have heard about it while out walking?' Harriest asked.

'I went to the posting-station to collect our letters. There was only one.' He took it from his pocket and tossed it to Harriet. 'It's from my uncle; you may as well read it. I met Southey there and it was he who gave me the marvellous news.'

'I can well understand how excited you must feel about it,' Eliza said diplomatically. 'But tell me, did you decide to write that letter?'

'I thought of nothing else while running back from the village,' he said, much to her amazement. 'Phrases sang in my mind the whole time. In fact, I shall capture them on paper at once.'

Immeasurably gratified, Eliza watched him as he flung himself down at the writing-table beneath the window, and her eyes lingered on him as he seized a pen, inked it and began to write at a frantic speed.

'I'll slip out and prepare the tea,' she whispered, 'but whatever you do, Harriet, I beg you not to disturb him.'

'I'll be quiet as a mouse,' Harriet promised, and began to read Captain Pilfold's letter.

By the time tea was ready Shelley had finished his task, and when Eliza came in with the teacups he bade her put them down, forget such mundane things as tea-drinking and listen to what he had written.

'*Your name*,' he began, '*has ever excited in me the deepest feelings of reverence and admiration. No sooner did I gain a real understanding of your principles than I felt an ardent desire to share them equally. I—*' he broke off. 'Why are you staring at me like that, Eliza?'

'You seem to be carrying dutifulness much further than I would have thought necessary,' she gasped.

'Nonsense. Be silent, please, and listen to the rest of the most important letter I have ever written.'

'Very well,' she said faintly.

'*Considering then my feelings*,' Shelley went on, '*you will not be surprised at the inconceivable emotions which stirred in my breast when I learnt of your existence, for I had enrolled your name in the list of the honourable dead.*'

'But your father *isn't* dead!' Harriet cried.

'Bysshe,' Eliza said sharply, 'is that letter really addressed to your father?'

Shelley flung up his arms in despair. 'Good lord, woman, are you completely out of your mind? This letter is addressed to none other than William Godwin.'

'We thought you were writing to your father,' said Harriet, in a small voice.

Shelley tossed the letter across the room and tore frantically at the neck of his shirt.

'Peace will never be mine until I do,' he said, in a strangled voice. 'I quite see that, heaven help me!'

'Captain Pilfold thinks you ought to,' Harriet ventured, 'and so does the Duke of Norfolk. Apparently the Duke visited Field Place with Captain Pilfold and urged your father to be forgiving and generous, but unhappily your father refused to listen. Both, however, are sure that if you write a conciliatory letter your father will relent.'

'So my father is no longer the Duke's *complete* toady,' Shelley exclaimed in amazement.

'It almost looks as if your father is showing a little of his son's good sense,' said Harriet brightly.

'It does indeed!' Shelley chuckled.

'Nevertheless,' said Eliza, knowing that more could be gained than lost by causing her brother-in-law to contradict her, 'I do understand that pride stands in the way of your writing a conciliatory letter.'

'Pride?' Shelley said reprovingly. 'Pride is an evil thing. Are you suggesting, Eliza Westbrook, that *I* am evil?'

'Why, Bysshe, of course not.'

He turned and walked slowly to the writing-table, Eliza and Harriet watching him breathlessly. He sat down at last, his shoulders quivering indignantly, and reached deliberately for a pen. He wrote this time, not in frantic haste, but slowly and carefully. Still watching him, Eliza and Harriet were afraid to speak or move. After a few moments he glanced at them over his shoulder.

'I am nothing if not inventive,' he said sternly.

He wrote solidly for five minutes, then glanced at them again. To their surprise there was an impish smile on his face.

'I quite understand,' he murmured, 'that I am being coerced. A man is rarely a match for one woman alone; when two are snapping at his heels he is lost, completely lost.'

When the letter was finished he signed it with a flourish and gave it to Eliza to read.

'I trust it meets with your full approval,' he said mockingly.

She saw that he had addressed his father formally as *My dear sir*, and concluded it dutifully *Yours respectfully and affectionately*. The tone of the first paragraph was far more conciliatory than she would have dared to expect. He told his father that when convinced of an error no one was more ready to own that conviction than he himself, nor to repair any injuries which might have resulted from a line of conduct he had pursued.

'This is really splendid, Bysshe.'

'Read on,' he commanded, looking over her shoulder.

Eliza read on, but not by any means so happily.

On my expulsion from Oxford you were so good as to allow me £200
per annum; you also added a promise of my being unrestrained in the
exercise of the completest free agency. In consequence of this last I married
a young lady whose personal character is unimpeachable. My allowance
was then withdrawn. I was left without money four hundred miles from
home, liable every day to be exposed to the severest exile of penury.

'Your father might well think that you are accusing him of
some criminal act,' she protested.

'Read on, read on,' Shelley said loftily.

Let me say that a reconciliation with you is a thing which I very much
desire. Accept my apologies for the uneasiness which I have occasioned.
Believe that my wish to repair any uneasiness is firm and sincere. I regard
these family differences as a very great evil. I much lament that I should
have been in any way instrumental in exciting them.

'Do my words convey any hint of sarcasm?' Shelley asked.

'No, I don't think so.'

Eliza, but with a sinking heart, read the final paragraph.

I hope you will not consider what I am about to say an insulting want
of respect or contempt, but I think it my duty to say that I can make no
promise of concealing my opinions in political or religious matters.

Eliza gave him back the letter. She was shaking with anger,
but feared that an angry word from her might cause the impetuous
young man to destroy what he had written. Better a letter of this
sort, she thought, than no letter at all.

'Well?' Shelley asked, prepared, she saw, for an argument.

'We can only hope for the best,' she said, diplomatically.

2

'A grey ghost swathed in mist?' Harriet exclaimed shrilly.
'I swear I can't see any such thing. Can you, Eliza?'

'Fortunately for my peace of mind, no,' Eliza laughed.

Harriet pouted prettily. 'Bysshe is teasing us as usual.'

Standing on a little mound, the three of them were looking
out across the waters of Lake Derwentwater. It was a bitterly

cold January day. Heavy clouds were drifting across the sky and a moaning wind was covering the surface of the lake with tiny white-caps.

'It was Southey's ghost I pointed out to you,' Shelley said gloomily, 'but only I can see it.'

'Mr. Southey was very much alive when last we saw him,' Eliza said cheerfully.

'The husk of his body lives on, I admit, but the spirit, that once so glorious spirit, departed long ago and now, restless and miserable, haunts the lake.'

'Have you quarrelled with Mr. Southey?' Harriet asked.

Shelley shook his head and heaved a deep sigh. 'Not that, but suddenly the scales fell from my eyes and the man who was once my hero fell dead at my feet. He has lost the enthusiasms of his youth. Where once he preached reform he now preaches tolerance. He takes the line that the mind cannot create, only perceive. He strives to please everybody, and *why*? I flung the reason at him and he made no attempt to deny it. He longs for one thing only, to be created Poet Laureate. I suspect that his downfall began with the granting of a Civil List pension a few years ago.'

'You may well be Poet Laureate yourself some day,' Harriet murmured, mistakenly hoping to please him.

'Not at such a cost, by God!'

'One must learn in this life to be prepared for disappointments,' Eliza said practically.

Shelley chose not to hear. 'The final blow came when Southey assured me that I would in time accept things as they are and become as he has become. Comfortable, he meant, and successful, and depraved! Far rather would I die today than let *that* happen to me.' He pointed a quivering finger at the ghost which no one else but he could see. 'Oh, Southey, Southey, how I weep for thee!'

Eliza looked at him with compassion. Still only nineteen, she thought, yet weighted down with what he considered the evils of society and at the same time burning with an intense desire to set things right.

'You still have Mr. Godwin,' she told him gently.

Shelley's eyes lit up instantly. 'Thank God for William Godwin!'

Not having expected so great a man to write to him, Shelley had been filled with wonder and gratitude when Godwin had replied immediately to that first enthusiastic letter. There had been other letters, other replies, and an exchange of views had convinced Shelley that Godwin, thinking as he himself did, was the only person in the world to whom he could turn for help and advice. William Godwin, his mentor, was indeed the only person in the world from whom he was prepared to suffer correction, and suffering it, regard it gladly as guidance.

'Godwin,' he said, 'agrees that I should go to Ireland, but warns me wisely that I must write and speak there with caution.'

Eliza looked at him in surprise. There had been much talk lately of the social conflicts that were taking place in Ireland, but this was the first mention of an actual visit.

'I shall begin by supporting Catholic emancipation,' Shelley asserted warmly.

Eliza laughed comically. 'Dear me, Bysshe, are we all, from being near-atheists, to become Roman Catholics?'

'Certainly not, Eliza! But with things as they are in Ireland, Catholic emancipation will be the first step towards complete freedom.'

'Much as I would like to visit Ireland,' Eliza said quietly, 'and happy as I would be to provide the money for the journey, my personal funds are far too low.'

She reflected that more than a month had passed since Shelley had written to his father, and as far as she or Harriet knew, no satisfactory reply had been received. There had been two letters from Mr. Shelley, but on receiving the first his son had been too immersed in writing to read it for several days, and having read it he had ventured no comment on its contents. As for the second letter, its arrival had found Shelley busily engaged upon the task of collecting his shorter poems together for eventual publication, and like the first, he had cast it aside as if it were of no importance whatever.

'Bysshe,' she pressed, 'did you hear what I said?'

'I did indeed, my dear Eliza, but we shall go to Ireland none the less.'

'Has your uncle been generous again?'

'He has, my dear, and to the extent of fifty pounds.'

'But even so, Bysshe—'

Shelley peered at her in surprise. 'Surely I told you the good news?'

'*What* good news, Bysshe?'

'My father has been generous also. Oh, but I *must* have told you! My allowance, the same sum of two hundred pounds a year, has been restored.' He chuckled richly at the memory of his father's second letter. 'The old rogue assured me that he was restoring it for one reason only, in order to prevent me from cheating the tradespeople.'

Eliza laughed in relief. She could now write to her father, and the young couple, with four hundred pounds a year between them, would be free of financial embarrassment. Free of it, that was, while she remained with them to manage their affairs.

'So we go to Ireland,' she said.

'Bearing the banner of freedom and ready to spread the Godwinian philosophy!' Shelley enthused.

'And ready also to be happy there for the rest of our lives?' Eliza teased.

Shelley laughed and tweaked her nose.

'For a few months, at all events,' he chuckled.

Nine

I

'The waiting,' said William Godwin sympathetically, 'is the worst part of it.'

Shelley looked at his friend and mentor with wild, unseeing eyes. 'For me, or for Harriet? *I* might wait in mental agony, but she, poor girl, waits and struggles in physical agony. Is it true, Godwin, that the first child is always the hardest to deliver?'

'An old wives' tale, no more,' Godwin said soothingly.

The Shelleys, with the ever-present Eliza, had taken temporary lodgings in Pimlico. Sixteen months had passed since they had left Keswick for Dublin. Shelley would be twenty-one in August and Harriet eighteen. Spurred on by Shelley's restlessness, the little party had visited many places during the sixteen months. From Ireland they had gone to Wales, from Wales to Devonshire, and from there back to Wales again. There had been visits to London, where Shelley had first met Godwin, a second visit to Ireland, and now they were in London once more, having stayed for a time with John Westbrook before coming here to Pimlico.

'Bysshe. . . .'

It was Eliza, entering the room on tiptoe.

'Eliza—!' Shelley cried, springing up from his chair.

She shook her head. 'Not yet, but the midwife thinks it won't be very much longer. I came down for a moment because Harriet is worried about you.'

'She needn't be,' Godwin told her. 'Am I not here to look after him?'

Eliza looked at him speculatively. She neither liked nor disliked him and thought it ridiculous that her young brother-in-law

103

should hold him in such high esteem. She saw nothing remarkable in his appearance, though of course it was his brain that Shelley admired. He looked older than his actual age, which was fifty-seven, and at times his eyes had a dull and brooding look. She thought of all she now knew about this man who, twenty years ago, shocked society with his book, *Political Justice*. The son of a Nonconformist minister, he had become one himself and had for a time held extreme Calvinistic beliefs. From that, influenced by the French philosophers, he had gone to the other extreme of philosophical radicalism, and through his writing had aimed at sweeping away all political, social and religious institutions. Yet he seemed to Eliza to be mild and gentle, and she had often heard him say that he hated any form of violence. A theorist, no more, she decided, and quite likely a disappointed one.

'Harriet wants to know if you have had dinner, Bysshe,' she went on.

'*Have* we?' Shelley demanded of Godwin.

'We dined together at the coffee-house on the corner,' Godwin said. 'I, substantially, but poor Shelley left everything untouched.'

'I can't tell Harriet that,' Eliza said crossly.

Shelley swung round on her. 'Tell her I ate a hearty meal, like the condemned man I am.'

'*Condemned?*'

'To loving her more than ever, and for the rest of my life.'

Smiling now, Eliza went back to her sister.

'Harriet is so brave,' Shelley told Godwin in a broken voice. 'And so proud, too.' He remembered how, in her delightful ignorance, she had expected that first night to become pregnant immediately. 'More than that, Godwin, she's quite convinced she's the cleverest young woman in the world, though I must admit she was beginning to doubt my own cleverness. Looking back, I must have doubted it myself at times. Getting a baby is obviously a difficult operation – for a man.'

'Since a man can't conceive one himself,' Godwin laughed, 'and since a woman has no hope of it without a man, you're talking nonsense.'

'And no doubt I shall talk a lot more nonsense before my own arrives,' Shelley wailed.

Godwin smiled affectionately. He sincerely hoped that the

baby's arrival would bring a settling influence to his young friend's life. He had the greatest admiration for Shelley and had recognized in him the seeds of real genius. The world, he thought, would be left all the richer for having known Percy Bysshe Shelley, provided he concentrated on expressing himself through poetry. Already his work, immature as it was, showed promise of a brilliant flowering.

'Let's pass the time,' Godwin suggested, 'in one of our lively discussions.'

'As you wish, but I warn you I shall contradict you flatly, whether or not I agree with you.'

Provoked by Godwin, Shelley forget his anxiety in a heated denial of what Southey had once said about the mind being unable to create, only to perceive. Provoking him still further Godwin asked for a simple example of mind's creation, upon which Shelley picked up a chair and thumped it down in front of Godwin.

'This, my dear Godwin, was first a vision in the mind of a cabinet-maker. His hands formed it but his mind created it.'

'If creation starts in the mind,' Godwin murmured, 'who then created the mountains and the lakes of Cumberland?'

'I refuse to fall into so silly a trap,' Shelley laughed. '*You* tell *me*.'

'God?'

'The personal God of men like my father – you mean that?'

'Perhaps.'

'Confound you, Godwin, you know as well as I do that a personal God was first created in the mind of man.'

'Ah, but God in an impersonal sense, and still in that sense the creator of the universe? Who created Him, or It?'

'I can't answer that unless you give me an explanation of the meaning and purpose of limitless space. Where does it begin and end? If truly limitless, how can it begin and end? If limited, what is beyond it?'

'Too deep a contemplation of space would lead to madness.'

Shelley tore at the neck of his shirt, found that by some mischance he was wearing a neckcloth and ripped it from his neck.

'I detest the conventional clothing we are compelled to wear,' he complained. 'Compelled because of what is called decency's sake. Nothing could be more restricting to clarity of thought.'

'I seem to have got the better of you in our little argument,' Godwin suggested wickedly.

'Nonsense! I was about to say that a full understanding of space might only be possible through what the world calls madness. Galileo was considered mad, remember, and—' he broke off. 'My God, what was that?'

Godwin had heard it too, and sprang eagerly to his feet.

'Your son, or daughter, whichever the case may be!' he cried.

Shelley dashed across the room, collided with Eliza at the door and seizing her by the shoulders shook her violently.

'A son or daughter?' he demanded.

'A daughter,' Eliza gasped.

2

Harriet covered her ears with her hands in mock horror.

'What an extraordinary noise, Bysshe,' she protested.

'Enough to waken the dead,' Eliza decided.

'Then frighten them back into their graves again,' William Godwin added.

'I'm singing to her and she loves it,' Shelley said mildly.

With his two-month-old daughter held lovingly in his arms he was striding up and down the small sitting-room of the furnished cottage the Shelleys had rented at Bracknell, in Berkshire, Shelley himself having decided that the country air would be much healthier for the baby.

'See how she frowns when I stop, smiles when I start again!' he chuckled, and broke once more into a tuneless repetition of the outlandish word he had invented: 'Yáhmani, Yáhmani, Yáhmani, Yáh-ma-neeee!'

'It's feeding time,' said Harriet practically. 'Do please give her to me.'

'Well, that's one thing *I* can't do for her,' Shelley laughed, and placed the baby in his wife's arms.

When Harriet had gone from the room Eliza looked at Godwin and coughed meaningly. It was she who had invited him to spend a few days at Bracknell, and taking him aside earlier had outlined the plan she had in mind and begged him to support her.

'Bysshe—' she began.

'Do you like my daughter's name, Godwin?' Shelley broke in eagerly.

'Ianthe . . .' Godwin murmured, dwelling on the name.

Shelley, taking the name from Ovid, had first used it in his narrative poem, *Queen Mab*. The Ianthe of his imagination was violet-eyed, whereas his fair-haired daughter was blue-eyed, but that, thought Godwin, meant nothing to the young poet. If the fancy took him he was just as likely to insist that the baby's eyes were black.

'Her second name is Elizabeth, or Eliza,' Shelly ran on, without waiting for an answer. 'I sincerely hope it pleases both my sister Elizabeth and my sister-in-law Eliza.'

'It certainly pleases me,' Eliza said, and tried again. 'Bysshe—'

'Ianthe shows signs already of deep mental power,' Shelley interrupted. 'I expect her in time to outstrip her poor father in both intellect and intelligence.'

'In my case,' Godwin laughed, 'my own daughter has shown dismaying signs of that all her life.'

'Ah yes, Mary, I must meet her sometime. How old is she now?'

'Fifteen, almost sixteen.'

'Splendid! I enjoy nothing better than a conversation with an intelligent child.'

'Bysshe,' said Eliza, growing desperate now, 'Papa said something when last I saw him that has worried me very much. Your friend Hogg, when he called last week, brought up the same subject, and that made me more concerned than ever.'

'Are you referring,' Shelley asked tartly, 'to the question of a second marriage for Harriet and me?'

'Yes, Bysshe, I am.'

'Hogg is an alarmist. Harriet and I may or may not be living in sin, but if everybody is so worried about it we can go back to Scotland and live there for the rest of our lives.'

Eliza looked hopefully at Godwin.

'My dear Shelley,' he said, coming to her aid, 'the most worrying aspect of the question is whether or not an English court would accept the legitimacy of your offspring.'

Shelley was beginning to look bored. 'If we take up residence in Scotland we can snap our fingers at the English courts.'

'Not as far as the inheritance laws are concerned,' Eliza put in warmly.

Shelley yawned. 'Inheritance laws?'

'Had Ianthe been a boy,' Godwin said, 'there would have been a grave doubt as to whether or not she would inherit the Shelley title and fortune.'

'Surely you mean "he", not "she"?' Shelley questioned sternly.

'Bysshe, do be serious,' Eliza begged. 'Your next child may well be a boy. We consider it imperative that you and Harriet marry again, in England, before a son is born to you.'

'By that you mean in the Church of England?' Shelley said dangerously.

'Why, of course.'

'Ah, you want to turn me into a hypocrite.'

'You went through a Christian marriage ceremony in the Church of Scotland,' Eliza pointed out.

'Nonsense! The Scots, as everybody knows, are barbarians.'

'Oh, Bysshe, how difficult you are!'

Shelley looked sadly at William Godwin.

'And you – you, my friend and mentor – are a part of this conspiracy,' he said reproachfully.

Godwin tried not to smile. 'If I say that in these matters one must conform you will accuse me of being as depraved as Southey.'

'By God I will!'

'Then I'll say no more for the moment. After all, looking at things as you do, you have right on your side. It would be folly to go through another marriage ceremony, here or elsewhere.'

'*Folly?*' Shelley challenged.

'Eliza is wrong to expect it of you.'

'Wrong? How *can* she be wrong? Eliza is a noble creature. The welfare of the son yet to be born to me is her sole concern.'

'Indeed it is!' Eliza averred, and gave Godwin a grateful look.

'Nevertheless,' said Shelley, 'Harriet is not yet with child a second time.'

'Oh, *Bysshe!*'

Shelley laughed gleefully. He had led them on, raised their hopes, dashed them to the ground again, and enjoyed the experience immensely. A most stimulating five minutes, he thought, yet the uneasiness, caused first by Hogg, still lingered. Being a father, it seemed, endowed a man with certain responsibilities, in respect even of the laws of a society which he hated. Perhaps Godwin was right in having once said that to achieve one's aim one must be prepared to use the little restrictions with which a frightened society sought to protect itself. If Ianthe were a boy—! he thought, and was about to say that he would conform, marry Harriet again without a moment's delay, when Eliza, quite losing her temper, attacked him harshly.

'You'll be twenty-one in less than a week, Bysshe. Legally a man. For heaven's sake try and behave like one.'

'That was precisely what my father said in his last letter,' Shelley told her tonelessly. 'Are you in the habit of reading my private correspondence?'

'Only when you show it to me.'

'Did I in this case?'

'You did.'

'Then you know that Father is anxious for a meeting with me, the purpose of which is to discuss the distribution of the Shelley fortune, my grandfather being in failing health.'

Eliza looked at him obliquely. 'You have no intention of going to Field Place, of course?'

'On the contrary,' Shelley said haughtily, 'I have every intention of going there. Have I not Ianthe to think of, and such other children as might be born to me?'

'And the re-marriage?' Eliza asked daringly.

'That, my dear woman, will depend entirely on what transpires at Field Place.'

'But Bysshe—'

'Enough!' he raged, and ran headlong from the room shouting that he hoped to find at least a little peace in the company of his wife and daughter.

'Bysshe will never grow up,' Eliza said despairingly.

'So much the worse for him if he does,' Godwin sighed. 'To grow up would be to condemn himself to the misery of disillusionment. Let him remain as he is, guilelessly angry at everything, often enough without cause. Not only angry, but charming and lovable, eager always to impose upon the world a joyous world of his own making.'

'A world of make-believe,' Eliza snapped. 'A fool's paradise.'

Godwin sighed again. 'And he, my poor Eliza, the only wise man in it.'

3

'You appear to be limping, Bysshe,' Timothy Shelley said gruffly, as his son, followed by Captain Pilfold, entered the study at Field Place. 'Is anything seriously the matter with your leg?'

'Elephantiasis,' Shelley replied promptly.

Timothy stepped back in alarm. 'My dear Bysshe—!'

'In the coach coming down I sat opposite a very large woman with abnormally fat legs,' Shelley explained. 'Obviously she was suffering from elephantiasis. Inadvertently I touched her on alighting, and that was fatal. Elephantiasis is a highly contagious disease. I do advise you, sir, to keep at a safe distance.'

'Confound you, Bysshe,' Timothy exploded, 'I expected you to come here in a serious mood!'

'But I *am* serious, Father. No man in his right mind would dare to joke about an affliction so desperate as elephantiasis. Would he, Uncle?'

'No,' said Captain Pilfold solemnly.

Timothy flung himself into a chair and looked angrily from his brother-in-law to his son. They had leagued themselves together, not only to oppose him but to taunt him. This meeting was doomed from the outset to end in failure.

'The old gentleman looks pale and ill,' said Shelley. 'Is he by any chance suffering from the after effects of delirium tremens?'

The Captain shook his head. 'Your poor father is suffering from something even worse.'

'*Is* there anything worse, Uncle?'

'The after effects of a sudden abstention from any form of liquor.'

Shelley looked at his father in horror. 'But what a waste, sir! Your cellar is one of the best in England.'

'I abstained for one purpose only,' Timothy said grumpily, 'that I might have all my wits about me during your visit.' He gripped the arms of his chair in sudden agony. 'Do my eyes deceive me, or are you actually wearing trousers?'

'Had I not been wearing them,' Shelley said mildly, 'I would surely have been forbidden entry, Field Place being an eminently respectable house.'

'Disgusting!' Timothy thundered.

'That I am respectably attired, sir?'

Captain Pilfold chuckled. 'Your father means that he would look upon you with greater favour if you were wearing breeches.'

'I most certainly would,' Timothy said warmly. 'I realize that some renegade introduced trousers ten or fifteen years ago, but no real gentleman would be seen dead in them.'

He himself was wearing knee breeches, knee-high leather boots, a plain buff-coloured waistcoat and a hopelessly old-fashioned tail coat. His son was not only wearing trousers and soft leather shoes, but a stylish dark brown *frock coat*.

'Your coat, too, is an insult!' Timothy shouted.

'My dear Father,' said Shelley, growing heated himself, 'the frock coat became fashionable long before I was born.'

'A fop, my son has become a fop!' Timothy exclaimed, shaking with an anger which he knew was ridiculous. 'Do you patronize the same tailor as that idiot Brummell? The last time I saw him in London he was mincing about in a sky-blue coat. Bonaparte will never suffer defeat while such creatures clutter up society.'

Shelley, who had ranted often enough about Beau Brummell, sprang instantly to his defence.

'Oh come, sir, Brummell has served society well in at least one respect.'

'And *that*?'

'He has made cleanliness fashionable. Because of him many people now take a bath once a week and change their linen two or three times a month.'

Timothy, speechless now, could do no more than sneer.

'Cleanliness is next to godliness,' Shelley added, 'though some people still consider it possible to be *un*clean and at the same time godly.'

Godliness! Timothy seized on that at once. The conversation must be brought sharply round to the negotiations which he found it imperative to enter upon with his son. Godliness, which had been the subject of many a letter, was an important condition.

'A full and amicable understanding will never be reached,' he said, as quietly as he could, 'unless you make a public declaration of your return to Christianity.'

'That depends on what you mean by Christianity,' Shelley told him earnestly. 'Was Christ, in the sense of orthodox Christianity, a Christian?'

'Blasphemy!' Timothy gasped.

'Father, I believe, and always have believed, in the teachings of Christ.'

'He's a good boy at heart,' Captain Pilfold put in. 'Give him his due, Timothy.'

Timothy shook his head in despair. For the life of him he didn't know what to think about this trouble-making son of his.

'Had Christ been on earth to lead the French Revolution,' Shelley ran on, 'there would be no Napoleon Bonaparte in France today, no debauched Prince Regent in England and, by heaven, not a single bishop in the House of Lords.' He paused for breath. 'Blasphemy again, Father, blasphemy again?'

But Timothy was staring at his son's frock coat. Crumpled as it was, it was obviously brand new.

'Are you in debt to your tailor?' he demanded.

'I owe my tailor not a penny,' Shelley said, fingering the lapels of his coat reflectively. 'I remember now that this coat, and the trousers too, was a present from Eliza. She considered, poor woman, that I was going about in rags. She bought all the clothes for Ianthe, too.'

'And who, pray, is Ianthe?'

'My daughter, of course.'

'Your—?' Timothy, badly shaken, turned appealingly to Captain Pilfold. 'Were you aware that Bysshe had a daughter?'

'Indeed I wasn't!'

Shelley looked from one to the other in surprise. 'Surely I informed you both by letter?'

'No doubt you intended to, and no doubt you forgot,' the Captain laughed.

'Tell me about the child,' Timothy begged eagerly. 'When was she born? Does she resemble the Shelleys or the Westbrooks? Heavens above, I can scarcely realize it – my first grandchild!'

Shelley gave his father the details of Ianthe's birth, said that she seemed at present to be more of a Shelley than a Westbrook, and dwelt at length, his voice soft with emotion, on the pleasure it gave him to watch the baby taking succour at her mother's breast.

'First one breast, then the other,' he concluded, 'and both so round and full. What amazes me is that they should be identical in size and shape, whether more milk is taken from one than the other.'

Timothy looked uneasily at his son. '*Really*, Bysshe!'

Captain Pilfold cleared his throat. 'I think we ought to trim our sails and embark on the real business of the day.'

Shelley bowed graciously. 'As you wish, Uncle.'

Timothy remembered his son's debts.

'Those insufferable post-obit bonds!' he cried. 'The money-lenders, damn their insolence, have been making inquiries embarrassing both to your poor grandfather and to me.'

Shelley looked surprised. 'I find nothing insufferable about post-obits. Those I have signed up to now have saved me from complete paupery.'

'Books!' Timothy shouted.

'I beg your pardon, Father?'

'You bought books to the value of one hundred pounds and committed yourself to the eventual repayment of two hundred and fifty pounds.'

'I was able to give excellent security, Father. Am I not eventually and inevitably to inherit certain Shelley estates worth six thousand pounds a year?'

'More than that,' Timothy corrected. 'Property values have increased.'

'They have? Oh, splendid!'

'You should have held your peace, Timothy,' Captain Pilfold chuckled. 'The young scamp is sure to sign a few more bonds now.'

'Enough have been signed already. I can't for the life of me imagine what he has done with the money.'

Shelley felt rather at a loss in this respect himself. Apart from buying books and travelling here and there with Harriet and Eliza he lived frugally enough. He had of course lent money to various needy friends, chief of whom was William Godwin, and

E

doubtless he would lend more. Wealth, after all, even wealth yet to be inherited, was meant to be shared.

'If you go on like this,' Timothy added, 'you will inherit an estate drained of all resources.'

Shelley cocked his head on one side and tried to be business-like. 'Surely the amount entailed on me is but a small portion of the whole?'

'It is, thank God!'

Shelley turned to his uncle. 'You will note, Uncle, how these Christians always thank God when the saving of a little money is involved.' He looked at his father again. 'Sir, I have only a hazy idea of the ramifications of the Shelley affairs. My mind, like the earth in the beginning, is without form – as far as money matters go. In a word, let there be light.' And after a moment's thought he added briskly, 'Genesis, one, three.'

Timothy shook a clenched fist at him. 'The devil can always quote scripture to his own advantage.'

'But think, Father, what a happy man you will be if you can see the light of your own creation and think it good. Genesis, one, four.'

'In the same verse,' said Timothy, determined not to be out-quoted, 'God divided the light from the darkness, and that as far as *you* are concerned is more than I can expect to achieve.'

'Ah yes, Father, but—'

'Let's push on with things before we're all three of us exhausted,' Captain Pilfold grumbled.

Timothy hesitated. A vision of not one but several bottles of his best port floated across his mind.

'The position is something like this,' he said, clearing his throat. 'The estate, in round figures, is valued at two hundred thousand pounds. Your dear grandfather has long wanted to make sure that his wealth, like the title, will pass from father to son for many generations to come, but because of your conduct, both at Eton and Oxford – at Eton, remember, you refused to fag – and at Oxford—'

'Stick to the point, Timothy,' Captain Pilfold muttered.

'I *am* sticking to it,' Timothy complained. 'Because of Bysshe's conduct at Eton and Oxford, and his hasty elopement and marriage with the daughter of a publican, our respected and sorely harassed head of the family has hesitated to entail the whole of the estate.' He looked sorrowfully at his son. 'Being cautious, yet at the same time loving you despite your many grave faults, and being also exceedingly generous, your dear grandfather settled upon you property to the estimated value of eighty thousand pounds which now yields in the region of seven thousand five hundred pounds per annum.'

'By settled,' Shelley asked brightly, 'do you mean that it cannot be taken from me under any circumstances?'

'Obviously it cannot, or those astute moneylenders would not have engaged in such scandalous traffic with you. At the same time, such being the legal aspect of the settlement – dear me, I'm no lawyer myself! – the entail cannot be carried further than you. Er – that is, without your own consent.' Timothy paused and looked plaintively at his brother-in-law. 'Where am I, my dear fellow?'

'In the soup,' Captain Pilfold chuckled.

Scowling, Timothy went on hurriedly. 'However, Bysshe, in view of your refusal to – hum – conform to decent Christian principles. we, your dear grandfather and I, are prepared to settle upon you the sum of two thousands pounds per annum for life, the yearly payments to commence from the moment of your agreement.'

'*And* pay his debts,' Captain Pilfold put in.

Timothy, his face that of a gargoyle rather than a saint, tried to beam upon his son.

'*And* pay your debts.'

'The moment of my agreement,' Shelley pondered. 'My agreement to . . . what?'

Timothy tried to beam again. 'Your agreement to the conferring of the entail on the property at the moment – hum – entailed upon you – dear me, I most certainly am not a lawyer – upon your son, should you have a son, or failing that upon your younger brother.'

Shelley smiled sweetly. 'Contrary to your denial, sir, you sound remarkably like a lawyer.'

'A handsome offer, Bysshe,' Timothy declared hopefully.

'Worth considering,' said Captain Pilfold.

Shelley shook his head. 'I don't agree. The money, from a personal point of view, means nothing to me. What I might be able to do with it for the good of mankind is the only consideration. Morally it would degrade me, once I inherited it, to keep it entirely for myself. And what if I have no son? My brother John, docile and obedient as he is, would guard it jealously for future generations of parasites.'

It was clear to Timothy that his son, speaking intensely but quietly, was entirely sincere in his views. A cunning look crossed his face.

'My dear Bysshe, you could print off a lot of pamphlets on two thousands pounds a year, and so, in your own peculiar way, such being your conviction, do much in the service of mankind.'

'Not as much as I could with seven thousands five hundred pounds a year.'

'To be yours only after your grandfather's death and mine, remember.'

'I can wait, Father.'

Timothy, perspiring freely, mopped his brow in desperation. 'You may well have to wait a long time,' he said. 'Your grandfather is eighty-five. I, sixty-three now, have every hope of living to ninety.'

Shelley glanced wildly about the room. He was beginning to feel trapped, trapped but not tempted. Fumbling at the neat starched cravat which Harriet had insisted on his wearing, he tore it from his neck.

'You had a weak chest as a boy,' Timothy said. 'You never wear enough clothes. You go hatless most of the time, and in winter I have yet to see you in an overcoat. Neglecting yourself as you do, you may die at an early age.'

'If I do, I shall at least die happy!' Shelley exulted. 'It's no use, Father. Nothing you can say will change my mind.'

And, laughing wildly, he ran from the room.

'Is he crazy, d'you think?' Timothy asked the Captain.

'Crazy in a sane sort of way.'

'A devil got into him the moment he was born.'

Captain Pilfold shook his head. 'Not a devil. Something strange and beautiful, Timothy. Unreal to hardened old sinners like you and me. Rare, too, so rare it makes me want to cry.'

Timothy began to feel uneasy. 'You'll be writing poetry next.'

'To throw away a certain two thousand pounds a year, that took real courage. He's a grand lad. There's more of a Christian

in him than there is in most people I know, you included,
Timothy. It's a rare great heart that beats in his breast.'

Timothy rose shakily. 'Talking like this won't help us.'

'What else can we do but talk?'

Timothy was silent and thoughtful for a few moments, then
he smiled bleakly. 'It was a mistake, my father settling that
property on Bysshe, and nothing can undo it, but he *can* alter his
will and safeguard the rest of the estate. I'll have a talk with the
lawyers. Who knows, there may be some way, a tricky clause
here and there, of safeguarding the whole of it. Damn the lot of
them, let them earn their money for once!'

Ten

I

ELIZA, candle in hand, went to the front door a second time, listened for a few moments without opening it, then returned to Harriet.

'You were right. That *was* Bysshe's voice you heard. He's arguing with someone farther down the street. I hope he doesn't forget he lives here and wander off again.'

'I grow so tired of his arguments,' Harriet sighed.

Eliza smiled approvingly. 'And well you might.'

Nine months had passed since Ianthe's birth, seven since Shelley had refused to agree to the proposition put to him by his father. There had been several more changes of residence, including a short period in Scotland, and now the Shelley household had been set up in a rented cottage at Windsor. Here Shelley had busied himself writing an essay in dialogue form, the subject being his views on deism. The printing of this most earnest work had served only to increase his debts, and this, with other creditors making constant demands, had been the cause of a quarrel between him and Harriet, a quarrel which had reduced her to bitter tears and wrung from him a promise to go once more to Field Place in the hope of reaching a compromise with his father. He had now been absent ten days and Harriet, distracted with worry one moment, resentful of what Eliza called his neglect the next, had come close to hardening her heart against him.

'He's coming in now,' Eliza whispered. 'Whatever you do, don't throw yourself into his arms.'

'I'll try not to,' Harriet promised.

'Remember all the things I've told you, darling. You must

take a firm stand, forgive him only if he really has been to Field Place, and then with every show of reluctance.'

Shelley came into the room before more could be said, but not with his usual hurrying eagerness. He was hatless and his shirt, in spite of the bitterness of the weather, was open at the neck. His shoes were caked with mud and his trousers wet to the knees. He glanced at Harriet and Eliza absently, as if he had last seen them but an hour ago, drew up a chair by the fire and sank into it.

'Who were you arguing with?' Eliza asked. 'I expected the neighbours to rush out thinking a fight was in progress.'

Shelley chuckled faintly. 'In a sense it was a fight, words being used, not fists. Ryan grew quite incensed.'

Captain Ryan, a handsome dashing young man who had recently bought an army commission, was a new acquaintance. Shelley had met him at a coffee-house and, as Shelley so often did with casual acquaintances, had brought him home to dinner. The two of them, Eliza knew, had little in common, but Ryan had continued to visit the cottage, being attracted, she suspected, by Harriet's pink and white loveliness rather than by Shelley's intellectual harangues.

'What was the cause of the quarrel?' Harriet asked crossly.

Shelley settled more comfortably in his chair. 'The scandalous practice of buying army commissions. Think of it, a nincompoop like Ryan has a commission, not because he has earned it, but because he could afford to buy it. But enough of Ryan. All I want to do is rest. I feel utterly exhausted.'

'By the look of you, you must have been walking for hours.'

'I walked all the way from London.'

'What a crazy thing to do,' Harriet said angrily.

'Oh, I enjoyed it. At least when the sun was shining, and when it rained I didn't take much notice of it.'

'But why choose to walk in the rain?'

'For the simple reason that I found myself completely without money.'

'Did you give it all away?' Eliza asked, remembering that Shelley had been known on occasion to empty his pockets for the benefit of some passing beggar. 'Or was it sheer absent-mindedness?'

'I gave it away. I remember now I kept a little for food, but the rest I gave to a poor woman who was too ill to travel outside the coach.'

'Apparently you gave her your own seat inside as well,' said Harriet, her voice rising shrilly.

'*Harriet!*'

'Don't sound so shocked,' she retorted. 'Very noble to give your money away and walk from London like some pious pilgrim, but did you stop to think that your wife might be in need too?'

Shelley laughed heartily. 'A pilgrim, yes, but not a pious one, heaven forbid!'

Eliza, studying the angry expression on Harriet's face, wondered how best to provoke her to further anger, yet at the same time remain apart from the quarrel herself.

'Did you go to Field Place?' she asked Shelley lightly.

'No,' he replied, regretting that he found it impossible to lie. 'I spent two or three days with Uncle at Cuckfield, the rest of the time in London with Hogg. It was very exciting. We studied Italian together. I want to master the language before visiting Italy.'

Harriet laughed with a harshness that appalled her. 'So it's Italy now! Well, at all events you won't be able to walk there.'

'Not with the Channel to cross,' Shelley said brightly, 'but a walking tour from Calais to Florence would be marvellous.'

'The three of us?' Eliza asked with a show of enthusiasm she hoped might please him.

'No, the *four* of us. Aren't you forgetting Ianthe?'

'Surely Ianthe is too young to travel?'

'She can ride on a mule. We'll need another mule for our baggage. We'll wait till the spring, of course. Everybody says the war will be over by the end of April, perhaps sooner.'

Where, as of old, his enthusiasm had always found a ready response in Harriet, she felt only impatience this time, not only with him but with Eliza.

'Try to be practical, Bysshe', she said. 'And you also, Eliza. Even a walking tour isn't possible without money.'

Shelley rose from his chair, yawned and stretched, and seizing a cushion for his head, settled down in his favourite position on the hearth-rug.

'I shall have two hundred pounds in a day or so. I remembered to negotiate another post-obit bond while in London.'

'You have debts far in excess of that amount.'

Shelley appealed comically to Eliza. 'What a wet blanket she is!'

Eliza, looking down on him, caught her breath sharply. Never before had his beauty caused her so much anguish. In spite of his exhaustion after the long walk, his brow was smooth and untrammelled, his features the finest she had ever seen in a man. She thought dizzily that no artist could ever capture the delicate shading of his complexion, and holding his eyes for a moment, eyes so large and guileless, she caught her breath sharply again. She knew now, in dismay and joy, why she was taking such pains to provoke Harriet's anger. She wanted Shelley for herself, and always had. For that reason she had taken of late to dressing more fashionably in an attempt to look young and gay. And for that reason also she had done her best during his absence to turn her sister against him.

'*Somebody* has to be what you call a wet blanket,' Harriet went on. 'Otherwise there would be no hope at all of making you see things as they are, not as you imagine them to be.'

'Dear me, how seriously you have begun to take life,' Shelley protested.

'Life is meant to be taken seriously, Bysshe.'

'You seem to have changed in other things too,' he said wonderingly.

'If you mean that I've grown up, then yes, I certainly have.'

'I'm sure *I* haven't changed in any way,' he said mildly.

Harriet nodded in indignant agreement. While she had become a woman, Bysshe had remained a boy. Eliza had drawn her attention to this and Eliza had been right.

'Oh, Bysshe,' she cried, 'can't you see how necessary it is that somebody in a family should develop a sense of responsibility? One usually expects it to be the husband, but in our case it has to be me.'

Eliza had said this, too, and again Eliza had been right.

'A sense of responsibility,' Harriet repeated heavily.

Shelley sat up in dismay. 'Harriet, we seem to be losing the intellectual sympathy which has been so precious to me.'

'What use is intellectual sympathy when I'm harrassed all the

time by debt-collectors, when I can't have the pretty clothes I
see other women wearing? You laughed once when I said I
wanted to take my rightful place in society, but I'd be ashamed
to now, with things as they are.'

'Ah, you want an argument on the subject of one's rightful
place in society,' Shelley cried with alacrity. 'There's nothing I'd
enjoy more! Tell me, to begin with, just what you mean by *your*
rightful place.'

'Harriet is thinking,' Eliza murmured, 'that she will some
day be Lady Shelley.'

'I am,' Harriet admitted, 'but how can I be sure of that
when I can't even be sure that Bysshe and I are legally married?'

'Heaven bless my soul,' Shelley laughed, 'I really had
intended going to Doctors' Commons while in London to apply
for a licence, but it quite slipped my memory.'

'And what if you *had* remembered it? Would re-marriage
make my position any the more secure?'

'You appear to be contradicting yourself,' Shelley pointed
out.

'I suspect that Harriet is thinking of your father's proposition,'
Eliza suggested quietly.

'Ah, I understand! Financial security to the extent of two
thousand pounds a year is more important to her than the
certainty that our marriage is legal. She has changed even more
than I thought. She agreed after my last visit to Field Place that
I had done the right thing, that a clear conscience was all that
mattered.'

'Only because my mind was clouded by your own ridiculous
idealism!' Harriet cried. 'Well, I can't exist on idealism for ever.
I had to wake up some day.'

Eliza, sure that Shelley was not observing her, caught her
sister's eyes and nodded vigorously. Harriet had uttered her own
often-repeated words and needed but a little prompting to utter
more of them.

'Liberty, equality, fraternity,' Harriet went on tearfully, 'how
I hate the sound of that meaningless phrase! Liberty is all very
well, but what liberty does your philosophizing permit me? And
equality! Do you realize, Bysshe, that your generosity at my
expense has made your friends superior to us, not equal?'

'Then, by heaven, they are no longer my friends!'

'They will be so long as you go on borrowing money and lending it to them.'

Shelley swept this aside uneasily. 'And what, my dear, is your interpretation of fraternity?'

Harriet could think of only one reply. 'Whatever it is I've seen more than enough of it.' She glanced round the room and seeing a pile of books on the sideboard snatched them up one by one and flung them to the floor. 'There! That's what I think of intellectual sympathy!'

An inexpressible wave of sadness swept over Shelley as he looked at her angry face. The change in her was heartrending, and try as he might he could find no reason for it. He knew he was often careless in money matters, that their joint income of £400 a year had long been insufficient for their needs, but with the moneylenders always eager to oblige, what point was there in worrying? Harriet had quite a lot of pretty clothes and more could be bought. She even had her own carriage; he had bought it for her in celebration of Ianthe's birth. Her real complaint seemed to be that there was no real certainty of her ever becoming Lady Shelley. Well, if the title ever did come to him – he was feeling now that he would die long before his father – he would refuse to use it. Harriet could be Lady Shelley if she wished; he would remain plain Mr. Shelley.

'I had thought you above the world,' he said woefully. 'Never had I dreamt that the world would drag you down.'

'Not the world, Bysshe – you.'

'We seem to be strangers of a sudden. I no longer understand you.'

'Oh, *Bysshe*!' Harriet cried, and picking up her skirts ran weeping from the room.

'Let her go,' Eliza said, when Shelley made to follow her.

'She can't be left in that condition!' he said angrily.

'Of course not, but this is a woman's business, not a man's. I'll do what I can to calm her, make her see reason.' Eliza placed her hand affectionately on Shelley's arm. 'Men are so *clumsy*. Sit by the fire. I'll come back presently and make you some tea.'

The bedroom – the connubial bedroom, thought Eliza, her heart leaping queerly – was in darkness. A sob from Harriet told her that her sister was lying on the bed, and going to it she took her gently in her arms.

'Go away,' Harriet cried.

'Darling, it's only me.'

'I thought it was Bysshe.'

'Were you expecting him?'

'It's the least he could do.'

'He needs a little more time, Harriet. Men are so stubborn. The best thing you can do is spend the night in the maid's room.'

'That's another thing. We haven't a maid to sleep in it.'

'Bysshe will get one for you. Act wisely now and he'll do anything you ask.'

'Because I refuse to sleep with him, you mean?'

Eliza laughed shakily. 'I'm only an old maid, but I have heard it said that it's the one sure way for a woman to get what she wants from a man. I'll take Ianthe in with me. She might wake when Bysshe comes and disturb you by crying.'

'Do you think he *will* come?' Harriet asked eagerly.

'Of course, darling, after lying awake for a time, alone and brooding.'

'He might think I'm sleeping with you.'

'I shall tell him just where you are sleeping.'

Harriet kissed her sister on the cheek. 'Thank you. I wouldn't tell him myself. I'm not speaking to him any more.'

'Speech won't be necessary,' Eliza told her excitedly.

When she returned to Shelley he was standing by the fire. He had brought the teacups from the kitchen but had forgotten the saucers, and he had put the kettle on the hob but from the way it was steaming had failed to refill it.

'Is Harriet still crying?' he asked miserably.

'Yes, but angrily, Bysshe. She says she'll never forgive you.'

'It could be said that *I* will never forgive *her*!'

'Nobody would blame you for that.'

'I was beginning to think that I might be at least a little to blame,' he said argumentatively.

Eliza laughed girlishly. 'How you love to contradict people! But for once I'm going to be bold enough to contradict you back. Harriet is at fault, not you. I thought it splendid, Bysshe, the way you gave your money to that poor woman and walked all the way from London.'

'I'm afraid I kept some of it back for food.'

'Oh come, Bysshe—'

'It was wrong of me. Christ would have given her everything he had.'

Embarrassed now, and at the same time confused, Eliza wondered how he could possibly model himself upon Christ and at the same time deny the reality of revealed religion. Then she remembered how fond he was of saying that to believe in the simple teachings of Christ was widely divorced from blind subservience to orthodox Christianity.

'To have kept money back for myself,' Shelley went on sadly, 'is proof that I am moved at times by the same respect for property that governs my father. You say Harriet is still crying, and angrily?'

Her anger won't last, Bysshe. She is determined not to—' Eliza shied away from the word 'sleep' and all its dark implications, then seized on it boldly. 'She is determined not to sleep with you tonight. She begged me to let her sleep with me.'

'Much joy to her, then.'

Joy, Eliza thought avidly, *joy*!

'I don't think you need worry,' she said, trying to keep the hoarseness from her voice. 'Harriet will lie awake, miserable and brooding, and when she can sustain it no longer will come to you. I know what women are, old maid though I am.'

'You're awfully wise, Eliza,' said Shelley, smiling on her gently.

Wise but unscrupulous, Eliza thought, realizing fully why she was acting in this strange and cunning manner. Struggling for a moment for self-restraint, she felt desire all the more.

'Why, you're blushing!' Shelley laughed.

'With anger, Bysshe. Anger at Harriet's stupidity.'

Shelley leant forward and kissed her on the cheek, murmuring that it was sweet and kind of her to be so concerned on his behalf. It was no more than a brotherly kiss, she was well aware of that, but it set her limbs trembling and filled her mind with confusion out of which came only one clear thought. Hogg, she found herself thinking, Thomas Jefferson Hogg, the love-crazed youth who had stolen silently into Harriet's room at York.

'I'm quite worn out with all this emotion,' Shelley said. 'Good night, Eliza.'

'Good night, Bysshe. Sleep well, if you can.'

She followed him to the door, watched him climb the narrow stairs and waited until she heard him moving about in the room above. It had occurred to her that Harriet might not have had time to move to the maid's room, or might have changed her mind, but on hurrying there herself she was vastly relieved to find that her anxiety had been misplaced. Harriet was in bed and amazingly enough half-asleep already.

'Did you take Ianthe to my room?' Eliza asked.

'Yes,' Harriet yawned. 'I thought you must have heard the noise I made moving the cot. Good night, Eliza.'

'Good night, darling.'

Eliza went to her own room and undressed slowly. Catching sight of herself in the cracked mirror, she thought hotly that no man could possibly find her anything but unlovely in the plain, even dowdy, nightgown. She let down her glossy black hair and spread it around her shoulders. That, she decided, made an immense difference, but catching her eyes in the mirror she looked hurriedly away, seized the brush from the dressing-table and began furiously to brush her hair.

She got into bed presently, took up a book and tried to read, for she knew that she must wait for at least an hour before going to Shelley. Finding concentration impossible she lay tensely in the bed, listening to the ticking of the travelling clock on the dressing-table. There was still time, she told herself, for her to come to her senses. Still time, the clock seemed to mock her, still time, still time, still time.

At last, unable to wait longer, she crept from her room and along the uncarpeted passage, so cold beneath her bare feet. The ticking of the clock still rang in her ears, but after only a moment's hesitation she ignored it and softly opened Shelley's door. Fearing that he might have left a candle burning, she came close to sobbing with relief to find the room in darkness. Closing the door softly she stood tensely with her back to it. Had he been counting on a reconciliation he would have left several candles burning, not in order that Harriet might find her way to him with ease, but because he preferred light to darkness for their love-making. Harriet, so free with her chatter of intimate things, had often said so, and Eliza had thought it shameless.

She began to move forward cautiously, groping for the bed-rail. The faintest sound of breathing reached her ears. Perhaps

Bysshe was asleep. So much the better if he were! Wakened by her kiss, he would have less chance of suspecting that the woman in his bed was not his wife. She shuddered deliciously at a new thought. Naturally he would soon discover that the woman he had taken in his arms was a virgin, but by that time, swept forward on a wave of passion, he would laugh triumphantly and make her fully his.

Her hand touched the bed-rail, and steadying herself against it Eliza submitted to a moment of dismaying doubt. He might push her away and turn on his side, whether or not he wanted a reconciliation. With his mind full of new and tremendous social reforms, he had grown less passionate. Harriet, shameless as ever, had complained of this, had shown a discontent which had made it easier for Eliza to provoke her to anger and resentment. But surely, after a bitter quarrel . . .! Eliza's heart pounded so violently that she could hear its rapid beating. There had been tremendous love-making in the past. Several times in one night, Harriet had laughed exultantly.

Eliza moved round to the side of the bed and almost tripped over the clothes which Shelley had scattered in all directions while undressing. In the morning, as was her usual practice, she would tidy the room, but now this disorder, so much a part of the man she desired, was as delightful to her as if he had reached out and caressed her. It was even possible, after tonight, that she would lose for ever her passion for tidiness.

'Harriet. . . .'

Soft murmur that it was, Eliza was taken so suddenly by surprise that she almost raised her own voice in reply. Silence on her part was imperative, absolutely imperative, except of course for a broken little sob or a cautious fit of weeping.

'Eliza was sure you would come,' he said dully.

Eliza emitted a tiny sob, waited for a moment and when he seemed disinclined to further speech, placed herself awkwardly on the edge of the bed. Irresolute now, she fingered her night-gown feverishly. He always went naked to bed and expected Harriet to do likewise. The nightgown would be an instant betrayal. She sobbed again, a real sob this time. Urgent messages flying from her brain to her hands, yet her hands remained wooden and unresponsive.

'I had thought,' Shelley said sadly, 'that our years together were the golden years of my life, but I begin to doubt it now. And if they were, what a fool I was to expect them to last for ever.'

The tragic beauty of his voice touched Eliza deeply. She wanted desperately to tell him that with *her* there would be nothing but golden years for the rest of his life.

'I have half a mind,' he went on sombrely, 'to become a country parson, find peace in some tiny village.'

Eliza stifled an hysterical laugh. Shelley a country parson! The vision thus conjured up got the better of her and she laughed outright, but obviously he failed to recognize her laugh, different as it was from Harriet's.

'Amusing, yes,' he said, with the faintest of chuckles. 'Imagine a country parson preaching liberty, equality and fraternity, and while preaching it refusing to offer up prayers for the local squire and all his beastly relations. Even if the Church accepted me at first, no time would be wasted in unfrocking me. Are you getting into bed or going back to Eliza?'

Eliza heard a queer, choking noise issuing from her throat, and instead of running from the room, as a nagging conscience urged her to do, she slipped hurriedly beneath the blankets.

'I had a remarkable vision while walking to Windsor,' Shelley said, moving to make room for her. 'As clearly as if she were walking at my side, I felt the presence of a woman. She was a stranger, yet so dear to me that I might have known her all my life. I reached out to touch her, but she disappeared. Later she was with me again, and all strangeness had passed. "Harriet is thinking of me," I told myself, "thinking of me so intensely that she is closer now than ever before." I hastened my steps, I ran on joyously, but when I reached you, and listened to your angry voice, you disappeared as surely as if, in the flesh, you were the vision that had eluded me. *Were* you that vision, Harriet? Had I been permitted a moment's glimpse of the future?'

Eliza stirred uneasily at his side. The insistence of his question demanded an answer. Emitting another little stifled sob she waited in an agony of suspense. The situation, she knew, was growing insupportable.

'What an amazing silence,' Shelley said in wonder. 'I've never known you like this before. When you're happy you chatter like a magpie. Even when you're sad you rarely stop talking. And when you're angry, as you were tonight, you rant like a veritable harridan.' His voice grew puzzled. 'Is there nothing I can do to provoke you to speech?'

More desperate than ever now, Eliza propped herself up on one elbow, reached out daringly and lightly stroked his brow. A moment later, with the feel of the smooth skin beneath her palm depriving her of all control, she flung herself heavily against him and kissed him on the lips. Shelley's arms went round her instinctively but remained there only a moment.

'Good Lord,' he cried, releasing her and sitting up, 'you're wearing one of Eliza's ridiculous nightgowns! Oh well, I expect she insisted upon it, prude that she is. I doubt if she would even have the courage to look at herself naked.' Thoughtful for a moment, he added in disgust: 'And the sight of another woman's body, to say nothing of a man's, would make her swoon.'

Eliza flung her arms round him. Prude, she thought – if only he knew! And still thinking her to be Harriet, surely he would tear the offending garment from her body any moment now. Oh, surely!

Shelley released himself and moved away.

'It seems to me . . .' he began slowly.

Eliza, her eyes accustomed now to the darkness, could see by his dim outline that he had brought up his knees and clasped his arms round them.

'Yes,' he went on, 'I'm sure I'm right. Eliza has been much too sympathetic lately. I ought to know better than to trust Eliza when she's sympathetic. Do you realize Harriet, that we have never been alone since we married, except for a few days in Edinburgh? There was Hogg to begin with, then Eliza, and Eliza, confound her idiotic tidiness, her soul-destroying tidiness, seems bent on living with us for the rest of our lives.'

Furious with him now, painfully aware that she had behaved with the utmost madness, Eliza sprang from the bed and hurried to the door.

'Come back, Harriet!' Shelley cried.

She groped for the handle, but Shelley was out of bed and dragging her back before she could find it.

'Darling, we must ask Eliza to go, we must *insist* on it! The golden years! How could they possibly have been really golden with Eliza cluttering up our lives?'

Beside herself with rage, Eliza spoke at last.

'Don't shout like that. You'll wake your wife.'

'My God, Eliza!'

'Keep quiet, Bysshe,' she whispered hoarsely, 'or I'll tear off this nightgown, scream for help and tell Harriet you attacked me. I – I swear I will!'

Shelley laughed softly. 'Eliza Westbrook, how you shock me! Still, I expect it's the dire result of having been brought up in a Methodist environment, that and remaining an old maid far too long.' He was beginning to enjoy himself and laughed again. 'What were you going to do, try and rape me?'

Eliza hammered at his chest with her clenched fists. 'How you make me loathe you.'

'Surely you mean yourself?'

'Myself, then,' she stammered.

Shelley moved away from her and after much fumbling lit a candle, turned with it and held it above his head. A statue, she thought, a beautiful male statue, golden in the flickering candlelight.

'Well, let's have a look at you,' he said mildly.

'For heaven's sake get back into bed, or at least wrap a blanket round yourself,' Eliza gasped.

'How wrong I was! You should be lying at my feet now in a deep swoon.'

'*Bysshe!*'

He tugged a blanket from the bed and swathed himself in it.

'I assure you, Eliza, I don't feel any of the shame Adam is supposed to have felt. How long will it take you to pack your possessions and go?'

'I've no intention of going,' she said stubbornly.

'I see no other way of retaining Harriet's love. Unless you go I shall tell Harriet what has happened tonight, and that will disgust her.'

'Bysshe—'

'Wait, Eliza,' he said earnestly. 'Harriet loves you dearly. Please don't force me to destroy that love. Harriet may visit you as often as she wishes. It would be heartless if I were to insist upon a complete separation simply because, in a moment of aberration, you lost your head.'

Aberration! The word roused Eliza's anger afresh.

'You never loved Harriet,' she said harshly.

'*Eliza!*'

'If you did you were trapped into it.'

'I rescued her from persecution at school and persecution at home.'

Eliza laughed wildly. 'The trap was set by Papa. The persecution at school was real enough, but not the persecution at home. That was pretence, mere pretence.'

'But – but *why*, Eliza?'

'Papa had your grandfather's title in mind.'

Shelley shook his head sadly. 'Poor misguided man. When did you discover all this?'

'I—' Eliza hesitated.

'You were in league with him?' Shelley asked indignantly.

'To my sorrow, yes.'

'To your *sorrow*? Why that, Eliza?'

'I wanted everything for Harriet. I thrust my true feelings aside. Indeed, I failed then to understand them. Had I been wise enough to look deep into my heart I would have known that I loved you far more than Harriet ever could.'

Shelley looked at her helplessly. 'I don't believe you.' A new thought struck him. 'And Harriet, was she a part of this trap? Was she only pretending also?'

Eliza hesitated again. She was sorely tempted to lie.

'*Was* she, Eliza?'

'No,' she admitted.

'Poor child, the misery you made her suffer, you and your father. And the senselessness of it all. The utter senselessness!'

'We felt that you would never marry her. It seemed to us that you must be made to imagine that you were rescuing her.'

'Why are you telling me all this?'

'I – I was angry. The words slipped out.'

Clutching the blanket round his body, Shelley ran to the door, but quicker than he was Eliza reached it first and stood with her back to it.

'If you tell her it will break her heart.'

'I have no intention of telling her.'

'Then what are you going to do?'

'I have no intention of telling her providing you promise to leave us.'

'I'll leave you on one condition only,' Eliza said, hoping that thus she might atone a little for what she had done.

'And *that*?'

'You must make the marriage legal in England.'

'How stupid you are, Eliza! As if I need any further urging now.'

Eliza held him back a moment longer. 'Promise not to tell her about tonight. I should die of shame if you did.'

'I promise,' he said impatiently, and thrust her aside.

Eliza followed him slowly along the passage, watching him dully as he flung himself into her bedroom and listened as he called her sister's name excitedly. A moment later he was in the passage again.

'She's not there! Eliza, she's not there!'

'She went to the maid's room,' Eliza told him bleakly.

Following him again she listened at the door of the maid's room, heard him assure what must be a startled Harriet that they would go to London tomorrow for a marriage licence, then returned to her own room. Ianthe was still sleeping peacefully, and gazing at her long and broodingly, Eliza remembered how much Harriet had meant to her at the same age. It seemed to her then that this child was hers rather than Harriet's. Separated from Ianthe, her life would be even emptier than when she had taken Harriet to the posting-station and given her into Shelley's care.

'I want them both,' she whispered, 'I want them both.'

2

Harriet laughed gaily as Shelley helped her down from the hackney carriage.

'There's no question now of my being Mrs. Shelley in Scotland and Miss Westbrook in England.'

'None whatever, darling.'

'It was a grand wedding,' said Eliza who, with the baby in her arms, was still sitting in the carriage.

'Grand, yes,' Shelley agreed.

They had just returned to the cottage at Windsor after a week at the Westbrook house in London. The wedding, a quiet enough ceremony had taken place at St. George's in Hanover Square, with only a few people present, including William Godwin and John Westbrook, the latter looking gleefully solemn, Shelley thought, in a new frock coat that was just a little too tight for him. On meeting his father-in-law again Shelley had come close to attacking him for the earlier misery he had caused Harriet, but for Harriet's sake he had managed to hold his peace.

The moment they were in the cottage he rushed from room to room, throwing open the windows. Clear and bright as the afternoon was, he had never felt more stifled, and it was not until a fire had been lit and they were all drinking tea that the reason occurred to him. Eliza was still with them. She had given her word but was still with them. And by the placid look of her face she was determined, come what may, to remain. Brooding over this he became fully aware of the difficulty of the situation. Harriet knew nothing of what had happened, and must never know. And yet, he thought, if Eliza by refusing to go provoked him too far and he told her, surely she, his wife, would be as eager as he was to see the last of Eliza. He looked at his sister-in-law hotly and for one brief moment she held his eyes mockingly.

'How are your friends at Southampton?' he asked, thinking himself cunning.

'Very well, I imagine,' she said.

'Didn't you say something about spending a long holiday with them?'

'I don't recall having mentioned a holiday in Southampton, long or short,' Eliza said tartly.

'Perhaps you said London, not Southampton,' Shelley went on desperately. 'You know what a poor memory I have.'

Eliza folded her hands in her lap. 'My dear Bysshe, I am much too happy here with you and Harriet.'

Shelley tried to control his temper. 'I thought your father was looking ill. He seemed lonely, too. He must have missed you sorely during the last two or three years.'

'He can manage very well without me.'

'Why, Bysshe, you sound as if you want to get rid of Eliza,' Harriet said, in surprise.

'And so I do!' he exploded. 'Moreover, we reached an understanding, Eliza and I, before we went to London. She promised to go. Promised, I tell you!'

Harriet looked distressed. 'Promised? But why?'

Shelley sprang up from the table and moved uneasily about the room. It disappointed him that Harriet, even without knowing what had happened, should cling so obstinately to her sister. True enough, Eliza had been more a mother to her than a sister, but did a man, however angelic he might be, expect a mother-in-law to live with him for the rest of his life?

'Shall I tell Harriet the reason?' Eliza asked softly.

He swung round and faced her. 'By all means, if you feel that confession is good for the soul.'

Eliza hesitated for a moment. She had rehearsed many times the things she had made up her mind to say when this scene was forced upon her. It seemed ludicrous that Harriet would believe her, but the growing desire to have Harriet and Ianthe entirely to herself was compelling her to take the risk.

'It was your soul I was thinking of, not my own,' she said, and looked sadly at Harriet. 'Darling, I find it very hard to tell you this, but I see clearly that you must be told. You haven't forgotten, of course, how you quarrelled with Bysshe – after all, it is only a week ago – and went to bed in the maid's room. Well, I found it impossible to sleep. I was so worried about it all. In the end I went to Bysshe. It was a silly, impulsive thing to do, I admit it now. But I wanted to plead with him, beg him to be sensible.'

Harriet smiled fondly at Shelley. 'And apparently he listened to you.'

'Wait!' Eliza said quickly. 'He did nothing of the kind. Indeed, he attacked me violently.'

Harriet giggled faintly. 'You mean, he lost his temper and banged your head against the wall?'

'I shall certainly lose my temper now if Eliza goes on with this nonsense,' Shelley said sharply.

Eliza rose from her chair and clasped her hands together as if in anguish.

'My poor Harriet, remembering how his friend Hogg attacked you at York, you will understand exactly what I mean.'

Taken completely by surprise, Shelley could do no more than stare incredulously at his sister-in-law, and Harriet was doing likewise.

'It was horrible, horrible,' Eliza went on hoarsely. 'I struggled with him desperately, but it was useless. I begged and begged for mercy, but he was deaf to my pitiful entreaties. There was a terrible pain in my chest. I felt as if I were dying. Finally, and mercifully, I fainted. When I recovered consciousness I was lying on the bed and felt' – she savoured for a moment the most telling phrase of all her rehearsing – 'and felt as if I had been torn asunder. It was all too clear that Bysshe had had his way with me.'

Shelley, being Shelley, and not for a moment expecting Harriet to take this ridiculous story seriously, immediately said the wrong thing.

'She means, Harriet, that she had suffered a fate worse than death.'

But instead of laughing, Harriet grew pale. She had quarrelled with Bysshe and had left his bed for the first time since their marriage in Scotland. That, in itself, must have made him furious. And Eliza, old maid that she was, was remarkably attractive with her fine eyes and shining black hair.

'Oh, *Bysshe*,' she cried, and burst into tears.

'It isn't that I didn't forgive him,' Eliza said nobly. 'You see, I remembered how he himself forgave Hogg.'

Shelley went quickly to Harriet and tried to take her in his arms. She flung herself away from him and ran to the other side of the table.

'And afterwards,' she sobbed, 'he dragged me back to the same bed and – and—Oh, Bysshe, how *could* you!'

'I expect it was remorse,' Eliza murmured. 'Or more than likely he was still incensed with passion.'

Harriet looked at Bysshe through her tears. 'Was it remorse that made you rush me to London for the second marriage?'

'No, not that,' Eliza said smugly. 'I forced him to do it. I threatened to tell you everything unless he agreed.'

'Harriet, listen to me for a moment,' Shelley said angrily, 'Eliza certainly came to me that night, but—'

'Ah,' Eliza interrupted sadly, 'I know what he's going to say. He's going to try and tell you that it was *I* who – well – attacked *him*. You can't believe that, can you, darling?'

'Of course I can't, not of a prude like you,' Harriet said crossly.

Eliza bit her lip, but on the whole remained well satisfied with the havoc she had caused.

'Now you understand why Bysshe wants me to leave,' she said, 'but I think it is he who should leave, not I.'

Harriet shook her head. 'No, Eliza, you must go.'

Shelley smiled instantly. 'I'll hire a hackney carriage for her at once.'

'And I must go, too,' Harriet added, struggling with her tears.

'Do you think that wise?' Eliza took the risk of asking.

'What else can I do?' Harriet sobbed.

Hiding with difficulty the triumph she felt, Eliza turned to Shelley.

'I want to be as gentle with you as I can, Bysshe,' she said quietly. 'Many things have been said this afternoon that would have been better left unsaid. But now it will be a long time before they can be erased from our memories. I think you will agree that meanwhile the best thing I can do is take Harriet and Ianthe home to Papa. Later, when we have all had time to think calmly and reasonably about this unfortunate situation, a compromise might be possible.'

Shelley turned angrily to the door.

'Bysshe—' Harriet said tremulously.

He opened the door without looking back.

'Bysshe, what are you going to do?'

'Hire a hackney carriage for you. What else?'

Eliza followed him to the front door. There was still something she wanted to say, something for his ears alone, for, in looking to the future her mind had seized upon what might yet be necessary in order to make the alienation permanent.

'Bysshe,' she said, calling him back as he stepped into the street, 'be good enough, please, to call on Captain Ryan and tell him that Harriet and I will be living for a while at Chapel Street.'

'What the devil does it matter to Ryan?'

'Captain Ryan is a good friend. He remained in Windsor only because we were here. He was a tower of strength when you went away, leaving us to wonder where you had gone, and whether or not you would come back. He has always been most attentive – to me, of course.'

'What a pity, then, that you didn't make him instead of me the object of your pitiful craving.'

Eliza shook her head sadly. 'What a tragedy that one so young as you should suffer such terrible delusions.'

She closed the door softly. More than likely Shelley would fail to give Captain Ryan her message, but that was of no account. She would write to him herself, telling him that Shelley had behaved so shockingly that she and Harriet, taking Ianthe with them, were obliged to seek refuge in her father's house, and that, without a doubt, would bring him hurrying eagerly after them. Smiling grimly, ignoring as best she could the feeling of guilt that gripped her, she went back to Harriet.

'Be as cheerful as you can, darling,' she said. 'Papa will look after us, and we shall have at least one good friend in London.'

'I can't imagine who that will be,' Harriet sobbed.

'You can't? Who else, Harriet, but Captain Ryan?'

PART TWO

Mary

Eleven

I

'You are Shelley, of course,' the girl said, looking up from the pile of books on the counter, 'Shelley the poet.'

Shelley, his mind in confusion, his one aim being to find William Godwin and confide in him fully, looked at her vaguely. He even felt a faint irritation that anyone, with the sole exception of Godwin, should presume at this moment to address him. In any case, her words, such was his preoccupation, had conveyed nothing intelligible to him.

'I beg your pardon?' he said politely.

'You are Shelley, of course,' she repeated, loudly and distinctly, 'Shelley the poet. Or would you prefer me to say "Shelley the atheist"?'

Shaken into attention at last, Shelley remembered sadly that Harriet, at their first meeting, had pointed a finger at him and called him 'Percy the atheist'. Thinking of this, he looked at the girl with unwilling interest. She was about the same age as Harriet at that first meeting, he thought, but there the resemblance ended. She was taller and more slender than Harriet. Her hair, darker than Harriet's, was shot with golden lights, and her brow was of a shape that people were in the habit, heaven knew why, of calling intelligent.

'You might as well call a pelican intelligent because of its ridiculous beak,' he burst out indignantly, 'or a parrot because it can talk, or a Member of Parliament because he can reel off platitudes by the hour.'

The girl looked at him gravely. 'Nevertheless, it's pleasing to be thought intelligent because of one's brow.'

'You seem to be able to read my thoughts,' Shelley exclaimed in wonder.

'You were staring at my rather large forehead,' she pointed out.

'And if I were to stare at your feet?'

She laughed deeply. 'Obviously you would then think that they too are rather large.'

'Do you ever go on walking tours? Large feet would be excellent for that sort of thing.'

'I was in Scotland recently and did a lot of walking there.'

'And enjoyed it?'

'Very much.'

'Would you like to go to Italy?'

'I have always dreamt of going there.'

'Splendid! We shall make a walking tour of it, starting off at Calais and ending up at Florence.'

The girl laughed delightedly. 'From intelligent brows to pelicans, parrots and Members of Parliament, from them to large feet, and now, in the twinkling of an eye, you are in Florence with a strange female.'

'A thousand apologies,' said Shelley, crestfallen. 'I was carried away, as ever, by a too lively imagination. To return to the beginning, my name *is* Shelley, and I am indeed a poet, but why were you so sure of it? What made you say "of course"?'

'Only a poet could dress as carelessly as you do, and of all the poets only Shelley could have your wild, distracted eyes.'

Shelley laughed joyously, the more so because it came upon him that, if only for a few moments, he had forgotten his domestic troubles. He wondered who the girl was. Clearly enough she had a deep interest in books, otherwise she would not be here now, browsing among the books in this bookshop which Godwin had established in Skinner Street.

'I'm looking for Mr. Godwin,' he said, glancing about the shop and seeing only two or three other customers. 'Is he upstairs?'

The girl shook her head. 'He received your letter, saying you were coming to London. He went at once to Cook's Hotel to see if you had arrived. He—' she broke off. 'Why are you staring at me?'

Shelley's attention had been caught and held by her eyes

which, set in a startlingly pale face, were large, candid, and hazel in colour.

'I know who you are,' he said. 'I should have guessed it at once. You are Godwin's daughter, Mary.'

The girl laughed wryly. 'In other words, the intelligent child you once thought you might enjoy conversing with.'

'Did I ever say that?'

'According to Father, yes.'

'Well, well, I must have said it, then. And I do, of course, enjoy talking to intelligent children.'

'In that case you are wasting your time here, Shelley,' she said dryly, but with laughter in her eyes.

'Dear me, have I offended you?'

'No, except that you appear to refuse to *see* me. Perhaps after my next birthday – I shall be seventeen in August – you will deign to glance at me properly and say, "Well, well, she isn't a child after all".'

Shelley began to feel real concern. 'Have you been here before and have I failed completely to see you?'

'No, this is our first meeting.'

Shelley laughed in relief. 'As if in any case I could have failed to notice you.'

'Ah, here comes Father,' Mary said.

'So he does – confound him!' Shelley grumbled.

2

Shelley threw down his pen. Never before had he found the writing of any sort of letter so difficult. He had half a mind not to write to Harriet at all, except when eventually he left Cook's Hotel and it was necessary to let her know his new address, whatever that might be. Having remained for a week alone at Windsor he had written briefly to Harriet, telling her that he would be at Cook's for an indefinite period, and this afternoon, on his return from Skinner Street, he had found a reply waiting for him. He picked it up and skimmed through it again. Harriet wrote that she had had time for much thought, but still her mind went round and round, and though she wanted with all her heart to forgive him, that seemed impossible. Nevertheless, she proposed to write to him frequently, for it was her duty to give him news of Ianthe. She gave him an address in Bath. She was going there to stay with some family friends, and would have left London by the time he received her letter. She had left hurriedly, he thought angrily, in order to prevent him from calling on her at Chapel Street. Either that, or Eliza had hustled her away. Eliza, of course, would have gone with her to Bath.

He took up his pen again. The lines of a stanza were running dirge-like through his mind, and catching them again on paper he addressed them reproachfully to Harriet.

> 'Thy dewy looks sink in my breast;
>   Thy gentle words stir poison there;
> Thou hast disturbed the only rest
>   That was the portion of despair—'

A knock at the door brought him impatiently to his feet. Feeling an impulse to hide until the unwelcome caller grew tired of knocking and went away, he glanced at the door which led from the sitting-room to the bedroom, but before he could move the outer door swung open and, to his amazement, he found himself face to face with Eliza Westbrook.

'I think you must have made a mistake,' he said angrily.

Eliza smiled faintly. 'Why that? I knew you were at Cook's.'

Shelley turned his back on her. 'Do you want me to call the landlord and ask him to remove you?'

'Oh come, Bysshe, what good will it do you to sulk? I know I have not always been a good Christian, but you must agree that in calling on you tonight I am showing at least a little Christian charity.'

'Cant, sheer cant!' he raged.

'Cant,' she murmured, 'that I should be ready to let bygones be bygones?'

He turned and looked at her hotly. 'I have nothing whatever to say to you.'

'As you wish.'

He saw in disgust that her dress was that of a much younger woman. The blue silk pelisse was much too high in the waist, and the bonnet, held in place with a velvet band, and with girlish ribbons hanging from it, made her look even more ridiculous.

Obviously she had convinced herself that she was in her teens, younger even than Harriet, not in her thirties. Remembering what had happened at Windsor, disgust gave place to uneasiness.

'I assumed you had gone to Bath with Harriet,' he blustered.

Eliza repressed a sharp retort. It had angered her that Harriet should have insisted on going to Bath without her, but anger was the last thing she must submit to now.

'I thought her in need of a complete change,' she said quietly. 'Indeed, I felt in need of a complete change myself, and am going to Southampton for a few days, after all.'

'Then why come here?'

'Harriet was anxious about you. She wanted to be sure that you were not neglecting yourself. Aren't you going to ask me to sit down?'

Shelley looked at her with increasing uneasiness, for she had accompanied her words with a tinkling little laugh. Backing cautiously to the writing-table, he watched her remove her grey fur gloves, move to a chair and sit down. Watching her still, he saw her draw up the skirt of the pelisse until her neat ankles, of which she had always been proud, were fully exposed.

'I hope Harriet will not be too lonely at Bath,' he said desperately.

Eliza hid a smile. He was making things remarkably easy for her.

'Papa's friends are old,' she said, 'but fortunately Harriet will have the company of at least one young person. It so happens that Captain Ryan is going to Bath also. A most happy coincidence.'

'You mean Ryan is following her to Bath?'

'Oh, scarcely that. He has friends there, too.'

'As you say, a happy coincidence!'

Captain Ryan called on us at Chapel Street,' said Eliza, frowning. 'I must admit that when he mentioned a proposed visit to Bath, Harriet seemed happier about going there herself.'

'You seem intent on linking her name with his!'

'Their names are already linked. When you were absent from Windsor they took many a walk together.'

'But Harriet and Ryan! I can't believe it.'

'She was neglected, Bysshe. Can you blame her for finding the attentions of an attractive young man pleasurable?'

F

'This, like the pitiful story you told Harriet, is a figment of your imagination.'

The old pain of hopeless longing stabbed at Eliza's breast as she looked up at him, and noting that his eyes were bright with anger she turned quickly to the real purpose of this visit.

'I wonder,' she whispered, 'if Harriet's second baby will be a boy or a girl?'

'Her *second* baby?' Shelley gasped.

'I thought she told you in her letter. *She* seems sure it will be a boy.'

Actually, Eliza knew full well that Harriet had said nothing about her second pregnancy, having been held back by her pride and the fear that the news would bring Shelley rushing to her side, and this was much to Eliza's liking. Alienate him altogether, she thought, and she would have not only Harriet and Ianthe to herself, but another child as well.

'Are you telling the truth?' Shelley asked violently.

'Why should I lie, Bysshe?'

'Then why did she refrain from telling me?'

Eliza pursed her lips. 'Could it be because . . . but no, of course not! And yet. . . .'

'Not my child, but Ryan's?' Shelley demanded.

'They were often together, but it would be wrong of me to suggest that anything improper happened.'

'How modestly you choose your words!'

Eliza rose and began to put on her gloves. 'Neglected as she was, there would be a certain temptation. Captain Ryan is charming and considerate, and he, my poor Bysshe, is not the sort of man who lives with his head in the clouds.'

She moved to the door, opened it and turned, but before she could say more Shelley rushed at her, thrust her aside and ran down the passage. Following him quickly, she came upon him in the street outside the hotel.

'Perhaps the best thing you can do,' she took the risk of saying, 'is go to Harriet and discuss the matter with her.'

'I shall only do that,' he said haughtily, 'when she has the grace to write and tell me about the baby.'

'As you wish,' Eliza said, satisfied now that she need say no more. 'Good-bye, Bysshe. We may or may not meet again, but in spite of everything, I wish you well.'

3

The yellow flame of a link-boy's torch, illuminating a familiar building on the corner, showed Shelley that his aimless wandering had brought him now to Skinner Street. Slowing his pace, he followed the bobbing light until he came to William Godwin's shop, and glancing up saw that candles were still burning in the living quarters above. Godwin, he knew, would welcome him gladly however late the hour might be, so he wasted no time in ringing the bell, and presently, as he peered through the window, he discerned a figure approaching with a candle.

'Godwin, my dear fellow!' he cried, when the door swung open.

'Father is out,' said Mary, for it was Godwin's daughter, not Godwin himself. 'How distracted you sound. Is anything the matter? Would you like to come in and wait?'

'Godwin seems always to be out when I need him most,' Shelley complained.

'Now you sound angry,' Mary laughed. 'How quickly your mood changes.'

Shelley laughed too. The sound of her voice, low and a little husky, was having a tranquillizing effect upon him. It would be pleasant, he thought, to talk with Mary while waiting for her father.

'Is your stepmother out, too?' he asked.

Mary shook her head. 'No.'

'A pity,' Shelley said, for he had never liked Godwin's wife.

Mary laughed again. 'From distraction to anger, from anger to disgust. What next, I wonder?'

'Delight,' he responded, 'providing I may wait in the shop with you for company, not upstairs with that fearsome stepmother monopolizing the conversation. Naturally, I never knew your real mother, but I feel sure that had she lived your father would be a different man today.'

'I never knew her either,' Mary said gravely. 'You may wait in the shop, if you wish.'

'Thank you.'

Shelley followed the girl into the shop and vaulting on to the counter sat there with his knees clasped in his arms. Mary, having placed the candlestick on a pile of books, stood straight and slim before him, a faint smile on her lips. He thought she looked older in the candlelight, while she for her part thought he looked younger, the more so because of his boyish attitude.

'You seem very anxious to lend money to Father,' she remarked.

'Anxious?'

'Rushing here again at this hour of night.'

Shelley recollected that he had not confided in Godwin this afternoon, as he had intended to, and it seemed more than likely now that he would not make a further attempt to do so when Godwin came home. It was strange and a little wonderful, he thought, that his personal worries should recede so swiftly when he was talking with Mary.

'How much money are you going to lend him?' she asked.

'Oh, two or three thousand pounds.'

'Is that wise?'

'When a friend is in need,' Shelley asked warmly, 'does one pause and ask oneself whether or not it is *wise* to help him?'

'Most people would, but not Shelley, obviously.'

Shelley stared at her curiously. 'You sound quite disapproving.'

'Not of your generosity, only of your impulsiveness. Yes, and your stupidity.'

'Stupidity indeed!' he cried. 'I care nothing for money, but you, apparently, regard it highly.'

'I was only thinking how much deeper in debt your generosity would force you. I know all about your nonchalant way of signing post-obit bonds, you see.'

Shelley laughed heartily. Her concern for him was pleasing, and he liked her use of the word 'nonchalant'. It was an apt description, he thought approvingly.

'Apart from my nonchalance in respect of post-obit bonds,' he said, 'what else do you know about me?'

'Little more than what I have learnt through reading some of your poetry. I think you might yet live to become a great poet.'

'Being only a mediocre one at present?'

'Not that, Shelley.'

'What, then?'

'Immature.'

'Ah, a child in years, but as far as judgement goes, a woman of at least fifty. What have you read of mine?'

'Some of the shorter poems, but it was *Queen Mab* that held my attention.'

'You actually understood it?'

'Better, perhaps, than you did yourself when writing it,' Mary chuckled.

'You should have been with me at the time to collaborate.'

'Do be serious,' Mary said sharply. 'I thought you dealt magnificently with the past, the present and the future. And I—'

'But immaturely?' he interrupted.

'Yes, immaturely.'

'I was well aware of that afterwards,' Shelley said miserably.

'And were you also well aware that you were writing about what you hate and what you love?'

'I was, but since you know so much about me, *you* tell *me*!'

'How cross you sound! Very well, then! What you hate is the past and present misery of mankind. Misery, of course, as *you* see it.'

'And what I love?' he asked eagerly.

'I think you love the shining vision you have of the future regeneration of mankind.'

'I offer you my apologies,' he said, after a moment of stunned silence. 'Never again shall I think of you as a child. Your perception is almost frightening.'

'Are you flattered by it?'

'Flattered?'

'Tell me the truth. It's very important that I should know.'

'Not flattered,' he said, her earnestness touching him deeply. 'but – well – humbled.'

'Humbled?' she echoed, and thought in disappointment: If only he had said *proud*!

'I admit,' he laughed, 'that humility sits oddly on my shoulders but in this instance I rejoice in it. Now tell me why it was "very important" that I should tell you the truth.'

Mary dwelt on this in silence for a few moments. She was surprised now that she should have been so earnest and could think of only one reason for it. The flesh and blood Shelley was even more attractive than the Shelley she had pictured in her mind after reading his poetry.

'It was important,' she said carefully, 'because I like to believe that my friends are always telling me the truth.'

'To believe and to know are two quite different things,' Shelley pointed out, 'but with me I think you will always know. But enough about me, entrancing subject though it might be. I want to hear about you. I don't know very much, so begin at the beginning.'

Mary jumped on to the counter and sat there at his side with her legs swinging lightly.

'The date of my birth was August 30th 1797 and I was named after my mother, who was Mary Wollstonecraft before she married Father. My full name is Mary Wollstonecraft Godwin. In actual fact I came close to being born a Wollstonecraft, not a Godwin. Mother was four months pregnant when the marriage took place.'

'I have heard of closer margins than that, Mary.'

'Yes, but there *could* have been more delay. Father told me once that he was disappointed in himself at not being quite able to live up to the principles of freedom which he had been at such pains to propagate.'

'And what of your mother? I always understood that she and your father were in complete philosophical agreement.'

'She wanted marriage, even before she knew she was pregnant. It had occurred to her, you see, that legal marriage, man-made as it is, is something that one must experience. Experience, I mean, as a test, but only, of course, after a long period of legally free association. She was sure of her love for Father and wanted to prove to herself and to him that not even legal marriage could destroy their happiness. Father, I think, was afraid that it might, he being so bound by his principles.'

'And did it?'

'The marriage didn't last long enough, Shelley. Mother died a few days after I was born. I wish with all my heart I could have known her.'

Shelley took her hand in his. 'Poor Mary, are you very unhappy with your stepmother?'

'Yes,' Mary admitted, 'when I allow myself to think about it, but mostly I can escape from her, even when she's there in the room, by reading a book. And sometimes I escape physically by taking a book to the graveyard at St. Pancras. Mother is buried there, and I often sit by her grave, reading. My stepmother thinks it a morbid thing to do, but I've never felt morbid doing it. I've felt at peace, always at peace, just as if Mother were there with me, laughing when I wanted to laugh, being serious when I felt serious myself. Do you think me too fanciful, Shelley?'

'No,' he said, an unaccountable lump in his throat.

Mary released her hand. Shelley's touch, though she knew he was unaware of it, was making her tremble.

'Please don't think I resent my father having married again,' she went on quickly. 'All I resent is that he allowed himself to be trapped into it. By "trapped" I mean flattered. I was only five when he met my stepmother, but that first meeting still stands out clearly in my mind. She was Mrs. Clairmont then, as you probably know, and a widow. She made a silly gurgling noise and said, "Is it possible that I stand in the presence of the immortal Godwin?" I can remember how sick it made me feel. I must have sensed then that she was a hypocrite. A few years later, long after the marriage, of course, I overheard Charles Lamb talking about her. He said she had bewitched Father, deprived him of his earlier powers and turned him into a child.'

'I know she is a disagreeable woman, and very few people like her,' Shelley said uneasily, 'but that was a harsh thing to say.'

'I know it was,' Mary agreed. 'My stepmother is a good housekeeper and has the common sense that Father lacks in everyday matters, so I suppose she could be called a good wife.'

'You don't sound very sure of it.'

Mary laughed ruefully. 'I was thinking that Father should have tried to find somebody more like Mother, but perhaps his intellectual powers would have declined in any case.'

'Please don't say that,' Shelley protested.

'It makes me sad, but I can't help saying it. Somebody once said that he is a worn-out philosopher who has survived his philosophy. That makes me sad, too, but you must admit that the William Godwin who wrote *Political Justice* no longer exists.'

Shelley's uneasiness deepened. He had long realized the truth of this. Godwin, whether or not his second wife was responsible for it, could think of nothing better to write these days than novels that were pitifully unreal and children's stories that no child could possibly take seriously.

'I honour him for what he was, not what he is,' he said brusquely, 'and I regret with all my heart that the privilege of knowing him at the height of his intellectual powers was never mine. And I can be thankful for one thing,' he added softly, 'I should not be sitting here now had it not been for *Political Justice*. Your father has been a very great influence in my life. I can even look upon him and call him Fate.'

Mary's heart missed a beat. It was pleasing to think that Fate, in the guise of her father, had brought Shelley into her life, yet she knew that even if the two of them had never met she would still have read Shelley's poems, and, having read them, found some means or other of seeking him out.

'*Political Justice*,' Shelley went on, tracing the strange pattern which it had etched in his life, 'caused me to write *The Necessity of Atheism*, and that, in its turn, brought about my welcome expulsion from Oxford. For the rest—'

He broke off abruptly. The expulsion had led to the bitter and still unresolved quarrels with his father. Moreover, it had been the cause of that first meeting with Harriet at Field Place, and all that had followed, even the devilish behaviour of Harriet's sister, Eliza. Yet how ridiculous to blame Godwin, he thought wryly. Or for that matter, Fate. He believed in freedom, as Godwin himself once had, and had acted freely, made decisions that were his own, not Fate's. He had been under no compulsion to follow the beckoning finger. Or *had* he? After all, Harriet's father and sister had set a trap and he had fallen into it.

'Is anything the matter, Shelley?' Mary asked.

He slipped from the counter and seizing the candlestick held it above his head.

'I want to look at you, Mary.'

She slipped down too and stood a few paces in front of him.

'I'm dressed as I was this afternoon, but I don't expect you to have noticed.'

Shelley looked casually at her gown. 'A tartan pattern. How very unusual in London. Are you trying to start a new fashion?'

'I bought the gown in Scotland. I never thought about starting a new fashion. Do a person's clothes really matter?'

'They do in your case, since they express your own unusualness. Keep still, Mary, I want to look at your face, your eyes, not your gown.'

Mary raised her eyes to his, and though he held them over-
long the candid expression which he remembered from this
afternoon never changed.

'Well?' she asked at length.

'I can see nothing but a blinding light,' Shelley whispered.
'A light that clothes you as never a woman was clothed before.'

Mary felt a little shiver of delight run down her back. Her
father and his friends, even though she had been brought up on
equal terms with them, still called her either a child or a girl. To
be called a woman now, especially in that all-embracing tone,
pleased her as never before.

'A light of purest intellect,' he added dreamily.

Her delight fading, Mary smiled wryly. Shelley was seeing
her as an adult rather than as a woman, was appreciating her
solely for her mental powers. I have a body as well as a brain,
she wanted to tell him, but saw that so bold a statement might
easily frighten him away.

Shelley laughed suddenly. 'I was quarrelling with Fate, but
how stupid of me!'

Before Mary could make any comment the shop door opened.

'Here comes Father,' she said, in disappointment.

'So he does – confound him!' Shelley grumbled, for the
second time in a day that to him now seemed as momentous as
a whole lifetime.

Twelve

I

'I SEE you are reading Shelley's *Queen Mab* again,' William Godwin remarked.

Mary looked up quickly. She could tell by her father's tone that he was in what she had come to call one of his 'dithery' moods. He had a problem on his mind and as yet had been unable to reach any definite decision. Moreover, she thought shrewdly, the problem concerned her and Shelley.

'I have read it several times myself,' he went on, 'and each time I have grown less impressed with it.'

Mary looked at him stonily. 'You said it showed infinite promise.'

'And so it does,' Godwin said hastily.

'You also said that, over-ambitious as it is, you recognized in it the hall-mark of genius.'

'Well, so I did, so I did.'

'And you meant it, Father?'

'Yes, I meant it, my dear, but Shelley, if he is to become a really great poet, will have to work much harder than he does at present.'

'Shelley will, if—' Mary broke off, realizing that she was speaking much too impulsively.

'If *you* have anything to do with it – is that what you were about to say?'

Mary smiled happily. 'Shelley takes a great deal of notice of anything I say to him.'

Godwin was silent for a moment, then went on hesitantly.

'Mary, you and Shelley have seen each other frequently during the past few weeks. You, being the sort of girl you are, have had ample time to make up your mind about something.'

'And that, Father?' she asked, determined to make him utter the words himself.

'Are you in love with Shelley?'

'Oh, Father,' she said, impulsively again, 'I feel that I was born for that purpose only, to be in love with Shelley.'

Godwin moved uneasily about the room. He had feared from the outset that the close friendship between Mary and Shelley would result in his losing Mary. Already they had grown apart, and daily the intellectual sympathy, which was his one link with the past, was slipping from his grasp. A faint enough grasp, he admitted angrily, and that served only to increase his resentment.

'Is Shelley in love with you?' he asked, as carefully as he could.

'If he is it has never occurred to him to tell me.'

'Do you propose to *make* him tell you?'

'I hesitate to do that, Father.'

Godwin came and stood by his daughter's chair. A startling thought had slipped into his mind.

'People can be in love without talking about it,' he said bluntly. 'Are you and Shelley lovers?'

She shook her head. 'I doubt if Shelley ever thinks of me that way.'

'But you think of him that way, obviously!'

'Yes, Father,' she said gravely.

'I know I have always preached the doctrine of complete freedom,' Godwin went on shakily, 'but the possibility of my daughter's embarking upon an *affaire* with a married man is – well, to put it mildly, disconcerting. If you do anything rash I shall be displeased, most displeased.'

Mary could see that his mood was growing even more 'dithery', and to confuse him further she made a remark which in normal circumstances would have brought from him a roar of laughter.

'Poor Father, how quickly the doctrine of sexual freedom falls apart when it comes to one's own daughter.'

Godwin rewarded her with a heavy scowl. 'This is not a joke, Mary.'

She agreed and said earnestly, 'You speak of an *affaire*, but I would embark on such a relationship only because of the intellectual and spiritual completion it would bring me.'

'You talk like a woman of experience,' Godwin complained. 'Whereas all you have to guide you is a noble-sounding theory. Intellectual and spiritual completion indeed!'

'The theory is your own, Father.'

Godwin ignored this. 'Shelley may be a genius but he is still a man. He may be highly intellectual but he is still flesh and blood—'

'I have yet to make certain of that,' Mary interrupted.

'—and flesh and blood,' Godwin went on insistently, 'combined with the madness of genius, are highly dangerous. Risking so much, your reward might be small. It might even be failure and a broken heart. You might suffer even more than his wife has been made to suffer. She wrote to me, Mary. Shelley began by neglecting her and has now deserted her.'

'Because of me, Father?'

'No,' Godwin was forced to admit. 'The separation took place before Shelley met you.'

'I can't believe that he deserted her,' Mary said warmly. 'He told me briefly what happened. They quarrelled, and Harriet went off with her sister.'

'Did he also tell you that Harriet is expecting another child?'

Mary shook her head, and Godwin saw by her face that he had gained some small advantage.

'It may be no more than a ruse to get him back,' she said quickly.

'If it is, it appears to have failed. I won't say any more now, Mary, except to ask you to promise me that you will think well before committing yourself to something that may bring you more sorrow than happiness.'

'Something that may never happen, Father, remember that.'

'But something you *want* to happen?'

'Oh yes, Father,' Mary cried joyously, 'yes!'

2

'Well,' said Shelley, smiling mischievously, 'do you, my sternest critic, still consider my poor efforts immature?'

Mary shook her head and began to read again the hastily

scribbled lines which he had thrust into her hand. Having found that they could never be alone together these days at Skinner Street, they had made it a habit to meet here in the churchyard and were sitting now on the grass near Mary Wollstonecraft's grave. Reading carefully, Mary felt deeply disappointed that the lines had not been addressed to her, as she had hoped, but were an expression of Shelley's feelings about the recent fall of Napoleon Bonaparte.

'You like them?' he asked eagerly.

'Oh, yes, Shelley. Your forcefulness here is shattering.'

'Are you impressed by any particular line?'

'Yes. This one, I think: *A frail and bloody pomp which time has swept—*'

'Splendid?' he interrupted. 'I was hoping you would seize on that. Our minds are more in tune than ever.'

Our minds, Mary thought, only our minds. . . .

'Never was I so inspired!' Shelley ran on. 'I want next to write a hymn—'

'Goodness,' Mary teased, 'are you turning of a sudden to religion?'

'To religion in its widest sense. My hymn shall be a hymn to intellectual beauty.'

'There are other sorts of beauty,' Mary suggested softly.

'Nonsense! I see beauty in your eyes, yes, but what else but *intellectual* beauty?'

'Can that sort of beauty thrive for long without a little earthiness to support it?' Mary asked.

'Ah, you want an argument!'

Mary shook her head, despairing that even the broadest of hints would make him see her as she really was, he being blinded, as he had said not once but many times, by a light of purest intellect.

'It was only a passing thought,' she said, and turning the sheet which she still held saw that other lines were written on the back. 'Why, what's this, Shelley?'

He snatched the sheet from her. 'Nothing of any importance!'

'Then let me see it.'

Shelley gave her a sulky look. 'I had quite forgotten that running out of paper I had used both sides of the sheet.'

'Whatever it is,' Mary challenged, 'are you afraid I might think it immature?'

'I do myself, in one respect.'

'Please let me judge for myself.'

'If you insist . . .' and he gave her back the sheet.

Mary saw at once that the verses, five of them, bore the dedication: 'To Harriet'; and two of them, the first and the last, told her that he was still in love with his wife. Clearing her throat, hoping that her voice would betray nothing of her feelings, she began to read aloud.

> 'Thy look of love has power to calm
> The stormiest passion of my soul;
> Thy gentle words are drops of balm
> In life's too bitter bowl;
> No grief is mine, but that alone
> Those choicest blessings I have known.'

Mary cleared her throat again. *These choicest blessings* . . . How stupid and unreasonable, she admonished herself, to be roused to so jealous a resentment of somebody she had never known.

> 'O trust for once no erring guide!
> Bid the remorseless feeling flee;
> 'Tis malice, 'tis revenge, 'tis pride,
> 'Tis anything but thee;
> O deign a nobler pride to prove,
> And pity if thou canst not love.'

Mary looked up indignantly. 'You sent her these verses?'

'Yes, but' – he smiled guilelessly – 'I thought them too good to be torn up, so I kept the original.'

Mary smiled too. After all, one must remember when dealing with a poet to make full allowance for poetic imagery, to say nothing of poetic licence.

'You expected Harriet to destroy them?'

'I thought it likely.'

Shelley stretched himself out on the grass and folded his hands behind his head. Harriet had written to him at last, telling him that she had been ill but was better again, and telling him also that she was expecting a baby in December. In despair at the impersonal tone of her letter – she might well have been writing to a stranger – he had worked all night on the five verses and sent them to her. Another letter, one in which the verses were not mentioned, had reached him this morning. Harriet was in London again, staying with her father, and hoped that even though he might not want to see her he might at least want to see Ianthe.

'I think you really need two women,' Mary remarked, smiling down on him.

'Two? Why two, Mary?'

'One for intellectual companionship, the other for – well – ordinary things.'

She still smiled down on him, hoping that he would spring to his feet, take her in his arms and declare that for intellectual companionship as well as everything else he need look no farther.

'What an excellent suggestion!' he cried, sitting up with shining eyes. 'I shall go and see Harriet at once.'

'I was only joking, Shelley.'

'Whether you were or not, it may well be the one way of solving all my problems. Dear Mary, only you could be so practical!'

3

'I nearly died,' Harriet said, in a low, monotonous voice. 'The physicians were in despair. Only one thing made me want to live and helped me to fight for my life. It was the knowledge, Bysshe, that my death would set you free. So I fought and fought, and slowly emerged from the shadow of death, and am left now, still far from well, to bring another child into this woeful world.'

Shelley, at a loss for words, looked at her helplessly. She was lying on a sofa in the sitting-room which, in earlier days, she had shared with Eliza, and to which a servant, whispering that Mrs. Shelley was too ill to talk for long with anyone, had conducted Shelley. He thought she looked prettier than ever in her cream silk morning dress, not only prettier but healthier, too.

'You thought I might like to see Ianthe,' he said at length.

'Well, would you?'

'That was one of my reasons for coming.'

'You have another, then?'

'Yes,' he said briefly, for the enthusiasm that had brought him rushing to Chapel Street was rapidly fading.

'You may as well tell me what it is, then I think you ought to go.'

'Let me see Ianthe first.'

'Eliza and Papa have taken her for a drive. If you care to wait you may see her when they come back, but I warn you that Papa will want to throw you out of the house the moment he sees you. He hates you for making me so ill with worry. Not only did I nearly die, but I nearly lost the baby as well. Even when I was getting better there were times when it seemed that I might lose it. Would you have cared, Bysshe?'

Her voice, far from being a monotone now, was growing increasingly querulous.

'Well, *would* you?' she insisted.

'As far as you yourself were concerned, I knew nothing about another baby.'

'Eliza told you. She told you, Bysshe, and still you remained unmoved. I know why, of course. You told Eliza that for all you knew you might not be the father. It was a dreadful thing to say. I think it was that as much as anything that nearly killed me.'

'Please believe me, Harriet,' he pleaded, 'it was Eliza herself who suggested that there might be any doubt.'

Tears welled up in Harriet's eyes. 'She warned me that you might blame her. She was afraid you might follow the habit you formed at Windsor of blaming her for everything.'

'Is it true?' he demanded furiously. '*Is* there a doubt?'

With tears streaming down her cheeks now, Harriet looked at him nervously. She knew he was suffering and exulted in the knowledge. She remembered the verses he had sent her, agony of mind expressed in every line. Well, he deserved to suffer. Eliza had said so, and Eliza, as usual, was right.

'Perhaps I can't be sure,' she whispered daringly.

'You mean there *is* a doubt?'

'You believe in complete freedom, you always have,' Harriet wailed. 'And isn't it part of the Godwinian philosophy that when husband and wife are what is called unfaithful they must tell each other?'

'*I* have nothing to tell *you*!'

'How surprising,' Harriet tittered. 'And whether you have anything to tell me or not, you should try to live up to your beliefs.'

'By doing what you have done, you mean?'

'If you feel you must.'

'But I *don't* feel I must, Harriet. It would be disgusting if, solely in a spirit of revenge, I sought physical satisfaction elsewhere.'

'Do you want to come back to me?' she asked, her heart beating excitedly.

'I don't know, Harriet, I don't know.'

'You mean you can't make up your mind whether you want a reconciliation or a permanent separation?'

Recognizing unhappiness and doubt in her voice, Shelley tried to feel compassion for her. Believing the things Eliza had told her, it was reasonable enough that she should regard him with loathing. That she did believe her sister was her only fault, but perhaps even in this he should make allowances, Harriet not being strong enough to set aside jealousy and possessiveness. Mary was different, of course, but Mary was unique among women. He remembered then the purpose of his visit and recovered some of the earlier enthusiasm.

'I want a reconciliation,' he said.

'Even after what I told you?' Harriet faltered.

'As you said, I should try to live up to my beliefs.'

'Oh, Bysshe—' she began, ready now to tell him that she had lied in order to hurt him.

'But on one condition,' he went on eagerly. 'Mary must be admitted into our household.'

'Mary? Who, pray, is Mary?'

'William Godwin's daughter.'

Harriet frowned over this. 'A mere child, surely.'

'She's older than you were when we eloped to Scotland.'

Harriet's face hardened. 'So you were lying when you said *you* had nothing to tell *me.*'

Shelley was appalled. 'Mary and I are good friends. We have everything in common, intellectually. Her companionship is so important to me that I doubt if I could live, really *live*, without it.'

'Intellectualism is usually a cloak for sensuality,' Harriet shrilled.

Shelley tried to be patient. 'Harriet, Mary is like a sister to me, a sister dearer than Elizabeth ever was. If you agree to this,

I shall have a wife and a sister living with me, just as earlier you had a husband and a sister.'

Harriet's eyes flashed angrily. She found it impossible to believe that Shelley could hold this Mary Godwin in so high esteem yet not want to touch her.

'Is she ugly, Bysshe?'

'Harriet!'

'Pretty, then?'

'More than that, much more.'

'Are you trying to tell me,' Harriet gasped, quite losing her temper now, 'that I am to keep house for you, sleep with you and bring up your children, and this Mary person, remaining in a state of virgin aloofness, is to provide you with nothing more than intellectual twaddle?'

Shelley's eyes were flashing angrily now. 'Your own virtue being frail, naturally you expect frailty in others.'

'Naturally I do. I know what women are, and men too. If Mary Godwin isn't your mistress already, she very soon would be, living under the same roof. And then you'd want to bring another girl in, and another, until you had a whole harem.'

'You overestimate my physical prowess,' Shelley said, trying to laugh.

Harriet sprang up from the sofa. Shaking now with rage and jealousy, she wanted only one thing, to hurt him more than ever.

'I was lying when I said there was a doubt about the baby's father.'

'I'm glad to hear that, Harriet.'

'Glad? But you're not the father, Bysshe, you're not, you're not!'

'Ryan?' he said dully.

'Ryan, or some other man.'

She was frightened the moment the words were out of her mouth, but before she could fling her arms round Shelley's neck and sob, as she wanted to, that she had been moved by jealousy to hurt him, he turned and went silently from the room. She waited until she heard the front door open and close, then ran to the window, hoping that he would turn and look up. If he did she would fling open the window and shout, 'Bysshe, I love you, I want you, come back!'

He moved on down the street, not breaking into a run as he

so often did, either in anger or excitement, but slowly, and so preoccupied was he with his thoughts – he was suffering more than ever, she hoped – that he failed to notice the approach of the Westbrook carriage. It would serve him right, she told herself, if she really had taken Captain Ryan to her bed. Yes, and a dozen others as well.

4

'You look exhausted, Shelley.'

'I feel exhausted, Mary, yet strangely triumphant.'

They were alone together in the Skinner Street shop. It was late evening and almost dark. Shelley, since leaving Harriet, had walked the streets, dwelling miserably on all that Harriet had said to him, all that he had said to her, and trying as never before to understand himself. In the end he had come to Skinner Street and by a lucky chance had found Mary standing at the door.

'Strangely triumphant?' she echoed.

'The sight of you made me realize that I was free at last of the despotism of marriage.'

Mary looked at him uncertainly. 'Did you and Harriet quarrel?'

'We did, inevitably we did.'

'About me?'

'In a way, yes. She failed to understand how I felt, refused to believe that a man, even a Shelley, could love a woman solely for her mind.'

'Oh . . .' said Mary, wanting to laugh and cry at the same time.

'Had you realized,' he said suddenly, 'that with the war at an end one may now travel freely in France and Italy?'

'Why yes, since many people are doing so already.'

'I feel stifled still, Mary. Only one thing can make my release complete. I must get away. Away from London, away from England. Why not come with me, Mary?'

'Are you serious, Shelley?' she asked carefully.

The idea had only just occurred to him, but he was instantly serious.

'Of course I am! The first time I met you I wanted you to go on a walking tour to Italy. Say you'll come, Mary, please say you'll come.'

'As an intellectual companion?' she asked, more carefully still.

'Of course!'

'The sole purpose being a pilgrimage in search of culture, the viewing of pictures, statuary and here and there a ruin?'

'My interest is in people, not in things.'

Mary came to a quick decision. 'Shelley, I want you to do something for me.'

'Gladly, gladly!'

'I want you to kiss me.'

Shelley moved towards her and kissed her on the brow.

'There!' he cried. 'We have made a bargain and sealed it with a kiss.'

Mary laughed ruefully. 'What sort of a bargain, Shelley? Have we agreed, you kissing me chastely on the brow, that we shall stand before a picture in the Louvre and exclaim, "How marvellous!"?' She reached for his arms and placed them lightly about her. 'Oh Shelley, Shelley, can a poet, frozen with chastity, write real verse, verse that will live for ever?'

After kissing her he turned from her abruptly.

'Have I disappointed you?' she asked in alarm.

He swung round on her instantly and took her in his arms.

'Now I know why I felt strangely triumphant! How stupid you were, Mary, to suggest that I needed *two* women! Surely you must have known that in you alone I could find *all* women?'

'It was important that you should know it too, Shelley.'

'So important that you needed to draw my attention to it, obviously.'

'Had I not been shameless I might have had to wait until I was a very old woman.'

'By which time,' Shelley chuckled, 'nothing but an intellectual union would have been possible. So everything is arranged. We leave for the Continent at the earliest possible moment.'

Mary drew away from him. She had remembered Harriet.

'Darling,' she said soberly, 'how can you and I elope when your wife is expecting a baby?'

'But not mine,' he said, and told Mary what Harriet had said.

'That does make a difference,' she admitted in relief.

'The one obstacle is removed?'

'Yes, Shelley.'

He made to take her in his arms again, but she pushed him gently away.

'I think you ought to go. Father is out but might return at any moment. He has a habit, remember, of catching us together, and if he did that now he would know at once from our faces what we are planning.'

'Does it show as clearly as that?'

'Yes, Shelley. Kiss me quickly, then go.'

He kissed her not quickly but lingeringly.

'I can't bear to be away from you for a single moment,' he said, when reluctantly he released her. 'Come with me to Cook's. I'll get a room for you there, the most sumptuous in the whole hotel.'

'How impractical you are,' she laughed, as she led him to the door. 'Would I not be missed? Father knows how I feel about you. We must make our plans carefully. I'll call on you at Cook's tomorrow morning at ten o'clock.'

Shelley took her in his arms again. 'You like it in the daytime?'

It was impossible not to understand what he meant. 'Oh, Shelley, I've never had an opportunity of knowing whether I like it or not, daytime or night-time.'

'No more you have! I was thinking of you as a complete woman, complete in every respect.'

'What nonsense you talk,' Mary chuckled. 'Not until today had you realized that I possessed more than a brain.'

'A brain on two legs! Are they shapely legs?'

'You shall discover that for yourself tomorrow, now go, please go!'

Shelley kissed her again, laughed in delight and stepped out into the street. Lingering at the door Mary watched him until he was lost in the darkness. He had broken into a run, she could tell that by the pounding of his footsteps, and he was laughing again, laughing so boisterously that people in the street would think him crazy. Well, perhaps he was, and she also, but it was a special sort of craziness.

'Tomorrow,' she whispered, 'tomorrow. . . .'

Thirteen

I

SHELLEY took out his watch and stared at it in horror. The last time he had looked at it the hands had pointed to five minutes to ten; now it was half-past four. Impossible! Surely six and a half hours could not have been taken up in running from his room to the street and back again? Unless of course he had fallen into a dead faint and remained unnoticed for hours. Such was his excitement that it did seem quite likely. He looked at the watch again and laughed in relief. He had been holding it upside down. The time was exactly ten o'clock.

He rushed down to the street again and pacing up and down in front of the hotel peered anxiously at everyone who approached. He had been up since dawn, and following his usual habit on rising had plunged his head into a basin of cold water, but even that had done little to steady him. He started at the sight of the hackney carriage which was drawing up in front of the hotel and leapt forward instantly.

'Mary!'

A stately old gentleman who was on the point of alighting drew back in alarm.

'A thousand pardons,' Shelley mumbled.

He was growing shortsighted, that was the trouble. Spectacles, which he abhorred, were an absolute necessity now. Obviously he had missed Mary, who was always punctual; she would be waiting for him upstairs, wondering what had happened to him, suspecting even that he had changed his mind and fled.

'Mary!' he cried again, as he flung himself into his sitting-room.

The girl who was standing at the window turned and smiled.

'Really, Shelley, I don't resemble Mary in the least.'

He ran his hands distractedly through his hair. 'Oh, it's *you*!'

The girl was Mary's step-sister, Jane Clairmont. Shelley had met her often but had never taken much notice of her. He knew she was a few months younger than Mary, though with her dark eyes and olive skin, and a figure that had matured early and voluptuously, she looked older. Mary had said that they had much in common, a love of literature and poetry, a mutual interest in all aspects of radical thought, but even that had failed to attract him.

'How ungracious you sound,' she pouted.

'I was expecting Mary.' A horrible thought struck him. 'Is she ill?'

'Not ill, but she remained in her room instead of coming to breakfast.'

Another horrible thought struck Shelley. Mary had changed her mind. She had offered him a full and glorious life and now had cast him into the depths again. There was only one thing left for him to do. He must rush to the park at once and drown himself in the Serpentine. It would be romantic to die young. All poets should die young, never grow old.

'There was a terrible quarrel last night,' Jane went on. 'I know nothing of the cause, but it must have been very grave. All I could hear was a confused shouting, with Mother making most of the noise. She sounded exactly like a second-rate actress in a melodrama.'

Shelley laughed in relief. 'I don't think you care much for your mother.'

Jane shrugged lazily. 'It displeases her that Mary and I should have grown up to be such good friends. And we *are* good friends, Shelley. You can trust me utterly. Mary said you could. She asked me to bring you a letter and swore me to secrecy, which I did, oh so solemnly, and for your sake as much as hers, dear Shelley.'

'On your bended knees?' Shelley demanded.

'Naturally,' Jane lied glibly.

'Give me the letter at once.'

'I carried it in a safe place,' she said, and taking it from between her breasts handed it to him.

Shelley read the letter hurriedly and with rising indignation.

Mrs. Godwin, creeping down the stairs, had heard part of the conversation last night, only part of it but sufficient for her to guess what was afoot. She had told her husband, and now, while Shelley was forbidden to enter the house, Mary herself was forbidden to leave it.

We can trust Jane, Mary concluded, *if only because she adores you. Had you noticed? I expect not, so I'm not jealous. She will carry our letters and by letter we can make our plans, but quickly, Shelley, quickly!*

Shelley glanced at Jane. She was watching him with her moist red lips slightly parted, her eyes alight with interest.

'Are you and Mary going to elope?' she asked eagerly.

'No,' said Shelley, thinking it foolish to trust her too far.

'It would be romantic if you did.'

'If you'll wait I'll give you a letter to take back to Mary,' he said curtly.

'A message by word of mouth might be safer,' Jane suggested.

Ignoring this, Shelley went to the writing table, and with Jane lounging gracefully on the arm of a chair, wrote rapidly and briefly that he would devise a plan of escape within the next twenty-four hours. Sealing the letter he turned and found Jane again watching him with interest.

'Do you think you can come here again at ten tomorrow?' he asked.

Jane stretched languidly. 'Tomorrow I shall go for another walk in the park. Mother doesn't like it because the redcoats always want to talk to me.' She stretched again. '*I* like it, of course, especially when they are intelligent as well as attractive. Do you see any harm in it, Shelley?'

'None whatever, providing you keep away from the trees and remember at all times not to stop talking.'

'What a strange person you are, Shelley! Are you sure you and Mary are not going to elope?'

Shelley darted at her, seized her by the shoulders and whispered hoarsely in her ear: 'Murder!'

Jane sprang away from him. '*Murder?*'

'Your mother is the intended victim. We plan to trap her in a dark alley, wring her neck, dismember the body and drop the pieces one by one into the Serpentine. Betray us by as much as one word and *you*, Jane Clairmont, will die too.'

Jane laughed shakily. 'For a moment I almost believed you.'

Shelley took the letter from the writing-table and gave it to her. 'Hurry to Mary with this, there's a good girl.'

'Must I go so soon?' Jane pouted.

He snatched the letter from her hand, thrust it down the neck of her gown, found that it stuck half-way and seizing her once more shook her until it disappeared from sight.

'*Well!*' she exclaimed in delight.

There was nothing for it then, since she seemed more disinclined than ever to go, but to hustle her to the door and push her from the room.

'Remember my warning,' he called after her. 'You are much too young to die.'

But turning, Jane had the last word.

'And much too beautiful, too, don't you think?'

She lingered for a few moments after he had slammed the door. Word of mouth, she thought; well, why not? In the hall downstairs she tore open the letter, read it, smiled her satisfaction and tore it into little pieces which she dropped, one by one, as if laying a paper trail, as she tripped along Fleet Street.

2

Shelley looked up from Mary's second letter.

'Jane,' he said angrily, 'I want to talk to you.'

The girl gave him a languishing look. 'I shall enjoy that, Shelley.'

'I doubt it! Mary says here that it was unwise of me to send a message to her by word of mouth. What happened to the letter?'

'I opened it, read it and tore it up.'

'And Mary said I could trust you!'

'But Shelley, you can. It's just that I like to know what is actually happening.'

'Jane,' Shelley said desperately, 'if I write another letter and give it to you, will you promise not to open it?'

'No,' said Jane, flatly. 'And please don't threaten to wring my neck and throw me in the Serpentine.'

'I feel inclined to do more than threaten!' he raged.

'But why? All I want to do is help you. I swore myself to

secrecy, didn't I? It's so romantic I simply *have* to know everything about it. The very thought of an elopement makes me feel
all weak inside. Why, at this very moment it feels as if my stomach
has been wrenched from my body. Now be sensible, Shelley. Tell
me the plans you've made and I'll tell Mary.'

Shelley shrugged helplessly. 'I see that I must. Tomorrow
morning, at four o'clock precisely, I shall be waiting with a post-
chaise at the Hatton Garden corner. At that hour Mary should
be able to escape unnoticed, and it will take her only a few
moments to reach the rendezvous. After that—'

'Yes, *after that*?' Jane asked breathlessly.

Shelley shook his head. 'It would be unwise to tell you more.
When Mary is missed, Godwin and your mother will question
you, so the less you know the better.'

'No torture, however vile, would induce me to speak.'

Shelley smiled at her romantic earnestness, took her by the
ear and led her squealing to the door.

'Off you go, you wretch,' he laughed.

He spent the rest of the morning packing. One portmanteau
was all that was needed for his clothes, which he bundled into
it in a matter of minutes, but his books and manuscripts presented
a real problem. Confident that he would never return to England,
he saw how necessary it was to take all his belongings with him.
Two large and overflowing boxes had been brought from
Windsor and now, since he had bought more books in London,
it was necessary to send out for a third box. Finally, with all three
packed and roped, he surveyed them with intense satisfaction.
In Italy, he told himself, he would be happy for the rest of his
life. So entranced was he with the thought of Italy that he sent a
porter out for a small quantity of black paint and later, having
forgotten to ask also for a brush, dipped his forefinger in the paint.
The words SHELLEY – ITALY, which he thus daubed on the boxes,
made him chuckle with glee.

He spent the afternoon walking feverishly in the park, and
on returning to the hotel learnt from the landlord that William
Godwin had called to see him. A lucky escape, he thought, and
hiring a post-chaise immediately, had his boxes and portmanteau
carried out to it. This done he settled with the landlord, which
left him short of ready money. Remembering the predicament
in which he had found himself in Scotland, he drove in haste to

Hogg's lodgings, only to find that Hogg was out of town for a few days. However, Hogg's landlady, a jolly, red-cheeked widow who had always felt a need to mother Shelley, lent him five pounds. He doubted if that would be enough and rushed next to the Old Bond Street premises of Thomas Hookham, a bookseller and publisher with whom he had become friendly. Hookham lent him ten pounds and promised, not very willingly, to send him another fifty to a Paris bank.

'Are you travelling alone?' Hookham asked curiously.

'Naturally, since the spirit of solitude beckons,' Shelley laughed gaily.

It was now six o'clock, and ordering the postilion to meet him at the rendezvous in ten hours time, at four a.m. precisely, Shelley wandered along Old Bond Street on foot. He had a meal at a coffee-house, forgot all about it and ordering another within an hour wondered why he had no appetite. The time was beginning to drag horribly, but happily, at yet another coffee-house, he fell into a joyous argument – the subject being that one should remember that France was no longer an enemy – with an army officer. After that, remembering that in France it would be necessary to speak French, he spent two hours practising French irregular verbs. When the coffee-house closed at midnight he engaged a link-boy and tramped the streets until the paling of the stars heralded the dawn. He reached the Hatton Garden corner at quarter to four, the post-chaise drew up ten minutes later, and at five past the hour Mary came hurrying along Skinner Street. She wore a light summer cloak and carried a small portmanteau, which Shelley seized and flung into the post-chaise.

'Darling,' he whispered, embracing her.

She was pale but her eyes were sparkling with excitement.

'All went well, Mary?'

'In a way, yes,' she said, looking back over her shoulder.

Another figure was approaching the post-chaise.

'Jane,' said Mary, and laughed helplessly.

'She's dressed for travelling and carrying a portmanteau too!' Shelley gasped.

Jane, her whole body shaking with excitement, thrust her portmanteau at Shelley.

'Put it with Mary's,' she giggled.

'By heaven, this is too much!' Shelley raged.

Jane giggled again. 'Would you like me to run back and give the alarm? After all, you and Mary need a chaperon. Not that I intend to be a very *strict* one.'

'I won't take you,' Shelley said flatly.

Jane turned on her heels. 'Very well, then!'

'Wait!' Mary cried.

Jane came back. 'I promise to be very good. The thought of such a glorious adventure was too much for me. I know I shall only be an observer, taking notes for a novel I intend to write, but I'm sure I shall enjoy every moment of it.'

Shelley flung her portmanteau into the post-chaise. 'A novel indeed! You'll never live to write it.'

'Oh, Shelley, not the Serpentine again!'

'No, the Channel, and so much safer, since your body may never be found.'

'You're laughing, I can see your shoulders shaking.'

'With anger,' he growled, but he was smiling now.

The two girls climbed into the post-chaise.

'Not the Channel,' Shelley said, leaping in after them. 'I have a crueller fate in store for you. Once in Italy I shall marry you to an Italian count, one who can't speak a word of English. A fierce count who will beat you three times a day for the rest of your life.'

'Oh, Mary, isn't Shelley funny!'

'He has a perverted sense of humour,' Mary smiled.

'And so have I,' Jane laughed. 'Imagine what will be said about Shelley when the news of our escape leaks out. Everybody will call him a bluebeard.'

'I bear no resemblance to Henry the Eighth,' Shelley said sternly.

They made good time to Dartford and there, while Jane was talking to the master of the posting-station, Mary slipped her arm through Shelley's and led him a few paces away.

'Shelley, I'm worried about something Jane said.'

'And that, darling?'

'Not really something she said, but something that occurred to me when she spoke of our escape. I want you to be sure, before we go any farther, that you are not merely rescuing me from a domineering stepmother.'

'Darling,' he said softly, 'whatever I might be rescuing you from, I am rescuing myself from so much more. I had thought once that the golden years had gone for ever, but how wrong I was! To me, because of you, a new great age is beginning in the world, and the golden years are returning.'

'That they should remain golden is my only wish,' said Mary, with tears in her eyes.

They turned and found Jane running to them excitedly.

'Shelley,' she gasped, 'that handsome post-master says we could be overtaken by someone on horseback. After all, we are still only fifteen miles from London.'

'You've been gossiping,' Mary reproved.

'I couldn't resist it, Mary. I simply had to tell somebody that Shelley is so insatiable he needs two beautiful girls, sometimes even three.'

'I can see that a most lurid novel is going to be the outcome of all this,' Shelley chuckled.

'And there's something else,' Jane ran on. 'In my excitement I quite forgot to tell either you or Mary that Mr. Hookham called at Skinner Street late last night. He had a long talk with Godwin. I didn't hear much, listening at the door, but I did hear mention of Paris, and something about Shelley going there.'

Shelley threw up his arms dramatically. 'Then pursuit has already begun. We must abandon the post-chaise, hire horses and reach Dover before we are caught.'

He hired four horses, the fourth to carry the portmanteaux, and instructed the postilion to proceed with the boxes.

'Leave them with the customs officers for shipment on to-morrow's packet,' he said. 'Inform the captain that I shall be waiting at Calais to receive them.'

'How can that be possible?' Mary asked.

'Darling, today's packet will have sailed before we reach Dover, yet to linger there until tomorrow would be disastrous. We shall hire a small boat the moment we arrive and cross the Channel like the brave souls we are. In a word, adventurously!'

3

'I don't think Jane has much stomach for adventure just now,' Mary whispered.

'Seasickness can be a very terrible affliction,' Shelley whispered back. 'I thought you were asleep, darling.'

Shelley and Mary were lying in each other's arms on the fore-deck of the small boat, a blanket beneath them, another drawn loosely over them. Jane, wrapped also in blankets, lay a few paces away. The seaman at the wheel, unseen in the darkness, was whistling *La Marseillaise* enthusiastically but tunelessly. It was midnight. The little party had reached Dover at four in the afternoon, dined hurriedly and sailed at six in the one small boat that was available. Though the sea so far was anything but rough, Jane had submitted instantly to the motion of the boat.

'She seems quieter now,' Shelley said. 'Perhaps the worst has passed.'

He got up and felt his way in the darkness to Jane's side, spoke her name softly and getting no response listened for a moment to her steady breathing.

'She's asleep,' he said, on returning to Mary. 'As for me, I never felt more wide awake.'

'I'm quite wide awake myself now.'

Shelley fell to his knees and bending over her kissed her lightly.

'I think you ought to remove your gown,' he whispered, 'otherwise it will become more crushed than it is now.'

'It is something of an encumbrance,' Mary said faintly.

She tried to still the trembling of her limbs as Shelley helped her, and failing, clung to him fiercely when presently she lay in his arms again, he for his part having removed his outer clothing.

'Jane is missing a splendid opportunity to take notes for her novel,' he chuckled.

'Not even our romantic Jane would have quite envisaged this,' Mary whispered, her head against his chest, the rapid beating of his heart loud in her ear.

'The night-time after all, Mary.'

'Is it too conventional for you?'

'Scarcely, with the hard deck of a boat beneath us.'

'Hard, yes.'

'Are you complaining?'

'I have no complaints whatever.'

'Ah, but I have, Mary.'

'That I should come to you so inexperienced?'

Shelley laughed softly. 'I was thinking of the seaman at the wheel. He should be singing an Italian love song, not whistling *La Marseillaise*. Do you think he might oblige if I asked him?'

'And asking him, waste so much time?'

'Darling!'

But after a moment Mary gently released herself and sat up. 'Mary, what is it?'

'Shelley,' she said, shivering in spite of the warmth of the night, 'do you believe in premonitions?'

'In the sense that premonitions are visions, yes. Have you had a vision of Godwin striding over the waves in pursuit?'

Unable to laugh, Mary shuddered violently. 'When you were kissing me I saw in my mind's eye another boat, smaller than this. You seemed to be alone in it. A heavy fog came down and I lost sight of you. A few moments later a wind sprang up, but the fog still clung to the surface of the water and I – oh, Shelley, I never saw you again.'

Shelley drew her down to him. 'You see what comes of not concentrating when being kissed.'

'Please promise never to go out in a small boat alone.'

'Darling, I give you my word I'll never go out in a small boat alone. Does that make you feel any happier?'

'Yes, a little.'

Shelley drew the blanket over them. 'Concentration now should give you a vision of infinite splendour.'

'All the golden years ahead, yes.'

'Are you afraid?'

'Not of *this*, Shelley.'

'Afraid, perhaps, that the circumstances being what they are I have no hope whatever of seeing whether or not your legs are shapely?'

With the vision fading now, seeming unreal and stupid, Mary

took his face in her hands and with her fingers lightly traced the outline of his features.

'Darling Shelley,' she whispered, 'I must be cleverer than you.'

'Why that, you conceited wretch?'

She clung to him and laughed shakily. 'Because I can see with my fingers – why else?'

4

The captain of the packet which had arrived less than an hour ago from Dover slapped his thighs and doubled up with laughter. He was short and stout, with shining red cheeks and bright blue eyes.

'You young dog!' he cried, straightening up and pointing a chubby finger at Shelley. I know all about you. Not content with a wife you've run off with two other girls.'

Shelley glanced mischievously from Mary to Jane. 'Do you blame me?'

'Can't say I do,' said Captain Davison, looking admiringly at the two girls.

It was now early evening on the first day of the little party's arrival in France. The latter part of the Channel crossing had been stormy. A contrary wind had driven the boat in the direction of Boulogne, but shortly before dawn a change had made a landing at Calais possible. Accommodation had been found at an inn near the beach and Mary, who in the end had been as seasick as Jane, had spent most of the day resting. Now, however, having enjoyed an appetizing French meal, she showed little sign of her earlier distress.

'News travels quickly,' said Jane, shamelessly ogling Captain Davison.

'Who told you this delightful story?' Shelley asked.

'One of my passengers. A fat lady who was seasick the whole way across. *She* got it from the postmaster at Dartford.'

Shelley shrugged easily. 'I'm not concerned about fat ladies, only the safe arrival of my boxes.'

Captain Davison roared with laughter again. 'They're here all right, an' so is the fat lady. Three boxes for Shelley an' the fat lady too. Boxes in better shape, mind you, but she's making a quick recovery. The sight of your name on the boxes helped a bit.'

'It sounds like Mother,' Jane said. 'Does she wear green spectacles, Captain?'

'Green as her face when she threw up.'

'Then it *is* Mother,' Jane cried in alarm.

'Was she travelling alone?' Mary asked.

'Far as I know she was.'

'And where is she now?'

The captain grinned and went to the window of the little apartment which was both a bedroom and a sitting-room. A deep chuckle shook his heavy frame.

'Rolling across the sand,' he said, and explained that he managed to out-pace her. 'Looks a bit drunk, but maybe that's only the temporary loss of her land-legs.'

Shelley and the girls ran to the window. The fat lady, now pausing for breath in the street outside the inn, was indeed none other than William Godwin's wife. She glanced up when Shelley threw open the window, recognized him and shook her fist angrily.

'Are you drunk, Mrs. Godwin?' he called down to her.

But before she could answer Jane and Mary dragged Shelley away from the window, and Captain Davison, excusing himself reluctantly, went chuckling from the room.

'The first door on the left,' Shelley heard him say, as he reached the bottom of the stairs.

'Mother always looks drunk when she's in a temper,' Jane said. 'Whatever are we going to do?'

Shelley laughed grimly. 'Listen to her. Even when she isn't in a temper one is always compelled to do that.'

'Can she force us to go back to England?' Mary asked.

'I doubt it. French law would be a stumbling block. She might, of course, be able to force her own daughter back, but she has no jurisdiction over you. In fact,' Shelley added, recognizing this opportunity of getting rid of Jane, 'I *know* she can force her own daughter to go home with her.'

'But not me?' Mary asked anxiously.

'Not you, darling.'

'I have no interest whatever in Mary,' said Mrs. Godwin,

stamping into the room at that moment. 'Jane is my only concern.' Gasping for breath she recovered it sufficiently to utter a terse instruction. 'Jane, pack your things.'

'What use would that be?' Jane said sulkily. 'The next packet doesn't sail until tomorrow. In any case I suffered too much coming over. Nothing will ever induce me to go to sea again.'

Mrs. Godwin collapsed heavily into a chair. Shelley, who had a habit of casting from his mind all things and people he disliked, realized in surprise that she was much stouter than he had previously thought. Her bonnet, much too small for so large a head, had slipped down over her left ear. Her heavy cheeks were dripping with perspiration and her green spectacles were balanced precariously near the tip of her nose. He rushed at her suddenly.

'Let me smell your breath.'

Mrs. Godwin half-rose in the chair. 'I *beg* your pardon?'

Shelley smelled her breath. 'Ah, you *have* been drinking!'

'Nonsense!'

'I can smell brandy.'

'A sip only. It revived me.'

'It made you drunk.'

Mrs. Godwin rose shakily. 'Jane,' she said again, 'pack your things. I'm well aware that the next packet doesn't sail until tomorrow, but meanwhile I have engaged a room at another inn.'

'Jane, do as you mother tells you,' Shelley said sternly.

Jane set her jaw stubbornly and looked at Mary.

'You have little choice,' Mary told her gently.

Jane scowled and turning flounced from the room, but she was chuckling to herself at an idea that had occurred to her.

'Have you anything else to say?' Shelley asked Mrs. Godwin. 'Nothing.'

'How disappointing,' he complained. 'We had anticipated an unending flow of recriminations.'

'Is it possible,' Mary asked tentatively, 'that Father has accepted the sitation?'

'Accepted it? Whether he has or not he has certainly disowned you. He agreed with me that no girl who has behaved as you have is fit to remain a member of a respectable family. Furthermore—'

'Ah,' Shelley interrupted, 'we are in for it now, Mary. When your delectable stepmother utters that ominous word nothing on earth or in heaven above can stop her.'

And nothing, during the next ten minutes, did stop her. Shelley was a vile and sinister seducer; Mary herself was no better than a common whore. As for Godwin, he was not entirely blameless. His theories were the prime cause of this lamentable and godless situation. Money came into it, too. Shelley had lent Godwin money, not out of the generosity of his heart, as everybody had first thought, but in a disgraceful attempt to place Godwin at an even more disgraceful and demoralized disadvantage. People would say, and nobody could possibly blame them for saying it, that Godwin, reduced to unspeakable depravity, had *sold* his daughter to Shelley and attempted also to do the same with his stepdaughter.'

Shelley clapped his hands over his ears and Mary, her cheeks red with anger, went to the window, opened it and leaning out tried not to hear. But still the voice went on and on. Shelley was the arch culprit. He had deserted his wife and child, his wife who was already heavy with a second child. Nothing was more certain than that this disgusting escapade would end in misery and degradation. Nor would she be surprised if Mary, deserted in the end by Shelley, deserted the moment he saw that she too was heavy with child, took her own life. It was more than likely that Harriet Shelley had already taken hers.

Mrs. Godwin paused for breath. 'And furthermore—'

'And furthermore,' said Jane, entering the room with a placid expression on her face, 'I have packed my things and am ready to leave immediately.'

'Thank goodness for that!' Mrs. Godwin gasped.

'I am, after all, a dutiful and obedient daughter,' Jane said solemnly.

5

Mary was the first to run out of the water, leaving Shelley to watch her as she padded up the soft sand of the beach. Reaching the top of a dune she turned to wave, her wet body gleaming in the sun, then with a laugh that came echoing back to him she disappeared.

'Mary!' he called, and wasted no time in running after her.

Finding themselves in this secluded part of the coast, with nobody in sight or likely to be, Shelley had suggested a bathe. Neither of them could swim, but with the sea almost flat they had decided that it would be safe enough if they didn't go out too far. It had pleased him to see her undress in a matter-of-fact manner, her movements the epitome of unstudied grace. Nevertheless, she had been rather shy while walking hand-in-hand with him to the water's edge, glancing at him quickly, blushing delightfully and finally breaking away to run ahead of him.

'Shelley,' she said, when he came upon her at last, 'I can't remember where we put our clothes.'

'Some child from the town has probably stolen them and is now selling them in order to provide bread for a starving grandmother.'

'Or wine for a thirsty but lazy grandfather.'

Shelley studied her with his head on one side. 'How handsome you look in light brown boots.'

Mary glanced down at her feet. They, like his, were covered in sand.

'You looked like a crazy long-legged duck when you ran up the beach,' he laughed.

'How impolite you are!'

'Or rather, you moved like one, with your bottom swaying from side to side.'

Mary pushed at him suddenly, but before he fell he caught her round the waist, dragging her down with him. They rolled over and over, shouting and laughing, and soon they were covered in sand. Deliciously exhausted they lay in the sun until they were thoroughly dry, then standing up they brushed the sand from each other's bodies.

'I feel like a lady's maid, Mary.'

'And I a gentleman's valet.'

'You look more like Venus to me, Venus newly risen from the waves.'

'Then you must be Adonis.' Mary's voice faltered. 'For I love you more than she ever loved him.'

They found their clothes, but stretching themselves out in the sun again neither of them felt any inclination to dress.

'Do you know what I wrote in our journal when I got up this morning?' Shelley asked, turning on his side and kissing Mary.

Mary smiled up at him. 'Did you write how glad you were that Jane is going back to England today?'

'The packet has already sailed. No, I didn't write anything about Jane. I wrote about us. I wrote, *We were too happy last night to sleep.*'

Presently, with seagulls swirling above them, making noises which Shelley said were evidence of resentment and jealousy, they brushed the sand from their bodies again and dressed.

'Is there enough earthiness in our relationship now?' Shelley asked in mock anxiety as they began to walk back towards the town.

Mary hesitated. 'I was about to say there was more than enough, but that would be untrue.'

They walked on in contented silence until they were within sight of the inn.

'By heaven,' Shelley exclaimed, 'here comes Jane!'

She was tripping towards them with a satisfied smile on her face, and for a moment affected to pass them without recognition.

'Jane!' Shelley roared.

She turned as if in surprise. 'Why, Shelley! And you also, Mary!'

'Has the packet been delayed?' Shelley demanded.

'Goodness, no. I watched it sail, and in considerable pleasure. Then I went in search of you. I must have walked for miles, asking people if they had seen you. Everybody knew who I meant, of course, because we all look so foreign in this country. Eventually I traced you to the beach and seeing footprints in the sand decided to follow them. Wasn't that clever of me?'

'Jane . . .' Mary said helplessly.

'Out of modesty I was obliged in the end to turn back. You may not believe it, but two people, a man and a woman, were running naked on the sand. A lovely sight, and so romantic, don't you agree?'

'You really did turn back?' Mary asked, blushing.

'I did, but reluctantly.'

'You said out of modesty!' Shelley reminded her. 'Modesty! You're the most immodest girl I know.'

'That was what Mother said.'

'And where is your mother?'

'On the packet, of course.'

Shelley, realizing that he was defeated, gave one arm to Mary, the other to Jane, and led them towards the inn.

'Tell me everything, Jane,' he said sternly.

Jane laughed reminiscently. 'Mother felt ill the moment she stepped on board the packet. I settled her in a cabin, made her put her feet up and gave her some brandy. After that I waited until sailing time, and with Mother in something of a stupor had no difficulty in slipping ashore without her knowing it.'

'But Jane,' Mary said angrily, 'she will come back by the next packet and try to find you again.'

'Oh no, she won't!' Jane laughed. 'I left a letter for her with the captain. Last night, when she was talking endlessly, as usual, she said that if I had behaved as Mary has she would waste not a moment in disowning me. That, naturally, gave me an idea.'

'Oh . . .' said Mary.

'It must have been a most interesting epistle,' Shelley chuckled. 'What precisely did you write?'

Jane sighed rapturously. 'Simply that in order to help me Mary was only pretending to be your mistress. It was you and I who had eloped, not you and Mary. Mary, I said, was the chaperon, not I. And I added a postscript for good measure in which I said that the worst had already happened. I had been ravished during the Channel crossing and was, therefore, a fallen woman.'

She glanced from Mary to Shelley and back again. 'I see I have left you both quite speechless. How delightful!'

'What are we to do with her, Shelley?' Mary asked.

Shelley laughed uproariously. 'Cut off her hands and rip out her tongue – what else?'

Fourteen

Paris
Aug. 8, 1814

My dear Hogg,

This morning Mary said, 'Shelley, have you remembered to write to your friend Hogg?' I had to admit that I had quite forgotten your existence and hasten now to put pen to paper. On second thoughts, I shall refrain from sending you this letter until we reach Italy and thus, by adding a few lines from time to time, give you a brief account of our wanderings. By now you will have seen Godwin and heard of our flight, so I need waste no space here in dwelling upon it. Sufficient to say that as far as my private life is concerned I am happy with Mary. Strange, is it not, that when one is truly happy one needs but a few words to describe so blissful a state! Unhappiness, on the other hand, would call for many pages.

We are, as you see, in Paris. We arrived six days ago and have lodgings at the Hotel de Vienne. The Tuileries gardens are too formal to interest us, and we find it ridiculous that they should be entirely without grass. At the Louvre we saw one picture – it depicted the Deluge – which impressed us, but in another, which depicted Heaven, the Blessed looked so stupid we were convulsed with irreverent laughter. I myself laughed more heartily than Mary and Jane, for one of the angels bore a quite frightening resemblance to my father.

There has been some difficulty in raising funds. Hookham, who promised to send me a remittance, did no more than write a cold and stupid letter. However, Travernier, who represents one of my London moneylenders, advanced me sixty pounds. This after I had been obliged to sell my watch and chain for the sum of 8 napoleons 5 francs. Jane accompanied me to the ass market earlier this morning to buy an ass. I must say that I was tempted to offer Jane in exchange for the ass, but forebore. Having grown used to her company I should miss her and look in horror at the ass.

Later today, leaving my boxes in store, we commence the first stage of the journey from Paris to somewhere in Italy. Mary and Jane will take turns at riding the ass; I myself intend to walk the whole way. It goes without saying that I shall be happier for the rest of my life in Italy.

Troyes
Aug. 13, 1814

The ass, my dear Hogg, proved so useless an animal that we sold him at Charenton and replaced him with a sturdy mule. Mary says I look more dignified leading a mule than an ass. The weather has been fine and the scenery beautiful, but we have suffered considerably from the filth of the lodgings we have been obliged to accept en route. At Nogent, for instance, we were disturbed during the night by rats running across our faces. Jane, who swore that there were more rats in her room than ours, was so frightened that we had to take her into our bed, placing her for safety between us.

Real progress has been hampered by my slipping and spraining an ankle, so now we have bought a voiture *at a cost of 5 napoleons, and in it will post to Neufchâtel. Mary tells me that in selling the mule for 40 francs and the saddle for 16 francs we have lost 15 napoleons since buying that wretched ass in Paris. This talk of napoleons one moment, francs the next, will be as confusing to you as it is to me. Apparently there are 20 francs to a napoleon, so we seem to be the worse off by 150 francs — no, 300 — but just what that amounts to in a civilized currency is more than I can say.*

Tomorrow morning at dawn we resume our journey.

I shall have more to tell you later.

Neufchâtel
Aug. 20, 1814

Vandeuvres, Bar-sur-Aube, Champlitte, Besançon, Mort, Pontarlier and now Neufchâtel. We are happy to be in Switzerland at last, carrying with us but one good memory of France. It was at Pontarlier that we had our first and only experience of sleeping in a clean bed. I am speaking, of course, of people and their habits, not of the magnificent scenery through which we have passed. But even that, varied as it was, and at times breathtaking, is little but a vague memory, for Hogg, my dear fellow, I am engaged upon the task of writing a romance which I shall call The Assassins, *and at every halt devote myself for an hour or two to my work.*

One thing I must tell you before I forget. I have written to Harriet, asking her to join us. Mary is worried about something her stepmother said, a suggestion that Harriet, in her present frame of mind, might be tempted to take her own life. I was filled with horror when Mary spoke of this, and then amazement that she should seem displeased at my issuing the invitation. I pointed out, as mildly as I could, that Harriet and I could never be more than friends, and would remain separated, even though she might take up residence with us. Mary, however, is convinced that Harriet will scorn the invitation. Believing what she does of me, I fear that that is more than likely.

Tomorrow morning at six we start out for Lucerne.

Brunnen

Lake Lucerne

Aug. 25, 1814

I cannot understand why I said that I should be happy for the rest of my life in Italy. Switzerland is glorious; I need travel no farther, and both Mary and Jane agree. We have rented a house for a period of six months. You shall visit us, Hogg. It is even possible, if Harriet is willing to come to Switzerland, that you, so old and dear a friend, might be her companion during the journey. I charge you, if that be the case, to take the greatest care of my little daughter Ianthe.

Brunnen

Lake Lucerne

Aug. 27, 1814

How is it possible to be happy anywhere when one is dogged by financial worries? That I should be reduced to such gross materialism will make you weep for me, but reduced to it I am. At a bank in Neufchâtel I was able to obtain some slight relief and staggered from the premises under the weight of a bag full of coins. Alas, the weight belied the value, for the coins were silver, not gold, and further relief will not be forthcoming. We are at a sore disadvantage in a foreign country. Only in London can I extend my credit substantially by means of post-obit bonds, so to England we must return.

When Mary suggested this, and reluctantly I agreed, Jane remarked, somewhat nastily, I thought, that Mary was afraid that Harriet might accept my invitation and was urging a return knowing that, in England, Harriet would never join us. The trouble with Jane is that she would do anything rather than go back to England, but the die is cast. Either we

G*

return or subject ourselves to poverty here such as the poorest peasants have never known.

In all other things I am happier than ever before in my life. I am still writing my romance and have in mind a long narrative poem dealing with the spirit of solitude. Mary is writing something of her own, and Jane, who has forgotten that she proposed earlier to write a novel, is keeping a journal, a record, in short, of our vicissitudes. Mary and I are keeping a journal also, the entries in which, unlike those in Jane's, are uncoloured by romantic notions. Jane, I fear, sees things not as they are but as she imagines them to be.

We leave early tomorrow for Lucerne and propose to travel back to England by way of Germany and Holland.

Ever your friend,

P.B.S.

P.S.: I keep referring to Jane as Jane when it should be Claire. She has taken a violent dislike to Jane and has decided that Claire suits her better. Clara to begin with, now Claire. Claire Clairmont. She refuses to answer to any other name and stares at us blankly if we forget and call her Jane. She swears that 'Claire' makes her feel quite excitingly different, but I can't say that I myself have noticed the slightest difference.

Fifteen

I

'You quite take my breath away,' Harriet cried furiously. 'After all this time, and all that has happened, you burst in upon me and declare, as if it were the most important thing in the world, that the one thing you regret about your travels is your failure to meet Beethoven. Who, pray, is Beethoven?'

Shelley smiled broadly. 'You must be speaking figuratively, Harriet.'

'Figuratively?'

'About my quite taking your breath away.'

Harriet, remembering her condition, remembering also that at the sight of Shelley she had decided to make the most of it, fell back limply in her chair.

'You are more impossible than ever, Bysshe.'

'Ludwig van Beethoven,' Shelley went on patiently, 'is a composer. I was thinking about him when I walked along Chapel Street. I admire him, not for the exquisite music he has written, but for his hatred of tyranny. He wrote a symphony which he dedicated to Napoleon Bonaparte. At that time Bonaparte had not revealed himself as a future tyrant. However, when Beethoven learnt that Bonaparte had declared himself Emperor of France he wept at the thought that his former hero was a mere mortal and exclaimed: "He will trample now on the rights of man and indulge only in his ambition." He then destroyed the dedication. The dedication only, mind you, not the symphony. Beethoven is a supreme artist.'

Harriet gave Shelley a sulky look. 'You have dedicated poems to me in the past. Do you intend now to destroy the dedication?'

'No,' Shelley said gently.

'Have you dedicated any to Mary Godwin?'

'Yes,' he admitted, and laughed softly. 'I wonder if I ought to find it embarrassing, having dedicated poetry first to one wife, then to another?'

Harriet's voice rose shrilly. 'Have you married Mary bigamously? Because if you have—!'

'Mary is more my wife,' Shelley said dreamily, 'than any marriage, bigamous or otherwise, could ever make her.'

Harriet resorted instantly to a fit of weeping. Obviously, Shelley, if he had noticed it at all, was unimpressed by her swollen stomach. More than likely he thought she looked in excellent health, which indeed she was, she thought resentfully. She had even been told, by none other than Captain Ryan, that her condition had increased her attractiveness, and thinking of this she grew more cheerful.

'Poor Harriet,' Shelley said contritely, 'I had no intention of hurting you. If I should seem to forget that you are in actual fact my legal wife, please remember that you have yourself to blame. Not that I want to reproach you. You were tempted, you believed the lies that had been told about me, and temptation was too much for you. All I ask of you is that you should remember that I have your welfare at heart. As I said in my letter, you will always find in me a firm and constant friend, one to whom your interests will always be dear.'

Harriet sniffed back her tears and looked at him curiously. His eyes were shining with benevolent enthusiasm. In a moment, if this ridiculous conversation was allowed to go on, he would be calling her his dear sister. She had missed him, at times terribly, yet now as she looked at him she realized that he was not the man she had pictured in her mind and *thought* she was missing. She compared him with Captain Ryan and felt vaguely comforted. Ryan, at all events, was a real man, not a hare-brained, would-be philosopher. She remembered that she and Shelley had had much fun together in the past, much laughter, but one could scarcely exist for ever on meaningless fun and empty laughter.

'I'd like very much to see Ianthe,' Shelley said. 'Where is she?'

'My sister has taken her to the country for a few days,' Harriet lied, for on Shelley's arrival Eliza had hurried the child from the house by the back door. 'How long have you been back in England?'

'Since the thirteenth.'

'You were not away as long as I thought.'

'From the twenty-eighth of July to the thirteenth of September.'

'What brought you back?'

Shelley laughed ruefully. 'A dire shortage of money.'

'No doubt you have raised more through post-obit bonds.'

'Indeed I haven't. The moneylenders are being damnably difficult. They want a certain three thousand, for instance, for an advance of one thousand.'

'Then you didn't come here today to offer me some small relief in my own desperate need.'

'I thought you were well cared for,' Shelley said, in genuine surprise.

'If I am, I see no reason why that should free you of your own responsibility.'

'I offered you a home. I came here today to repeat the offer.'

'Oh, Bysshe, what a simpleton you are!'

'I see that I am,' he said sorrowfully. 'And obviously Mary thinks so too.'

'Mary?'

'She was sure you would refuse.'

That was almost enough to make Harriet say at once that she would accept his offer, but she restrained herself. To feel jealous still was ridiculous, and to have people saying that she was sharing her husband with a loose woman would be too humiliating.

At the door now, Shelley turned and smiled hopefully. 'How long will Ianthe be away?'

'Till the baby is born.'

'And that will be—?'

'The end of December.'

'May I know where she is? I'd like to visit her.'

Harriet shook her head. 'We all consider that your influence would be bad for her.'

Shelley flushed angrily. 'Whereas your influence, you carrying another man's child—!'

'Oh, Bysshe—!' Harriet cried, on the point now of begging him to believe that she had lied to hurt him.

'Yes, Harriet?'

She held up her head disdainfully. Did it matter what he believed? She no longer loved him.

'If your need is as great as you say,' she said, 'I can lend you twenty pounds.'

But even then, to her vast annoyance, he failed to recognize the scorn in her voice.

'You can, Harriet? How very generous of you!'

2

'That sounds like Shelley's knock this time,' Claire said.

'Wait!' Mary warned. 'We must be absolutely sure before we go to the door.'

She and her stepsister were unpacking a box of books and other personal belongings which had been sent from Skinner Street to these furnished rooms which Shelley had found in Margaret Street, Cavendish Square. They were small and dingy, and it was hoped that soon it would be possible to rent a house in the country.

The knock came a second time and with it Shelley's voice demanding admission. Both girls ran to the door. Claire opened it quickly and Mary, the moment Shelley had entered, locked it without delay.

'Are you afraid of burglars?' Shelley asked mildly.

'Not burglars,' Mary said, 'creditors.'

'Goodness, have they been pestering us again?'

'Three came while you were out. It was anything but amusing.'

'Dear Mary, how cross you sound!'

'Do please try to be serious,' Mary begged. 'We were all but penniless when we arrived in London, and the position has not improved.'

'Ah, but it will, it will. The quarterly payment from my father is due within a few days, and meanwhile we are as rich as the Prince Regent. Nay, richer, for *he* owes hundreds of thousands and probably hasn't two pennies to rub together in his pocket, whereas *I* have twenty pounds in mind.'

'I can't believe it!'

'Nor can I, but there it is! Harriet was generous enough to offer me a loan, which I accepted gladly and gratefully.'

Shelley took a sovereign from his pocket, tossed it in the air, caught it and pressed it into Claire's already outstretched hand.

'Off you go and buy some oysters, and anything else we might need. I think I ought to eat a substantial meal before being flung into prison, don't you?'

When Claire had gone Mary said, 'Shelley, I still want you to try to be serious.'

'But why?' he asked in surprise. 'The debts can take care of themselves. All we need is ready money, and for the time being we have plenty of that. Besides, being serious makes you frown, and I hate to see a frown on your face. It gives me indigestion.'

Mary tried not to smile. 'Shelley, two of the creditors were trying to collect money owed by my father and by Harriet, not by you personally.'

'Well, what of it? I seem to remember that I made myself responsible both to your father's creditors and Harriet's.'

'Yet Harriet gave you twenty pounds.'

'Yes, most peculiar, when you come to think of it.'

Mary decided to say no more for the moment about Harriet. 'Father's attitude is even more peculiar.'

'We must try to be reasonable,' Shelley said warmly. 'I lent him money and made myself responsible for his debts before our elopement. The fact that he considers that I have wronged you has nothing to do with a business agreement.'

Mary went back to her unpacking. Shelley's extraordinary sense of fairness, lovable trait that it was, bewildered her. And her father's attitude disgusted her. He had disowned her and refused to communicate with Shelley, except through an attorney, yet was willing, through his own improvidence, to see Shelley fall deeper and deeper into debt. She wondered if it amused him to think that Shelley, with Claire and herself to keep, was more embarrassed financially than he was himself. So much for the Godwinian philosophy, she thought angrily.

'I wonder if Harriet thought I would be too proud to accept money from her?' Shelley asked.

'You know her better than I do,' Mary said cautiously.

'I shall pay it back, of course. And as soon as possible I'll make her a regular allowance.'

'She isn't coming to live with us, then?'

'No, but you do agree that I should make her a regular allowance?'

'Of course, Shelley.'

'She'll need more money when the baby comes. It might not be mine, but I am still responsible for it. I wonder if it will be a boy or a girl? If a boy it will eventually receive the Shelley title. Imagine my father's face if it is and I told him that a future Shelley baronet had no Shelley blood in his veins.'

'Would you actually tell him?'

Shelley shook his head. 'Why should I hurt an innocent child?'

Mary straightened up with a book in her hands. 'Yet my child, if a boy, will have no hope of inheriting the title.'

'Pooh! You care no more for titles than I do.'

Mary smiled affectionately. Shelley had failed to understand what she was trying to tell him. Turning the pages of the book she began to wonder why she should have delayed as long as this. She wondered if it had been an unconscious fear that Shelley, under the circumstances, would not be pleased. Her own attitude puzzled and disturbed her. She had been brought up to believe in complete freedom. Convention meant nothing to her, yet nagging at her and disgusting her was the thought that to bring an illegitimate child into the world would be shameful. She remembered something she had said to her father: *How quickly the doctrine of sexual freedom falls apart when it comes to one's own daughter.* Trying to forget this she told herself that she must be stronger than her father. To cast aside her principles at seventeen would be admitting a weakness even more pitiful than his.

'How clever you are,' Shelley laughed, 'reading a book upside down.'

Mary laughed too. 'I do it frequently, Shelley. The exercise is good for one's eyes. You should try it yourself, though I admit it could never cure your absent-mindedness.'

'Dear me, what have I forgotten now?' he asked in deep concern. 'Not your birthday, I hope?'

'Not that. You remembered it, much to my amazement, when we were in Germany. It isn't what you have *forgotten*, only what you have failed to *observe*.'

He peered at her closely. 'Ah, you're wearing a new gown!'

'I wore it yesterday and the day before, and countless times while we were abroad.'

'I still claim that my observation is more than ordinarily acute.'

'And *I* claim that it is the very reverse.'

'Then prove your words!'

'Had you, for instance, observed that nothing whatever has prevented us from sleeping together since the day we eloped?'

'Naturally I had, though Claire's presence has made it difficult at times.'

Mary laughed helplessly. 'Oh Shelley, how dense you are!'

'Great heavens!' he cried. '*Now* I know what you mean!' He swept her into his arms. 'Darling, how splendid!' He kissed her, then held her from him. 'Are you absolutely sure?'

His joyous enthusiasm brought tears to Mary's eyes.

'There should have been the first interruption the day we reached Nogent, the second a few days ago. I think I can say that I am absolutely sure.'

Shelley was looking at her intently. 'Do you mind?'

'No, darling. Do you?'

'Oh, Mary, what a stupid thing to ask! The very thought of it makes me immeasurably happy.'

Mary flung her arms round his neck.

'You make me feel that I should apologize,' she said.

'Apologize?'

'Not to you,' she whispered, 'to myself, my real self.'

3

John Westbrook himself opened the door and admitted Shelley with an amazing air of friendliness.

'Eliza said you wouldn't come, I said you would,' he chuckled.

'And Harriet?' Shelley asked politely.

'In two minds about it, she was.'

'She must have been, having waited a week before writing to tell me the news.'

'Wasn't well enough to write, poor girl.'

'*You* could have written.'

'Harriet wouldn't let me. "No," she said, "it's me or nobody." Mind you, I wouldn't have let it go on too long. Too important, young fellow, eh? A boy this time. Charles Bysshe, we've called him. Makes me as proud as punch, it does. Just think of it, one of these days he'll be Sir Charles.'

Shelley had received a letter from Harriet that morning. There had been several other letters during the seven or eight weeks that had passed since he had last seen her, all written in a complaining tone. In one she had threatened him with legal action, in another she had said that she was so ill that once again the doctors despaired for her life. Alarmed by this he had sent his own doctor to attend her and had learnt later that she was mentally distressed rather than physically ill. The final letter, which he had hesitated to open, had conveyed the startling news that a week ago, and a month before her time, she had given birth to a son.'

'Like to go up right away?' John Westbrook asked.

'Of course, providing I can see Harriet alone.'

'If you're thinking about Eliza, I'll see to it she won't disturb you.'

'Thank you.'

'There's Ianthe, but you can see her afterwards.'

'Thank you again. Would you care also to kill a fatted calf?'

Westbrook slapped Shelley on the back. 'Always one for a joke!'

Shelley found Harriet propped up on a number of lace-covered pillows. Her eyes narrowed at the sight of him and she greeted him with a hesitant little cry.

'So Papa was right, Bysshe.'

'A well brought up daughter should always say that.'

A tentative smile touched Harriet's lips. 'Even when she has a husband?'

Shelley suspected an archness in her tone, and this alarmed him.

'Poor Bysshe,' she went on, 'you look pale and drawn. Are you ill?'

'My health is excellent.'

'Still worried by debts, then?'

'Nonsense!'

Actually the financial position had grown much worse after Harriet had lent him the twenty pounds. Unsuspected creditors had leapt up on every hand, like pikemen of old, but flourishing writs, not pikes.

'Somebody told me,' Harriet murmured, 'that you had left Mary Godwin.'

Shelley shook his head, and smiling reminiscently failed to see Harriet's face harden. The rumour that he had deserted Mary had been caused by his going into hiding. Leaving her at Margaret Street to spread the story that he had fled abroad, he had taken a room at a small and quiet inn in St. John Street and there, on many occasions, he and Mary had secretly spent a night together Finally, after Mary had been obliged to make another move on her own account, a suitable house had been found in Nelson Square, and there, because a new and surprisingly eager money-lender provided sufficient temporary relief, he and Mary were now living in open defiance of both hated convention and barely satisfied creditors.

'I heard another story, too,' Harriet said viciously.

'Apparently I am becoming quite notorious.'

'Notorious is indeed the right word. I heard that having deserted me for Mary Godwin, you had now deserted her for her stepsister.'

'Good lord, Harriet,' Shelley laughed, 'it would take a dozen men, not one, to cope with Claire.'

'I thought her name was Jane.'

'She decided that Claire suited her temperament better.'

Harriet tried to smile sweetly. He had provoked her into a harshness which she had not intended, for a strange thing had happened at the birth of her second child. It had come upon her that she wanted Shelley and was prepared to forgive him.

'I thought it very dutiful of you,' she said softly, 'to send me an address every time you moved.'

'Merely dutiful?'

'I meant kind and considerate,' she said hastily.

'I shall always be interested in your affairs, you know that.'

'It was also kind and considerate of you to come and see me today,' she added.

'You say that, Harriet, even though you know I must have guessed your reason for asking me to come?'

Harriet sighed as pathetically as she could. 'I didn't ask you to come. I only hoped that you would.'

'I don't want to quarrel with you, but are you afraid that I might disclaim the child and in some way make it impossible for him to inherit the title?'

'*That* isn't being kind and considerate, but never mind. I don't want to quarrel with you, either. Much rather would I forget all our differences and be – well – good friends.'

'You really mean that, Harriet?'

'With all my heart, Bysshe. And now, would you like to see little Charles?'

'If you want me to see him,' Shelley said gruffly.

Harriet rang a bell which stood on the table near her bed and a few moments later an elderly nurse brought in the baby. Shelley peered at him reluctantly as he lay in the nurse's arms, then, startled by a facial resemblance he found it difficult to place, moved closer.

'Give him to me!' he commanded.

The nurse did so and at a word from Harriet withdrew.

'Good lord,' Shelley burst out, 'he looks ridiculously like my father.'

'I'm glad you noticed,' said Harriet, in considerable satisfaction. 'When he smiles he looks exactly like your father.'

'He's frowning, Harriet. It's the frown that attracted my attention, probably because my father frowned at me far more than he ever smiled.'

Forgetting everything except the baby in his arms, and carried back in memory to Ianthe at the same age, Shelley began to walk up and down the room.

'Poor little fellow, such a puzzled frown,' he murmured. 'Is the world too much for you after only a week in it? Well, well, we must change all that.'

The baby squirmed in his arms and began to whimper.

'Now, now, enough of that,' Shelley admonished.

'Why not sing to him?' Harriet suggested.

'Ah yes, that silly old song of mine!' And tunelessly he began the half-remembered chant: 'Yáhmani, Yáhmani, Yáhmani, Yáh-máh-neeeee! There, he likes it, just as Ianthe did. A most beatific smile now, not a frown. He— Great heavens, Harriet, how carried away I was. Is it possible that this Shelley look is only a coincidence? Answer me, confound you, answer me!'

'Now you've upset him,' said Harriet, for the baby was crying lustily.

She rang the bell again and when the nurse came hurrying into the room she told her to take the baby away and pacify him.

'I don't think he likes the look of his papa,' she added in mock concern.

Shelley gave the baby to the nurse and when he was alone again with Harriet he approached the bed uncertainly.

'I was a beast,' Harriet said tremulously.

'Are you trying to tell me now that you lied when you told me I was not the father?'

'Yes,' Harriet admitted, recognizing both confusion and indignation in his voice.

'But why, Harriet, *why*?'

'I wanted to hurt you, Bysshe. I had suffered horribly and wanted to make you suffer too.'

'And *now*?'

Harriet fumbled for the right words but failed to find them.

'I'm sure you've been punished enough,' she said. 'I'm more than ready to forgive you now.'

'And yourself? Are you more than ready to forgive yourself?'

'You made me do what I did,' she said stubbornly.

'I thought it was Eliza, Eliza and the lies she told.'

'Oh, Bysshe, why must you continue to insist on that? Why can't you see that I want to forgive you for what you did to Eliza as well as what you did to me?'

'I did nothing to Eliza.'

'Very well, then. I forgive you for having done nothing to Eliza.'

'You still don't believe me.'

'How can I? Eliza might tell a small harmless lie on occasion, as so many people do, but never one so monstrous as that. But does it matter after all this time? I see I should have forgiven you ages ago, but better late than never.'

'How splendid to be forgiven for something one hasn't done.'

'You make things very difficult for me, Bysshe. All I want is that we should both forget the past and be happy together.'

'Are you actually suggesting a reconciliation?'

'Of course I am! I thought I was making it obvious that I wanted you to come back to me.'

Shelley looked at her in despair. 'It's too late for that, Harriet.'

Her eyes flashed angrily. 'Because of Mary Godwin?'

Shelley hesitated. 'Mary comes into it, but I was thinking of all that had happened between you and me. Neither of us is the same person. We've changed and grown apart.'

'I thought change was the breath of life to you,' Harriet sneered.

'Then why argue about it? So much simpler to accept it.'

Harriet tried to speak quietly. 'I don't want to argue, and I don't want to accept it. I was confused by the memory of something you said when we were going to Scotland. You were talking about mutability, you and that Scottish attorney. I wasn't quite sure what you meant until you said that nothing endured but change.' She laughed bitterly. 'I thought how wrong you were. I was sure that whatever else might change, love never would.'

'And you were right,' Shelley said eagerly.

She looked at him doubtfully. 'You – you really mean that?'

'Not love in the all-embracing meaning of the word,' he ran on, caught up now in a grand new philosophy. 'Love has always been and always will be. It touches everyone, though few can hold it, and grasp instead at hate. Love is so shining a jewel that it blinds people and makes them afraid. It blinded us, even though for a time it enriched our lives. The world isn't ready for love, but love is ready for the world, glorious and unchanging.'

'What nonsense you talk,' Harriet said scathingly. 'How can you say that love is unchanging when, if you ever did love me, you love me no longer?'

'You don't understand a word I said,' Shelley sighed.

'I doubt if your precious Mary would. Or if that's the sort of talk that goes on between you and she thinks she understands, she'll wake up with a horrible start when you turn from her to somebody else.'

'Oh, Harriet, I wasn't talking about individual love.'

'What, then?'

'Impersonal love, of course.'

'How charming! How grand! I'd rather have a man who said

he loved me and meant it, than a man who talks so crazily about a sort of love that you can't feel and probably doesn't exist. I want to live, not merely stagnate. I only *thought* I loved you, I see that now. Please go, Bysshe. I don't want to see you again, ever.'

'You said you wanted to be good friends; you said you meant it with all your heart.'

'An excellent example of mutability.'

'Harriet, for the sake of the children—'

'Ianthe and Charles are mine. I won't have them contaminated by your influence. Ianthe has forgotten you and Charles will never know you.'

Shelley looked at her sadly. 'You threaten me with legal action. Could I not now threaten you also? I want my children, Harriet.'

'Take legal action, then. Stand up in court and tell the judge that you have a fine home waiting for them. Tell him that you are living in sin with two disreputable females and want the children to learn by your own example and the indescribable joys of free love.

'No, wait!' Harriet cried, as he moved to the door.

'Haven't you said enough?' he asked, turning.

Harriet laughed disdainfully. 'I only wanted to remind you that you still owe me twenty pounds.'

Shelley smiled in the way that had always appealed to her so much in the past, but merely infuriated her now.

'I had quite forgotten,' he laughed, 'but you shall have it tomorrow, even if I have to go into hiding again immediately after sending it to you.'

When he had gone she lay back panting. And to think that she had been ready to forgive him, had even deceived herself into believing that she wanted him! Well, perhaps she *had* wanted him, but that sort of want could be satisfied by others. There was Captain Ryan, for instance, ever attentive and ready to wait patiently for years and years, or so he had been gallant enough to say. Ryan would do to begin with, but she was too young and beautiful to tie herself ever again to one man. Yes, and too ambitious also. Falling into an exciting day-dream she fancied she could see people nudging each other and saying, 'There goes the exquisite Harriet Shelley, I wonder which of the royal dukes is keeping her now?' She knew that the women were looking at her enviously and the men in despair, for it was rumoured that soon she would have the Prince Regent himself at her beck and call and through him become the most powerful royal mistress in English history.

'I shall offer to make Shelley the poet laureate,' she whispered, 'and then, at the last moment, laugh in his face.'

Sixteen

I

'I DOUBT very much if you were listening, Claire,' Shelley said severely.

'I was, Shelley, I swear I was.'

'Then tell me what I said.'

'Do you expect me to repeat everything, word for word?' Claire protested. 'You walk so fast and talk so fast that my legs fail me and my mind is in utter confusion.'

'Then sit down, rest your legs and collect your thoughts.'

'Here in the street?' Claire laughed.

Shelley laughed too. 'Forgive me. I was so immersed in what I was saying I thought we were still in the park.'

It was the second Sunday in January and he and Claire were returning to Nelson Square after a brisk walk in St. James's Park, Mary herself not having felt well enough to accompany them.

'What I like best about Sunday,' he chuckled, 'is that a bailiff on so holy a day has no legal power to arrest a poor debtor.'

'Goodness, are you going once more in fear of arrest?'

'I shall be if I fail to raise a little more money within the next week. But enough of that! I was talking about the first principles of true philosophy and I repeat, my dear Claire, I doubt very much if you were listening.'

Claire thought very hard for a moment, then laughed triumphantly.

'One of the first principles of true philosophy,' she quoted in a deliberately sing-song voice, 'is the acceptance of the in-ev-it-a-bil-ity of change.'

'Proceed,' he said, trying not to laugh at her childish lisping.

'A person whose mind is unformed may change. Only in the event of his refusing to change is he utterly lost.'

Shelley bowed in mock humility. 'I apologize. You were paying attention after all.'

'I expect you were thinking about *my* mind,' Claire pouted.

'Indeed I was.'

'Oh dear, do you still consider it unformed?'

'By no means. Have you not studied, and are you not continuing to study diligently under my direction?'

Claire sighed elaborately. 'How nice to know that I am not yet utterly lost. And how splendid to think that when my mind is fully formed the new Claire Clairmont will be Shelley's creation.'

Shelley chuckled and took her arm. 'I see I have assumed a great and terrible responsibility.'

Claire drew him back a little, slowing down his pace and matching her step with his. Smiling up at him archly she wanted to tell him that if he took as much interest in her body, which no one could possibly call unformed, as he took in her mind, she would rapidly become the most attentive pupil in the world. The search for truth, as he called it, was all very well, but one was apt to grow a little tired of a search that took up twenty-four hours of every day, a search that often seemed to lead from nowhere to nowhere.

'I'm getting a little tired of waiting,' she said, her mind on anything but philosophy.

'Of waiting for what?'

'Well—' Claire's nerve failed her. 'Of waiting to discover truth.'

'How impatient you are! One may well have to wait a whole lifetime, testing many theories, discarding them and testing others, before stumbling upon the grand discovery.'

'But I want to know *now*.'

Shelley decided to say no more. Claire's stupidity was irksome at times, but one must be patient with her. For the rest, as far as ordinary things were concerned, he found her a friendly and companionable creature, willing always to go for a long walk, to accompany him on any sort of expedition, to restore his equanimity with a merry laugh, to turn grim reality into a side-splitting comedy.

'I've been thinking . . .' Claire began.

'You have? My heartiest congratulations!'

'I've been thinking,' she went on, resisting the impulse to giggle, 'that Mary must trust me to a ridiculous extent.'

'What do you mean by that?'

'The way she permits our walks together, saying she's too tired to walk herself, saying "You go, Claire, I don't like to think of Shelley walking too much alone, he may get lost".'

'In other words, I need a keeper and you feel the responsibility too great for you?' Shelley laughed.

Claire all but gave up; his denseness was absolutely infuriating.

'Nevertheless,' he went on, 'I see nothing ridiculous in the trust Mary places in you.'

'I was thinking of you, not myself,' she tried again.

'Why me?' He was thoughtful for a moment. 'Ah, I understand! Mary trusts me to see to it that you never run after an attractive redcoat.'

Claire seized on this happily. 'On the contrary, Shelley, she trusts me to see to it that you never run after a pretty girl.'

'What nonsense!'

'Are you never tempted? Come, be truthful!'

'Judge for yourself, you with your sharp eyes, you the apparent keeper of my morals. *Am* I ever tempted?'

Claire recognized defeat but still pressed on. 'For all I know, you might be hiding your feelings from me skilfully. And yet, at a time like this, Mary being too ill for – we-ell . . .'

Thinking that she might be speaking too boldly she let her voice trail away and waited anxiously for an indignant reprimand.

'Poor Mary,' Shelley said at length, 'all was going well until the third month, but now – Claire, you've talked to the doctor yourself. Is anything serious being kept from me?'

'Nothing,' she assured him.

'Thank heaven for that.'

They had reached Nelson Square now but Claire, defeated as she felt, rallied for a final assault.

'How strong of you to resist temptation, Shelley.'

He stopped, as so often he did when he wanted to make a telling point, swung Claire round to face him and looked at her earnestly.

'I do not resist, for there is nothing to resist. How then can it be said that I am either strong or weak? With nothing to resist I see no virtue in what you call my strength.'

'Ah, you are like Caesar's wife, above suspicion.'

'The exact quotation, my dear Claire, is that Caesar's wife *must* be above suspicion.'

Claire laughed prettily. 'So temptation is there but must be set sternly aside.'

They had now reached the house but Shelley, having opened the door, turned to look thoughtfully at Claire. He saw clearly the meaning behind all this talk of hers. Most of it had seemed nonsense, but obviously it was anything but that. Claire had been expressing thoughts and feelings entirely personal to herself.

'This is a desperate situation,' he said.

Claire could scarcely believe her ears; Shelley had understood at last!

'Desperate indeed,' she exulted.

'Mary and I,' he proclaimed, 'must waste no time in finding you a husband.'

'A *husband*?' So taken aback was she that she could have slapped his face. 'What nonsense you talk,' she said angrily. 'You know very well that I have been brought up to regard marriage as something almost sinful, made necessary only by bigotry.'

'I doubt if your mother believes that.'

'Perhaps not, for she married Godwin, but I was brought up, remember, as was Mary herself, to believe wholeheartedly in the Godwinian philosophy.'

'And how much of it do you understand?' Shelley asked sternly.

'Sufficient to know that a woman should be free to take a lover without any thought of legal ties.'

'Really, Claire,' he said indignantly, 'your tone suggests that you subscribe to looseness of morals, not freedom.'

'Is there any difference?'

Shelley stared at her in horror. 'My dear child, neither Godwin nor I have ever preached that a man should shun legal marriage in order to be free to go capriciously from mistress to mistress, or a woman from lover to lover.'

'What, then?' Claire asked stubbornly.

'The virtue of our philosophy is that a man, or a woman, should be free to find love without bigotry, and finding it, live nobly and freely.'

'But Shelley, how is a woman to know that her first lover, or for that matter her first husband, will live up to expectations?'

'Oh . . .' said Shelley, for the moment nonplussed.

Claire tossed her head and swept past him haughtily, leaving him, still nonplussed, to follow her into the house.

'Did you have a pleasant walk?' Mary asked.

'Instructive, at all events,' Claire said brightly.

'Ah, Shelley has been lecturing you. What was it this time?'

'Morality, I suspect, though he spoke in riddles.'

Mary laughed lightly. 'Morality is, I admit, one of the greatest riddles of the ages.' Lying on a sofa she had been reading the Sunday newspaper, and turning to it again remarked that Lord Byron had married an heiress. 'A certain Miss Milbanke,' she said. 'Do you know anything about her, Shelley?'

'*I* do,' said Claire, who was well acquainted with all the gossip about the notorious Lord Byron. 'Eminently respectable and extremely dull.'

'I can't believe,' Mary laughed, 'that Lord Byron's reputation will become any the less unsavoury by his possessing an eminently respectable and extremely dull wife.'

Shelley frowned reprovingly. 'Oh come, Mary, that is scarcely kind. His private life is his own affair. Our interest in him is centred solely in his poetry. We must meet him sometime, you often say that.'

'*I* certainly want to meet him,' Claire chuckled, 'and not because of his poetry. All my friends are obsessed with thoughts of his wickedness. At least three of them are making plans to snare him, if only for one night, and all but swooning at the thought of it.' She folded her hands dramatically over her breast. 'Not that *I* would swoon, however intense the pleasure. I'd relish every moment of it and ask for more and more and more!'

'Have you ever thought of going on the stage?' Shelley asked.

'You think I have dramatic ability?' Claire demanded eagerly.

'Possibly, but what I really had in mind, assuming that you really do want to meet Lord Byron, is his connexion with Drury

Lane Theatre. He, as the manager, must be pestered again and again by girls as crazy as you.'

'How dull of me not to have thought of it! Thank you very much for the suggestion.'

'Shelley!' Mary cried, looking up from her paper.

'I was only joking,' he laughed, 'and Claire knows it.'

'I wasn't protesting, if that's what you mean. There's a notice here of your grandfather's death. He died two days ago.'

Shelley snatched the paper from her. 'I can't believe it! Why wasn't I told he was ill? Why have I been left to read the news in a public paper? Poor old man, I should have liked to see him again before he died.'

'Let's not be hypocrites,' Claire said brightly. 'Let's remember what it means to you, and rejoice.'

'What it means to me? It means, of course, that never again shall I need to go into hiding!'

2

'He's still out there,' a voice whispered hoarsely.

Shelley looked up from his book and the front door of Field Place closed sharply. Shrugging, he resumed his reading of Milton's *Comus*. Sooner or later his father would be obliged to admit him. Not for ever could the black sheep of the family be left sitting on the steps of the new baronet's country mansion.

Determined to be present at the reading of his grandfather's will, Shelley had journeyed in haste to the near-by village of Slinfold, where he had prudently left Claire, his excited and eager travelling companion. On reaching Field Place he had learnt that the will was indeed about to be read, but he had also learnt that his father had given orders that he was not to be admitted.

The door opened again and a servant, a stranger to Shelley, approached nervously.

'Well, what is it this time?' Shelley asked amiably.

'I'm sorry, sir,' the man stammered, 'but Sir Timothy says unless you take yourself off he'll be forced to swear in some special constables.'

Shelley roared with laughter. 'Special constables notwithstanding, tell the old gentleman that I'm determined to see him and will sit here till doomsday if he doesn't admit me.'

Comus held his attention for another ten minutes, upon which the door opened slowly and the family doctor, old, fat and quivering with agitation, crept cautiously out.

'Your father is very angry with you,' he ventured.

'I can scarcely remember a time when he was anything else.'

'Angry with you myself. Just look at you, sitting in the cold. No overcoat and shirt open at the neck. Disgraceful!'

'Are you concerned about my health, or my improper mode of dressing?'

'One and the same thing, young feller. D'you want to kill yourself?'

'If I expire here from cold and hunger Father will have only himself to blame. Tell him that.'

'He won't see you, no matter what I tell him, and that's the truth.'

After the best part of an hour, during which time Shelley had contined to read Milton with growing admiration, the door swung open once again, and this time it was William Whitton, Sir Timothy's attorney, who appeared.

'I feel like Horatius,' Shelley greeted him gaily.

'God bless my soul, why Horatius?'

'A severe stretching of the imagination, I admit. *He* held a bridge; all *I*'m doing is holding the front door of Field Place, not against the Etruscan army, but sorrowing relations who must be growing tired of waiting to escape. Surely you finished reading the will ages ago?'

'I did,' Whitton said testily.

'Is the old gentleman satisfied with its contents?'

'Scarcely, since they present him with a number of difficulties.'

'I being the cause of the difficulties?'

'Indubitably.'

'That,' said Shelley brightly, 'is a word I never use, but I rather like the way it trips off your tongue. Is my father prepared to see me now?'

'Sir Timothy will never see you.'

'I'm still prepared to wait till doomsday.'

'Be sensible, young man,' Whitton begged. 'Sir Timothy—'

'Does he like the sound of it?'

'The sound of *what*?'

'The title, of course.'

'Enough of this nonsense,' Whitton said fussily. 'Your father slipped out of the house half-an-hour ago and is now well on his way to London. In so far as the affairs of the estate are concerned, you must deal with me or nobody. Nevertheless, I am not prepared to negotiate with you now. If you will be so good as to meet me in London tomorrow, the offer I am empowered to make you shall be discussed then.'

'That sounds as if a certain amount of bargaining lies before us.'

'For want of a more dignified word, yes.'

'The law is nothing if not dignified.'

'Confound your impudence, young man!'

Shelley rose and stretched his cramped limbs. He felt cold and hungry. What he needed most was exercise. If he ran all the way to the inn at Slinford, then ate a good meal, he would feel in better shape.

'I deny impudence,' he said, 'but I do admit a temporary defeat.' He turned and began to run. 'Tomorrow, in London.'

3

'Too many details will only bore you,' Shelley told Mary, after many days of 'bargaining' with Whitton. 'The position, in brief, is this. According to the terms of the will I am offered the income from one hundred thousand pounds, providing I agree to entail the whole estate.'

'Have you agreed, Shelley?'

'Tell me first if you would want me to agree.'

Mary shook her head. 'I know how you feel about entail.'

'Darling, I love you more than ever. But think for a moment what a large income I have refused.'

'So large an income might have a corrupting influence on us.'

'It might,' Shelley admitted, 'though one would have to submit to the tyranny of so much money to find out.'

'You don't propose to take the risk.'

'Indeed I don't. We shall know one way or the other when the settled estates, which cannot be taken from me, come to me at my father's death. As far as the question of complete entail goes, the terms of the will allow me a year in which to make up my mind.'

'And meanwhile our position is unchanged?'

'Does that worry you?'

Mary laughed wryly. 'I should like to be free of debts. It doesn't amuse me to think that you might have to go into hiding again. It would be nice if you had an income sufficient for our needs.'

'Would a thousand a year be sufficient?'

'More than sufficient!'

'The income we can actually count on will be eight hundred. You see, out of the thousand I feel bound to pay Harriet two hundred. With that and the two hundred her father still allows her she will be in comfortable circumstances. I have, in fact, instructed my banker to make that payment and an immediate two hundred to cover her debts.'

'But the thousand—?'

'This, darling, is how the agreement was reached. I decided to offer to sell my father the reversion of some of the settled estates, then I discovered that he was anxious himself to propose such an agreement. Naturally, I pretended, being really cunning for once, not to be interested. Thus I gained a stronger bargaining position. The result is gratifying. My debts, which amount to perhaps five thousand pounds, are to be settled and I am to receive a thousand a year. We really must celebrate. I shall slip out at once and buy a bottle of champagne.

'And Mary,' he said, turning at the door, 'how would you like to go abroad again?'

'In my condition?' she laughed.

'Darling, what a thoughtless idiot I am!'

'If your heart is really set on it—'

'No, I can wait, but we shall leave for Geneva as soon as convenient.'

'And do you think,' Mary asked teasingly, 'that at Geneva you will be happy for the rest of your life?'

Shelley shook his head and laughed. 'Never again will I say that in this place or that I'll be happy for the rest of my life. And do you know why?'

'I couldn't even guess.'

'Darling Mary, for the simple reason that I am happy anywhere if you are with me.'

Seventeen

Hotel de l'Angleterre
Geneva
May 15, 1816

My dear Hogg,

I find it hard to believe that a period of fifteen months separates the day I decided to come to Geneva from the actual day of my arrival here. But in Geneva we are at last, and in this clear, clean air (such a heady feeling it gives me!) the things that delayed me seem of little importance now. What indeed were they? I shall strain my memory in an effort to list them.

To begin with, there was the first baby. Poor little mite, the hopes we placed in her, even though we knew that born so prematurely she had no chance of surviving. Then there was Bonaparte's escape from Elba and his invasion of France, happily unsuccessful. From a personal point of view, however, the delay caused by the Court of Chancery was more irritating than that caused by Bonaparte's last campaign. Just when I thought everything neatly arranged I learnt that I could sell only a small part of the settled estates to my father. Fortunately the income from that is sufficient to cover the thousand a year annuity, but insufficient (unfortunately) to cope with all my debts. Some have been paid, others have yet to be paid. Negotiations are still going on between my father's attorney and mine, and meanwhile I am happy to be living in a country where one can live more cheaply than in England. You can scarcely blame me if I have failed to make my financial position entirely clear. It isn't entirely clear to me either.

Finally, there was the second baby, our darling William, who, by the way, is 15 weeks 5 days old today. Pray don't exclaim that Shelley has of a sudden become a mathematician; I was obliged to ask Mary before telling you, and she in her turn was obliged to ask Claire who, having counted laboriously on her fingers, succeeded in arriving at the exact number of weeks and days.

This hotel is beautifully situated in a suburb called Sêcheron. From our windows we look out across the waters of the lake, which today is a mass of countless diamonds sparkling in the sunshine. Mary is entranced, particularly with the distant view of Mont Blanc, but Claire remains unmoved. More than ordinarily anxious to come with us, she is now, on arrival, behaving very oddly. In high spirits and wellnigh hysterical one moment, she is subdued and plunged into the depths of gloom the next. Were she not so young I would suspect her of suffering from the first stage of the change of life!

May 25, 1816

I left this letter unfinished ten days ago and have now decided to make it more a diary than a letter, and will dispatch it to you only when it is of sufficient length actually to resemble a diary.

The Claire Clairmont mystery is solved! Claire is in love, not with a mere mortal, as she herself exclaimed, but a beautiful young god. When she added that he was also a poet I thought for one horrible moment that she meant me! But no, she is in love with none other than Byron. The truth came out when his lordship arrived unexpectedly this afternoon. Judge for yourself my shocked amazement when Claire threw herself into his arms. Hurriedly, and full of apologies, I tried to tear her from him, but to my further amazement I perceived that Byron was embracing her as heartily as she was embracing him. A crowd gathered instantly and an English visitor, exclaiming that it was scandalous behaviour, informed the landlord that he would seek lodgings elsewhere.

I began to feel that perhaps there was something scandalous about it, but when Claire later explained that she and Byron were not actually meeting for the first time, I grew more tolerant. Byron in any case is travelling without his wife and appears to be separated from her. Claire said proudly that she was the cause of the estrangement, but Byron told me privately that Claire, as usual, was permitting her imagination to run riot.

'As usual, my lord?' I asked politely.

'I first experienced her flights of imagination many months ago,' he said.

'And I, her guardian, knew nothing about it!' I gasped.

'Which suggests, my dear Shelley,' he laughed, 'that you are an extremely poor guardian.'

'My dear Lord Byron—!' I protested.

'And,' he added, with that coarse yet peculiarly attractive chuckle of his, 'a very poor judge of female beauty.'

'I am well aware,' I said stiffly, 'that Claire is a beautiful young woman.'

'Are you made of ice, then?' he asked.

'Ice, my Lord?'

'According to Claire you spurned her, made her life a misery, all but broke her heart.'

However, before I could fully comprehend the unjustness of this statement, Byron dismissed Claire from his mind, told me that he had been much moved by Queen Mab *and was anxious to read more of my work. We became firm friends instantly, and during a drive in his travelling-coach we talked our heads off about Godwin's* Political Justice. *The coach, by the way, is a monstrous thing of luxury. It contains a bed large enough for two people, a small library, and a sort of tiny sideboard complete with a full dinner service. He had it built at a cost of £500. He is, of course, as mad as the winds, and even though I like him he fills me with a certain indefinable disappointment. One should never meet one's heroes, but should remain afar to worship.*

May 26, 1816

Claire was absent from her room last night. It was obvious that she had undressed, for her clothing was scattered about the floor. I was on the point of rousing the hotel and leading a search-party when Mary, wiser than I, restrained me.

'She might have come to some harm,' I protested.

'Dear Shelley,' Mary said, 'any harm she might have come to is her own concern. It all began some months ago.'

'Byron?' I asked.

'Byron, who else?'

'Is she with him now?'

'I should imagine so.'

Mary then told me the full story, for Claire had confided in her yesterday. If anyone is to blame, I am, for it was I who jokingly suggested that Claire should seek out Byron at Drury Lane Theatre. This she did, on the pretext of wanting to become an actress. She even told him, confound her, that I had insisted on her taking up a stage career in order to prevent us all from starving. Whether by this or some other means, she quickly won his sympathy, his admiration and, if love it can be called, his love. She became his mistress. They met secretly. She was aware some weeks ago that he proposed to leave England for Switzerland, hence her own urgent desire to accompany us to Geneva. Mary fears that Byron's interest in Claire is but a passing one, yet we both hope that the love of this pure and beautiful girl will bring about the moral regeneration of a man stigmatized by the world as the personification of evil.

> Campagne Mont Alègre
> Coligny
> June 5, 1816

You will note the new address. Campagne Mont Alègre, grand as it sounds, is merely the name of a humble cottage near Coligny, a distance of perhaps two miles from Geneva. We moved here for economy's sake and hope to remain for several months, if the lawyers in London will leave us in peace and not insist on our returning. Five or six minutes' walk from here is the Villa Diodati, which Byron has rented. When he takes possession on the 10th we shall do much boating together, for that is one joy we have in common. We have already decided to sail completely round the lake, Mary not being very happy about it because of a dream or vision she once had. I reminded her that I had promised not to sail alone, and with that she is resting content.

The Campagne Mont Alègre has a small garden which runs down to the edge of the lake. We miss the view of Mont Blanc, for we are on the southern shore, but we can see the Jura mountains to the north, a magnificent sight at all times. I sometimes wish I were a painter, able to capture on canvas what I fail to capture fully in words.

Claire is immensely happy and no longer the somewhat silly girl she used to be. Byron shows her every consideration and appears to be in love with her. He finds it irksome, by the way, that wherever he goes in Geneva little groups of English tourists should gather to gape at him.

Mary and I are well, and busy with our reading. She intends to write a novel and I a lyrical drama in four acts. Young William is blooming and happy. He has the bluest of blue eyes. If I could have my other children with me I'd count myself the most fortunate man on earth.

> July 1, 1816

Byron and I are newly returned from circumnavigating the lake, an expedition which lasted for nine joyous days. We sailed in our own boat, for we have bought one between us. Our companions were two boatmen and one of Byron's servants, an indispensable valet. Claire wanted to come and on being forbidden sulked to such an extent that she refused to wish us god-speed.

I need only report one exciting incident – a hurricane! I felt in no danger whatever until one of the boatmen did a stupid thing. We were scudding in a south-easterly direction with only one sail set and he persisted in holding it when the boat was on the point of being driven under water. A mighty shout from Byron acquainted him with his mistake, he let the sail go and the boat refused to obey the helm. (Is my nautical language confusing to you, Hogg?) The rudder was now so damaged as to render its management difficult. One wave fell in upon us, then another and another. I thought then of Mary's vision, but took comfort from the fact that I was not alone. Byron, an excellent swimmer, calmly took off his coat. I did the same, but not so calmly. Byron's valet screamed that the end had come, and it did indeed seem more than possible. Expecting every moment to be swamped, we sat with our arms crossed, a ridiculous picture of British stoicism. (No, I mean phlegmaticism, if there is such a word.) I must admit that terror touched me as we waited, and in one single moment many incidents of my early life flashed through my mind. Is it true, I wonder, that when a man is drowning the past becomes rapidly and starkly clear to him? However, I was not drowning, and a few minutes later, the sail being held again and the boat obeying the helm, we reached the shelter of the little port at St. Gingoux.

'*Now you have really lived,*' Byron commented.

'*More important,*' I said faintly, '*I am still alive.*'

Both Mary and Claire wept when we told them about this little adventure, and Claire, sulking no more, threw herself into Byron's arms.

July 19, 1816

*I have had a long talk with Claire. She told me soberly that she had at last learnt the difference between looseness of morals and sexual freedom. She begged me to believe that there is nothing licentious about her. Quoting some words of my own, she said: '*I believe only this, that a man or a woman should be free to find love without bigotry, and finding it, live nobly and freely*'. She added, with tears in her eyes, that she had in Byron found the one true love of her life.*

'*I am proud and happy to be able to tell you,*' she concluded, '*that I am now with child by him.*'

And what of Byron himself?

I have had a long talk with him also. Somewhat diffident at first, I began by introducing the new gossip which is being circulated in London, and which has brought more tourists than ever to gape at him. It is being said, as no doubt you are aware, that he drives forth every night with a new girl, seduces her, throws her from the coach and leaves her, either to walk home in sorrow to her parents or throw herself into the lake.

'In sorrow?' *he asked, with a chuckle.*

'Do be serious, Byron,' *I begged.*

'Do you actually believe the gossip?' *he asked.*

'Of course not,' *I said warmly,* 'but I thought it possible that you might have two or three mistresses tucked discreetly away in and about Geneva.'

He shook his head. 'It grieves me to disappoint you, Shelley, but for months now I have had only one mistress.'

'Claire?'

'Who else?'

'Her love and devotion are very touching,' *I murmured.*

'I'm well aware of that,' *he said sharply.*

'So you are not in love with her.'

He gave this only a moment's thought. 'She forced herself upon me at Drury Lane. I did everything possible to discourage her. I failed, and failing found her naïveté extraordinarily appealing, and her attempts, shall we say, to unphilosophize me, amusing. She was so adept that I found it hard to believe that she had come to me, as indeed she had, a virgin. I – and this was a shattering novelty – found myself well and truly seduced. But am I in love with her? No, Shelley, I am not. I doubt if I have any love left for any woman.'

'But some little kindness, Byron?'

'That,' *he said gently,* 'is another matter.'

Our talk then turned to other things and I was left to hope that when the break comes, as come eventually it must, Claire will have the fortitude to face the situation with a brave heart. I curse myself, nonetheless, for my capricious suggestion that she should seek out Byron at Drury Lane.

Aug. 4, 1816

Today is my birthday, my 24th, Mary tells me. She herself will be 19 at the end of the month. Old age is creeping upon us, my dear Hogg, and with it, as far as I myself am concerned, a longing to see my birthplace again. Amazing that I, who truly aim at internationalism, should in this foreign land find tears in my eyes at the thought of the rolling downs of Sussex. To be practical, however, my attorney is pressing me to return, for the legal difficulties in connexion with the Shelley estates are mounting daily. Claire is desolated at the thought of parting from Byron, but Byron assures her (sincerely, I hope) that a short separation will be good for both of them.

We propose to leave towards the end of the month, and travel home by way of Dijon, Versailles, Rouen and Havre.

Till we meet again,
Ever your friend,
P.B.S.

P.S.: Mary is much engrossed with her novel. She conceived the idea after listening to Byron and me discussing galvanism, reanimation of dead bodies and the creation, by some scientific means or other, of life. She began it as a short story, but is now going to make a real novel of it. The title is Frankenstein.

Eighteen

I

Eliza Westbrook laughed harshly. 'Of course Harriet is in debt, and much more deeply than ever before. I saw to that myself.'

'But why?' Shelley asked in surprise. 'You were always so careful in money matters.'

'Are you not responsible for your wife's debts? I know something of your financial position. The harder I can make things for you the better. I would ruin you completely, if possible.'

Shelley looked at her sadly. Her face was pale and drawn. He had heard that she had suffered a severe attack of smallpox, and this was evident from the marks on her brow and cheeks. She looked ugly now, positively ugly, not because of the pockmarks but because of the hatred that gleamed in her still magnificent eyes.

'Did you invite me to come to Chapel Street in order to tell me that you wanted to ruin me?' he asked.

'That was one reason.'

Shelley had been back in England since September, and it was now late November. Arriving at Portsmouth, he had taken his little family, as he called Mary, Claire, the baby William, and a Swiss nurse, to Bath, Mary having judged it necessary, since Claire's condition was beginning to show, to keep well away from London. Having found temporary lodgings in Bath he had come on to London alone, and since then had been moving constantly between London and Bath. Negotiations between his own attorney on the one hand, his father's on the other, had at last shown him that, while the thousand pounds a year would be his for life, there was little possibility of acquiring additional lump sum payments. Depressed by this, for there were other debts as well as Harriet's to be settled, he had been on the point of rejoining Mary when Eliza's letter reached him.

'I should like to see Harriet,' he ventured.

'Harriet is away,' Eliza said shortly.

'Has she taken the children with her?'

'The children are here.'

'Then let me see them.'

'I don't mean here in the house. I sent them out with their nurse.'

'I can't believe that Harriet would go away without them. Why are you lying to me, Eliza?'

'I'm not lying!' Eliza cried angrily.

'Then give me Harriet's address.'

'I don't know it, Bysshe.'

Shelley saw then that Eliza was shaking with something more than anger. Her eyes had a distracted look and her face was twitching horribly. She tried to control herself and, partly succeeding, spoke again.

'Harriet went away without telling either me or Papa where she was going. She had been behaving queerly for months. She went away often, and alone, for several days at a time, but she always left an address. This time she slipped away without warning and we've neither heard from her nor seen her since. I was so worried that I felt compelled in the end to apply to you for help.'

'Did you drive her away, you and your father between you?' Shelley asked angrily.

'How unjust you are! You know how much I love her.'

'Have you made any efforts at all to find her?'

'Naturally I have. I wrote to all her friends, those with whom she was supposed to have stayed from time to time, but—'

'*Supposed?*'

'She had stayed with none of them. Captain Ryan, to whom I first appealed for help, was good enough to go to the various addresses, just to make absolutely sure, but the result was the same.'

'Ryan,' Shelley said, in disgust.

'He is just as anxious as I am to find Harriet.'

'Has he made any other inquiries?'

'Indeed he has, but not even a trace of her has he been able to find.'

'You said Harriet had been behaving queerly for months. What did you mean by "queerly"?'

'She would laugh as if at nothing at all, sometimes excitedly, sometimes quite hysterically. When questioned she either smiled secretively or burst into tears. We assumed that *you* were the cause of it, and for all we know you were. Be that as it may, Harriet must be found. You understand, Bysshe, she *must be found*. I'm nearly out of my mind with worry.'

'I'll do anything I can,' Shelley promised, deeply worried himself now. 'I'll begin by having a talk with Ryan. Please tell me where I can find him.'

'The Captain is spending a few days in Bath. I'll get his address for you.'

'Splendid! I shall be back in Bath myself tomorrow.'

2

Shelley reached Bath in the late afternoon. He had intended seeking out Captain Ryan immediately, but decided now that he must see Mary first and discuss with her the mystery of Harriet's disappearance. On arriving at the lodgings, which were situated above a circulating library at No. 5, Abbey Churchyard, he found no one at home but Claire, who burst into tears at the sight of him.

'I've been weeping all day,' she told him mournfully. 'That was why they went out. To find a little peace, Mary said. I thought it most unkind.'

Shelley looked at her helplessly.

'Mary was angry with me, of course.'

'Continual weeping does get on one's nerves,' he suggested.

'I expect you'll be angry with me too, when she tells you.'

'When she tells me – what?'

'I opened a letter of yours. It was from Byron. I recognized the writing. I know it was a dreadful thing to do, but I couldn't help myself.'

'You've done that sort of thing before and not thought it dreadful,' Shelley reminded her.

'Byron promised to write to me,' she went on, ignoring this, 'but has he? You know very well he hasn't. He promised to come back to England, but seems to have forgotten that, too. I had to know what he said in the letter, I *had* to, Shelley.'

'And what did he say?'

'Nothing of any consequence, and no mention whatever of me. I – I wish it were possible to hate him, but it isn't.'

Shelley reflected that though he had written several times to Byron, giving him news of Claire, Byron in his own infrequent letters had ignored her completely. And apart from this he had said in an earlier letter that he had no intention whatever of returning to England.

'Byron has abandoned me,' Claire burst out. 'I think I do hate him now.'

Shelley racked his brains for something else to say.

'Claire, you quarrelled with him just before we left Geneva. Neither you nor he told me what the quarrel was about, so for all I know that might be the reason for this seeming neglect.'

'We quarrelled about my baby.'

'Did he deny being the father?'

Claire fought back her tears. 'It was the baby's future we quarrelled about. He said he wanted it to be brought up by his sister. Can you imagine anything more callous? I know I can't be with Byron all the time, but I want to keep my baby.'

'And so you shall. Byron can't take it from you by force.'

'Byron can do anything, anything!'

'Did you reach an agreement in the end?'

Claire smiled wanly. 'Yes, after I had quite worn him down with my tears. He promised that the baby should remain either with me or with him until the age of seven.' She paused. 'Shelley, how soon can we go back to the Continent?'

'You expect the baby in January. I don't think it would be wise to travel before then. March would be a good month, so March it is.'

'You don't mean it!' Claire gasped.

Shelley smiled wryly. 'I'm a queer fellow. When I'm abroad I long to be in England, and when I'm in England I long to be abroad.'

'March is a promise?'

'A promise, Claire, and a solemn one.'

3

Captain Ryan looked at Shelley with distaste. 'If I knew where your wife was I'd tell you at once. To accuse me of hiding her from the world is ridiculous.'

Shelley looked at Ryan with equal distaste. He had forgotten that the man's eyes were so close together and the bridge of his nose so thin, but what really aroused his contempt was the fanciness of his dress. Looking more preposterous than Brummell had ever looked, and possessing none of Brummell's gracefulness, he wore a sky-blue coat, a pink waistcoat, light grey trousers and dark scarlet shoes.

'Tell me when you last saw Harriet,' Shelley demanded.

'Control your temper, Shelley, or I'll throw you out,' Ryan said curtly. 'I'm a great deal more upset than you at Harriet's disappearance. Please understand that I love her and want to find her.' Lifting Shelley from his feet he thrust him roughly into a chair. 'I have seen Harriet twice only in recent weeks, and that is the truth. The first time was at Chapel Street just before she disappeared.'

'And the second?'

'I'm coming to that. The Chapel Street meeting was a brief one, with her sister and her father present, for by then Harriet had ceased to show any interest in me. Believe me or disbelieve me, as you please, but her indifference grieved me deeply.'

'You sound sincere,' Shelley admitted gruffly.

'I fell in love with Harriet when I first met her at Windsor.'

'Did she return your love?'

'Not until after the birth of your son. It was then that we became lovers. We met secretly, and later, still secretly, we fell into the habit of spending a few days together, often here in Bath.'

'A hole and corner business!'

'That was Harriet's wish, not mine. I wanted her to live openly with me but she refused. I noticed nothing at the time, I was far too besotted for that, but looking back I think I can say that she appeared to be waiting for something better.'

Knowing that he was behaving badly, but unable to help himself, Shelley murmured with a sneer that she was surely not compelled to wait too long. And having delivered himself of this he made a quick apology.

'Better in the sense of rank and money,' Ryan went on gloomily. 'She met through me a titled gentleman whose name I need not give you. She was attracted to him chiefly because he is one of the Prince Regent's friends. I know this, for I talked to him as soon as I began my search. He amused himself with her for a short time, then threw her over. He said he found her both too tedious and too demanding. She went to his house several times, but was always forbidden entry.'

'Poor little Harriet.'

'After that I begged her to go abroad with me, but she only laughed, and scornfully at that.'

'And then she disappeared.'

'Not immediately.'

'Could she have gone abroad with somebody else?'

Ryan shook his head. 'No, Shelley. You see, I did succeed in tracing her, but in order not to hurt the Westbrooks I refrained from telling them.'

'Then you know where she is, after all!'

Ryan shook his head again. 'I only wish I did. What happened was that I saw her by accident. She was riding in a hackney carriage with a soldier, a lieutenant. I followed them to a house near Knightsbridge Barracks. They entered the house, a dingy place where single rooms are let. I waited for two hours, then the lieutenant came out alone. I regret now that I didn't ask him his name, but I was too anxious to see Harriet. I found her much changed. She was despondent, yet defiant. She said she was enjoying the mode of life she had adopted, then contradicted herself by saying she loathed it but found it impossible to change. I tried to reason with her, and weeping a little she appeared to be impressed with what I said. To my joy she gave me a half-promise, saying that if I called again that evening she would tell me whether she had made up her mind to return home or remain on the town.'

'On the town!' Shelley exclaimed.

'The words were her own. I see now my mistake in leaving her, for when I returned she had gone. The landlady had been paid her rent in full and thought that Miss Smith, for that was the name Harriet had given her, had said something about moving to Bath. That, Shelley, is why I am here now. You may join me in my search if you wish, but I am beginning to fear that her mention of Bath was only a ruse.'

Shelley rose shakily. Why had Harriet chosen that sort of life, he asked himself, *why*? She was not in want. She had £400 a year, and when her father died she would inherit a half-share of an estate worth £60,000. He remembered Ryan's words. Harriet had appeared to be waiting for something better. Yet, not having waited very long, she had accepted something worse.

'Am I to blame for what Harriet has become?' he asked pathetically.

'Eliza Westbrook would say you are, certainly.'

'Eliza caused much trouble, told many lies.'

'So I believe.'

'How can you possibly know that?'

'Harriet told me when I last saw her three days ago. She said she no longer believed the things Eliza had said about you. She had had time to think, to remember you as you really were.'

'Thank you for telling me,' Shelley said emotionally.

'She also said that it didn't much matter, it was too late now. She said something else that might make you feel a little easier in your mind.'

'And that?'

'She had discovered, she said, a sad little philosophy of her own. However much people may be provoked by others they only have themselves to blame for allowing things to happen to them. Then she quoted some poetry. I'm not much of a hand at reciting, but it went like this:

> Virtue, how frail it is!
> Friendship how rare!
> Love, how it sells poor bliss
> For proud despair.'

'For proud despair,' Shelley repeated.

'She said they were your lines.'

'Yes. Part of a poem I failed to complete.'

Self-conscious now, Captain Ryan led Shelley to the door, asked for his address and promised to communicate with him at once when or if he had more news.

'Thank you,' Shelley said dully, 'thank you . . .'

4

Sensing that something was amiss, Mary looked up from the shawl she was knitting for Claire's baby. Shelley, with the letter clutched tensely in his hands, was staring fixedly at the fire. More than two weeks had passed since his talk with Captain Ryan, and a few days ago, in desperation, he had written to Hookham, asking the publisher if he had heard anything at all of Harriet. He had done this because Harriet had sometimes communicated with him through Hookham, and now Hookham had replied.

'Shelley . . .' Mary said anxiously.

He thrust the letter into her hand. 'Read it for yourself.'

The letter, dated 13 December, had been written two days ago. The writer, addressing Shelley formally as 'My dear Sir', said that he had experienced some difficulty in obtaining information about Mrs. Shelley. To read Harriet thus described gave Mary a twinge of resentment, and angry with herself she read on rapidly.

While I was yet endeavouring to discover her address, news was brought to me that she was dead – that she had destroyed herself. You will believe that I did not credit the report. I called at the house of a friend of Mr. Westbrook; my doubt led to conviction. I was informed that she was taken from the Serpentine on Tuesday last, apparently in a state of pregnancy. Little or no information was laid before the jury which sat on the body, and the verdict was 'found drowned'.

'Oh, Shelley, what a dreadful thing to have happened.'

'Ryan said nothing about Harriet being pregnant.'

'He might not have known.'

'He *must* have known!'

'I think Harriet would only have told him had she been certain he was responsible.'

'Of course, there were others. Why are we talking like this, Mary, *why*?'

'Perhaps because we are afraid to contemplate the real issue.'

'The suicide itself, yes.'

'And being afraid, fail to look at it squarely.'

'*Squarely?*'

'You blame yourself, I know, but Shelley, try and believe, as I do, that Harriet took her life because she was afraid of her condition being discovered.'

'Society, how I loathe it!' Shelley burst out.

That was better, Mary thought. The angrier he grew the easier it would be for him.

'Remember her upbringing,' she said carefully. 'She must have found herself in a position from which she could see only one means of escape.'

'Society again!' Shelley raged. 'Why in heaven's name did she not turn to us? We would have helped her and sheltered her, as we are now helping and sheltering Claire.'

Mary wondered about this. Shelley, yes, but what of herself? I, she thought, the mistress, and at times a jealous one, being asked to give shelter to the legal wife, and she with child by another man, known or unknown. She was glad that she had not been forced to submit to so rigorous a test, for, inspiring as Shelley's noble simplicity might be, she was coming to regard it as entirely unreal, something not of this world.

'I think it likely,' she said quietly, 'that Harriet believed she was acting honourably. Rather than foist the baby on Ryan, or have it born legally a Shelley, she did what she did.'

This reminded Shelley of the children, Ianthe and Charles.

'I asked Hookham to inquire about the children,' he said. 'Does he make any reference to them in his letter?'

Mary glanced at it again. 'He says they are well and apparently in Eliza's keeping.'

'By God, Eliza! We can't have that! You agree, I'm sure, that they must be taken from her at once.'

'Yes, Shelley, I agree.'

'You really are willing to accept them into our own household?'

'Oh, darling, of course, and happily.'

'It won't make any difference, their not being yours?'

'Dear Shelley, are they not yours, and being motherless now, mine also?'

5

Shelley hesitated for a moment at the front door of the Westbrook house in Chapel Street. Before leaving Bath, Mary had warned him that the Westbrooks might prove difficult to deal with, and begging him to keep his temper under control had advised him to move with the utmost caution. That was all very well, he thought, but it was cunning that was called for, not caution. He saw then that the door was slightly open and decided to enter unannounced. Pausing in the hall and listening intently, he heard a low murmur of voices in the front parlour and then, surprisingly enough, a giggle, which was followed by complete silence. Lingering, he waited until the murmur of voices rose again. One was a man's, the other Eliza's. It occurred to him then that there was nothing to prevent him from creeping upstairs to the nursery. A post-chaise was waiting farther along Chapel Street and in it a nurse whom he had engaged for the journey back to Bath. Ianthe and Charles might scream in alarm, but that was something he would have to risk.

He reached the nursery on tiptoe, opened the door silently and found the room empty. Agitated now, he went hurriedly from room to room and even ran up the narrow attic stairs. The house, except for the occupants of the front parlour, seemed to be deserted. Returning disconsolately to the hall downstairs, he came upon Eliza, but she neither saw nor heard him, for she was clasped firmly in the arms of a man who looked considerably younger than herself.

'Good lord!' he exclaimed.

Eliza and the man sprang apart.

A most touching sight,' Shelley added mildly. 'Young love always is.'

Eliza was the first to recover at least a little composure.

'My brother-in-law,' she said, with a formality that rang idiotically in Shelley's ears. 'Bysshe, this is Mr. Farthing Beauchamp.'

'What an extraordinary name.'

'Extraordinary or not,' Mr. Beauchamp tittered, 'Eliza is soon to accept it as her own.'

'She is? How splendid! I can only hope that you have considerably more than a farthing to your name.'

'Mr. Beauchamp is heir to a large fortune,' Eliza all but simpered.

'As are you, my love,' Mr. Beauchamp added.

'Yes, we are very fortunate.'

Shelley looked at Eliza indignantly. Harriet was dead. She had drowned herself. The inquest had been held four days ago. Her attitude now was callous as well as crazy.

'How did you get in here?' Eliza demanded.

'The door was open.'

'A fortuitous meeting,' Mr. Beauchamp said pompously. 'Come, Shelley, I want a word with you in private.'

Grimly, but recovering some of his old spirit, Shelley took him by the shoulders and hustled him to the door.

'Be warned, my good man,' he said hoarsely, 'this woman is a notorious vampire.'

Eliza tried to intervene, but a moment later Mr. Farthing Beauchamp was out in the street, and Shelley, slamming the door, had locked it.

'High-handed as ever!' Eliza screamed.

Shelley turned to face her. 'What could that microbe possibly have to say to me in private?'

'Microbe! He's a very good-looking man.'

'Round-shouldered and short-sighted, I saw that at a glance.'

'Poor boy, he spent many years bending over a desk.'

'Really.'

'He used to be a bank clerk.'

'Then why not penny, or crown, or even guinea?'

'What on earth are you talking about?'

Shelley sighed wearily. 'Since this situation is crazy, if nothing else, I'm talking nonsense. Nonsense is probably more acceptable to both of us than reality. You did say Mr. *Farthing* Beauchamp was a bank clerk, didn't you?'

'He also has considerable knowledge of something more important than banking.'

'And that?'

'The law. That was why I empowered him to speak to you on my behalf. We agreed, he and I, that it would be too humiliating for me to have to deal with you myself. I can't tell you how splendid it is, having a man to protect me. And the children too, of course.'

Shelley began to understand her at last. 'By heaven, Eliza—!'

'You came for the children, didn't you?'

'Of course I did.'

'We expected it, of course, and sent them for the time being to the country. I and my future husband propose to give them a home. Already their father is no more than a name to them, and soon they will forget their mother. Nor will they ever know that she took her own life. If you care to study the details of the inquest – it was reported in *The Times* – you will find that it was held on the body of a young woman by the name of Harriet Smith.'

'Where is Harriet Smith buried?'

'I have no intention of telling you. Why, in any case, should you or I be interested in a person of that name? Harriet Shelley, who was once Harriet Westbrook, died of natural causes, *of natural causes*, Bysshe.'

'Your insistence suggests that you have much with which to reproach yourself.'

Eliza held Shelley's eyes for a moment, then looked quickly away.

'Self-reproach would only be possible,' she said woodenly, 'if I did nothing to protect the children from scandal and gossip.'

'Eliza,' Shelley said quietly, 'I want you to look at me again.'

She did so unwillingly. 'Well?'

'Are you trying to protect the children, or just you yourself? Yourself from yourself, I mean.'

Startled, Eliza tried to hold his eyes unwaveringly. His steady gaze all but compelled her to scream that she and no one else had brought about her sister's suicide.

'Bysshe,' she said quickly, 'I want you, too, to do all you can to protect them from scandal and gossip.'

'I give you my word that I'll never tell them the truth.'

'I don't mean that.'

'What else, then?'

'I have no intention of delivering the children into your care.'

'You have no right, moral or legal, for refusing to do so.'

'The legal right is the only right in question.'

'Are you forcing me to take the matter to court?'

'No, Bysshe, I am asking you, for their sake, not to do that. Go to court and you will cause more scandal, more gossip.'

'I think you are asking me for your sake, not theirs.'

'Very well, do your worst!' Eliza cried.

'No, Eliza,' Shelley said warmly, 'not my worst, my best.'

Nineteen

I

My dearest Mary,

I wrote to you yesterday – perhaps it was the day before – telling you about my frustrating talk with Eliza Westbrook. Such is my confusion that I cannot remember what else I told you. Did I, for instance, mention my visit to the Westbrook attorney? He suggested a compromise, Eliza to keep Ianthe, I to take Charles. I refused absolutely.

Earlier – and this I think I did mention – I had a long consultation with my own attorney. He resembled a war-horse scenting the smell of battle and expressed a lively interest. Nevertheless, he said we must proceed with the utmost caution and resoluteness. There are many ticklish aspects, yet he feels confident, should I decide to take the case to the Court of Chancery, that our position would be a stronger one if you and I were married. I told him instantly that I was under contract of marriage to you, and he said brightly that this would be soothing intelligence to you. Soothing indeed! Are you ill with a pain in your stomach, and am I about to apply a medicinal plaster?

It occurs to me now, Mary, that my impulsiveness may not be pleasing to you. For that reason I shall make this a short letter, dispatch it at once and thus give you time, before my return to Bath, for much serious thought. Knowing me as you do, knowing me indeed better than I know myself, you will understand that a contract, a legal tie, will make no difference whatever. I write this with a full heart, knowing that you have already blessed me with a whole world of real happiness.

Mary, I love you,

Shelley.

'Darling,' Mary laughed gently, 'you are talking pompously, really you are.'

'Pompously?' he ejaculated.

'Can you remember the last involved sentence you uttered?'

'Every word of it!'

'Repeat it, Shelley.'

'As you wish,' he said huffily. 'Er – It is through you, Mary, that I can entertain without despair the recollection of the horrors of unutterable villainy that led to this dark and dreadful situation, and – er – it is at least consoling—'

'It is, to say the least, consoling—'

'It is, to say the least, consoling to know that its termination in your nominal union with me, a mere form appertaining to you, will not be barren of good, nor—'

He broke of abruptly.

'You had every right to laugh at me,' he said dolefully.

'Dear Shelley, I wanted you to laugh at yourself.'

'Pomposity, I admit it. A result, you see, of having dealt so lengthily with lawyers.'

'Can you not laugh at least a little?'

'I have too much on my mind for that.'

'Oh dear, are you depressed at the thought of nominal union?'

'*Mary!* Have I not been trying to tell you how much you mean to me?'

'You told me in your letter, darling. You said, "Mary, I love you". Why, after that, was there any need for a jumble of words?'

'I – well – perhaps because I was nervous.'

Mary thought she understood now. 'Are you afraid I might not agree to – what was your phrase? – a mere form appertaining to me?'

'Well, yes,' Shelley admitted.

'Had it not occurred to you that I myself might be afraid that "a mere form" would be offensive to you also?'

'It would be, ordinarily, but I have a valid reason.'

Mary saw that she would have to be careful. 'Ah yes, a means of strengthening your case, if you decide to apply to the Court of Chancery.'

'A decision has been made already, not by me but by the Westbrooks. They had announced their intention of filing a Bill of Complaint.'

'In that case we must marry without delay.'

Shelley looked at her doubtfully. 'I'm still not sure that you want it.'

Mary remained silent for a few moments. To reproach him with the accusation of only wanting it himself because of the legal battle now looming up before him would not be wise. And to tell him that she had often dreamt of what, until Harriet's death, had seemed impossible, would be even more stupid. He might well accuse her then of having become a slave to convention. Better, she thought, to agree at once, yet how to convince him that her reason for wanting it had nothing to do with convention? Shelley, unlike the horse that could be led to water but not forced to drink, must be persuaded gently that he was drinking willingly of the waters of legal union. Happily, she remembered the letter which she had received that morning from her father.

'Darling, I have a valid reason of my own.'

'You have?' he asked eagerly.

Her father, though he still refused to see her, had written many times, and she had begun to suspect that, stubborn as he was, the continued separation pained him as much as it pained her.

'Would you despise me if I said I still loved my father?' she asked.

'But I love him myself, Mary. I respect him for what he once was, and I love him for the excellent reason that you are his daughter.'

Mary's eyes filled with tears. 'You can understand, then, how it would please me to end the long and senseless quarrel and be able to meet him freely again?'

'Of course I can.'

'I received a letter this morning. He suggested that with marriage now possible, marriage, if we were not too pigheaded to accept it, would put everything right.'

'Pigheaded indeed!'

'I see I have said the wrong thing.'

'Godwin said the wrong thing, not you.'

'No, the word was my own.'

'Really, Mary.'

'I seem to have said the wrong thing twice.'

'I was never pigheaded, never!'

'Then perhaps I have said the right thing twice.'

'Ah,' Shelley laughed, 'coercion, but of a subtle order! Make me angry, force me to say that I am not pigheaded when I know quite well that I am, and there you are!'

'Thank you for laughing, Shelley, and at yourself, too.'

He laughed again. 'A cunning little coercionist, this wife of mine. I'll go back to London and apply for a licence.'

Mary tried not to show the satisfaction she felt. 'If you are absolutely sure . . .'

'We have a valid reason, each of us. For the rest, did I not say that a legal tie would make no difference whatever?'

Mary sensed in this an uncertainty, a doubt, even a fear, which he was trying not to recognize.

'Shelley,' she said, 'do you remember why my mother wanted to marry my father, but only after a long period of legally free association with him?'

'I do indeed. She wanted to prove to herself and to him that not even legal marriage could destroy their happiness.'

'Then you understand what I am trying to say.'

'A test and a challenge, by heaven, yes!'

'So you see, apart from valid reasons which concern us separately, we have a reason that concerns us jointly.'

'The legal tie would have been necessary in any case, yes!'

Mary smiled at him fondly. His wholehearted enthusiasm filled her heart with joy, yet as she savoured it the dismaying thought came to her that her mother had not lived long enough to prove anything, either to herself or to her husband.

'Why are you frowning?' Shelley demanded.

Mary laughed as gaily as she could. 'Like all women when a wedding has been arranged, I was thinking about new clothes. I'd like at least a new hat. Can we afford it, Shelley?'

3

Mr. Longdill, Shelley's attorney, arrived at Skinner Street only to discover that Godwin's bookshop had been closed for the day. 'Tut, tut,' he said to himself, for it seemed to him that a bookshop which had been closed to the public would create in the minds of any would-be customers an unwelcome mystery.

Shelley himself answered his knock. 'Longdill, my dear fellow, what happened to you? I expected you at the church.'

'Come, come,' Mr. Longdill protested, 'you know quite well that I refused the invitation. A quiet wedding, that I insisted upon. And secrecy, that I also insisted upon. If we are to surprise the Westbrooks, who will surely claim that your association with Miss Godwin is both irregular and – hum – sinful, secrecy is absolutely essential. I – er – trust, my dear Shelley, that she is Miss Godwin no longer?'

'Mary Godwin is now Mary Shelley.'

It was now the afternoon of 30 December. Shelley and Mary, leaving William with Claire and the nurse, had come up to London on the 27th, and the next day, after an amicable talk with Godwin, Shelley, accompanied by his father-in-law to be, had gone to Doctors' Commons to obtain a marriage licence. The marriage itself had taken place that morning at St. Mildred's Church in the City of London.

'I do trust,' Mr. Longdill went on, 'that not too many people were present at the ceremony.'

'Four players only.'

'*Players*, my dear Shelley?'

'The principal actor and actress, supported by Mr. and Mrs. Godwin, each playing the minor part of witness.'

'Were any members of the public attracted to the scene?'

'Not to my knowledge.'

'No representatives of the newspapers?'

'I saw none.'

'Thank heaven you are not yet as notorious as Lord Byron.'

Laughing, Shelley led Mr. Longdill to the living quarters above the shop.

'As you see,' he said, pointing to the table in the small dining-room, 'what might be called a wedding breakfast has just been concluded. We have had much feasting, much drinking and even, heaven help us, a little speech-making. Would you care to make a speech yourself, Longdill?'

'Thank you, no,' that gentleman said, with dignity.

Mary, her father, and her stepmother were still seated at the table. Shelley's eyes lingered for a moment on Mrs. Godwin. Flushed, she had drunk a little too much champagne, and as a result her inevitable green spectacles were perched at a jaunty angle on her nose. Both she and her husband had been oozing satisfaction, as Shelley termed it, since the ceremony at the church, and she herself had made a speech punctuated at intervals by the formidable 'Furthermore', a speech in which, surprising everyone, she had referred to Shelley as her dear and long-cherished stepson-in-law.

At the sight of Longdill, Godwin rose and, his speech somewhat slurred, invited him to partake of what was left of the champagne. Longdill protested that never before had he touched strong drink in the middle of the afternoon, but graciously allowed himself to be persuaded that the strictest of rules could on such an occasion as this be broken with equanimity.

'I do trust, Mr. Godwin,' he said anxiously, 'that you have given out a convincing excuse for the closing of your shop on a Monday, of all days.'

'Convincing enough,' Godwin laughed. 'I told everybody that I was celebrating the completion of a novel.'

'I take it that that is not the exact truth, sir?'

'By a happy coincidence, it is.'

Mrs. Godwin, maudlin now, burst suddenly into tears.

'Oh come, my dear,' Godwin chided her, 'my novel is not as bad as that.'

'It's Claire I was thinking about,' she sobbed. 'Claire, my own poor daughter. I can't imagine why she isn't here, not with everything nice and tidy now and the past forgotten.'

Shelley glanced quickly at Mary. Claire had begged them to keep her secret, at least until the baby was born.

'She stayed at Bath to look after William,' Mary said soothingly. 'It was very kind of her.'

Accepting this, Mrs. Godwin rose, stumbled and clutched at her husband for support.

'Everything's going round and round. Put me to bed, Godwin, I'm feeling real poorly.'

Mr. Longdill watched disapprovingly while the Godwins went on uncertain feet from the room, then he looked at his champagne, which he had scarcely touched, and put the glass down firmly.

'I must hasten back to my chambers, Shelley. I called for a few moments only, my purpose being to tell you that Mr. John Westbrook, acting on behalf of your children, Ianthe and Charles, proposes to file a Bill of Complaint on the eighth day of January next. In short, nine days from now.'

'On behalf of my children?' Shelley echoed.

'They are the real complainants, but being minors . . .' Mr. Longdill's voice trailed away.

'How disgusting that words which they are incapable of uttering should be put into their mouths!' Shelley burst out.

'We must be prepared for something even more disgusting, the nature of the Bill itself. Knowing something of the Westbrook vindictiveness, I anticipate the raking of much unpleasant mud. Not, of course, that mud of that sort is ever – hum – pleasant.'

'You are anything but encouraging, Mr. Longdill,' Mary said faintly.

'It is my habit, Mrs. Shelley, to prepare for the worst and hope for the best. Once we have heard the Complaint we shall know how best to answer it. And remember, my dear, we have one valuable card up our sleeves. You and your husband are no longer living in – Dear me, forgive me, please! You and your husband are – well – *married*!'

Utterly confused now, scarcely knowing what he was doing, Mr. Longdill seized the glass he had placed so firmly on the table, raised it to his lips and drained it.

'Flat,' said Shelley, absently.

'I beg your pardon?'

'Not a bubble left in it.'

'Goodness gracious, does that mean it will have a bad effect on my digestive system?'

'Indeed it does, and if you drink any more somebody will have to put you to bed also.'

Mr. Longdill laughed archly. 'But not with Mrs. Godwin, heaven forbid!'

Upon which, shocked at his own words, he hurried from the room.

'Dear Shelley, what nonsense you talk when you're deeply disturbed,' Mary remarked, trying to laugh light-heartedly.

'Deeply disturbed, yes.'

'You care nothing for scandal, and nor do I.'

'Less than nothing, when I have right on my side.'

'Which you have, darling. Remember that, *which you have*!'

'How often do law and justice mean one and the same thing?'

Mary looked at him despairingly. 'Oh, Shelley—!'

He smiled wanly. 'I'm not a very cheerful bridegroom, am I?'

Mary seized on this hopefully. 'Could it be that you are just a little nervous?'

He laughed half-heartedly. 'Being so young and inexperienced, and wondering what is expected of me, perhaps.'

Encouraged a little, Mary tried again. 'Darling, I have a confession to make. I'm not inexperienced myself.'

Shelley's eyes twinkled. 'A shameful admission, to be sure. Nevertheless, since I shall obviously be in good hands, it puts me a little at ease. Do you think we could escape from here before Godwin comes back?'

'I'd like nothing better, except one thing.'

'And that?'

'I was thinking of the sand dunes at Calais.'

'The golden sands, the golden days.'

'They're golden still, Shelley.'

'And always will be, Mary. That I vow.'

4

'The Westbrooks have engaged Romilly,' Mr. Longdill said. 'I, on your behalf, have engaged Wetherell.'

'Which is the better man?' Shelley asked.

'Had it been possible I would have engaged Romilly myself, and yet, I *wonder*. . . . Romilly, when it comes to argumentative ability, might be thought shrewder than Wetherell, but Wetherell is considerably more voluble than Romilly. Time and again it has delighted me in court to witness the triumph of volubility over argumentative shrewdness. Much will depend upon the judge.'

'And he—?'

'None other than the Lord High Chancellor, the Right Honourable John, Lord Eldon, Baron Eldon of Eldon, in the County of Durham. As you know, the Westbrooks filed their Complaint on the eighth. As you also know, we filed our Answer on the eighteenth. I can now tell you that the case will be heard before Lord Eldon on the twenty-fourth.'

The 24th, Shelley reflected, would be his son William's first birthday, a happy omen, he could only hope. Today was the 21st, and once again Mary was in Bath and he separated from her in London. He was staying for convenience at Skinner Street where Godwin, kindly and courteous, had already proved a surprising source of comfort and encouragement.

'One small but important point,' Mr. Longdill went on. 'You told me in confidence that your wife's step-sister, Miss Clairmont, had given birth to a baby, the father being Lord Byron.'

'Yes. A girl, and amazingly beautiful.'

'Be that as it may, the news must not be allowed to leak out.'

'Indeed?'

'My *dear* Shelley, Miss Clairmont is living under your protection. Imagine what Romilly would make of that in court!'

'I can well believe,' Shelley laughed, 'that he would render our voluble Mr. Wetherell quite impotent.'

'A pity Lord Byron, in another sense, wasn't rendered *quite impotent* years ago,' Mr. Longdill snapped, and took up some papers from his desk. 'I have here a copy of our Answer, but want first to run through the salient points of the Complaint. First we have this: that father of the children, Ianthe Eliza Shelley and Charles Bysshe Shelley, deserted his wife, Harriet Shelley *née* Westbrook, in order to cohabit unlawfully with Mary Wollstonecraft Godwin, daughter of William Godwin, author of *Political Justice*. Next we have: the said father, Percy Bysshe Shelley, is an avowed atheist who was expelled from Oxford for writing and causing to be published a pamphlet entitled *The Necessity of Atheism*, and further wrote and caused to be published a work entitled *Queen Mab* in which he blasphemously derided the truth of Christian revelation and denied the existence of God as Creator of the universe.'

'I am applying for the custody of my children,' Shelley said hotly, 'not standing trial on a charge of blasphemy.'

'Come, come,' Mr. Longdill said soothingly, 'the Westbrooks have as much right to try and blacken your character as we have to try and – hum – polish it up a little. We come now to this point: Westbrook and his daughter, speaking on behalf of the children, pray that they shall be placed under the protection of the Court of Chancery. The Westbrooks, showing a suitable if hypocritical respect for law and order, are not asking in so many words for the custody of the children but are hoping that Lord Eldon will find in their favour. To add strength to this neat point John Westbrook has set up a trust fund to provide in part for the children's education.

'And now,' Mr. Longdill went on, 'we have what to us is the most important point of the Complaint. The said father, Percy Bysshe Shelley, still cohabiting unlawfully with the said Mary Wollstonecraft Godwin, has had several illegitimate children by her. *Several*, mark you, whereas you have had two, and only one is now living. We cannot deny illegitimacy, but we *can* deny that you are cohabiting unlawfully with any woman.'

Mr. Longdill beamed on his client. 'As for the Answer, you, the defendant, separated yourself from the late Harriet Shelley because of certain differences of opinion arising out of the aggressiveness and possessiveness of Eliza Westbrook. It will be pointed out that she, while looking upon herself as her sister's guardian, failed in her guardianship by permitting the elopement. More than that, she thus brought about all this trouble and is by no means a fit and proper person to be the guardian of your children. Indeed, you did not desert your wife but were driven from her by Eliza Westbrook.'

'And what of the polishing up of my character?'

'Ah yes, *that*. I have made light, my dear Shelley, of your early writings. Think how young and impulsive you were. And whatever you wrote and published about the married state, have you not married twice already before the age of twenty-five? As for your religious opinions, goodness gracious me, my dear boy, everybody knows that views such as yours are fashionable these days among the – hum – *literati* of Europe.'

'*Fashionable!*' Shelley was deeply shocked.

'And the same as any other fashion are likely to change. As

for your adherence to unorthodox principles – early growing pains, no more. However, the main point is the simple and undeniable fact that you are not cohabiting unlawfully; you are respectably married. And in so far as Mr. John Westbrook's sudden and remarkable generosity is concerned, you are well able to provide for the children yourself.'

'You are beginning to sound exceedingly confident, Mr. Longdill.'

The attorney laughed cagily. 'Perhaps, but we must not lose sight of this: everything will depend on Lord Eldon and his lordship's interpretation of the law.'

5

Mr. Charles Wetherell bowed to the Lord Chancellor, blinked vaguely at his learned friend, Sir Samuel Romilly, and reseated himself. The case, as far as he and Romilly were concerned, was concluded; all that was now required was Lord Eldon's decision.

'He may not feel disposed to give an immediate decision,' whispered Longdill, who was seated at Shelley's side.

Lord Eldon cleared his throat, and a tense hush fell over the courtroom.

Here it comes, Longdill thought.

'In a case such as this,' his lordship announced, 'I feel bound to say that I should be guided by that excellent rule, *festina lente*. Therefore, I shall indeed hasten gently, even slowly, and give my decision at a date yet to be announced. Meanwhile, further hearings, which I judge to be necessary, shall be heard in private.'

Romilly rose instantly and protested that since the case had begun in public it should continue in public.

'It is not my wish, Sir Samuel,' Lord Eldon said with a gentle sigh, 'that a young man's follies should be brought to light and exhibited in public.'

Romilly bowed. 'I assume, my lord, that "in private" does not mean the exclusion of the representatives of the newspapers now gracing the court with their presence?'

Lord Eldon smiled thinly. 'A singularly obtuse remark, Sir Samuel.'

Romilly bowed again and muttered something about the sacred freedom of the Press.

Lord Eldon cupped his left hand over his ear. 'I beg your pardon, Sir Samuel?'

Romilly shrugged and sat down with a scowl on his face.

'I must confess,' said Longdill, when he and Shelley were leaving the court a few moments later, 'that his lordship's attitude puzzles me. This kindly insistence on privacy – is it a good sign or a bad one? That, my dear Shelley, is the question.'

'A good one, surely!'

Longdill pursed his lips. He had not been heartened by the tone of Lord Eldon's voice when he had pronounced the phrase 'a young man's follies'.

'One thing is certain,' he said, 'the prohibition will bring forth a howl of rage from the newspapers.'

6

'I think you must have forgotten your promise,' Claire said tearfully.

'I never forget a promise,' Shelley said indignantly.

'You promised to take me to the Continent in March, and it is now almost the end of the month.'

'For heaven's sake be reasonable, Claire,' he begged. 'How can I possibly leave England when Lord Eldon has not yet announced his decision? And how, in any case, can I possibly take you in pursuit of Byron when his attitude to the birth of the baby is not yet known to any of us?'

Shelley was worried almost as much about Claire's affairs as he was about his own. Mary had written to Byron the day after Claire's confinement, he himself a week later, but so far the letters had not been acknowledged. Mary was as resentful of this as was Claire herself, for she was talking constantly these days of her desire to have a settled home, a home entirely to themselves, and was anxious to be free of Claire. Shelley thought this a little unkind, but had refrained from saying so, for Mary was expecting another child in September.

'I don't think you care what happens to me,' Claire said brokenly.

'My dear, what a silly thing to say.'

'Byron doesn't, that's clear enough.'

Shelley turned from her abruptly.

'I'm going for a walk,' he said. 'Tell Mary I won't be long.'

He walked for an hour, his mind occupied solely now with his own problems. Seven weeks had passed since Lord Eldon had reserved his decision. It had been expected that he would make up his mind at the conclusion of the private hearings, yet he had delayed again and again, and still delayed, and Shelley had returned to Bath to wait. Longdill, gloomy now, was of the opinion that the delay was caused by a protracted and careful study of the arguments concerning the Shelley views on marriage, for Romilly, setting aside all else, had seized upon these views as a more than sufficient reason for depriving Shelley of the guardianship of his children. Shelley had married twice, to be sure, but had he not written, and was not that writing in the possession of the court, that the institution of marriage, as it existed in the opinions and laws of England, was a mischievous and tyrannical institution? Had he not also written that men honest enough to express such an opinion lived in terror lest a court of justice should be converted into an instrument of private vengeance? Such words, Mr. Longdill feared, might be regarded by the Lord Chancellor as a direct challenge.

When Shelley returned to the lodgings, he noticed a post-chaise outside, and on running up the stairs found Mr. Longdill solemnly drinking tea with Mary and Claire.

'My poor Shelley—' he began, rising hurriedly from his chair.

Shelley looked at him stonily. 'Be as brief as you can.'

'Lord Eldon gave his decision this morning. I hastened to Bath at once.'

'An adverse decision, obviously.'

'Adverse, yes, but try and find a little consolation in this: the Westbrooks have not got the children either.'

'That, I admit is something, but if neither myself nor the Westbrooks—?'

'Do please come to the point, Mr. Longdill,' Mary begged.

The attorney bowed uncomfortably. 'This then is the position in simple language. . . . Lord Eldon refuses to believe that Shelley is capable of bringing up his children without instilling into them his own principles, and has issued an injunction the purpose of which is to prevent him from – hum – intermeddling with them until a further court order is made.'

'A *further* court order?' Shelley demanded.

'Earlier, as you know, the Westbrooks placed the children in the care of the Reverend John Kendall of Warwick, and there they are for the time being to remain. The Westbrooks have access to them, but not you, but I repeat, my dear Shelley, the Westbrooks have not got them and will not be appointed guardians. However, both you and they may put forward the names of suitable persons, and one of the Masters in Chancery will inquire further into the matter.'

Shelley turned away. 'Have I no redress?'

'None.'

'I shall leave this country of civil and religious tyranny and never return.'

'When?' Claire asked quickly.

Angry with her, Mary took her by the arm and led her un-willingly from the room. Longdill then approached Shelley who was now standing at the window.

'Try not to take this defeat too hardly, Shelley,' he said gently. 'Would it please you if Mrs. Longdill and I became the children's guardians?'

Shelley turned and looked at him woodenly. 'Would the court accept you?'

Longdill smiled faintly. 'I think I may say that our characters are unimpeachable. We – hum – go to church twice every Sunday, rain, shine or hail.' He waited for a moment, hoping that Shelley would smile, then, disappointed, went on hurriedly. 'Perhaps if we were to approach your father—'

'Ah, yes. He might be even more acceptable. *He*, if I remem-ber rightly, goes to church *three* times every Sunday. Not even a blizzard would hold him back.'

'After all, Shelley, your son Charles is Sir Timothy's next heir after you.'

'He has shown no interest in the boy.'

'What opportunity has he had?'

'Very well, approach him if you wish. No, wait! I doubt if the court would accept him.'

'My dear Shelley, the children's grandfather, and in addition a man of such high standing in the community—'

'You miss my point. The old gentleman failed to instil into me the orthodox principles which Lord Eldon holds in such high esteem. It might well be considered that my father is lacking in real strength of character.'

Longdill looked at Shelley doubtfully. 'Are you – hum – joking?'

'Yes, Longdill, I am, but the extraordinary thing about it is that I can't laugh. Be a good fellow and laugh for me.'

Mr. Longdill shuffled his feet, tried to laugh and failed miserably.

'I don't think I'll ever laugh again, not in England,' Shelley said.

Twenty

———————

I

Albion House
Great Marlow
Bucks.
England
Sept. 3, 1817

My dear Byron,

I am addressing this letter to you at Venice, for having heard that you had left Venice for Rome, I now hear that you are in Venice again. I also heard that you had suffered a severe attack of fever, so possibly that is why you have failed to answer my previous letters.

You will note my new address. It might be said that the Shelleys have come up in the world, for Albion House is really a house, not merely a cottage, still less some poky lodgings. There are five best bedrooms. Best, mark you well! In addition there are two nurseries, six attics, a drawing-room, dining-room and a library, all of them spacious. Moreover, there is the abandoned luxury of a water-closet. Great Marlow, as you may know, is less than 35 miles from London, while Albion House itself stands on the edge of the country and is close enough to the river.

Claire is still with us, and it is about Claire and her baby that I am now writing once again. The child is eight months old and still we await your instructions, happy as we are to give both mother and child shelter under our roof.

I have news of another birth. Yesterday Mary was safely delivered of a daughter. We have called her Clara Everina, and I dote on her already. I hesitate to speak of my other children, Ianthe and Charles. Indeed, their names are rarely mentioned here, for Mary and Claire have entered into a conspiracy of silence, hoping thereby to make the anguish I feel less difficult to bear. Ianthe and Charles are still with the Reverend

Kendall. The detestable Westbrooks proposed that he should become their permanent guardian; I for my part put forward Longdill's name; and Lord Eldon decided against both of them. And so the weeks and months drag by, with nothing known except that I am not to have and never will be permitted to have my own children In fury and despair I wrote a few lines which shall be dedicated to Eldon:

> *By thy most killing sneer, and by thy smile –*
> > *By all the arts and snares of thy black den,*
> *And – for thou canst outweep the crocodile –*
> > *By thy false tears – those millstones braining men,*
> *I curse thee – though I hate thee not.*

The Westbrooks have, of course, made another proposal, their champion this time being a certain Reverend Cheesborough who in their opinion is more God-fearing than Kendall. I, at my father's suggestion, have proposed Dr. Hume and his wife, the doctor being an even more God-fearing gentleman than Cheesborough. Moreover (and this should impress Eldon) he was once physician to his Royal Highness the Duke of Cambridge. The Humes will surely win the day. Let the final decision be hastened so that –

> *We shall soon dwell by the azure sea*
> *Of serene and golden Italy*
> *Or Greece, the mother of the free.*

Mary at long last has completed her novel Frankenstein, *and soon we shall have the task of correcting the proof copies. I am working hard myself, but still publishing at my own expense, of course. I doubt if ever I shall be able to command, as you do, the munificent sum of a thousand guineas per canto.*

I look forward to your reply to this letter.
> *Your friend,*
> *P. B. Shelley.*

2

Shelley, immersed in the task of correcting the *Frankenstein* proofs, had the sudden feeling that unseen eyes were watching him. Smiling at the thought that the eerie passages he was reading were playing fantastically upon his imagination, he went on eagerly with his work.

'Shelley.'

Startled, he looked up and saw that Claire was standing in front of his desk. He wondered how long she had been there, and if by some mischance she had noticed the letter which had arrived that morning from Byron. Rearranging his papers he did his best to hide it without drawing her attention to what he was doing.

'You know I don't like to be disturbed when I'm working,' he said crossly.

'Your pensioners are waiting at the door,' she told him.

'Goodness, is it Saturday night? I'll go out at once.'

Claire followed him slowly to the front door, by which time he was already emptying his pockets and dividing such money as he could find among the little gathering of women and children who had come to receive what was now being called the Shelley bounty. Her eyes filled with tears as she watched him. Sublimely happy, he cared nothing for the fact that soon, with his resources strained to the limit, he would be obliged once more to borrow money at exorbitant interest rates. Helping the poor of the town had become an engrossing occupation, and not only did he distribute money every Saturday night, but food and blankets as well.

Leaving him with a child in his arms Claire slipped back to the library and found the letter which she had seen him trying to hide, but before she could do more than recognize the handwriting Shelley joined her, saw what she was about and shook his head reproachfully.

'I have a right to know what Byron says,' she protested.

'Indeed you have, and let me tell you at once that he accepts full responsibility and is willing to maintain Allegra.'

'Allegra?'

'The name he wants the child to bear.'

Claire began to read the letter. It pleased him, Byron said, to know that his daughter showed promise of great beauty. Having acknowledged her, he added, it was his intention to breed her himself, and he would give her the surname of Biron, not Byron, in order to distinguish her from Little Legitimacy.

'What does he mean by Little Legitimacy?' Claire asked.

'He has a daughter by his wife,' Shelley reminded her. 'It seems likely, since he and Lady Byron will never live together again, that he is to be deprived permanently of that other daughter. Hence, perhaps, his growing interest in Allegra.'

Reading further, Claire learnt that Byron would maintain the child on certain conditions. He wanted sole custody. Any promises he might have made before Allegra's birth were set aside. He had no interest whatever in his former mistress and intended to separate her from her child. Assuming that his conditions would be accepted he asked that Allegra should be sent to him at Venice.

'Byron is a monster,' Claire whispered. 'He knows I'm penniless and thinks he can take my daughter from me. What were those lines of yours? *By thy most killing sneer* . . . They apply to Byron more than anyone else. *By all the arts and snares of thy black den* . . . How can I give my baby up to Byron, how can I?'

Shelley looked at her uneasily. She wasn't raging, as might have been expected; her voice was growing quieter and quieter.

'Byron lives in a palace, not a black den.'

'Fool,' Claire whispered.

Shelley took her arm. 'We'll go for a walk. There's plenty of daylight left. It's peaceful by the river. We can talk there.'

'Mary might object.'

'She'll understand when I tell her later.'

'She doesn't like our going for walks together. She used not to care about gossip, but now, being a respectable married woman—' She broke off. 'I'm sorry, Shelley. Forgive me.'

Shelley was well aware that gossip worried Mary, but only because she had got it into her head that the Court of Chancery might be able to take William as well as Ianthe and Charles.

'She refuses to understand,' he said, speaking of this now, 'that the court can't do any such thing.'

'Not unless some enemy of yours makes a complaint.'

Shelley laughed lightly. 'What enemies have I, apart from the Westbrooks?'

'You have creditors. You also have debtors, and they, in their ingratitude, are likely to hate you. Godwin, for instance. He was furious when you were unable to meet his last demand for money.'

'You really are trying to alarm me, Claire. Or – he laughed

shortly – 'or are you merely trying to force me to rush abroad at once and take you with me?'

'Perhaps I am, but dare I go near Byron now?'

'He can't take Allegra from you by force.'

'He knows I can't live on you for ever.'

'He knows nothing of the kind.'

'But I can't, Shelley. You might think this strange, but I seem of a sudden to have discovered a sort of pride. Surely I can find some way of earning a living. I have a good voice. Perhaps if it were properly trained – Oh, Shelley, I want my child to have the best of everything.'

'Only Byron could give her that.'

'Ah, you want me to accept his inhuman terms!'

'Indeed I do not, Claire! It had merely occurred to me that Byron's conditions are rooted in fear.'

'*Fear?*'

'I think he fears that if he saw you again he might weaken. I know I would if I were Byron.'

'I can't believe that Byron will ever want me again,' she said unsteadily, 'but I'm willing to find out. I'll go to Italy whenever you're ready to take me. But promise me one thing, Shelley, promise you won't let Byron rob me of my daughter.'

'That,' said Shelley confidently, 'is the easiest promise I've ever been asked to make.'

3

It seemed to Mary as she surveyed the piles of books and the empty boxes that she had spent the greater part of her life with Shelley in packing and unpacking. Would they ever have a settled home? She was beginning very much to doubt it. She went to the library window and looked disconsolately at the wintry scene outside. The denuded trees, black against the sky, were bending beneath the force of an icy February wind. Shelley, newly returned from a search for temporary London lodgings, came into the library and joined her at the window.

'I can well imagine your thoughts,' he said gaily.

Mary looked at him guiltily. 'Can you?'

ı*

'You're thinking that in a matter of a few weeks only all this will have given place to the sunshine of Italy.'

'They have winter in Italy too.'

'I refuse to believe it.'

'There are so many things you refuse to believe.'

'Darling, how cross you sound. Is it the packing? Packing often makes me cross, too.'

'It does nothing of the kind. It fills you with new hope, always with new hope.'

'Better that than new despair, Mary. Is it the thought of leaving England never to return that upsets you?'

'Never to return?' Mary echoed.

'I feel as Byron did when he decided to leave for ever.'

'Byron!' she exclaimed angrily.

'You sound as if you hate him. It isn't like you to hate people.'

'I hate him for what he is trying to do to Claire. His last letter, for instance. Bring the child but leave the mother.'

'I do hope you haven't told her.'

'Naturally I haven't. There was a PS., remember?'

'Yes,' Shelley laughed. 'He warned me playfully to bring Claire only if I particularly wanted her for myself.'

'Do you?'

Shelley looked distressed. 'Dearest Mary, how stupid you are.'

'Yet Claire is with us and apparently always will be.'

'You still sound cross. I'm sure it's the packing.'

'What a difficult man you are to quarrel with!'

'Goodness, do you actually want to quarrel with me?'

'You know very well I don't, I'm simply trying to make you see that I want a settled home, one entirely to ourselves.'

'We shall have a settled home in Italy.'

'And Claire a part of it.'

'Byron will want her when he sees her again.'

'Shelley, how blind you are!'

He sighed gently. 'I admit to certain doubts, but what can we do? Can we leave her behind, penniless and unhappy?'

'No,' said Mary, shaking her head miserably.

'Can we separate her from Allegra and take the child with us?'

'Would *you* do that, Shelley?'

'By heaven I wouldn't!'

'Nor would I,' Mary admitted.

'Can we send her alone with the child and remain behind ourselves?'

Mary shook her head. 'That would be worse than leaving her in England.'

'Well, there you are! And apart from Claire and Byron, we have our own reason for wanting to go to Italy. Your fear that William, and perhaps the baby too, might be taken from us is greater even than mine.'

'Yes,' Mary agreed, and went back to her packing.

It was a ridiculous fear, she told herself, yet it still persisted, causing her often to lie awake at night, brooding over it, while in sleep there were horrible dreams in which the baby, Clara Everina, was taken first, then the boy, William, soon after.

'I had a brief interview with Alexander, the Master in Chancery,' Shelley said, joining her and beginning to help with the packing. 'He said that he himself had accepted Dr. and Mrs. Hume, and was sure that Lord Eldon would do likewise.'

'One small victory over the Westbrooks,' Mary commented carefully.

Shelley shrugged. 'Precisely what my father said. I met the old gentleman in London, by accident. He was staying at Cook's. He said brusquely that the hopes he had once placed in me he now placed in my son Charles. And he asked me angrily if I was aware that the gossips were now spreading the story that I had murdered Harriet.'

'Oh Shelley, how horrible!'

'He said the best thing I could do to kill the scandal was get out of England. That, naturally, was almost enough to make me decide to stay.'

Mary gathered up some more books and placed them in the box. The growing scandal was another reason why she herself wanted to go abroad, but she had been careful not to aggravate Shelley by saying so. Lord Eldon's ban on the newspapers had made things worse, not better. One newspaper, *The Times*, had protested in an editorial that all judicial proceedings should be public property, and less scrupulous journalists had invented many vile and infamous stories. In London Shelley was sometimes followed in the street and jeered at, and even here at Marlow, where he was loved at least by the poor, it was now being said that Allegra was his and either Claire or the Swiss nurse, Elise, the mother. He had a handful of good and worthy friends, but nobody would listen to them. It was much more amusing to believe the worst of a man than the best. But what hurt her more than anything else was the refusal of the critics to acknowledge Shelley's poetical genius. Either they ignored his work when it appeared or, more deeply versed in the art of sneering than Lord Eldon, killed it with a sneer.

'I forgot to tell you about the lodgings I found,' Shelley said. 'They—' He broke off, overcome for several moments by a paroxysm of coughing. 'These books are covered in dust,' he complained, when able to speak again. 'The lodgings, Great Russell Street, not far from Tottenham Court Road. Please don't laugh, but the landlady's name is Godwin. Please *do* laugh, for she had never heard of your philosopher father.'

Mary was looking at him anxiously. 'Darling, did you see that new doctor while you were in London?'

'Did I? Ah yes, of course I did. I remember we had a long talk about music. He prefers Mozart to Beethoven, which is of course quite ridiculous. He—'

'Shelley, I want the truth,' she persisted.

'There's no need whatever for anxiety.'

'Did he, for instance, say that only a warmer climate could save you from consumption?'

'Very well, then, he did, confound him.'

Knowing that it would anger him to talk further about his health, Mary went on with the packing.

'Shelley,' she said briskly, 'by the look of things we shall need at least three more boxes.'

Twenty-one

I

Lyons
France
March 22, 1818

My dear Byron,

We are, as you see, at Lyons and have just arranged for a voiturier
*to take us to Milan. The weather is fine and pleasant and my health is
much improved already. We propose to settle for a time at Pisa, where
the climate is mild, but will remain in Milan until I receive your reply
to this letter.*

*Our last few weeks in England were spent in London, and with one
exception they were remarkably enjoyable. Godwin was the cause of the
only distress we were called upon to suffer. His attitude reduced Mary to
tears, and Mary, as you know, does not weep easily. He resented the fact
that we were leaving England, admitting shamelessly that, at a distance,
I might remain unmoved by his demands for further financial assistance.
It is as difficult now to love him for what he once was as it is not to hate
him for what he has become.*

*London was enjoyable in the first place because a few good friends,
including Hunt, Keats and Hogg, gathered about us to wish us godspeed,
and in the second because we were able to go several times to the opera.
We enjoyed* Don Giovanni *and* Figaro, *I myself taking back an earlier
assertion that it was ridiculous to prefer Mozart to Beethoven, for it
seemed to me as I listened that Mozart's music came from the air and
returned to it, magically. We were also much amused by* The Barber of
Seville, *which was presented for the first time in England. My increasing
appreciation of music will, I feel sure, bring about an immense improvement in my work.*

I must be frank with you, Byron, and tell you that Claire is with us.

It was as impossible to leave her behind as it was to separate her from Allegra, and knowing that you are not the heartless fellow you would like us all to believe, I feel sure that a compromise acceptable both to you and to Claire, can yet be reached. Would you like us to join you at Venice, or would you prefer to visit us at Pisa? I long again for the happy association which we all enjoyed in Switzerland.

Your friend,
Shelley.

2

'I can't believe that you brought me out at this hour of night for no better purpose than to look at Milan cathedral in the moonlight,' Claire said quietly.

'No *better* purpose!' Shelley exclaimed. 'Did I not tell you when we admired its beauty this morning that it would look even more beautiful by moonlight?'

'You did, and it does.'

'How unmoved you sound! Your heart must surely have turned into a cabbage. Look at those clustered spires, Claire. Are they reaching up to the stars, or are the stars reaching down to them?'

'When did you receive the letter?' she asked.

'To which letter do you refer?' Shelley evaded. 'I received several this afternoon, including an unpleasant one from Godwin. He—'

'What did Byron say?'

'Oh come, Claire—'

'You brought me here to tell me about it. I know you did. Please don't delay any longer.'

'Very well, then,' Shelley sighed. 'Byron is obdurate. He refuses to come to Milan. He refuses to receive us in Venice, that is unless – well—'

'Unless you leave me behind somewhere?'

'Yes.'

'Don't sound so distressed,' Claire said calmly. 'I expected him to be obdurate.'

Shelley found her calmness frightening. Her face, pale in the moonlight, showed no emotion whatever. He took her hands in his and found them cold and lifeless. It was the calmness, he thought, of despair.

'Does he still want Allegra?' she asked.

'Yes, and he expresses a livelier interest than ever.'

'But his conditions are the same.'

'Except that he mentions the sum of five thousand pounds which he proposes to settle upon Allegra.'

'Does he expect me to be tempted by that?'

'If he does, and if you are, I urge you not to be.'

Claire looked at the cathedral. 'As you say, more beautiful by moonlight.'

'My dear—'

'Why does he hate me so much.'

'I think he hates himself, not you.'

'And for that reason wants to take Allegra from me?'

'I find him extremely difficult to understand,' Shelley complained.

'I don't think I do,' Claire said slowly. 'It isn't hatred he feels for me, merely contempt. Remember, Shelley, that he never loved me. I was one of many who for a time had amused him. He told me once that my pestering efficiency – those were his words, Shelley – had made it possible for him to prolong the *affaire*. Even so, he made it clear to me that I meant no more to him than the most casual of mistresses. Life was pleasant and tranquil at Switzerland, otherwise our association would have ended sooner.'

'I do wish you would either weep or scream,' Shelley said helplessly.

Claire laughed gently. 'If I did either a crowd would gather. You know how curious and excitable Italians are. To scream would convince them that you had spurned me, and to weep would on the other hand convince them that you had already betrayed me.'

'I wish you really meant that as a joke, Claire, then we could both laugh heartily.'

'As for his interest in Allegra,' she went on, 'I can explain that, too.'

'A daughter to comfort him, as he said, in his old age?'

'Partly, but it goes deeper than that. He brooded often on the possibility that even a woman who had spent only one night with him might have become pregnant. Pride of blood was the cause of it. He wants Allegra because he knows without question that Allegra is his. I take what little comfort I can from the fact that he has never disowned her. That is one reason why I decided before we left England to accept his terms.'

'Claire—'

'You said yourself that only Byron could give my daughter the best of everything, and—'

'If you feel compelled to part with her because of something *I* said—!' Shelley began heatedly.

'Please don't be angry with me, Shelley. I have thought about everything very carefully. If I continue to allow you to support Allegra, more and more people will believe that she is yours. If I give her up to the man who has acknowledged her, you and Mary will be saved from that embarrassment.'

Shelley remained silent. Mary *was* embarrassed. He had to admit it, though it pained him that she should be.

'What really influences me,' Claire went on, 'is that Byron *wants* her. He hasn't broken his word. He said she should remain either with me or with him until she was seven. A lot might happen in the next five years. Byron might grow tired of having a child, and then I shall take her back. I can, you know, any time I wish. It would be a different matter if he were demanding to adopt her legally.'

Shelley remembered how once she had said, Byron can do anything, anything! He looked at her admiringly, thinking that she had since then gained a remarkable strength of character.

'How soon can you take Allegra to Venice?' she asked.

'I think it would be wiser if I sent her with Elise. I doubt if I could face Byron without losing my temper. Allegra is used to Elise, so Elise may as well stay on with the child as long as Byron thinks it necessary. On second thoughts, I shall insist upon that.'

'Whatever you wish.'

'Tell me one thing, Claire. Are you doing this because you fear Allegra is a burden to me and Mary?'

'No,' Claire lied. 'I'm thinking only of Allegra's future welfare. But seriously, Shelley, am I myself not a financial burden to you?'

'What an idiot you are,' he laughed. 'Both Mary and I have

plans for an enormous amount of work. We need a secretary, and you were always very good at transcribing. Please say no more about it.'

They turned and began to walk back to their hotel.

'Promise me one thing, Shelley,' Claire said presently. 'When all is ready, just tell me that Elise is taking Allegra for a drive. It will be easier for me that way.'

3

'You look depressed, Mary,' Claire said. 'Is it because of *Frankenstein*?'

She and Claire, having left the children with Shelley, had been out for an hour's drive, during which Mary had uttered scarcely a word. News had reached them yesterday that *Frankenstein*, published at last in London, had been violently attacked in *The Quarterly Review*.

'*Frankenstein* may be attacked in every journal in London, for all I care,' Mary said indifferently. 'If you must know, I was wondering if I had a settled home at last, wondering and doubting.'

Claire, though she liked travel and change herself, was ready to sympathize with her stepsister. They had not settled at Pisa, after all, for Shelley, seeing chained gangs of prisoners working in the streets, had declared that he could not live in such a monstrous place. They had remained there until the Swiss nurse, Elise, had written to announce the safe arrival in Venice of Allegra, and had then wandered on to Leghorn. Lucca had been their next brief resting place, and from there they had come here to the Baths, the Bagni di Lucca, where they had found a charming little house, the Casa Bertini.

'Would you like to remain here permanently?' Claire asked.

Mary shrugged. 'It's pleasant enough, and Shelley's health is improving daily. The Baths are doing him a lot of good.'

'And what a scandal he causes,' said Claire, trying to make her laugh, 'by sitting naked on the rocks.'

Mary smiled in spite of her depression. 'Waiting for the perspiration to subside before leaping into the water.'

They had now reached the Casa Bertini, and descending from the carriage found Shelley playing with the children in the garden. Mary's eyes softened at the sight of them. Shelley was lying on his back with William, now two and a half, and the eleven-months old Clara swarming over him. Claire herself tried to smile, but her heart grew heavy with longing for her own Allegra. Shelley rose with a laugh and took a letter from his pocket.

'From Elise, by the look of it,' he said, and gave it to Claire. 'I must say it's good of Elise to write so regularly.'

Claire, who lived for these letters, took it eagerly. It was now over three months since the nurse and the child had reached Venice, and Allegra, now nineteen months old, had apparently been happy from the first with her father. Byron himself, as well as all his Venetian friends, was much taken with her, and the appearance of the two of them together on the Piazza always caused a sensation. It was a happy state of affairs, Claire thought, for everyone but herself.

'Well, what is the latest news?' Shelley asked.

Claire opened the letter and stared in horror at Elise's opening sentence.

'Shelley, Allegra is no longer with Byron. She has been taken by Mrs. Hoppner, the British Consul's wife.'

'*Taken?*' Mary asked.

Claire nodded and read more of the letter. 'Elise is almost incoherent, but it seems clear that Mrs. Hoppner, obviously a kindly woman, is shocked at the licentiousness of Byron's life in Venice. The Palazzo Mocenigo, she said, was no fit place for a child. Elise gives very few details, but apparently Mrs. Hoppner insisted on taking Allegra and Byron agreed. Oh, Shelley, what are we going to do? The thought of Allegra being with strangers, however kindly they might be, is more than I can bear.'

'She must be taken from them,' Shelley said instantly. 'Byron has broken his word.'

'Would it not be better,' Mary said stiffly, 'to write first to the Hoppners?'

'Allegra *must* be taken from the Hoppners,' he insisted, 'but since Elise might possibly be exaggerating I'll write at once to Mr. Hoppner.'

Mr. Hoppner's reply bore out all that Elise had said. Byron

had quickly gained an evil reputation in Venice. In earlier days he had caused a scandal by seducing the young wife of an elderly count, and it was now known without question that he kept what might be called a harem at the Palazzo Mocenigo. Hoppner felt strongly that Allegra, a child he and his wife had grown to love very much, should be with her mother, but he knew that Byron, who visited her often and appeared to dote on her, would be hard to persuade. He therefore suggested that Shelley should come to Venice, bringing Claire with him secretly, thus enabling her to see her daughter at the consulate while he himself called on Byron.

Shelley looked hopefully at Mary when both she and Claire had read this letter.

'The Bagni di Lucca no longer attracts me,' he said. 'Let us all go to Venice for a few months.'

Mary could but smile. Shelley, knowing that she might object to his travelling to Venice alone with Claire, was trying to be cunning. Nevertheless, a foreboding of evil descended upon her as she contemplated this proposed change of residence. She argued with herself that it arose from nothing more serious than her growing dislike of being obliged once more to pack their belongings, but since it clung to her depressingly she sought for an excuse. Remembering the Gisbornes, old friends of her father whom they had met at Leghorn, she reminded Shelley that they were about to arrive at Bagni di Lucca for a prolonged visit.

'They shall go with us to Venice,' he said promptly.

'Shelley, do be practical,' she protested. 'I had looked forward to entertaining the Gisbornes here. How can we possibly command them on arrival to go with us to Venice? If you really insist upon Venice, we can go there later.'

'And would you call *that* being practical?' said Shelley, thinking miserably that Mary cared more for social activities than for Allegra's welfare. 'The situation calls for instant action.'

Mary looked at Claire, who had remained silent and unhappy, and reproached herself for contributing in part to her misery.

'Very well,' she said, 'perhaps the best thing you can do, Shelley, is take Claire to Venice, and if you can, bring Allegra back with you.'

'You mean that, Mary?' Claire asked eagerly.

'Darling, of course I do. Allegra and William adore each

other, and William misses her. I miss her myself. She has always had a place in my heart, so why not in my home as well?'

Laughing happily, Shelley embraced both Mary and Claire.

'So to Venice it is,' he cried, 'and by heaven, I shall lecture the wicked Lord Byron as sternly as if I were the Lord High Chancellor of England.'

4

Venice
Aug. 24, 1818

Dearest Mary,

We reached Venice two nights ago and are staying at an inn, the name of which I can pronounce but cannot spell. We travelled from Padua by water, in a gondola. My first gondola and my first view of Venice, but a Venice blanketed in rain. How we shivered, Claire and I, in that unromantic gondola!

Yesterday morning, immediately after breakfast, we went by gondola to see the Hoppners. Allegra was brought in immediately by Elise. She has changed so much in three months that you would hardly recognize her. Clinging to Elise, she was at first a little shy of Claire, but presently, sitting on her knee, she laughed charmingly and asked if Papa was coming to see her today. Her attachment to him, after so short a time, is most profound.

Mr. Hoppner told me privately that Byron must not be told of Claire's presence in Venice, for he had said that if she came here he would leave at once and take Allegra with him. Hoping that I could induce Byron to see reason in the matter, I went at once, and of course alone, to the Palazzo Mocenigo.

Byron, I must say, was strangely pleased to see me, and talked eagerly of our time together in Switzerland. As soon as I was able, I reminded him of the purpose of my visit. He turned this aside with a joke about the evilness of his reputation. Had I heard that he now kept a harem? I said I had, but could scarcely believe it. He assured me that it was true enough.

'My poor Byron,' I said, 'surely such doubtful pleasures grow wearisome?'

'My constitution was becoming undermined,' he laughed, 'but now, since I have rearranged the order of things, I am as fit as a fighting cock.

You see, my dear Shelley, I now spend my days in the harem and my nights alone.'

I again reminded him of the purpose of my visit, upon which he grew truculent and told me to mind my own business. Yet the next moment he was all apologies, and thereafter was amazingly reasonable one moment, harsh and cruel the next. He said he had no right over Allegra; Claire could take her back if she so wished. Then he laughed unpleasantly and asked how Claire proposed to support the child. I pointed out that he was rich. It would cost him little, I said, to make Claire an allowance sufficient for herself and Allegra. He shook his head at that and made it clear that he intends, by forcing Claire to remain penniless, to retain the upper hand.

'Claire may have access to the child whenever convenient,' he said, his mood changing again.

'And when will that be?' I asked.

He shrugged, said that he needed time for a little thought on the matter, and insisted upon taking me across to the Lido, where we found horses waiting on the beach. After an exhilarating ride across this long sandy island which defends Venice from the Adriatic, he announced that he had come to a decision.

'You shall have the use of my villa at Este,' he said, 'and take Allegra there, but she must be returned to me the moment I ask for her. I expect this is a foolish weakness on my part. Claire will perform like a thousand devils when called upon to part with her a second time.'

I accepted this offer at once, being obliged to make up my mind without consulting you. You must scold me if I have done wrong and kiss me fondly if I have done right. Este is not far from Arqua and is within easy reach of Padua. The villa, the Casa Capucini, is ideally situated in the Euganean Hills. I shall take Claire, Allegra and Elise there without delay and want you to waste no time in joining us. Our manservant, who is efficient and trustworthy, shall be your courier. Knowing your own efficiency, I give you two days from the receipt of this letter in which to pack. If you rise at four o'clock on the morning of the third day you will reach Lucca at six. Thus, by private carriage, you will reach Florence before nightfall. The journey from Florence to Este will occupy three full days, and then, my dearest Mary, we shall be happily reunited.

I realize in some dismay that you will probably spend your birthday packing, and being your twenty-first birthday, what an important one it is. That you should come of age at last makes me fear that you might also become something of a termagant. In other words, a bold, boisterous and *brawling wife. No doubt I am trembling without cause, for did you not, in a very real sense of the word, come-of-age four years ago during our first Channel crossing?* Four years! *Can you believe it, Mary? Years of much sadness, yet years of much joy. Forgetting the sadness, thinking of the joy, and thereby thinking only of you and our children, I shall ever remember them, my dearest, as four of the most golden years of my life.*

Mary, I love you,

Shelley.

5

Having decided that today he must work, Shelley was finding concentration impossible. How, he asked himself, could he settle down to work when Mary, already two days late, had not yet arrived at Este? More restless than ever, he sprang up from his writing-table and hurried from the summer-house which he had turned into a study. A few quick steps along the trellised path brought him to the front door of the villa. Pausing for a moment, he smiled as he heard the laughter within. By the sound of things Claire was romping merrily with Allegra. Feeling calmer now, he walked down to the garden. Below him in the distance lay the wide flat plains of Lombardy. Turning he gazed with pleasure at the Euganean hills, rising above a purple haze. Beneath, the waveless plain, he thought; above, sailing like strange ships through the broken mist, the hills. He felt like work, he *wanted* to work, and by heaven, work he would!

An hour later, having been vaguely conscious of excited voices, he looked up with a start to find Mary in the summer-house.

'You're late by two days, nay, almost three,' he accused.

'Am I indeed?' Mary asked, much taken aback by his manner.

Scattering papers in all directions he sprang up and embraced her hungrily.

'My God, what a way to greet you! Please forgive me, darling. I was immeasurably anxious, but kept trying to tell myself that nothing dreadful could possibly have happened to you on the way.'

'There were lice at one inn, rats at another.'

Shelley embraced her again. 'Darling, you must have had a

very trying time. Are you as cross as you sound at my wanting you to come to Este?'

'I didn't intend to sound cross,' Mary said wearily. 'It was a difficult journey, and to make things worse Clara was so ill at Florence I thought I might have to remain there for several days.'

'The children!' Shelley cried. 'My joy at seeing you had made me forget even them.'

Rushing headlong from the summer-house, he came upon William in the garden. Allegra was with him, and so delighted was he to see her again that he gave his father no more than a casual smile. Shelley then hurried into the villa and found the year-old child lying listlessly in Claire's arms. Her forehead, which he stroked gently, burnt hotly beneath his fingers.

'There seems a slight improvement,' said Mary, joining him at that moment.

'Nevertheless, I don't like the look of her,' he said anxiously. 'I'll get the local doctor at once.'

The local doctor, who knew no English and had difficulty in understanding Shelley's Italian, expressed the opinion that the child was suffering from nothing more serious than teething trouble.

'You're a stupid fellow,' Shelley said heatedly in English. 'The Shelley's have never been known to suffer from teething trouble.'

Clara was put to bed at once, and the next day and the next showed a slight improvement. Meanwhile, both Shelley and Claire complained of pains in the stomach, and Mary had three patients on her hands. Shelley was the first to recover, upon which, with no faith in the local doctor, he hurried Claire to Padua. Claire, however, grew a little better without further treatment, but by this time a message had been received from Mary that Clara, never having fully recovered, was dangerously ill. Not teething trouble, but dysentry was suspected. Frantic now, Shelley remembered that Byron had a clever and reliable doctor in Venice.

'Do you feel well enough to travel back to Este alone?' he asked Claire.

On her saying that she did, he begged her to return with all speed and send Mary and the sick child to Padua. He gave her a letter to Mary in which he said briefly that there was only one thing for it, they must take the child to Dr. Aglietti in Venice. It meant that Mary must start out from Este at not later than four o'clock in the morning and this, so great was her own anxiety, she did without complaint. The child, when Shelley saw her again, was showing signs of convulsions, and grew worse as the hurried journey to Venice proceeded.

It was five o'clock in the afternoon when they reached the inn at which Shelley had previously stayed, and leaving Mary to engage a room he went in search of Dr. Aglietti. The physician was out and not expected back for several hours. More frantic than ever Shelley returned to the inn where, to his relief, he found that another doctor had already been summoned, but his relief was short-lived. There was no hope whatever, the doctor said, and Clara died in her mother's arms an hour later.

'I can say nothing to comfort either of us,' Shelley said brokenly.

Mary, her heart feeling cold and dead within her, looked at him dumbly.

'The golden years. . . . Do you still call them that, Shelley?'

PART THREE

Jane

Twenty-two

—————

Palazzo Galetti
Pisa
Jan. 17, 1821

My dear Hogg,

On opening a box which had not been unpacked during our travels I found two letters which I wrote to you, one seven years ago, the other five, and apparently forgot to send. I really am the most absentminded of fellows. I wonder how many other letters have suffered a similar fate? In view of this possibility, perhaps I had better dwell briefly on the things that have happened since we left Byron's villa at Este, which is more than two years ago.

We are, as you see, at Pisa, but pray do not imagine that we have an entire palazzo *to ourselves. Sufficient to say that our lodgings are spacious, with an excellent* mezzanino *and a secluded room on the fourth floor, which I turned instantly into a study and in which I am now writing. We pay thirteen sequins a month, but please don't ask me what a sequin is worth in English currency.*

During the last two years Mary has been sorely tried at times by my restlessness, but is happier now since at Pisa she has made many friends and is able to go about in society. From Este we travelled slowly to Rome, spent a week there with daily visits to the Forum and the Coliseum and moved on to Naples. Three months later we were in Rome again, and after five months there we travelled to Leghorn. Florence, I think, was our next resting place before coming here to Pisa. Mary and I have never ceased to read voraciously, and I have worked and worked, finding in travel a haunting inspiration.

It was while we were in Rome the second time that William became desperately ill. It was high fever and we were warned that there was little hope for him. I watched by his bed for sixty hours and when death claimed him I refused to believe it. Mary's depression was pitiful, Claire and I failing to cheer her, until, five months later, she was safely delivered of another son. We dote on him, the more so since three other children have been taken from us. His name is Percy Florence, Florence because he was born in that city. How fortunate, my dear Hogg, that he wasn't born in Naples or Leghorn!

Claire is not with us, but is in Florence, where she found employment as a governess in the family of a professor who rejoices in the impossible name of Bojti. The poor girl was miserable at first but from her letters seems happier now. She has had several offers of marriage but declares she will never marry. Byron took Allegra from her a second time before we left Este. He objected to our nomadic way of life and in part to my un-Christian beliefs. He, old lecher that he is, declared that he had every intention of his daughter becoming a Christian and, if possible, a married woman.

'Which do you consider the more important?' I asked sharply, when discussing this with him.

'That she should become a Christian,' he said.

He was ill at the time and, as you know, the Devil, when ill, believes himself to be a saint. Allegra is with the Hoppners again, and there is talk of her being educated at a convent.

The only news I have of my dear Ianthe and Charles is that they are well, and happy with Dr. and Mrs. Hume. The doctor, out of the kindness of his heart, writes to me from time to time, but my father, who visits them, has never yet replied to any letter of mine. If you could catch a glimpse of Ianthe and Charles sometime, as if by accident, and write to me about them, I should be eternally grateful.

There are times, Hogg, when I long to be in England again, yet what does it mean to me, my native soil? Why should happiness be in any way concerned with geography? My England, my soil. What progress have I made to think such thoughts? Mine. A matter of possession, and that is one of the human frailties I loathe with all my heart. When I think of England with longing I remind myself of Lord Eldon, yes and of William Godwin also, Godwin who wrote so cruel a letter to Mary when he heard of William's death in Rome.

And when I think of England I think too of the sufferings of the working people, the children in the factories, the hanging of a woman for stealing potatoes, the Manchester Massacres. Yet what can I do to help but write, and writing be accused of stirring up the sort of restlessness that leads to anarchy?

> Men of England, wherefore plough
> For the lords who lay ye low?
> Wherefore weave with toil and care
> The rich robes tyrants wear?

Have I thereby achieved anything worth while? I doubt it, Hogg, I doubt it. For this and much more important work have I been castigated by mean ltttle men plying mean little pens. They notice me, these reviewers, more often than not to mock me. When my Prometheus Unbound *appeared, one of them concerned himself only with the title, suggesting that the volume was likely to remain unbound, that an age would be spent in finding anyone weak enough to pay for the binding. I could but laugh, and laughing reproached him as gently as I knew how:*

> *Alas, good friend, what profit can you see*
> *In hating such a hateless thing as me?*

Do you realize, my dear Hogg, that I shall be twenty-nine next August? An incredible thought, for I feel as if I have lived at least ninety years already. Perhaps even longer. Time, in relation to myself, is difficult to grasp. Sometimes it seems as if I have always been, and always will be; and again, that I never was. How my thoughts wander! The plain fact is that I find it good to be ninety years old in experience, yet possess the body and health of twenty-eight.

In closing I must tell you that we now have some new friends. I call them friends though we met them only two days ago. Perhaps it flatters me that they should have come to Pisa for the express purpose of meeting me, not out of curiosity, but a genuine admiration of my work. Let me be honest, I am flattered. Their name is Williams. The husband, Edward, I liked instantly and feel that we shall discover many things in common. As for the wife – her name is Jane – she affects me so strangely that I find it impossible to make up my mind about her.

Write as soon as you have the time.

Your friend,
P.B.S.

Twenty-three

I

'How monotonous it becomes, this constant talk about boats and sailing,' Mary said plaintively.

Shelley and Williams protested warmly, Shelley saying that she was a born land-lubber, Williams claiming that there was no more entrancing a subject under the sun. Mary looked at Jane Williams for support but Jane, smiling serenely, remarked that though she was a little timid, especially in rough weather, she loved to lie in the bottom of a gently rocking boat with nothing above her but the sky.

'A most heavenly feeling,' she added.

Shelley looked at her gratefully and wondered why he had at times thought her stupid. Nevertheless, he still found it impossible, even after four months, to decide whether or not he really liked her. Sometimes he found her calm and restful, yet again vaguely irritating. Younger than Mary, she was pretty and graceful, and dressed with a deceptive simplicity which enhanced her attractiveness. He wondered now, as his eyes held hers for a moment, if she irritated him because in some indefinable way she reminded him of Harriet.

'Mary hates my interest in sailing,' he explained indulgently, 'because she fears I might some day be drowned at sea.'

'You came close to drowning in Switzerland, and again here only a few weeks ago,' Mary said sharply.

'I was never in danger,' Shelley laughed. 'I had Byron to protect me in Switzerland and Ned Williams here.'

'He behaved remarkably well,' Williams commented. 'Instead of struggling in the water as most people would, he kept perfectly still. I hauled him out as easily as if he were a floating piece of timber.'

Edward Williams was a year or so younger than Shelley. He too had been at Eton, after which he had joined the Navy, though later, tiring of the sea, he had applied for a commission in the Dragoon Guards. His Army career had taken him to India where he had met Jane, whose brother was a general in the Indian Army. Out of the Army now, and with sufficient private means for his needs, he was content, he said, to spend the rest of his life loafing in Italy. Loafing, however, meant more than sailing a boat, for with an interest in literature he was writing a play – playing at play-making, he called it – and as an amateur painter he had an especial aptitude for portraits. His affection for Shelley had grown steadily since their first meeting, and he liked to deceive himself that he remembered well the young fellow who at Eton had shocked everybody by refusing to fag. Shelley, to him, was a poet of astonishing genius, and as full of fun, in spite of all he had suffered, as a carefree, mischievous boy.

'I'd feel happier about all this sailing,' said Mary, 'if only Shelley would learn to swim.'

Shelley laughed softly. 'It was different at Calais, darling. It didn't trouble you then whether or not I could swim.'

It pleased him immeasurably to see Mary's face soften at the memory, for it was so difficult these days to make her recall even the happiest things of the past with any signs of real joy. She was much too serious, even in the pursuit of social pleasures, while in her insatiable pursuit of learning her determination had assumed a grimness which in anyone else would have been laughable.

'Are you quite comfortable at Pugnana?' Mary asked Jane.

'Yes indeed. It's very healthy for the children.'

Jane and Edward Williams had taken a villa at Pugnana, which lay only four miles from the Baths of Pisa, where Shelley, tired for the moment of Pisa itself, had rented a villa for the summer. Jane and Edward, visiting the Shelleys today, had come as usual by boat, their children being left behind in the care of a reliable English nurse. They had two children, a boy of about two, and a baby girl who had been born only two months ago.

'Is it not past feeding time?' Shelley asked, thinking now of Jane's baby. 'You must hurry Jane home at once, Ned. That poor little daughter of yours will be getting quite desperately hungry.'

'We have a wet-nurse,' Edward Williams explained, smiling at Shelley's seriousness.

When the Williams had gone, and it had been agreed that the Shelleys should dine with them later in the week, Mary announced that she was going to study Greek for an hour and went off to the little room which was her own private study, leaving Shelley to reflect that her shortness of temper had been distressingly evident during the last few weeks. She was worried, of course, about Claire, who in her turn was miserable because Byron had at last placed Allegra in a convent, yet she had no desire, or so she said, to ask Claire to come and live with them again. Perhaps she was studying too hard. Greek was a damnable language, and the long hours she spent at it would be enough to upset anybody's nerves. She was indoors far too much. What she needed now was a short brisk walk.

'Mary!' he shouted, running to her study. 'Put your books away. Come out for a walk!'

He saw, as he approached the writing-table, that she wasn't studying after all, but writing in her journal.

'You're cheating,' he said, glancing over her shoulder.

'I know I *said* I was going to study—'

'I don't mean that. Entering two weeks all at once isn't actually cheating, I admit, but how can you possibly remember exactly what you did ten or twelve days ago?' He peered closer. 'And what cryptic entries, darling. Just look at that. *Write. Read Greek. Walk. Arrange.* Now what on earth does "arrange" mean?'

'It means,' Mary said crossly, 'that I arranged those new books which arrived from London.'

'I don't believe you,' Shelley teased. 'More than likely you have a secret lover and arranged that day a new meeting place.' He kissed the back of her neck. 'You won't ever take a secret lover, will you, darling?'

'Shelley, *please*. I want to bring my journal up to date.'

Disgruntled now, he snatched the journal from her. 'Let me see what other intriguing mystery I can find. Good lord, here's that wretched word "arrange" again. Almost a year ago, too. Can you really remember what it was you arranged then? Of course you can't! Ah, here's something more explicit. A long sentence, in fact.'

'Give it back to me,' Mary all but wept. 'One's journal is meant to be private.'

Shelley looked at her aghast. 'Mary, we used to write in this same journal together.' He looked at the entry again, and reading it aloud grew more troubled with every word. "*We have now lived five years together; and if all the events of the five years were blotted out, I might be happy; but to have won and then cruelly to have lost the associations of four years is not an accident to which the human mind can bend without much suffering.*" He looked up in dismay. 'Mary, I don't understand all this.'

Mary bit her lip. 'I wrote it almost two years ago. Perhaps I don't understand it myself, now.'

'You had lost Clara, and William too,' Shelley said gropingly, 'and so had I. We shared the unhappiness, and sharing it, or so I thought, found it easier to bear. But Mary, to want to blot out everything, to believe that you could only be happy by doing so . . .'

'You're reading more into it than I intended,' she said sombrely.

'What had you intended?'

'Oh, Shelley, I don't *know*.'

'To suggest that I have caused you much suffering breaks my heart.'

'It wasn't you I was thinking of, please believe that. It was life.'

He looked at the entry again. ' "*To have lost the associations of four years.*" . . . What does that mean?'

Distressed as she now was at Shelley's misery, she said resentfully, 'I suppose I was brooding over all the many changes, the making of friends here and there, then losing them, the hopes which were proved hopeless as far as a settled home was concerned.'

Shelley looked utterly bewildered. 'But Mary, I thought you believed as I do, that the home we share is within ourselves, not a material state depending on geography.'

'For a time I did, but I soon realized that I was living with my head in the clouds.'

'What a trite thing to say.'

J

'The truth is often trite.'

'Mary, are we . . . quarrelling?'

'It would seem so,' she said wearily.

'But we can't be. People always shout when they quarrel.'

'Let us assume, then, that we are not quarrelling.'

Shelley looked aggrieved now. 'You seem to be looking upon me as a little boy who ought to be spanked. Spank me if you must, but tell me first what I have done to deserve it.'

'Oh, *Shelley*—' Mary said, trying not to laugh.

'I know! You're still cross about Emilia Viviani.'

'I was never cross about poor Emilia.'

'Amused, then? Yes, you must have been.'

'Partly,' Mary admitted, 'but mostly I tried to remain aloof.'

'Weren't you afraid I might be falling in love with her?'

'Of course not,' Mary laughed.

Emilia Viviani was an amazingly attractive girl of nineteen who had been placed by her mother in a convent where she still resided as a *pensionnaire*. The Shelleys had met her at the house of a mutual friend, and Shelley himself, learning of her plight, had grown indignant. She had been placed in the convent by a cruel mother who wanted to hide her beauty from the world, or so the girl had led him to believe. Eagerly making plans for her rescue he had met her whenever it had been possible for her to escape for an hour or so from her prison. He thought her sweet and innocent, and regarded the situation in which she was placed as a sad yet highly romantic one. Gradually the true story had come to light. Emilia was anything but innocent. She had been placed in the convent because her mother's lover was showing a lively interest in her, an interest much appreciated by the girl. And while 'imprisoned' she had, none the less, succeeded during the restricted spells of freedom in taking several young lovers of her own, had, in fact, thought it might be amusing to add a poet to the list.

'What a fool I made of myself!' Shelley burst out.

'Well, never mind,' said Mary. 'While the dream lasted you did at least write some pretty verses.'

'How condescending you sound.'

'I'm sorry,' Mary said contritely.

He looked at her hopefully. 'Is the evil mood passing? Please say it is!'

Mary came to him quickly and put her arms round his neck. She had remembered something which her father had once been fond of saying. If Shelley ever really grew up he would find himself condemned to the misery of disillusionment. That had not yet happened, and she found herself praying that it never would. It had been close enough at times – in part Godwin himself had disillusioned him, and Byron also – but the boyish optimism had always prevailed.

'I suppose it was just indigestion,' Shelley said, after kissing her. 'Come to think of it, indigestion might well be the cause of all the ills of the world. Napoleon suffered a bad bout and made a wrong decision. Indigestion and ambition are a fearful combination.'

'If it was indigestion in my case,' Mary said, 'it was the mental kind.'

'Caused by devouring too much Greek, naturally.'

No, Mary thought sadly, the cause was her feeling of failure as far as Shelley was concerned. Disillusioned by life herself, she had ceased to provide him with the help and comfort he needed as a means of keeping that noble head of his in the clouds. He had not yet realized it himself; she could only pray that he never would.

'Come, darling,' he cried merrily. 'Take up your pen and complete today's entry. Add two words. *Shelley*, and that inscrutable little *arrange*.'

'And what is one to suppose it means this time?'

He embraced her warmly. 'Can't you guess, my sweet?'

2

'Jane,' Shelley said suddenly, 'I want to be frank with you.'

'That sounds ominous,' Jane Williams smiled.

'I also want *you* to be frank with *me*.'

'Have I ever been anything else?' she asked calmly.

It was late afternoon and the two of them were returning from a long walk together. Jane and her husband had come over from Pugnana early that morning, sailing, as usual, along the canal which connected Pugnana with the Baths of Pisa. The Williams enjoyed walking as much as the Shelleys, and often enough the four of them went on long rambles together, but today, with Edward Williams intent on finishing the miniature portrait of Mary which he had begun some time ago, Shelley and Jane were left to walk alone.

'Why,' Shelley went on, 'do I enjoy your company so much and yet at times still find you irritating?'

'That,' Jane laughed softly, 'is certainly being frank with me.'

'I do hope,' he added anxiously, 'that I have never revealed my irritation.'

Jane shook her head. 'You have always been so courteous and gentle that I find it impossible to believe what you say about irritation.' She laughed again. 'I must admit that before I met you I was prepared for quite a monster. I had heard so many stories about you. Not that I quite believed them, for your work disproved all the vicious gossip. On the other hand, I was more than a little taken aback at the sight of you.'

'Ah, you found me frightening after all!'

'By no means. I found you mild and guileless, and you looked so much younger than your actual age.'

'Mild and guileless!' Shelley cried indignantly. 'Am I not supposed to be at war with the whole world?'

'*Supposed* to be?'

'I *am* at war with the whole world, and always have been, but only, apparently, in a mild and guileless way.'

'Am I irritating you now?' Jane asked curiously.

'No,' he chuckled, 'you are making me laugh at myself.'

'Could it be my appearance that irritates you?'

'I never saw a prettier young woman.'

'The way I dress, perhaps?'

'You dress with the utmost taste.'

'My voice?'

'I never heard a more soothing voice.'

'Goodness, Bysshe, you are making me feel like a spoonful of cough mixture.'

'Answer my question,' he said sternly, 'or I shall indeed liken you to cough mixture, which I utterly abhor.'

'How *can* I answer it, when I am I and you are you? You must find the answer for yourself.'

He looked at her searchingly. 'Does it distress you that I should sometimes find you irritating?'

Jane shrugged lazily. 'Not in the least.'

'Confound you,' he burst out, 'I am growing irritated now with the irritation.'

'That might be the best way of ridding yourself of it.'

'How calm you sound about it all. Indeed, Jane, your calmness is the most remarkable thing about you. Never, in all the months I've known you, have I seen you in any way disturbed. I find it quite uncanny.'

'And . . . irritating?'

'And *irritating*!'

Jane smiled at him affectionately. 'And so the riddle is solved.'

Shelley looked at her in amazement. 'So it is, by heaven!'

'But how strange,' she chuckled, 'that calmness should irritate you.'

'Oh, I can explain that now, my dear. I was thinking all along that a person as untrammelled as you couldn't really have lived. That is, experienced life to the full.'

'How wrong you are,' Jane said lightly. 'My calmness was achieved only after much suffering. Edward rescued me from an unhappy marriage. My first husband—' She broke off. 'But why should I speak harshly of a man now dead?'

'But to have suffered and yet to have found tranquillity. How I envy you!'

'I have Edward to thank for it. You know how kind and gentle he is. My life with him is perfect.'

Shelley frowned over this. 'Because of your gratitude?'

'I can think of no sounder basis for enduring love than gratitude.'

'Love without passion?' Shelley questioned.

'How you like to probe and analyse! With my first husband it was passion without love.'

'That is scarcely answering my question, Jane.'

'First it was gratitude, then it was love, and later ' – Jane chuckled again – 'have I not two children, Bysshe?'

'But even so. . . .'

'But even so, my inquisitive friend, the conceiving of them was accompanied by something more enjoyable than a grim feeling of duty faithfully performed. Are you still inquisitive? Would you like precise details?'

Shelley laughed heartily. 'That, my dear Jane, would be carrying frankness a little too far.'

On reaching the villa they found Mary deep in a study of Homer, and Edward plucking idly at the strings of Jane's guitar. Mary, after glancing up vaguely, went on with her reading, but Edward, asking if they had enjoyed their walk, sprang eagerly from his chair and presented Shelley with the miniature.

'I hope you like it, Bysshe?'

Studying it carefully, it seemed to Shelley that his friend had captured an expression which he himself saw but rarely on Mary's face these days. The characteristic graveness was there, but not the now familiar look of severity. Carried back over the years, he was reminded strongly of Mary as she had been at their first meeting.

'It's an exquisite piece of work,' he said shakily.

Williams looked relieved. 'I was afraid I might spoil it by hurrying to finish it in time.'

'In time for what, Ned?'

'This rather special day, of course.'

'Special? What's special about it?'

Jane and her husband laughed, and Mary looked up from her book again.

'We may as well tell him,' she said. 'It happens to be your birthday, Shelley.'

'Well, fancy that! How old am I?'

'Twenty-nine.'

'Amazing!'

'I think we ought to make a real party of it,' said Jane.

'Indeed, and why not!' Shelley cried enthusiastically. 'I'll run out at once and ask all the people we know to spend the evening with us.'

Mary closed her book with a snap. 'What an unreasonable suggestion.'

'But Mary, you *like* parties.'

'Yes, but I prefer to plan them carefully in advance.'

Shelley looked at her aghast. An ordered life, that had of late become her dictum. Trying to find a reason for it, he wondered if this passion for planning things in advance gave her a feeling of security.

'The four of us can spend a pleasant evening on our own

account,' Williams said soothingly. 'Jane brought her guitar. I'm sure she'll be glad to play and sing for us.'

'But on your boat, not indoors,' Shelley decided. 'We'll pack a hamper, take a bottle or two of wine. I can see it's going to be a beautiful evening and a glorious sunset. Mary can plan a party for me one day next week.'

Shelley had heard Jane sing many times before, but that night, as they drifted on a light wind along the canal, he listened with a new awareness. Her voice, clear and true, seemed to him the one perfect medium through which he could enjoy the grace of her body and the calmness of her spirit. Fancifully he told himself that tonight Jane was making him the slave of her music, and so intense was his joy that at times it turned to pain.

Watching him as he listened, Mary thought that never before had she seen so rapt an expression on his face, and growing impatient with him when again and again he pleaded for just one more song she remarked that the night air was bad for Jane's throat.

'How thoughtless of me,' he said contritely. 'Please forgive me, Jane.'

He had been so entranced, Mary thought, that he had failed to notice her impatience, but Edward Williams had, she knew that by his look of kindly reproach. She had seen that look before and now, as always, it made her feel ridiculously guilty. Loving his wife and all but worshipping Shelley, it was clear that he in no way shared her own suspicion that Shelley, quite likely without knowing it, was falling in love with Jane. Here then was another problem, she thought, but it was neither hers nor Edward's, perhaps not even Jane's, for Jane had no room in her heart for any man but Edward. If problem it really was it would be solely Shelley's.

'Do you intend going back to Pisa for the winter?' Williams asked.

Shelley turned to Mary. 'Do we, darling?'

'It would amaze me,' she said dryly, 'if you remain content with merely Pisa.'

'My dear Mary,' he said stoutly, 'I have had my fill of travel for the rest of my life.'

She smiled faintly. He sounded as if he meant it, but then he always sounded as if he meant it when he declared that he had found in this place or that the perfect resting place. Impatient with him again, she made a longer entry than usual in her journal that night.

Saturday, Aug. 4: Williams all day. Read Homer. Walk. Edward finishes my miniature. Sail. Shelley's birthday. Seven years are now gone. What changes! What a life! We now appear tranquil; yet who knows what wind . . . But I refuse to prognosticate evil; we have had enough of it. When we came to Italy I said all was well if it were permanent. It was more passing than an Italian twilight. I now say the same. May it be a Polar day; yet that, too, has an end.

Another thought came to her, but she hesitated to enter it. Why am I so disgruntled? Could it be that I ache for a life of my own, am tired of being merely a part of someone else's life? If that were true, she thought sadly, she had failed both herself and Shelley.

Twenty-four

I

'INCREDIBLE,' said Claire, 'that Byron should be living there across the river, almost within hailing distance.'

Shelley, alarmed at the note of hysteria in her voice, joined her quickly at the window. It was now April, in the year 1822, and the Shelleys had been here at Pisa since last October. They had taken a top floor apartment in an old building known as the Tre Palazzi di Chiesa, and the Williams, happy to join them, had taken a smaller apartment on a lower floor. The building stood on the south bank of the River Arno, while facing it on the opposite bank was the stately Palazzo Lanfranchi, which Byron had rented some months ago.

Claire laughed on a high note. 'Would Byron pack up and leave if he knew I had arrived?'

'My dear Claire,' Shelley said uneasily, 'it will be better for all our sakes if your visit remains unknown to him.'

Claire had arrived from Florence an hour ago and had not yet seen Mary, who was out walking with Jane and Edward Williams, and though Shelley was delighted to see her – it came upon him now as he looked at her tense, unhappy face, how much he had missed her – he could but view her sudden arrival with the utmost apprehension.

'What made you some so suddenly?' he asked, knowing quite well what her answer would be.

'I want to see Allegra. Oh, Shelley, I *must* see her. Unless Byron relents I won't be able to answer for the consequences.'

'Allegra isn't at Pisa,' Shelley said helplessly.

'Are you telling the truth?'

'If Allegra were here it would be possible to contrive a secret meeting, but the child is still at the convent.'

'Then you must help me to kidnap her.'

'Oh, Claire, such a wild scheme would have no hope of success,' he said gently. 'Please don't think I intend to reproach you, but you gave her up of your own accord, and she is as happy as possible where she is. I visited her, remember.'

Claire looked at him wildly. 'Yes, yes, you told me in a letter. You laughed with her, romped with her. Is it too much that I, her mother, should ask the same privilege? Just an occasional visit will make things easier for me. If Byron would only relent a little I wouldn't pester him so much. Please talk to him, Shelley, and plead with him.'

'Very well,' said Shelley doubtfully, 'providing you promise not to force yourself upon him. I don't ask it for his sake, my dear, but yours.'

'I promise. And tell him that I have been offered a position in Vienna, and will take it gladly, providing I can see Allegra before I go.'

Mary arrived with the Williams at that moment, and while Mary seemed vaguely glad to see her stepsister the Williams, with whom Claire had once stayed at Pugnana, were delighted. Percy Florence, now two years old, was brought in, and when Claire bent to embrace him he flung his arms affectionately round her neck. She wept a little, thinking with greater longing of her own child, but gradually felt herself growing calmer. She was with friends again, and it seemed to her that after much wandering she had come home and was surrounded once more with love and kindness.

While Shelley went off to see Byron, Mary and Claire talked quietly together, Mary saying that except for the proximity of Byron she was very glad indeed to have her stepsister with her again. Nevertheless, Claire began to suspect from Mary's manner and her depressed way of speaking that all was not well in the Shelley household. Mary was thinner and obviously in poor health, and was inclined to start nervously at any sudden noise. She confided in Claire that she was pregnant again, had not yet told Shelley and was uncertain whether she was pleased about it or sorry.

'Shelley has got it into his head,' she went on, 'that I am

depressed at the thought of going back to the Baths for the summer. I denied it, but he thinks a change imperative and has set his heart on the Gulf of Spezia. Jane and Edward – they like the idea, too, you see – have already made a search but so far unsuccessfully.'

'You propose to share a house with the Williams?'

Mary shrugged indifferently. 'The idea is Shelley's, not mine. I like them, of course. Jane in particular is a very restful person to be with. It will amuse Shelley to have her even closer than she is now.'

'Is he in love with her?' Claire asked frankly.

'Yes, I think he is, but pray don't tell him. It would only make things difficult.'

'It would not be pleasant for you, I quite see that.'

Mary shrugged again. 'Say rather that it would not be pleasant for Jane. You know how she adores Edward. An impulsive declaration from Shelley would embarrass her deeply.'

When Shelley at length returned he said briefly that Byron was away for the day. Later, alone with Mary, he admitted that he had lied. Byron, who so far had no suspicion that Claire was at Pisa, had uttered an uncompromising no to her entreaty, and had laughed dryly that Siberia would be a better place for her to go to than Vienna.

'Then what are we going to do?' Mary asked.

'I shall try again and hope meanwhile that he won't hear about her presence here. I don't like the thought of her going off to Vienna alone. Can't we keep her with us for the summer?'

'If you wish. She can make herself useful by copying and correcting my novel.'

Mary, setting aside her Greek lessons for the time being, had written another novel, and while not being entirely pleased with it she had enjoyed during the writing of it the sensation that she was making for herself a life entirely her own. Now she was preoccupied with Greek again and was determined to master that most difficult language.

'Byron,' said Shelley, with an impish laugh, 'asked me if I was aware that my wife now goes regularly to church.'

'And what did you tell him?'

'I said,' Shelley chuckled, 'that you were only pretending to go to church, for I had reason to suspect that you were in actual fact meeting a secret lover.'

'That must have amused him.'

'It did, but he said he had sat near you in church on the memorable occasion when Dr. Nott preached his equally memorable sermon against atheism.'

Mary looked curiously at Shelley. He spoke mildly, even teasingly, showing no sign whatever of annoyance. Yet he must have known that Dr. Nott, an English clergyman now resident in Pisa, had in his sermon been obliquely attacking the author of the still remembered pamphlet on the necessity of atheism. And I, she thought comically, sat and listened attentively instead of rising and walking out indignantly.

'Do you object to my going to church?' she asked.

'Darling, are you not free to come and go as you please?'

'Would you accompany me if I asked you to?'

'To do that,' Shelley frowned, 'would be to ask me to insult your Dr. Nott, I being so violent an unbeliever.'

Mary laughed shortly. 'Wasn't it Byron who said you were the complete Protestant?'

'Yes,' Shelley chuckled, 'but only because, by force of habit, I protest against every known religion.'

'Those who protest as you do often become in the end the most pious of converts.'

'Good lord,' he cried in dismay, 'is that what you have in mind, my eventual conversion?'

'It might well be the solution to all your problems,' Mary said seriously.

'Have you found in religion a solution to all yours?'

'No, but in going to church I do find rest and consolation, and a certain freedom from the need to grope blindly, the need to ask myself so many unanswerable questions.'

'So your search for Truth has ended in blind faith.'

'It might well have begun again in that and led me to a greater faith, one that is anything but blind. Are you disappointed in me, Shelley?'

'How can I be when in part I envy you?'

'Why do you envy me?' Mary asked.

He considered this for a moment. 'I am only an atheist in

that I have never been able to believe in a personal God, but I believe in God in a wider sense, you know I do.'

'Yes, I know. God is Truth, God is Beauty.'

'And also Love,' Shelley said softly, 'yet my search goes on and on, unendingly. Yours has stopped, and whether or not you have found the God I seek, you have, as you say, found rest and consolation. Of course I envy you.'

'Envy, not in any way pity?'

Shelley looked at her uneasily. It was unfair of her to try and put it like that, and unworthy of him, even for a moment, to suspect that pity did come into it.

'If I were still the young firebrand who wrote *The Necessity of Atheism*,' he said lightly, 'I might indeed say I pitied you. Now, while envying you, I can only say that I pity myself, forced as I am to stand alone.'

Mary saw then that they were talking, not about religion, but about themselves, each being unwilling to admit it, each turning hurriedly from the realization that they were growing farther and farther apart.

'Oh, Shelley,' she cried, 'what has happened to us?'

Seeking a means to avoid this unwelcome question, he pointed his finger at her in mock sternness.

'I can at least tell you what has happened to *you*, happened in a down-to-earth biological sense. Why, you little idiot, have you been afraid to tell me?'

'But it doesn't show, and won't for ages,' Mary said, relieved that he had refused to answer her question. 'How could you possibly know?'

'You went to a physician. I saw the man myself this morning. He congratulated me. Come, Mary, why this mysterious reluctance?'

'I don't know whether to be glad or sorry,' she admitted miserably.

'But we have always wanted another child, a companion for young Percy.'

'Because— Oh, Shelley, I'm tormented by a nagging foreboding of evil. I fight against it, but I can't free myself from it. I keep remembering what happened to Clara and William.'

'Percy is healthy enough. This other child will be just as healthy.'

'Clara and William were healthy children. They would be alive today if we hadn't come to Italy. What worries me most at the moment is this new outbreak of typhus fever in Romagna. It could so easily spread here to Tuscany.'

'Who told you about it?' Shelley asked sharply.

'Trelawny, I think.'

'Then I urge you when next you see him to beg him not to spread the story. I hadn't heard it myself, but Byron had. Ravenna is hit very badly, and Allegra's convent, remember, is only a few miles from there. Byron is very worried, and Claire, if she knew, would become quite frantic.'

'She could scarcely feel more frantic about typhus than I do.'

'Would you like to go back to England?' Shelley asked quickly.

Mary hesitated for a moment. The thought of the long journey appalled her, and she knew that even if she were able in her present state of health to sustain the rigours of so much travelling they would be no more settled in England than they were here. Possibly they would be a great deal more *un*settled, for Shelley, apart from his enthusiasm about the Gulf of Spezia, had grown surprisingly content with this part of Italy.

'No,' she said shortly.

'Then the sooner we find a house in the vicinity of Spezia the better,' he said eagerly. 'A complete change of air – what could be more delightful for all of us?'

'What indeed,' Mary said ironically.

2

'I must have missed Shelley by a matter of moments only,' Trelawny said. 'As a matter of fact I thought I heard that quick step of his while I was in the Williams' apartment.'

'Jane and Edward are away,' Mary told him.

'So the maid said.'

'Shelley won't be long, if you care to wait.'

'Nothing would please me more,' Trelawny laughed. 'I'd much rather have a quiet talk with you than a heated argument with Shelley about morality, or some such thing.'

Smiling, Mary invited him to sit down, and for a time they discussed the Williams and Claire, all three of whom had left that morning for Spezia to make another search for a suitable summer residence. Claire, suspecting that Shelley wanted her out of the way, had at first refused to accompany Jane and Edward, but had agreed reluctantly when he had promised to have another talk with Byron. Claire had been at Pisa for six or seven days, and, as far as Mary knew, Byron was still unaware of her presence. Except for brief walks after dark with Shelley she had remained hidden indoors and had met only Trelawny and the Williams who, sympathizing with her, had promised not to tell Byron or anyone else that she was in Pisa.

'I saw Byron last night,' Trelawny remarked. 'He was talking of bringing Allegra here.'

'Pisa would be safer than Ravenna, certainly.'

Edward John Trelawny, a friend of Edward Williams, had come to Pisa three months ago and had become immediately popular with all the other members of the Shelley circle. He was Shelley's age, Mary reflected, but much more mature in appearance. He was tall and muscular, with a quantity of dark, flowing hair. Some people called him the Arab because of his swarthy complexion, others preferred the Pirate because of the adventurous life he had led, but in the Shelley circle he was usually addressed simply as Trelawny. Mary wondered why she should feel drawn to him, for he was anything but an intellectual. Action meant more to him than analytical thought, and often enough he acted without pausing to think of the consequences. Like Shelley, he had rebelled at an early age against established authority, had been expelled from school and had later been disowned by his father, chiefly because, as far as Mary could gather from his many stories of adventure in various parts of the world, he had deserted the Navy soon after joining it in order to become a privateer. 'As terrible and lovely as a tempest,' Shelley had said of him, and Mary, allowing for poetic licence, thought it an apt description. Whatever her reason for liking him, she knew now, as his grey eyes rested upon her inquiringly, that his flamboyance was almost the only thing capable these days of dispelling the depression which swamped her.

'By the look of you,' he chuckled, 'you're thinking I'm an odd sort of chap to be mixing with your little gang of intellectuals.'

'*My* little gang indeed,' Mary countered, faintly nettled.

'Sorry,' he apologized. 'I shouldn't have said that, you being the only sane one among them. Not that you don't think things out; it's plain enough you do; but you don't spend the whole time dreaming. It's all very well wanting to reshape the world, but the way I look at things it's important first to see the world as it is, not as you *think* it is. I don't mind telling you I wouldn't have stayed here five minutes if it hadn't been for you.'

'Really,' Mary said faintly.

'Don't get it into your head I'm making love to you,' he said bluffly, 'because I'm not.'

'Am I supposed to be cast down by that, or relieved?' Mary asked, feeling an idiotic urge to flirt with him.

'Cast down if you think I'm irresistible, relieved if the thought of it revolts you.'

'What an extraordinary conversation this is!'

'Seems normal enough to me, Mary. Whether or not I start making love to you depends on one thing.'

'And that?'

'I can't make up my mind if you need rescuing.'

'Rescuing from what?'

'A situation that's beginning to bore you.'

Yes, Mary thought, perhaps boredom is the cause of all my dissatisfaction.

'And once you do decide,' she said lightly, 'and assuming the decision is that I *do* need rescuing, that will be the signal for you to start making love to me. How ridiculous!'

'Nothing of the sort,' he chuckled.

'My poor Trelawny, you're as crazy as the rest of my gang.'

'Now wait a minute,' he said warmly, 'I've had lots of affairs and I've been married twice. I'm not regretting any of it, but nothing ever lasted, partly because I was foot-loose myself, partly because the women concerned were foreigners, every damn' one of them. Exotic and exciting, I'm not denying it, but that sort of thing sort of sticks in the throat. What I'm after now is stability. Next time, if there is a next time, it's got to be permanent.'

'In short, a woman of your own race.'

'That's right.'

'And I, providing you decide I need rescuing, am marked down as the next and final victim?'

Trelawny looked puzzled for a moment, then he laughed uproariously.

'Seems to me *I* might be the victim, so I'd better watch my P's and Q's.'

Mary laughed too, and they were still laughing together when Shelley entered the room. Mary saw at once that his face was pale and drawn. He spoke neither to her nor to Trelawny and walked with unaccustomed slowness to the window.

'Shelley, what is it?' Mary asked anxiously.

He turned and looked at her. 'Mary, that foreboding of evil . . .'

'Has something happened to Claire, or the Williams?'

'No, to Allegra,' Shelley said, speaking with difficulty. 'Byron had just received the news when I called. I can't tell you how grieved he is. I stayed for a while, trying to comfort him, but it was hopeless.'

'Typhus?'

'Yes. The poor child died three days ago.'

Mary bowed her head and wept bitterly, the more so because her first reaction had been relief that it was Allegra, not her own child. She remembered Claire's face when she had said before leaving that morning that the conviction was growing upon her that she would never see her daughter again. Byron, however grieved he might be, had much to answer for.

'When do you expect Claire back in Pisa?' Shelley asked tonelessly.

'I can't be sure.'

'One thing is certain, Mary. She must not be told in Pisa, not with Byron so close at hand. She'd force herself upon him, make a terrible scene.'

'Would you spare him that?' Mary asked angrily.

'I'm thinking of Claire, not Byron. He's capable still of treating her harshly. Perhaps even more harshly than ever, because of his grief.'

'But what can we do? She has to be told.'

'I can't think clearly, but we must find some way of getting her away again, and as quickly as possible.'

Claire, with Edward and Jane Williams, returned to Pisa

two days later. The Williams were excited about a vacant house they had found, though Claire herself remained indifferent. Known as the Casa Magni, it was the one large house at the fishing village of San Terenzo on the Bay of Lerici not far from Spezia.

'What you'll like best about it,' Edward told Shelley, 'is the veranda. It's practically on the water's edge and there's a delightful view of Lerici across the bay.'

'We'll take it,' Shelley said promptly.

'Perhaps you ought to see it first,' Jane suggested.

'We'll take it,' Shelley insisted, 'and move there at once.'

Leaving Jane and Claire to tell Mary more about the Casa Magni, and pretending a vast excitement himself, he hurried Edward down to the Williams' apartment where he broke the news of Allegra's death. Edward agreed that Claire must not be told while in Pisa and began to make hurried plans. Trelawny was called in and made a number of practical suggestions.

'First, there's the house,' he said. 'I take it a lease hasn't been signed yet?'

'No,' said Edward Williams.

'Then there's Claire. You want to get her away at once. I'm yours to command in both respects. Where does the owner of this Casa Magni live?'

'Spezia.'

'Then if you're agreeable, Shelley, I'll make the first move by taking your wife, your boy Percy and Claire to Spezia. That'll get Claire out of the way and give Mary time to negotiate for the house before you and the Williams arrive. You can deal with all the packing and be off in a couple of days, I take it?'

Shelley glanced at Edward. 'I'm sure we can.'

'Is the house furnished?'

Edward shook his head. 'We'll have to take everything with us.'

'In that case, make for Lerici and have the stuff sent by boat. Easier and cheaper that way. I think that deals with everything.'

'Everything,' Shelley said gratefully.

'Except that boat of ours,' Edward pointed out.

He and Shelley, sharing expenses, had ordered a boat from Captain Roberts of Genoa. The captain was also building a larger one for Byron who, when a summer residence in the Gulf of

Spezia had first been mooted, had expressed a wish to spend a few days now and then with the Shelleys and the Williams. Both boats, according to the captain's latest report, were nearing completion, and delivery could be taken of the smaller one within two or three weeks.

'I'll look after the boat for you,' Trelawny offered. 'There's nothing to stop me from going off to Genoa, once I get my little party settled at Spezia. Agreed?'

'Agreed,' said Shelley.

Mary, when told that she must be ready to leave with Trelawny early tomorrow, agreed reluctantly, for to her dismay the foreboding of evil still clung to her. Claire herself proved difficult for a time, declaring that she would rather remain in Pisa until Byron had been persuaded to allow her to see Allegra. In the end she too agreed reluctantly, Shelley having told her, and hating himself for the need to lie, that Byron, learning of her presence in Pisa, had grown more stubborn than ever.

'What a nuisance I am to you,' she said wryly, when Shelley bade her good-bye the next morning. 'You should have wrung my silly neck ages ago.'

'You're my dearest friend,' he said emotionally.

'Dearer even than Jane Williams?' she asked.

It pleased yet saddened him to recognize in her voice a haunting echo of the teasing, provocative Claire of the past.

'Jane is an inspiration, I admit it,' he laughed, 'whereas you— Oh, confound you, Claire! A nuisance, yes! You always have been, and doubtless you always will be, and – confound you again – I love you for it.'

3

'We seem to be in a devil of a mess,' Edward Williams said cheerfully.

'Chaotic,' Jane murmured, in no way upset.

'I shall wave my magic wand,' Shelley declared, 'and turn chaos into well-regulated order.'

He and the Williams, having reached Lerici soon after midday, had found temporary accommodation at what, as far as they could see, was the only inn. Shelley rushed to the window of the room in which they were having a light-hearted council of war. There, across the waters of the bay, stood the Casa Magni, looking, he thought rapturously, like a tiny dream palace.

'That's what it is,' he declared, 'a tiny dream palace.'

'Tiny is an apt description,' Edward said ruefully.

In the hurry and confusion of the departure from Pisa the fact that the Casa Magni was much too small for two families had been nonchalantly set aside. Easy enough, Shelley had declared, with his usual optimism, to find a second house on arrival; the thing to do was to get to Lerici without a moment's waste of time.'

'Not another suitable house closer than Spezia,' Edward added.

'Spezia isn't such a great distance away,' Jane pointed out reasonably.

'But what about our boat?' Shelley said warmly. 'We can't chop it in half, Ned sailing one half, I the other. How many rooms has the Casa Magni? No, don't tell me! We'll all fit in comfortably enough, I'm sure of that.'

'So much for the magic wand,' Edward grinned. 'Swish it to the left and we have an extra bedroom; swish to to the right and we have a banqueting hall.'

'And swish it in the middle and we have that most solemn gentleman, the harbour master of Lerici,' Jane laughed.

'That,' Shelley admitted, 'is where my magic wand is most needed.'

The harbour master, a portly Italian with large sombre eyes, black curly hair and fat, expressive hands, had waited on them only a few minutes ago. Taking a glass of wine with them he had warned them sorrowfully that to land their furniture and and other possessions would cost them in duty a vast amount of money. On their asking how much he had quoted various currencies and had at last, after another glass of wine, arrived at the understandable but dismaying figure of three hundred pounds.

'There's only one thing for it,' Edward Williams said. 'We must send the stuff back the moment it arrives and buy a few sticks and pieces locally.'

'I'm attached to my own furniture,' Shelley said promptly. 'I refuse to part with it.'

'I'm rather fond of ours,' Jane sighed.

'Think of the cost of bringing it here, then sending it back to Pisa,' Shelley said indignantly. 'I'll have another talk with the harbour master. I've just remembered how his eyes lit up when I inadvertently mentioned my friend Lord Byron. I'm a straightforward fellow as a rule, but for once I'm going to practise a bit of low cunning.'

Leaving his wife with their children, Edward Williams followed Shelley from the room, lost him as he ran nimbly down the stairs and only caught up with him again because the harbour master had not yet left the premises. Indeed, he looked as if he had taken up permanent residence, for he and the landlord, who in appearance might well have been his twin brother, were sitting contentedly at a little table with a bottle of chianti between them. Shelley immediately called for another bottle and drew up a chair to the table.

'Chianti – Lord Byron's favourite wine,' he pronounced.

Leaning against the whitewashed wall, Edward Williams watched and listened while Shelley, in fluent enough but somewhat crazily phrased Italian, regaled the harbour master and the landlord with stories, some true, some sheer invention, of the shocking exploits of the incredibly wicked Lord Byron. He asked them to imagine for a moment the great benefit Lord Byron's presence would bring to the community of Lerici. He was well known for the lavish way in which he flung his money about, but better still, crowds and crowds of tourists would descend upon the place, fighting each other in an effort to gain a glimpse of the notorious lecher. They would have to be housed and fed. They would drink much wine. The tradespeople of Lerici would in the twinkling of an eye grow fat and prosperous.

Edward hid a smile. The landlord's eyes were gleaming greedily and there was a thoughtful look on the harbour master's face. Remembering that he had earlier expressed an interest in the arts, Edward himself joined in the attack, even though he could only guess what Shelley had in mind. He pointed out that their own presence, as well as Byron's, assuming that Byron could be induced to come here, would make Lerici famous throughout the civilized world. He himself was a painter, Shelley was a poet. Other painters and poets would flock to Lerici, the former to paint the local scene in brilliant colours, the latter to sing about it in such verse as had never before been written.

'But alas,' said Shelley sadly, 'everything is lost. Tomorrow my friend and I depart, never to return. Byron will go elsewhere and Lerici, unpainted, unsung and shrouded in its accustomed poverty, will slumber on to dream in vain.'

'To raise our hopes, then dash them to the ground!' the harbour master protested.

'How can we remain at the cost of three hundred English pounds?' Shelley asked warmly.

The harbour master and the landlord held a hurried consultation, speaking so rapidly and in such agitation that neither Edward nor Shelley could understand more than a word here and there. There seemed to be an argument about the impounding of the baggage and furniture if it were landed and duty not paid on it, then again an argument about storage space, of which it seemed certain, there was little to be had.

'The Casa Magni!' the landlord cried shrilly.

'The Casa Magni!' the harbour master laughed gleefully.

He rose, beamed and shook Shelley and Edward by the hand, then bowing sweepingly he indicated that the Casa Magni, as far as he was concerned, had now become a customs depot. Everything could be placed there. Impounded if they wished, but he himself preferred to say stored.

'So we are going to live in a sort of customs shed,' Jane laughed, when Shelley and Edward told her the story. 'How delightful!'

'There's still one problem facing us,' said Edward, sobered by a sudden thought. 'We don't know yet whether or not Mary has completed negotiations. The furniture is expected hourly. What are we to do with it if the house isn't actually ours?'

'I'll write to Mary at once,' Shelley said.

This he did, sending the letter by a fisherman who, after haggling about payment, agreed to row round the headland to Spezia. Mary replied that the house had been secured and a lease signed. Shelley had asked her to come back with the fisherman, but she said she was in such low spirits and poor health she preferred to wait until she could move at once into the Casa Magni. Trelawny, she added, had been a great comfort during the journey, but had now taken his departure.

'Once we take possession of the Casa Magni,' Shelley said optimistically, 'Mary, I'm sure, will be completely happy again.'

4

'It's much smaller than I thought,' Mary complained.

She and Shelley, with the others busily unpacking, had just completed a thorough inspection of the Casa Magni, and even Shelley had to admit, though only to himself, that living space was very much restricted. The lower floor, which was open to the weather at the front, was useful only as storage space, and Shelley had already envisaged it crammed with fishing and boating gear, envisaged it to so great an extent that he could smell the tar of the ropes and the brine of much used lines. The upper floor, reached by two staircases, consisted of an entrance hall, large enough to be used as a dining-room, and four small rooms, which would have to serve as bedrooms, one for the Shelleys, one for the Williams, one for Claire and the fourth for the children. In addition there was a poky little kitchen, the only room in the house with a fireplace, while in the garden stood an outhouse scarcely large enough for the servants.

'Call them bedrooms if you must,' Mary said, 'but they look more like cells to me.'

'The Casa Magni was once a Jesuit convent,' Shelley laughed, 'but I don't think we need let that depress us. We've no intention, I'm sure, of living like monks and nuns.'

'Where are you going to work?' Mary asked, unsmilingly. 'You can't have a study to yourself here.'

'So long as we're all happy together I can work in any hole or corner,' Shelley said cheerfully. 'There'll be the boat, remember. That should make an excellent outdoor study.' He led her eagerly to the veranda. 'You can't complain of a lack of space here, Mary. It's a terrace rather than a veranda. Isn't a veranda supposed to be covered at the top? We can dine out here in warm weather. Isn't it a glorious view? I never thought I'd have the opportunity of living so close to the water. Think how delightful it's going to be sitting out here at night, or pacing up and down. Jane can play and sing to us, and there'll be the additional music of the waves breaking on the beach.'

'And breaking over the terrace itself in rough weather,' Mary pointed out querulously. 'I'm not going to enjoy that. It's a pity

Jane and Edward didn't give us a clearer account of the place. It's so isolated.'

She was beginning to feel desperate. The Casa Magni was not at the fishing village of San Terenzo, as she had expected, but on the outskirts, and the village accessible only by a rough and broken path. Another equally difficult path led to Lerici which by land was a mile away.

'I hate the place already,' she said.

'You're tired, darling,' Shelley said patiently. 'A good night's sleep will make all the difference in the world to you.'

'I hope it will,' Mary said wearily, 'but I haven't slept properly for days. If it hadn't been for the need to get Claire away from Pisa I wouldn't have agreed to the Casa Magni without first seeing it.'

'It isn't quite fair to blame Claire for your disappointment,' Shelley protested.

'When are you going to tell her about Allegra?' Mary asked.

'Must I be the one to tell her?' he asked unhappily.

'I haven't the courage myself, and the longer we leave it the harder it's going to be.'

'It's the one thing that's making you miserable, isn't it, darling?'

'No, Shelley, there's something else. I can't free myself of the fear that the same thing is going to happen to Percy. I feel it more strongly than ever in this dreadful place.'

By early evening, when most of the unpacking had been done, the sky had darkened and a wind was moaning in the hills at the back of the house. Nightfall brought a squall sweeping across the bay. Sleepless during most of the night, Mary lay listening to the wind and the rain. The Casa Magni, she thought, might well be a ship at sea, a ship in constant danger of foundering. And this impression, symbolizing her fear of the future, still clouded her mind the next morning, even though the storm had passed and the sun was glittering on the surf.

Shelley took Claire for a walk immediately after breakfast, hoping in the solitude of the hills to be able to speak calmly of Allegra's death, but still his courage failed him.

'You're troubled about something,' Claire said once.

'My dear . . .' he began.

'Is it Mary?'

'Her poor health is a constant worry, yes.'

'There's more to it than that, Shelley. I can sense it. An atmosphere of strain, of waiting for something horrible to happen.'

'Claire—'

'The move from Pisa was much too hurried. That was upsetting for Mary. No real plans were made. Taking the Casa Magni without knowing how small it was— Shelley, it occurred to me last night that Mary might be happier with one person less in the house.'

'If you mean yourself—'

'I do, Shelley, and please don't try to stop me from leaving. I'm no happier here than Mary is. How could I be when my thoughts are with Allegra? I've decided against going to Vienna, but there's no reason why I shouldn't go back to Florence. Professor Bojti was always kind. He goes to Ravenna from time to time. I could travel with him and call at the convent. I'm not known there, and if I said I was Allegra's aunt the mother superior would have no reason for disbelieving me. I can't imagine why I didn't think of so simple a plan before.'

'It's not as simple as you think,' Shelley told her desperately 'I really must insist on your remaining at Casa Magni. Mary would be more depressed than ever if you left. We need you here until the baby arrives.'

'That won't be for months.'

'Claire, I—'

'Are you conspiring with Byron to keep me from Allegra?' she broke in angrily. 'You went to see her yourself. You could easily have taken me.' She turned from him quickly. 'I'm going to pack. I'll leave for Florence first thing in the morning.'

Shelley followed her dejectedly. He had tried and failed, but would have to try again. It was out of the question that she should be allowed to leave without being told. He wondered then if Jane, always so calm and resourceful, would undertake the sorry task, but Jane, whom he approached the moment he reached the Casa Magni, said in a troubled voice that she had neither the heart nor the courage.

'We can't let her go without telling her,' Shelley said. 'As I love you, Jane—'

'Quietly, Bysshe,' she said. 'Claire might hear you.'

Shelley looked about him hastily. They were standing in the

entrance hall. He could hear Edward moving boxes on the floor below. The children were with him and by the sound of their shrill voices were clearly enjoying themselves.

'Is Claire in her room?' he whispered.

'Yes, packing.'

'And Mary?'

'In your own room.'

'Fetch Ned and join us there. We'll decide between us how best to tell her.'

'Well, if you think it will do any good . . .'

A few moment's later the four of them were arguing fruitlessly and miserably. Mary refused point blank to be the one to break the news.

'You're Claire's stepsister,' Jane pointed out.

'It's not a matter of who tells her, but how we tell her,' Shelley said. 'If I could think of some gentle, consoling words I wouldn't hesitate for another moment.'

'Nor would I,' said Edward.

'I've just remembered something,' Mary said, after a moment's silence. 'Claire had a dream last year about Allegra. She told me about it in a letter. In the dream somebody had written to tell her that Allegra was ill and not likely to recover. If you could begin by talking to her about that dream—' She broke off and stared in horror at the door. 'Claire!'

Claire was standing on the threshold, one hand still grasping the door handle.

'Claire, you were listening,' Mary said stupidly.

Shelley sprang forward. 'Claire, my dear—!'

'It's a funny thing,' she said in a whisper, 'but my hand seems to be stuck to the handle.' She stared at her hand for a long moment. 'My fingers seem to be locked.' Her voice rose shrilly. 'Shelley, I can't move them!'

As gently as he could, Shelley forced Claire's fingers from the handle.

'Why, thank you,' she said, and began to laugh.

'Claire!' he said sharply.

Still laughing, she turned and ran through the entrance hall, reached one of the stairways and disappeared down it. Shelley and the others rushed out to the terrace, and a moment later they caught sight of Claire running along the beach. She stumbled in the soft sand as they watched and for a moment lay face down, her whole body quivering.

'She can't be left alone,' Shelley said. 'I'll go after her.'

By the time he reached the beach she was running again.

'Claire!' he shouted. 'Claire, wait for me!'

She was making for the village, but at the sound of his voice turned sharply right and was quickly lost to view among the undergrowth. Reaching the spot where he had last seen her, Shelley paused to listen, and presently he caught the sound of her body brushing through the tall grass of a little clearing farther up the slope. In pursuit again he caught up with her on the edge of a small plantation of walnut trees.

'Oh, Shelley . . .' she said numbly.

He took her in his arms, but instantly she began to struggle with him, and so frantically that a moment later they were rolling together in the long grass. Exhausted at last she lay passively in his arms, but when he made to release her she clung to him fiercely.

'Shelley, don't leave me.'

He stroked her brow gently. 'It might make things easier for you if you cried.'

'I want to but I can't.'

'Then curse me for bringing all this sorrow upon you.'

'I brought it upon myself.'

'Dear Claire, what can I say to comfort you?'

'Nothing, Shelley. Tell me how she died.'

'There was an epidemic. Typhus fever.'

'You knew before I left Pisa, didn't you? That was why you hurried me away.'

'If it means anything to you at all, Byron's grief is as deep as your own.'

'He's a queer man.'

'He promised to send you a lock of Allegra's hair.'

Claire flung herself away from him. 'Shelley, don't!'

With tears in her eyes now she lay tensely on her back, digging her fingers into the grass on either side of her. Shelley watched the struggle with tears in his own eyes. Never had he seen so heartrending a sight. No grief of his own had ever affected him so poignantly, nor isolated him from the whole world with such shattering force. Not quite knowing what he was doing he bent over her and lightly brushed her lips with his. She responded instantly and violently, at first with her fingers still clinging to the grass, presently with her arms frantically about his shoulders. Yet gradually a strange, sweet calmness descended upon her. It was like the striking of a summer storm which, passing swiftly, left the world drenched in peace and beauty.

'Thank you, Shelley,' she said, when at length they drew away from each other.

'How wonderful,' he said shakily, 'that we should be joined together like that by grief. And yet how horrible that only through your loss should I have learnt that grief even more than love can heighten one's feelings, raise them to a pitch of sheer impersonal exultation.'

Claire looked at him doubtfully. He sounded like a man who was trying to explain away something which, though scarcely recognized, he was afraid to accept, and she knew now that as far as she was concerned there had been nothing impersonal about that little storm of passion through which they had passed. Grief had done more than heighten her own feelings, it had called to life a past dream of what might have been. Byron had merely dazzled her; he had said as much himself. Her heart was Shelley's, and always would be; Byron had said that too, and Byron was right.

'Are you ready to go back to the others?' Shelley asked gently.

'Yes, I think so.'

'You do see now that there's no need for you to go off to Florence?'

She rose to her feet, finding it difficult to say either yes or no. Concerned as Shelley was on her account, she could see that he had quickly recovered his equanimity. No doubt he would write a verse or two about death and grief and heightened feeling, and that would be that. To go would be less agonizing than to remain.

'Grief is a personal, private sort of thing,' she said quietly. 'I shall recover from it more quickly among strangers.'

Twenty-five

I

'Oh, there she is,' said Edward, shipping the oars.

Shelley squinted in the sunlight. 'It doesn't look like Claire to me.'

'She's wearing a ridiculous new bonnet. Probably the latest fashion in Florence these days.'

Leaving Edward to tie up the boat at the steps near the Lerici inn, Shelley leapt out and ran along the seawall to greet the young woman who had waved to them.

'Ah, so it *is* you! That silly bonnet deceived me. Take it off at once.'

Claire obeyed demurely. 'Shall I throw it into the sea?'

'No, give it to the inn-keeper's wife. She'll look ravishing in it. Dear Claire, how happy I am to see you again. I'm so glad you thought of coming on to Lerici by road. Ned and I hoped you would, once you saw how rough the sea was. Mind you, we tried to get the boat in at Via Reggio but were driven back again and again.'

It was a month since Claire had left for Florence, and soon after her departure Mary, her health deteriorating, had written begging her to return as soon as possible. For a time Claire had argued with herself, but in the end she had decided that Mary's health was as good an excuse as any for doing what, in her heart, she wanted so much to do. Shelley had then written enthusiastically about the new boat – his latest love, he called it – and had promised to meet her in it at Via Reggio.

'If that's the *Don Juan*,' Claire said, looking down at the frail craft from which Edward Williams was waving to her, 'thank heaven you weren't able to meet me at Via Reggio. Nothing would induce me to out to sea in a cockle-shell like that.'

Shelley looked hurt. 'What an idiot you are! *That* is our landing craft. We row about the bay in it too. However, if you don't think it's safe enough you may *walk* to the Casa Magni.'

'I'll risk my life in your cockle-shell.'

'And later you'll risk it in the *Don Juan*.' He pointed to a two-masted boat lying at anchor in the bay. 'There she is! Isn't she a beauty!'

The boat, which had been delivered from Genoa soon after Claire's departure, was smaller than her schooner-rigged construction suggested, being less than thirty feet long and no more than eight feet wide.

'I can't see any sign of a cabin,' Claire said.

'There's no deck either. We're rough seamen, not aristocratic amateurs. She carries more than enough sail for her size – we made the trip to Spezia and back in ninety minutes – and if you're nervous she might overturn in a storm we have two tons of iron ballast in the bottom to hold her firm in any sea.'

His enthusiasm was so infectious that Claire found herself laughing gaily. He sounded happier and more carefree than she had ever known him, and looked amazingly healthy. His face and neck and forearms were deeply sunburnt. Dressed in a tattered shirt, open at the neck and the sleeves rolled up, and a shabby pair of trousers wet to the knees, he might well have been taken for a boy of sixteen rather than a man of twenty-nine, or even an overgrown Italian urchin, for he wore no shoes.

'We intended to call the boat *Ariel*,' he said, frowning, 'but that high-handed Byron took it upon himself to have the name *Don Juan* painted on the mainsail. We tried spirits of wine, everything we could think of, but failed utterly to get rid of it.'

'Byron, being what he is,' Claire laughed lightly, 'should have called his own boat *Don Juan*.'

Shelley looked at her quickly. 'I'm sorry I mentioned him. Please forgive me.'

'Byron to me is dead,' she said lightly. 'Far more so than Allegra ever could be.'

'You can talk about her now without hurting yourself too much?' he asked anxiously.

Claire looked at him as steadily as she could, her heart aching for him more than ever before. It was unwise of her to have come back, she knew that now; and it was the height of

folly to believe that having come back she could convince him
that he needed her as much as she needed him.

'The past is dead,' she said quietly. 'The present is all that
matters.'

Shelley's face clouded. 'And the future of no account?'

'Oh Shelley, I've looked too often to the future to want ever
to think of it again.'

'So many high hopes, Claire, then bitter disappointment.'
He turned and centred his gaze on the Casa Magni. 'If the past
is really dead, and one could obliterate the future, perhaps the
present would be sufficient.' He laughed jauntily. 'But I'm
talking nonsense. It's far too glorious a day for gloomy thoughts.'

Claire looked at him closely. He was not then as happy and
carefree as she had first thought. *Perhaps the present would be
sufficient. . . .* She dwelt on this during the rest of the day at the
Casa Magni. What, she asked herself, did the present, of which
he seemed to have many doubts, actually hold for him? Mary
on the one hand was depressed and querulous; Jane on the other
was calm and aloof, yet still held Shelley entranced. It seemed to
Claire that he was torn between the two of them and, because of
Mary's frowns and complaints, was turning more and more to
Jane, looking at her always as if begging her mutely to smile
upon him. Did he realize what an intolerable situation it was?
And did he long to obliterate the future because he saw it as
nothing more than an unchanging extension of the present?

One thing seemed certain; Shelley was only really happy
out of doors. Or was it excitement he felt, not happiness? He
insisted on taking Claire out in the *Don Juan* immediately after
a midday meal. Edward Williams, addressed solemnly as
Captain Williams, was in charge, for he knew far more about the
handling of boats than Shelley. Jane accompanied them, but
Mary, saying she was too unwell to lie tossing perilously on the
ocean in what she called 'Shelley's plaything', preferred to remain
at the Casa Magni reading. They sailed halfway to Spezia.
Shelley would have gone farther, in spite of a change of wind,
but Edward insisted prudently on turning back. Claire, who
remembered sailing in the boat which Shelley and Byron had
shared at Geneva, thought the *Don Juan* rather sluggish in the
water and, in spite of the ballast, a little top-heavy.

There was another trip that night, but only up and down the

bay. Mary once again refused to join them, calm and beautiful
as the night was. She had been studying Greek most of the day
and wanted now, by way of a change, to read a few chapters of
Madame de Staël's *Vie de Necker*. Jane brought her guitar, and
with Shelley lying at her feet she sang some Neapolitan love
songs. Fishermen were busy in the bay, their bobbing lanterns
dimmed by the brilliance of the moonlight, while on the beach
a group of village girls danced and sang at the water's edge.

'On a night such as this,' said Shelley, when Jane at last grew
tired of singing, 'one can almost believe that this earth of ours
is another world, free of strife and pain, sailing serenely in the
peace of limitless space.'

He spoke, Claire thought, with a dreamy sombreness, and
after a moment, frowning now, he went on in a whisper that
scarcely reached her ears.

'If the past and the future could be obliterated the present
would content me so much that I could say, as Faust did,
"Remain, thou art so beautiful".'

He was troubled still about time, Claire thought, and about
Jane too, for he had looked beseechingly at her while speaking.
For a moment Claire caught the graceful shrug of Jane's shoulders
the slight inclination of her pretty head. She looked, Claire
thought angrily, like a goddess accepting and rejecting the
homage of a mere mortal.

'Nothing could be more beautiful than the bay tonight,'
Claire said, trying to keep all sign of harshness from her voice.

'A beauty that hurts,' Shelley murmured, as if to himself.

'How can anything that hurts be really beautiful?' Jane
asked.

What a fool she was, Claire thought angrily. Beauty could
hurt exquisitely. There had been beauty in the grief she had
shared with Shelley, and yet, intense as the pain of it had been,
that strange, sweet calmness had replaced it. That, too, they had
shared if only for a fleeting moment. To share it again, and sharing
it hold it. . . . To convince Shelley, to make him realize how much
she, above all other women, could give him. . . .

'Beauty that hurts,' said Shelley, as if answering himself
rather than Jane, 'is beauty that turns to ugliness.'

'Time can do that to a beautiful woman,' Jane laughed.

'Even a woman whose beauty has hurt no one?'

But Claire was scarcely listening now. Let them argue; Shelley would only grow more confused and unhappy. It would serve her purpose well, make the struggle which lay before her, and upon which she was determined to embark, all the easier. She saw it as a contest, her opponents Mary and Jane, and Shelley himself the prize.

Later that night, when talking with Mary in her room while the others sat out on the terrace, it occurred to Claire that it might be easier to free Shelley of Mary than of Jane. Mary had retreated into a life of her own. She had her work, as Shelley had his. Neither was now an inspiration to the other, for inspiration had given place to obstruction. They were divided by conflict, resentment, perhaps even unacknowledged jealousy. The long-dead Harriet, with no literary life of her own, could have kept Shelley for ever, had she not been such a fool. Jane, by all appearances not really wanting him, held him firmly enslaved. Shelley, as far as Jane was concerned, must be sharply and swiftly disillusioned. Everything would be remarkably easy, Claire thought, if only she could decide how best to act.

'Trelawny hasn't seen the Casa Magni yet,' Mary was saying. 'When he does I'm sure he'll be shocked at the primitive conditions under which I am forced to live.'

Claire wondered then why she hadn't thought earlier of Trelawny as a possible weapon. She had noticed while at Pisa that he and Mary were more than ordinarily attracted to each other, but absorbed in her own troubles she had failed to attach real significance to it. And during the journey to Spezia Mary had remarked more than once that without Trelawny she would have been utterly lost.

'Do you expect him on a visit soon?' she asked.

'Any day now,' Mary said, a faint edge of interest to her voice. 'He intends to spend a few days here on his way from Genoa to Leghorn. Byron wants his new boat at Leghorn, which is close enough to Pisa, and Trelawny is going to sail it there from Genoa. Boats! How sick to death I am of all these boats. The men are like children playing with floating bits of paper in a pond.'

'Even Trelawny?'

'He,' Mary said sharply, 'is a professional sailor.'

Claire let it rest at that.

'Mary,' she said presently, 'I keep wondering why you hate this place so much. I know you were rushed here because of me. Could that be part of your reason?'

'Darling,' Mary said contritely, 'I would have done anything at that time to make things easier for you. I hate it for its isolation as much as anything else. You know how ill I am. If I grow worse, is there a really good doctor within reach?'

'Isn't it a sickness of the spirit rather than the body?' Claire asked quietly.

'It might be, but it's not really myself I'm thinking of, it's my son. I'm so afraid that what happened to Allegra might happen to Percy. Shelley says I'm obsessed with an unreasoning fear, but I can't help it if I am. I was once obsessed with a fear that Shelley might be drowned, yet if I dwelt on that these days with all this childish interest in boats I'd go crazy.'

'And so,' said Claire pityingly, 'you have found another fear, one even more unnecessary.'

Mary looked at her stonily. 'I want to go back to Pisa, but Shelley won't take the slightest notice.'

'Perhaps he doesn't want to leave Jane.'

'Jane?'

'You suggested once that he was in love with her without knowing it. You begged me not to tell him.'

'Tell him if you must. Wake him from his little dream. Force him to realize that Jane, in her own unemotional way, wants no man but Edward. It won't make the slightest difference. Shelley will remain here.'

'Surely disillusionment would send him back to Pisa more quickly than anything else.'

'Leigh Hunt is the problem, not Jane.'

Claire remembered then that Leigh Hunt, with whom Shelley had become friendly in London, had been persuaded to settle in Italy. He had not yet arrived, but was expected soon at Leghorn. In earlier days, when Hunt, a poet and essayist, had been fined and imprisoned for libelling the Prince Regent, Shelley had wanted to lend him five hundred pounds, and had been prevented from doing so only by his failure at that time to raise the money. Intent on giving him real help now Shelley, with Byron, had suggested that the three of them should in Italy publish a periodical in which all their work would appear.

As a result, Shelley would be faced soon with the task of finding a house for Hunt and his large family.

'Byron could quite easily look after the Hunts unaided,' Mary said, referring to this now. 'Shelley is entirely unreasonable.'

'Since the idea was his, he probably feels responsible for their welfare.'

'Responsible for theirs, but not his wife and son's, apparently.'

'Oh come, Mary, there's no epidemic in this district. All in all, Percy is safer here than at Pisa.'

Mary picked up a book. 'Good night, Claire. I shall read for an hour before going to sleep.'

2

'Shelley is a complete duffer at handling a boat,' Trelawny said scathingly, 'and Ned Williams isn't much better. As for the boat itself, I'm damned if I'd risk *my* life in it in a really heavy sea.'

'You're trying to alarm me,' Mary exclaimed.

'Sorry,' Trelawny said gruffly. 'Not much sense in doing that when I haven't made any sort of fist of alarming Shelley.'

He had arrived that morning in Byron's magnificent yacht, the *Bolivar*, had taken lodgings at the inn at Lerici and had then been rowed over to the Casa Magni by Edward Williams. He was sitting now on the terrace with Mary, both of them watching Shelley, Edward, and Jane, who were rowing out for a close inspection of the *Bolivar*.

'It's not my place to insist on anything as far as you are concerned,' Trelawny went on, 'and you can tell me to go to the devil if you feel like it, but I won't rest easy unless you promise me you'll never make a trip outside the bay in the *Don Juan*.'

Mary, surprised that Trelawny's arrival should have cheered her so much, gave him a grateful smile.

'It's kind of you to be so concerned,' she murmured. 'Rest assured, I won't tell you to go to the devil.'

'You don't think I'm interfering?'

'Of course not, Trelawny.'

He looked at her thoughtfully, well satisfied with the colour that had come to her cheeks at the sight of him. He had made up his mind in Pisa that he wanted her, and was as sure now as he had been then that a rough and ready approach would do more to make her his than any romantic, poetic nonsense.

'It's not my fault if I feel responsible for you,' he said.

'Whose, then?'

'In the first place, Shelley's.'

'And in the second?'

'Yours, Mary. That is, unless you've deliberately set yourself to look pathetic and helpless.'

'I'm sure I look neither!' Mary said indignantly.

Trelawny chuckled richly. 'Best way to shake you out of it is to make you angry. I can see that. Will it make you angrier still if I tell you Shelley had no right to bring you to a place like this? Casa Magni! What a damn silly name. It's not much better than a boat-house. Practically uninhabitable in rough weather, I'd say.'

'It's frightening in a storm,' Mary admitted.

'Much too cranky in the breeze, like the *Don Juan*. How long does Shelley propose to keep you here?'

'For ever, apparently.'

This, Mary had to admit to herself, was a gross exaggeration. Shelley had promised to take her back to Pisa for her confinement, but that would not be until early November. Five months was so long to wait that it certainly seemed like for ever.

'If it's as bad as that, Mary, I'd better make up my mind about rescuing you.'

She wanted him to say something like that, but now that he had said it she began to feel unhappy about the position in which she was allowing herself to be placed.

'Trelawny,' she said uncertainly, 'you once spoke about a situation that was beginning to bore me. To rescue me from boredom might lead to further boredom, for both of us.'

'There's more to it than boredom. Way I see it now, it's a situation that's killing you.'

'Yes,' she said, 'I think it is.'

'This illness of yours – what is it but mental depression tearing you to pieces physically?'

'I expect you're right in that.'

'Of course I am. I'm right in this too. You're a different

woman when I'm about. Once I get you away from all this you'll start to live as you've never lived before.'

'You've made up your mind, then?'

'That's for you to say,' Trelawny chuckled. 'A woman likes to think she's the cause of a man doing what he *thinks* he wants to do. I hope I'm man enough to let her keep on thinking that way.'

Mary looked out across the bay. It really was a beautiful scene, she told herself, but only because, through Trelawny, she was hovering now on the brink of a new sort of happiness. She must be, because even the ghastly obsession was forgotten. Trelawny's straightforward manner had given her a new confidence in herself, a glimpse of the security she would surely be able to find with him. *What I'm after now is stability*, he'd said at Pisa. And again: *Next time it's got to be permanent.* Shading her eyes from the sun she looked at him as steadily as she could. There was more to it than all that; there was a tremendous and so far unacknowledged physical attraction.

'Well?' he asked, deeply moved by the questioning softness of her eyes.

'There's at least one complication,' Mary said hurriedly. 'You know I'm going to have a baby.'

'All the more reason for having a man who knows what he's about to look after you.'

'I need time to think,' she faltered.

'I'll be here for four or five days, and Leghorn isn't all that far away.'

'They're coming back from the *Bolivar*.'

'So they are. By the way, where's Claire? I haven't seen her yet.'

'She went for a walk. She'll be back presently.'

But Claire was standing just within the entrance hall, afraid to move lest she should draw attention to her silent presence. She had come in quietly from her walk, so absorbed in thoughts of Shelley that she had failed at first to notice that Mary and Trelawny were alone together on the terrace. Yesterday and the day before she had taken the same walk, which she had now come to regard as a pilgrimage. Lying in the grass on the edge of the small plantation of walnut trees, she had recalled again and again the pain and pleasure of the grief which she and Shelley had shared there. She would make the pilgrimage daily until

her hopes were fully realized, bowing as it were before an altar
of her own creation. This she was telling herself when, about to
step out on to the terrace, she had heard Mary say, *I need time to
think*. Those words alone had made her smile with satisfaction.
She had thought of Trelawny as a weapon, but it was clear now
that he was a weapon which she need not grasp. She felt immensely grateful both to Mary and Trelawny. What she had
heard had freed her mind of self-accusation, even the slightest
pricking of conscience. Jane Williams was now the only obstacle.

She drew back a pace, then stepped quickly on to the terrace.

'Mary—' she began, and then, as if in complete surprise,
'Why, Trelawny! How nice to see you again.'

3

'That noise on the beach is quite barbaric,' Mary complained.

She was sitting out on the terrace with Claire and Trelawny.
So still was the night that the singing and laughter of the fishermen and their girls on the beach might well have come from the
other end of the terrace.

'But attractive too, don't you think?' Claire suggested.

'I find nothing attractive in that sort of savagery,' Mary said
plaintively. 'They'll keep me awake all night.'

'I'm sure they won't,' Claire laughed. 'They'll start dancing
soon, as well as singing. According to Shelley it's a primitive
ritual. They'll grow quiet when they reach a certain pitch of
excitement, and by next year the population of San Terenzo
will have increased considerably.' She rose and stretched.
'Oughtn't you to go to bed, Mary?'

'I'm quite happy here, except for that howling.'

Claire was worried about her stepsister. She had been much
brighter during the last two days, with Trelawny a constant
visitor, but her physical health had deteriorated yet again.
Feverish that morning, she had complained of a violent headache
and vague pains in the stomach. The local doctor, summoned
hurriedly by Shelley, had found nothing seriously the matter
with her and had advised her, as usual, to rest.

'I'll go and see what Shelley is up to,' Claire said.

She found him on the lower floor, busy untangling fishing lines in the light of a lamp. Jane, sitting nearby on an empty packing case, was looking unaccountably sulky. She had refused earlier to go with her husband to Lerici, and Edward, keen to see Captain Roberts, who had come with Trelawny in the *Bolivar*, had gone off alone.

'Won't you change your mind, Jane, and come out in the boat?' Shelley said.

'No,' said Jane, uncompromisingly.

'It's ages since we were out in the bay alone. I'd like to hear that new song you were learning. You haven't sung it for me yet.'

'Don't *pester* me, Bysshe,' Jane begged.

Shelley tossed the tangled mass of line aside. He too was looking sulky now.

'I'll go for a row on my own,' he said, and went out without having noticed Claire.

'Poor frustrated little boy,' Jane murmured.

'It's not like you to be in a temper,' Claire remarked mildly.

Jane shrugged and smiled. 'It's the time of the month. The only time, come to think of it, when I dislike people.'

'Even someone who absolutely adores you?'

'Shelley?'

'Weren't you aware of it, Jane?'

'Naturally I was,' Jane said smugly.

Claire's breathing quickened. Here, she thought, was the opportunity for which she had been waiting.

'I wonder if you realize how cruel you are to Shelley?' she said carefully.

'Cruel?' Jane asked in amazement. 'Simply because I wouldn't go out in the boat tonight? I can't play court minstrel all the time.'

'I'm sure you can't, and I'm sure Shelley doesn't expect it. Has it never occurred to you that you yourself would be a welcome change from your guitar and your pretty voice?'

'Are you suggesting,' Jane said complacently, 'that I should on occasion play the mistress as well as the minstrel?'

'For all I know you might have done that already.'

Jane flushed. 'You really are being insulting, Claire.'

This, Claire thought, was splendid; Jane was becoming quite angry now. Nevertheless, she gave her next move some quick and careful thought. Up to now she had agreed with Mary that Jane would never take Shelley as a lover, but she knew her own sex well enough to take into account the possibility of Jane becoming contrary if provoked too far. How great was the risk? She remembered the reason for Jane's shortness of temper. Tonight, at all events, there was no risk whatever.

'Do you give me your word, Jane,' she asked lightly, 'that you are not Shelley's mistress already?'

'If it's any business of yours, yes.'

'No wonder Shelley is so depressed and hurt these days.'

'Are you actually suggesting that he wants to make me his mistress?'

'You've been tantalizing him for months,' Claire countered. 'What do *you* think?'

'I never meant to tantalize him,' Jane scowled.

'I think you did, and I think you were enjoying it.'

'I love him only as a friend,' Jane said furiously.

'But smugly, since you feel so impregnable. An intolerable situation has developed. Unless something is done about it the friendship which exists between you and Edward and Shelley won't last much longer. You may even be in danger of losing Edward.'

'What nonsense,' Jane cried in alarm. 'Edward trusts me.'

'Will he go on trusting you? You're alone often enough with Shelley. Edward must feel a certain suspicion at times. Any husband would. Of course, if you don't care about Edward's feelings . . .'

'I care more about his than Shelley's. I'll never be alone with Shelley again. Never!'

'To break the intimacy abruptly, without explanation,' Claire sighed, 'would be more than cruel. Would you like me to tell Shelley that you care for him only as a friend?'

Jane considered this for a moment.

'I'll tell Shelley myself,' she said, jumping down from the packing case.

'Be gentle with him,' Claire begged.

'I'll choose my words as carefully as possible,' Jane promised.

Claire followed her from the house and, lagging back a few

paces, down to the beach where Shelley at that moment was pushing the small landing craft into the water.

'Wait!' Jane called. 'I'll come with you. I want to talk to you.'

Claire, remaining in the shadow of the house, watched Shelley help Jane into the boat. The waning moon, newly risen, was casting a faint orange glow over the bay. A romantic night, she thought, for an unromantic revelation. She waited until Shelley had pushed the boat through the surf and leapt in, then she began to walk slowly along the beach. Her only fear now was that Jane, in disillusioning Shelley, might bring her own name into it. There were only a few men and girls on the beach now, some lying in the soft dry sand, others splashing up to their thighs in the surf. She retraced her steps after watching them for a few moments. Shelley, to her surprise, was already rowing back to the beach. With the moonlight stronger now she could see Jane sitting stiffly in the stern and sensed that Shelley was rowing in grim silence. He beached the boat, jumped out and offered Jane his arm. Ignoring him, she waited till the surf receded, stepped quickly out and ran up the beach. Meeting her near the house, Claire looked at her anxiously. She was flushed and looked quite frightened now.

'I never knew such craziness,' she said. 'He wanted to tip up the boat and drown us both, said something dramatic about solving the great mystery together that way.'

Leaving her to hurry into the house, Claire walked down to the boat, smiled uncertainly at Shelley, thought it wise to respect his silence and helped him drag the boat up beyond the reach of the tide. This done, he kicked off his sodden shoes and began to take off his shirt.

'Shelley, what are you going to do!'

'Walk out into the water until I can walk no farther.'

'You'll change your mind when the water is up to your chin.'

'Don't mock me, Claire.'

'Drown yourself if you must, but come for a last walk with me first.'

He gave her a shame-faced look. 'You think I'm play-acting, don't you?'

'No, Shelley, I think you're desperately serious.'

K*

'Liar,' he said sombrely.

He buttoned up his shirt, ignored his shoes and began to walk along the beach with Claire. Kicking off her own shoes she matched her step with his. Walking in silence they kept to the water's edge, their feet sinking at every step into the soft wet sand.

'What did you say to Jane?' he asked at length.

Claire hesitated. So Jane *had* brought her name into it.

'I told her she was being cruel to you.'

'So you did. I was too confused and disheartened to remember. I myself had thought her cruel many times, but not despicable as well.'

'I don't understand what you mean, Shelley.'

'It appears that she misunderstood me from the first. The shock of it was all the greater because I had thought her far above the ordinary female vanity. It had never occurred to her that what I was offering her was far removed from the thing that men call love. She wasn't prepared to give me physical love, she said, and had decided, for all our sakes, to tell me so. Thus, in a few brief words she shattered the lamp that I had thought burnt so brightly. The light, even if it was only part of my imagination, lies dead in the dust.'

Claire, for the moment, could think of nothing to say. Things had turned out differently from what she had expected. Shelley, thwarted spiritually, not physically, was in need of spiritual comfort. Could she give it to him? She doubted it very much. What a perplexing nuisance a poet could be! More than likely the pressure of her warm lips on his would at this moment revolt him. And yet, she pondered, had not she received from him, in a moment of grief-inspired passion, a comfort that was gloriously spiritual? He had been quickly dejected, could he not be just as quickly elated? She knew to what extremes his moods could fly. It was all a question of finding the right words.

'There are other lamps yet to be lit,' she said.

'Never would I take the risk of lighting them. I have been condemned to darkness, and in darkness I shall remain.'

Claire all but laughed. By the sound of his voice he was enjoying his own misery, clinging to it like a faded flower the beauty of which had delighted him yesterday. Soon, if she didn't find the right words, he might find them himself and have no need of her.

'Let's walk into the hills and look down on the bay in the moonlight,' she suggested.

It had been in her mind all along to lead him to the spot on the edge of the walnut plantation, and this she did without Shelley realizing where they were.

'My feet aren't as hard as yours,' she said ruefully, and sat down in the long grass. 'I don't think I can walk any farther.'

Shelley sat down at her side. 'I didn't know you were bare-footed. I hope you haven't injured yourself.'

She held up her left foot. 'Not seriously.'

'Why, it's bleeding!'

'I must have stepped on a sharp stone. I thought my big toe was burning.'

Showing instant concern Shelley took off his shirt, the back of which was in rags. Making it worse he tore out a strip and began with gentle fingers to bind up Claire's toe.

'I'm making a better job of it than that incompetent doctor would,' he chuckled.

Claire drew her skirt a little higher. 'How ridiculous, Shelley, that because of my injured toe you should of a sudden feel easier in your mind.'

He looked up at her in surprise. 'Ludicrous, yes.'

'You must regard it in future with becoming reverence. A toe, my dear, has freed your enslaved spirit.'

'Am I expected to genuflect every time I catch sight of it?' he laughed.

This, Claire thought, was terrible. She had made him laugh, and to comfort him with laughter was the last thing she'd intended. Worse, she was finding it hard not to laugh herself. Laugher, she thought angrily, would make them carefree companions, that and no more.

'Shelley,' she said, striving to be utterly serious, 'is it possible that you don't want to obliterate the future any more?'

'Why do you ask that?'

'Because the future, in spite of the pain Jane caused you, is no longer an extension of the unbearable present. No,' she added quickly, 'I mean *because* of the pain she caused you.'

Shelley tied the bandage in a neat little knot.

'You're an amazing person, Claire. How did you gain such terrific insight?'

'I've suffered too,' she reminded him. 'But never mind me, it's you we are concerned with. Jane inspired you, yes, but how deeply? As deeply, perhaps, as Mary?'

'Mary inspires me no longer,' he said, miserable again.

'It's Jane we're talking about, not Mary. Jane inspired you, but it was a limited inspiration. That was part of the present which you feared might go on and on into the future. Jane held you back – held you back, Shelley, at a time when your career as a prophetic poet was only just beginning.'

'I was still able to dream, Claire. Such grand dreams, too. Long narrative poems singing in my mind. History in verse. The ugliness of a decaying civilization. A protest against what man has made of the thing he calls Christianity. Looking backward, that. Showing, if only I had the skill, that Christ has rarely been a part of the religion to which his name was given. Then looking forward, Claire. Christ, the only real Christian, driving the hypocrites from all the temples of the world—' He broke off. 'Do you think I'm talking nonsense?'

'If all that is to remain no more than a dream, yes.'

'Since I stand alone, what else can I do but dream? It isn't possible to be a complete individualist. That's one sorry lesson I've learnt. A man alone is a pitiful, helpless creature.'

'So is a woman.'

Shelley stretched himself out on the grass at her side. 'Women are stronger than men.'

'Only because of the need men have of them.' Leaning over him Claire lightly touched his smooth bare chest. 'It's a funny thing, Shelley, but until tonight I'd been thinking that I was the only one who stood alone. Now it seems we both stand alone. Silly, isn't it. . . .'

He took her hand in his. 'Ludicrous.'

'Infamous.'

'Preposterous!'

'Perfidious!'

They both laughed, as if delighted at a little game they were playing.

'In short, not to be borne any longer, Claire.'

'The trouble with me is I talk too much.'

They laughed again, Shelley drawing Claire down beside
him. It began to seem to her then that laughter was better, after
all.

'It's your fault, Shelley. You told me years ago to keep away
from the trees and not stop talking.'

'You're close enough to the trees now.'

'But still talking.'

Turning, Shelley took her fully in his arms and kissed her, but
holding back with difficulty from a blind emotional response she
pushed him gently away. Laughter had brought him to this, yes,
but laughter alone might not be enough to hold him. It was
necessary still, she thought, to play upon his poetic, romantic
and tragic imaginings.

'Dear Shelley, do you recognize this place?'

'There's something vaguely familiar about it, but—'

'If only you knew how much it means to me,' she went on
quickly. 'When I saw how desperate you were I knew I must
bring you here, the more so if this is to be our last meeting. Silly
of me, but this has become a hallowed place.'

'Why Claire, of course. . . !'

'Yes, Shelley, this is where you consoled me in my grief,
shared it with me, became a living part of it. I' – her voice
shook; she knew now that she was practising this shameless
trickery with the utmost sincerity – 'I couldn't bear to come here
again and again alone. If you must go back and walk out into the
sea, I'll come with you. I too, with nothing else left in life, would
want to solve the great mystery.'

'Dear Claire,' he whispered, drawing her closer, 'it seems to
me now that we have a more important mystery to solve, a warm
and living mystery.'

'If you think I can console you as you consoled me. . . .'

She kissed him then of her own accord, holding back in no
way, and submitting to the intensity of his response she began to
feel that the struggle, bringing her victory, was all but over.

'Not joined by grief any more,' Shelley murmured presently.

'By what, then?' she asked tremulously.

'An understanding so deep it frightens me.'

'If anything frightens me, Shelley, it's the love I feel all about
us.'

'One shouldn't be afraid of love.'

'Nor of understanding.'

'For heaven's sake, woman, stop talking!'

'Darling Shelley,' she chuckled softly, 'you're the only one who knows how to silence me.'

Later, when they were walking down to the beach, Claire complained that her clothes were full of grass seed. Shelley told her sternly that there was no grass seed at this time of the year, but to make absolutely sure he found it necessary to undress her again.

'You're probably full of grass seed yourself,' Claire laughed, and leaving him in the act of shaking out her clothing ran back up the slope.

When at last they started off a second time for the beach Shelley asked her if the fear she had felt still clung to her.

'It does in a different sense,' she said seriously. 'I'm afraid that this lovely thing, which it has taken us so long to find, may be taken from us.'

'We weren't either of us ready for it before, but it's ours for ever, now.'

'Not if we remain at the Casa Magni, Shelley.'

'It would be an impossible situation, yes.'

'Impossible in every respect. We would be forced to hide our feelings, become furtive, and furtiveness kills love. But worse than that, what hope would you have here of turning those dreams of yours into reality? None at all, Shelley.'

'Where shall we go?' he asked briskly. 'Paris, perhaps? Geneva might be better. I prefer a lake to a river. Though best of all I like the sea. Perhaps we could stay here after all, providing we were alone. Mary wants to go back to Pisa, and Jane said tonight she would make Ned take her away as soon as possible. Mary . . .' He dwelt uneasily upon the name. 'It isn't going to be altogether easy, is it, Claire. . . .'

This, Claire thought, was the time to tell him about Mary and Trelawny, but before she could speak a figure came hurrying towards them along the beach. It was Edward Williams, and it was clear the moment he spoke that he was deeply agitated.

'I've been looking for you everywhere! Where have you been? Didn't you hear me calling? Mary is desperately ill and Trelawny has gone to fetch the doctor. By the look of things there's every danger of a miscarriage.'

Twenty-six

I

'When did it happen?' Mary asked.

'It would be better not to talk,' Claire whispered.

Mary closed her eyes again, but still struggled to remember all that had happened since last night. Or was it the night before? Her mind, unnaturally clear one moment, was clouded with hazy half-memories the next. Listening as she lay tensely in her bed, she heard a voice outside. Trelawny's, of course! She had been sitting on the terrace with Claire and Trelawny. Claire had gone out, Jane had come in. There was that dreadful howling noise in the beach. The wind? Another storm blowing up? *And by next year*, someone had said, *the population of San Terenzo will have increased considerably*. It was really indecent that the wind should make so much noise about that sort of thing. She tried to sit up, her mind clear for a moment.

'It was a miscarriage, wasn't it?'

'Yes, Mary. Please try and rest.'

'Tell me when it happened.'

'At eight this morning. You were terribly ill all night but there's no danger now. Shelley saved you. The doctor couldn't be found. When he did arrive the danger was past.'

'And how, pray, did Dr. Shelley save me?'

'He used ice to stop the bleeding. Luckily there's still a store of it in the ice-house at Lerici. We were afraid of it ourselves, but Shelley insisted. There's nothing wrong with you now that rest won't cure.'

'You sound like a doctor yourself. Ice! How ridiculous. You think I'm hysterical, don't you. I'm not, you know.'

'A little delirious still, darling, but not hysterical.'

'What time is it now?'

'Six in the evening.'

Mary sank back on the pillows. A miscarriage. All to the good, perhaps. One less child to worry about. Only two now instead of two and a bit. Two? She tried to sort out her thoughts. Percy was one, but the other . . . ? Why, Shelley himself, of course. More trouble than any child of her womb. Fruit, that was. Fruit of her womb.

'Claire, ask Shelley to get me an orange.'

'They're out of season, Mary.'

'So are we all. Why isn't Shelley here?'

'We made him go to bed. He was up with you all night.'

To Claire's relief Mary grew drowsy and fell soon into a fitful slumber. Claire went to her own room where Shelley had promised to rest, but he had wandered off, Jane told her, to the beach, Edward going with him to make sure he came to no harm. Later Mary was able to sit up and take a little broth. She was sleeping again when Shelley and Edward came back, Shelley flushed and wild-eyed, and declaring, almost incoherently, that he had seen a naked child rising out of the sea.

'Ned saw it too,' he claimed.

Edward, standing behind him, caught Claire's eye and shook his head.

'We'll all start seeing apparitions if we have another sleepless night,' she said sharply. 'I'm going to regard myself as the mistress of the house and order you all to bed.'

'Is it safe to leave Mary?' Edward asked.

'She's sleeping now, and I've put up a camp bed for myself in her room.'

Claire and Jane put the children to bed, by which time Shelley had gone meekly to Claire's room. Trelawny called when Edward and Jane had bidden Claire good night, but smiling good-naturedly allowed himself to be ordered back to Lerici.

'I'll come over again first thing in the morning,' he said.

Claire herself, uncomfortable on the camp bed, spent a restless night. The night-light troubled her, and from time to time, anxious about her stepsister, she got up to look at her. At dawn, when at last she had fallen into a heavy sleep, Mary roused her by calling her name sharply.

'Darling, what is it? Are you feeling worse again?'

'No, I think I feel a little better,' Mary said, 'except that I'm troubled by a dream. At least, I think it was a dream, or were you really shaking me and reproaching me about Trelawny?'

'I wouldn't shake you, Mary, and I wouldn't reproach you about anything.'

'You know about Trelawny and me, I can see it in your eyes.'

'I suspect you of having a certain interest in him, yes.'

'He wants me to go away with him. I can't make up my mind. But perhaps I *had* made up my mind just before I was ill, and was reproaching myself in the dream. It – oh Claire, it's so hard to know whether the things I dream are real, or the real things just a dream.'

'Try not to worry about it, Mary.'

'I'll try,' Mary said doubtfully, 'but you must promise not to tell Shelley about Trelawny and me.' Her voice rose shrilly. 'Promise, Claire!'

Claire hesitated for a moment.

'Very well,' she said helplessly, 'I promise.'

'I'll tell Shelley myself, once I know what is real and what isn't. Can *you* distinguish reality from phantasy, Claire?'

'Not always,' Claire admitted.

She went back to the camp bed, but had lain there only a few moments when Shelley burst into the room. He had, he said, sat up most of the night writing, had finally gone to bed in his clothes and had now, with excruciating difficulty, emerged from a horrible nightmare.

'I dreamt that I was dreaming,' he said hoarsely, 'and in the dream within a dream Jane and Ned came into the room and woke me violently. They were in a horrible condition, with blood on their faces and their bones sticking through their bruised flesh. Edward said the sea was rushing into the house and the house was crumbling away. Jane, stronger than he, was supporting him. He could hardly stand. I was sure he was dying. Then I was awake but still dreaming. I was alone with you, Mary, and, dear heaven, I was strangling you. I had to wake up, I had to!'

'And you did,' Claire said soothingly. 'Do please go back to bed before you give poor Mary a relapse.'

'Poor Shelley,' Mary said pitifully, when he had rushed from the room as wildly as he had entered it, 'have I treated him so badly that he should want, even in sleep, to strangle me?'

She was brooding over this when Trelawney called soon after breakfast. She sent Claire from the room and was able for a few moments to talk with him alone. He said at once that he must leave that morning with the *Bolivar*, otherwise Byron, who had expected the boat at Leghorn the day before, would grow alarmed and send out a search party.

'I go with the greatest reluctance,' he said.

'But I want you to go,' Mary told him.

'Go and not come back?'

'I don't know, Trelawny, *I don't know*. It might be easier for me to make up my mind when you're not here, tempting me.'

'Nice to know you find me as attractive as all that,' he chuckled. 'Still, I won't pester you now. It wouldn't be fair to you, or for that matter to myself.'

'Why the last, Trelawny?'

He chuckled again. 'In your present weak condition you might make the wrong decision.'

Or the right one, Mary thought. But which was which?

'I'll write to you,' she said. 'Please be patient.'

2

Later that morning Shelley and Claire stood together on the terrace watching the *Bolivar* sail out of the bay. There was a good and favourable wind, and Trelawny had been confident that he would reach Leghorn, a matter of fifty miles by sea, in well under five hours.

'I've just had a letter from Leigh Hunt,' Shelley remarked. 'The innkeeper sent it over from Lerici. Hunt is at Genoa. I shall write and tell him to remain there until I join him.'

'I though he was going to Leghorn,' said Claire, alarmed at the strained note in Shelley's voice.

'And from there to Pisa, yes. Byron has offered him an apartment on the ground floor of the Palazzo Lanfranchi.'

'Then why join Hunt at Genoa?' she asked carefully.

'I must get away from the Casa Magni for a few days, you know I must, Claire.'

'Because of me?'

'Because of *us*. Neither of us can think clearly, not while seeing each other every moment of the day. Obviously my own confusion is greater than yours. That dreadful nightmare, those visions. Claire, I think I'm going out of my mind.'

'Nonsense!' she said sharply. 'It's only the strain of Mary's illness.'

'That naked child I saw rising from the sea was Allegra,' he went on tensely. 'She laughed and clapped her hands, and told me how much happier I'd be if I joined her. Then there was another vision early this morning. After the nightmare. A vision, Claire, not a dream. I went out to the terrace and there I came face to face with myself. I tried to run from myself, my ghost, my phantom. Even when I succeeded my own voice echoed after me, asking me how long I expected to remain so foolishly content.'

'But are you content, Shelley?'

'I was when we found each other, but now— Claire, I must go to Genoa, *I must*!'

Claire looked at him sadly. The nightmare and the visions, she thought, were nothing more than a reflection of his state of mind. He hated the present, feared the future and wanted to escape from both. She came close then to telling him about Mary and Trelawny, but found herself unable to break the promise she had made.

'A few days with Hunt will be good for you,' she said quietly. 'You'll have such a lot of talk about after all this time.'

'Yes, and the sea trip will be marvellous. I'll sail the *Don Juan* to Genoa. I always know my own mind best with nothing but the sea all about me and the sky above.'

'I know *my* own mind, Shelley, in spite of all this strain.'

'How fortunate you are.'

'Let me come with you to Genoa. The two of us together, no one else. The sea all about us, the sky above. . . .'

'I can't, Claire, *I can't*.'

Edward Williams, when told of Shelley's plan, agreed to go with him. He felt, he said, in need of a change of air, and wasn't willing to let Shelley embark for Genoa with only their boat-boy to help him.

'Good lord, Bysshe,' he laughed, 'you'd probably end up at Elba, or even Corsica.'

Mary herself thought it a stupid idea and said so without hesitation. The Hunt family were in any case going to Leghorn, why then must Shelley rush off to Genoa? Shelley, more distracted than ever, grew violently stubborn. There were arguments, pitiful little outbursts of temper, and Mary, who had been regaining her strength, suffered a serious relapse. The trip to Genoa was then out of the question, and Shelley, writing to Hunt, promised to join him as soon as possible at Leghorn or Pisa, whichever was the more convenient.

'But only for a few days?' Mary begged.

'Only for a few days,' Shelley promised.

3

Mary, who had dressed today for the first time since her illness, was lying on her bed listening to the voices of the others in the entrance hall.

'Everything in readiness, Ned?'

'There's still a cask of water to put aboard, but the boy is seeing to that.'

'Tell him to hurry. If we don't make a start soon we won't reach Leghorn before sunset. You know what the health authorities are like there. No work after sunset. We don't want to be cooped up on board all night.'

'There's a fair breeze. We should reach Leghorn in less than seven hours.'

Both Shelley and Edward were speaking jauntily, Mary noticed, trying their best to ignore the strained atmosphere which had mounted steadily during the last few days. Or perhaps she was imagining it; perhaps such strain as there was existed solely within herself. Shelley or Trelawny, Trelawny or Shelley? The struggle went on unendingly. Leigh Hunt was now at Leghorn and Shelley had written to say that he would join him there today. It was ridiculous, she thought, that he should rush off to Leghorn when Byron was capable of looking after Hunt unaided, ridiculous and inconsiderate, though she was forced to admit that she was well enough now to be left for a few days. Shelley or Trelawny, Trelawny or Shelley? Perhaps it was better after all that Shelley should go. Free of both his influence and Trelawny's she might have more chance of making up her mind.

'I'd feel happier,' she heard Jane say, 'if you went direct to Pisa by road. Since Hunt is going to live at Pisa he could join you there without any trouble at all.'

'Why go by road when we have a perfectly good boat at our disposal?' Shelley asked crossly.

A little boy who refused to be thwarted, Mary thought sadly, and began to worry herself about the trip by sea. Shelley's nightmare had troubled her many times. Jane and Edward with blood on their faces, the sea rushing into the house, the house crumbling away. Foolish, of course, to regard it as a vision of the future, or to associate it with the boat. Jane wasn't making the trip to Leghorn, and Shelley hadn't seen himself in danger in the nightmare.

'Trelawny doesn't think it a perfectly good boat,' she heard Claire say anxiously.

'Captain Roberts does,' Edward said equably.

'*He* built it,' Jane reminded him.

'*And* he's coming with us to Leghorn,' Shelley said impatiently. 'That shows his faith in it. As for Trelawny, he's only jealous because he can't afford a boat of his own, and supercilious too, with Byron's *Bolivar* to play with. We've been out in some pretty rough seas and come to no harm. And look at the weather today – perfect! We're wasting a lot of time arguing. I'll go and say good-bye to Mary.'

He came into the room scowling and looked more like a boy than ever. Trying her best to smile at him, Mary felt a need to tell him that his shrunken trousers were a disgrace and his stained shirt no better than a beggar's.

'They'll throw you out if you try to enter Byron's fine palace in that condition,' she said severely. 'For heaven's sake take some civilized clothes with you.'

'Claire packed a suit for me, and some clean shirts.'

'Why not take her with you? She'd make a good valet.'

Shelley looked at Mary uncertainly. Claire had wanted to make the trip and he had wanted to take her, but that, he had seen unhappily, would in no way help him to make up his mind. Mary or Claire, Claire or Mary? He still couldn't think clearly and was growing increasingly afraid that it would be just as bad at sea.

'Good-bye, Mary,' he said, and bent to kiss her.

She called him back when he reached the door, and as he turned she saw him, not as a boy any more, but as a man older even than his years. His shoulders had a hunched-up, rounded look and there were a few grey streaks, scarcely noticed before, in his hair.

'Please don't stay away too long, Shelley.'

'Hunt's affairs may occupy me longer than I expect,' he said doubtfully.

'You can go to Pisa again later. Two or three days should be enough this time. Today's the first of the month. Promise to come back on the fourth.'

'Mary, I *can't* promise.'

'If you don't come back on the fourth I'll follow you.'

What she meant, or thought she meant, was that if he didn't come back on the fourth she'd follow Trelawny. An ultimatum, yet a childish way of reaching a decision.

'You're not fit to travel,' Shelley said.

'Then promise to try and come back on the fourth.'

That, he thought, was easier. 'Very well, I'll try.'

She called him back a second time. 'Shelley, only if the weather is safe. It would kill me with worry if there was a storm blowing on the fourth.'

'Only if the weather is safe,' he promised.

Claire followed him from the house and walked down the beach with him to the little landing craft. Jane and Edward were walking ahead, beyond earshot, but even so there was only time for a hurried exchange of half-whispered words.

'You're not really anxious about the boat, are you?' Shelley asked.

'No. It's a perfect day, as you said. I'm only concerned about whether you come back. It's what you said last night, isn't it? If you leave Edward to come back without you I'll know what to do?'

'Join me in Pisa, yes.'

'Shelley, I love you.'

'I love you, Claire.'

And Mary too, he thought desperately, and Mary too.

Claire and Jane remained on the beach watching Shelley and Edward row out to the *Don Juan*. The boat-boy, an English youth of eighteen, was swimming near by. Greeting them with a cheery shout he hauled himself into the *Don Juan*, his wet body gleaming in the sun, and tied up the landing craft. Trelawny had said that they should employ a local boy, one well acquainted with the coast, but both Edward and Shelley, confident that they knew the coast well enough themselves, had only laughed at him.

Later, Claire and Jane, with Mary between them, stood on the terrace. Captain Roberts had been picked up at Lerici, and any moment now the *Don Juan* would disappear from sight in the direction of Spezia.

Mary shivered involuntarily. 'To see the sun set on this scene, the stars shine, the moon rise. . . . A wondrous beauty, would you say? Perhaps, but now more than ever it will add only to my wretchedness.'

She was talking as if to herself, Claire thought, torn this way and that, as Shelley was, by the need to make a decision.

'I can't watch any more,' Mary said, and went indoors.

4

'I've never been disturbed by dreams and visions before,' Jane said nervously, 'but—'

'If you're worrying about Shelley's nightmare—' Mary interrupted harshly.

'I am, and more than ever, now!' Jane cried. 'I had a nightmare myself last night. It – it was so vivid I can't believe it was merely a dream.'

Claire, remaining silent herself, looked sharply from Jane to Mary. It was hard to decide which of them was suffering the more from nervous tension. Nor was she free of it herself, for the atmosphere which had developed at the Casa Magni since the non-appearance of the *Don Juan* on the fourth, bright and calm as the day had been, made her feel at times like screaming. Everything tore at their nerves; the slightest rattle of a window, the happy cries of the children at play, and, as far as Mary herself was concerned, the incessant singing of the villagers at night.

Not even Shelley's letter, which had reached Mary on the fifth, had done much to ease the tension, though all three of them had laughed at Shelley's description of Byron's reaction to the arrival of the Hunt family. There were, it seemed, six Hunt children, and Mrs. Hunt, disgruntled and in poor health, was expecting a seventh. According to Byron, the Hunt children were screeching, savage little Cockneys. He regretted having given the Hunts the use of the ground floor of the Palazzo Lanfranchi, and to protect himself had placed a large bulldog at the door of his own apartments on the first floor. For the rest, Hunt had arrived penniless, and something, Shelley wrote, would have to be done about it immediately. By 'something', Mary had said bitterly, he obviously meant that the Shelleys themselves would fall into debt once again. Hunt's financial predicament, Shelley had concluded, made it necessary that he should remain away a little longer. This, Claire thought now, was a hopeful sign. He could do no more by remaining at Pisa than by returning; he was wavering still, and the longer he wavered the better.

'I've had more than enough of dreams and visions,' Mary said. 'Do you really have to inflict one of your own upon us, Jane?'

'It might be amusing,' Claire suggested brightly.

'*Amusing!*' Jane protested shrilly.

Shelley should be here now, Claire thought. He would no longer be irritated by Jane's tranquillity, for it no longer existed. She had changed amazingly, was surely more highly strung than Mary herself.

'Tell us, in any case,' Claire said soothingly.

Jane looked at her with loathing. 'I dreamt that the *Don Juan* and the *Bolivar* had sailed together from Leghorn. I was immensely excited about it and got up at dawn to watch for their arrival. I—'

'You mean you actually got up, or were still dreaming?'

'I was still dreaming,' Jane said tersely. 'Is my command of the English language so poor I fail to make myself clear?'

'I was beginning to wonder,' Claire murmured.

'Don't interrupt!' Mary said angrily.

'I got up at dawn,' Jane went on, 'and there, to my surprise, only the *Bolivar* was in the bay. I strained my eyes but there was no sign whatever of the *Don Juan*.'

'Shelley wants us to call it the *Ariel* in future,' Claire interrupted.

'What a hateful creature you are!' Jane cried, and burst into tears.

'Really, Claire!' Mary protested.

'Proceed, my dear Jane,' Claire said calmly.

Jane found a handkerchief down the neck of her dress and blew her nose.

'The *Bolivar* hoisted more sail,' she sobbed, 'and disappeared.'

'I don't call *that* a nightmare,' Claire laughed. 'Had you not wakened up Shelley and Edward, Trelawny and Byron would probably have come ashore from the *Bolivar*.'

'In which case,' Jane snapped, 'you would have been able to resume your despicable *affaire* with Byron.'

'And that,' said Claire, still calmly, 'would indeed have been a nightmare. Really, Jane, I can't imagine why you should be so upset by a dream like that.'

Jane looked at her resentfully. 'I can't help connecting it with the vision I had the night before Mary's miscarriage.'

'A vision as well as a dream!' Claire chuckled.

'You might be interested when I tell you it concerned Shelley,' Jane said nastily. 'It was the same night that you forced me to quarrel with him. I realized afterwards what you'd been trying to do. Did you succeed? You were with him for a long time after I left him.'

'I don't understand what all this is about,' Mary said dismally. 'Claire forced you to quarrel with Shelley?'

'Not quarrel with him, disillusion him.'

Mary nodded. 'I think I understand now.'

'She was jealous and wanted to make him turn from me to her.'

'Did that actually happen?' Mary asked.

'No,' Claire lied.

'I don't believe you.'

'Very well. I succeeded.'

'After almost eight years? Congratulations.'

'Mary, I can't be certain that I succeeded.'

'In that case I must withdraw my congratulations. And yet—' Mary looked at her stepsister strangely. 'Did you break the promise you made me?'

'No, Mary.'

'Had you done so, complete success might have been yours?'

'Perhaps.'

Mary sighed deeply. 'Forgive my sarcasm.' She looked without interest at Jane. 'You may as well tell us about your vision.'

Jane made a visible effort of concentration. 'I was sitting in the hall with Trelawny. You had gone to bed. Edward was still at Lerici. Shelley passed the open door, glancing in at us as he passed. He was walking from right to left. A moment later, without having retraced his steps, he passed again, still walking from right to left. He couldn't have done that without jumping over the wall, a drop of twenty feet or more, and scrambling up again at the other end of the terrace.' Her voice rose shrilly. 'In any case there wouldn't have been time for that. Trelawny said he'd been watching the open door all the time and hadn't seen Shelley. But I had! He was stripping off his shirt the first time, carrying it the second. He gave me such a sad, lost look each time.'

And at the moment of this 'vision', Claire thought, Shelley could easily have been stripping off his shirt. If Jane were really gifted with second-sight she would have seen a great deal more, Shelley tearing a strip from the shirt, binding up her toe, Shelley—Grass seed, she thought tenderly, that imaginary grass seed. . . .

'You had disillusioned him,' Mary said sharply. 'This vision, as you call it, was your conscience.'

'Oh nonsense!' Jane snapped.

Later that day Jane received a letter from Edward. He was at Leghorn and growing tired of waiting for Shelley to return from Pisa. If Shelley continued to hang on indefinitely he would hire a felucca on Tuesday the ninth and leaving the *Don Juan* at Leghorn come back alone to the Casa Magni. Claire wondered then if Edward knew Shelley's real reason for delaying the return. Not that it mattered; she knew it herself. If Edward returned alone she would understand and leave at once by road for Pisa.

During the next two days Mary, Claire and Jane avoided each other as much as possible. Mary was angry that Shelley should have made no real effort to return on the fourth, Claire was tormented by the suspense of waiting and Jane alone regained some semblance of calmness. Tuesday the ninth was a wet and depressing day, and by nightfall there was no sign either of the

Don Juan or Edward's hired felucca. Wednesday and Thursday were calm clear days, and still the three women were left without word of any sort. Jane grew frantic again when, on Friday morning, a rumour reached them from the village that there had been a storm farther down the coast.

'Shelley is safe at Pisa, of course,' she raged, 'but Edward has been drowned.'

'You've no reason for saying that,' Mary told her angrily.

'I'll leave at once for Leghorn,' Jane ran on. 'One of the fishermen shall take me.'

'If you must go, Jane, go by road.'

'How can I look for wreckage if I go by road?'

'Jane, control yourself,' Mary shouted.

Jane allowed herself to be persuaded to wait until midday. It was more than likely, Mary said, that today being the regular day for the arrival of letters, one would reach Lerici, either from Shelley or Edward. A servant was sent across to Lerici in good time and returned soon after midday with two letters, one for Mary from her father, the other addressed to Shelley.

'It's from Hunt,' said Mary, staring at it fearfully. 'Why should he write to Shelley here if Shelley is still at Pisa?'

So Shelley had made up his mind, Claire thought exultantly. Obviously he had left Pisa and was now waiting for her at Leghorn. But what of Edward Williams? Had Shelley sent a message by Edward, and had Edward—?

'For God's sake open it!' Jane cried.

Mary did so with trembling fingers, but before she could read the letter Jane snatched it from her. Watching her, Claire saw her face stiffen as she read, and when at last she looked up her eyes were expressionless.

'Edward and Shelley left Leghorn four days ago,' she whispered. 'Hunt wants to know how they got on. He addresses Shelley as "Shelley Mio". Such a stupid affectation. Is that the only Italian word he knows, *mio*?' She thrust the letter into Mary's hands. 'They sailed in the *Don Juan*. Four days ago. A little voyage of fifty miles. Seven or eight hours. It shouldn't have taken more than that. Oh, my God, Mary, *four days*!'

5

Mary came into the room to find Claire bending over one of the boxes which had arrived from the Casa Magni. Lifting bundles of papers and casting them aside, she appeared to be searching for something with desperate haste.

'Those are Shelley's manuscripts,' Mary said angrily. 'Leave them alone, Claire. You have no right to touch them.'

Claire glanced up with tears in her eyes. 'I'm looking for a poem. I knew it by heart, but I can't even remember the first line now. Please be patient with me, Mary.'

Mary sank wearily into a chair. She, with Jane, Claire and the children, had come to Pisa. Trelawny had insisted upon it – the desolate Casa Magni was no place for any of them now – and had found them temporary accommodation. Claire intended going to Vienna, Jane back to England, while Mary herself, afraid to look too far into the future, knew only that she must remain in Italy until Shelley's remains had been placed with those of his son William's in Rome.

'Trelawny should arrive soon from Via Reggio,' she said, thinking aloud.

Trelawny had been remarkably gentle and helpful, the only one of the Shelley circle who had really kept his head. She would love him always for that, but she knew now that he would never be anything else but a dear friend, nor ever could have been. Ironical, she thought sadly, that it should have taken Shelley's death to bring her to her senses.

Earlier Trelawny had gone to Via Reggio to identify the bodies which had been washed up farther along the coast. He had scarcely recognized them at first, Edward Williams' being more mutilated than Shelley's. Now, with Byron and Hunt, Trelawny had gone again to Via Reggio, his grim task being to watch the burning of the bodies and collect the ashes. A funeral pyre, Mary thought; Shelley would have liked the idea of that. But it was a matter of necessity, no more. The Italian authorities, fearful always of the spreading of a plague, had insisted upon cremation, had even refused permission for the bodies to be removed from the beach.

'Haven't you found it yet?' Mary asked, indifferent now.

Claire shook her head and went disconsolately to the window. Jane, still frantic and inconsolable in her grief, was pacing up and down in the street below. Was she trying yet again, Claire wondered, to find somebody to blame for the tragedy? She herself had dwelt often on this. Was Hunt to blame for coming to Italy, or Shelley for asking him to come? She knew she need no longer blame herself. Shelley, in spite of the problem she had inflicted upon him, would in any case have gone to Leghorn at that time. As for the delay, it was clear from a talk she had had with Hunt that that had been caused by arguments with the contrary Byron. Blame Byron, then? Or why not Edward Williams? Captain Roberts had begged the travellers not to sail that day. There'd been a thunderstorm in the morning, another was threatening and the currents were treacherous. But Edward had insisted upon sailing. Edward, not Shelley. Shelley, impatient as he was to go home, would have waited till the next morning. He was amazingly happy, Roberts had said, at the thought of seeing his wife and child again and had quoted two lines from one of his earlier works:

'The world's great age begins anew,
The golden years return—'

Fruitless, Claire thought, to attach blame to anyone in particular. All of them had had a hand in it, each in his own way contributing to the inevitability of this ghastly tragedy, even Shelley himself when he had bought his first boat.

She stirred herself at the sight of a post-chaise drawing up at the door.

'Here's Trelawny,' she said. 'He doesn't seem to have noticed Jane.'

It was clear when he entered the room that Trelawny was deeply shaken by what he had witnessed at Via Reggio, and it was some moments before he could speak coherently.

'I have the ashes in two separate boxes,' he said at last.

Mary inclined her head. She felt amazingly polite, like a well-trained little girl.

'It's a remarkable thing,' Trelawny went on, 'but the heart, Shelley's heart, wouldn't burn. The flames barely touched it. Byron swore that they recoiled from it.'

'People as well as flames have recoiled from that great Shelley's heart,' Mary said emotionally.

Trelawny nodded eagerly. 'Byron said much the same. He said the whole world was brutally mistaken about Shelley. Shelley, he said, was the best and most unselfish man he had ever known.'

'Shelley now being dead,' Claire said harshly. 'Does the tender-hearted Byron propose to write a splendid epitaph?'

'The best was written three hundred years ago, by Shakespeare. The lines kept running through my mind all the way back from Via Reggio:

> Nothing of him that doth fade
> But doth suffer a sea-change
> Into something rich and strange.'

'Thank you,' said Mary. 'If the heart didn't burn—'

'I took it from the flames myself. See, my hands were scorched. My hands, but not the heart.'

Claire laughed hysterically. 'What did you do with it, Trelawny?'

'The quarantine officers were furious. Present in full force, they were. In the end they allowed me to place it in spirits of wine. After that Hunt took it from me, said he had a prior claim, he being an older friend. Byron wanted it too, but in the end he promised to get it from Hunt and give it to Mary.'

Mary's insane politeness deserted her; she laughed as hysterically as Claire had laughed.

'Imagine it, the three of you quarrelling about Shelley's heart!'

Trelawny looked at her uncertainly. 'We realize, of course, that it belongs to nobody but you.'

Mary struggled to control herself. It belonged to nobody but her, even though for a time she had rejected it, recoiled from it, indestructible as it was.

'Please leave us, Trelawny,' she said unsteadily.

The moment he had gone, saying as he went that he would make all arrangements for the funeral in Rome, Claire took Mary in her arms, and there for a time she remained, weeping quietly.

'I've remembered the first verse of that poem,' Claire said presently, and quoted it broodingly:

> 'Like the ghost of a dear friend dead
>   Is Time long past.
> A tone which is now forever fled,
> A hope which is now forever past,
> A love so sweet it could not last,
>   Was Time long past.'

Mary smiled sadly through her tears. 'To you Claire, and to me, and to all who knew him, *A love so sweet it could not last*.'

FOOTNOTE

And afterwards?

Mary, only twenty-five when Shelley died, never remarried. She died at the age of fifty-four. Sir Timothy Shelley withdrew all financial help after Shelley's death, but, difficult as life was for her, she was able to earn a little money by writing for various magazines, and later published three novels. On the death of Charles Bysshe, Shelley's son by Harriet, Mary's son Percy Florence became heir to the Shelley baronetcy, and Sir Timothy made Mary an allowance of £300 a year. Opening his purse-strings still farther, he allowed his heir £400 a year at the age of twenty-one. When Sir Timothy himself died Mary's circumstances became considerably easier. Her son married, but died without issue, and the title passed to a Shelley cousin. Ianthe, Shelley's other child by Harriet, made a happy marriage and lived to the age of sixty-three.

Claire, a few months younger than Mary when Shelley died, never married. For several years after the tragedy she earned a frugal living by teaching in various parts of Europe, but under Shelley's will, which became effective at Sir Timothy's death, she benefited to the extent of £12,000. She died at the age of eighty.

Jane Williams found consolation, five years after her husband's death, by marrying Shelley's old friend, Thomas Jefferson Hogg. According to some authorities she was no more legally married to Hogg than she had been to Williams. Very little is known about her, except that she spread unkind stories about Mary's failure fully to appreciate Shelley, and that she lived to a very great age.

Eliza Westbrook eventually married her Farthing Beauchamp, but not until the year of Shelley's death. His surname was originally Farthing. An old lady had made a will in his favour, and providing he took her own name, which was Beauchamp, he would inherit her estate. According to some, the infatuated old lady was in love with him. It might well have been that he and Eliza waited for her to die before marrying. In any case Eliza, at a later date, inherited the whole of her father's estate, which was valued at £60,000.